Praise for

NOBODY'S MAGIC

LONGLISTED FOR THE CENTER FOR FICTION
FIRST NOVEL PRIZE

A *GOOD MORNING AMERICA* BUZZ PICK

A MOST ANTICIPATED BOOK BY *ESSENCE* • *THE MILLIONS* • *ATLANTA JOURNAL-CONSTITUTION* • *BUSTLE* • *BOOKPAGE* • *NASHVILLE SCENE* • *MS. MAGAZINE* • *PARNASSUS MUSING*

A BEST BOOK OF FEBRUARY BY *WASHINGTON POST* • NYLON • BOOK RIOT

"The magic here is not the supernatural kind, but rather an attention to the grace of the ordinary. It is the magic of watching these women come into their power." —*New York Times*

"Birdsong's novel is a searing meditation on grief, female strength, and self-discovery, and is perfect for fans of the film *Moonlight* by Barry Jenkins." —*Good Morning America*, GMA Buzz Pick

"Birdsong has brilliantly crafted three coming-of-age stories that glimmer with passion and purpose." —*Atlanta Journal-Constitution*

"A powerful portrait of womanhood and the beautiful mess that comes along with it…It's a stunning read." —Associated Press

"Destiny O. Birdsong brings poetic beauty to her first novel, NOBODY'S MAGIC... The book is a feat of voice and storytelling."
—Shondaland

"[Birdsong] hasn't just written good stories, but searing ones with unforgettable characters. These three women are so distinct and real they will undoubtedly be remembered by readers years later, the hallmark of iconic characters. Readers will come to love and know these three women so deeply, they'll immediately recognize NOBODY'S MAGIC's characters if they see a Suzette & Maple & Agnes T-shirt—and likely want one, too."
—*Chicago Review of Books*

"Hopeful and powerful."   —*Ms. Magazine*

"Bold."   —Nylon

"Birdsong's writing challenges readers to reimagine what is magic in a work that is sure to become a new favorite in Southern literature."
—*Deep South Magazine*

"Birdsong imbues the characters with palpable emotions and crafts spot-on dialogue, conveying vernacular speech with layers of pathos and wit. It's a stunning achievement."
—*Publishers Weekly* (Starred Review)

"Birdsong excels at evoking savagely strong emotions... [She] portrays her main characters as individuals with their own heart and soul, searching for family, love, acceptance, and independence."
—*Library Journal* (Starred Review)

"Birdsong is a masterful storyteller with a powerful voice that will keep readers captivated."   —*Booklist* (Starred Review)

"A thoughtful examination of a subject rarely addressed in contemporary literature."   —*Kirkus*

"Masterfully crafted…NOBODY'S MAGIC is worth reading simply to spend time with these women, but the thoughtful and unexpected way that Birdsong combines their three unique stories into one is what makes the book unforgettable."   —*BookPage*

"The characters' personalities are so distinct and written so realistically, you'll feel like you've been invited into a friend's life, and you're rooting for them to make it."   —*Book Riot*

"A book that transfixes and mesmerizes, so much that you find yourself staying up until the wee hours of the morning so enthralled you can't put it down."   —*Electric Literature*

"With NOBODY'S MAGIC, Destiny Birdsong has given us a devastatingly beautiful, sexy, searing gift. I fell in love with the women Birdsong conjured so brilliantly. These are stunning, irresistible stories of Southern Black womanhood that I will return to again and again."

—Deesha Philyaw, author of National Book Award 2020 finalist *The Secret Lives of Church Ladies*

"From the very first page of NOBODY'S MAGIC, when I could hear the voice of the protagonist as if she was sitting next to me, I knew I was in the hands of a confident, one-of-a-kind storyteller. Here is a world full of complex, memorable characters who feel real, with stories unlike any I've read before. Destiny O. Birdsong has a gift; how lucky we are as readers to benefit from it."

—Angela Flournoy, National Book Award finalist and *New York Times* bestselling author of *The Turner House*

"The women of NOBODY'S MAGIC are unforgettable. These are deeply moving stories of love and longing, mourning and discovery, getting unstuck and moving toward freedom. Birdsong captures the unexpected grace of everyday life in sharp, vibrant prose, and the power of these characters—their courage and willingness to reinvent themselves—stayed with me long after the last page."

—Naima Coster, *New York Times* bestselling author of *What's Mine and Yours*

"NOBODY'S MAGIC is a captivating triptych of three unforgettable women. Each of their voices will ring in my memory for a long time—they have so much to say of love, loss, desire, and the city that knows them best. Together, their perspectives illuminate a prismatic portrait of how possible it is to feel intimately bound and a stranger to the places that have created you, and the people you call home."

—Melissa Febos, national bestselling author of *Girlhood*

"NOBODY'S MAGIC is an ironic title because Destiny O. Birdsong's prose is, in fact, magical. The characters' wisecracks are as delicious as a po' boy, the situations are textured and sticky as the Southern heat, and the histories are as thick as the bayou. We, as an audience, are ever so lucky to be along for the ride."

—Morgan Jerkins, *New York Times* bestselling author of *Caul Baby*

"As with Destiny Birdsong's poetry, the stories in NOBODY'S MAGIC are striking and original, full of down-home hilarity, Black love, truth, grief, and the sometimes-uncertain roads one travels to accept the self. Birdsong's is a powerful voice I'd follow anywhere."

—Dantiel W. Moniz, author of *Milk Blood Heat*

"NOBODY'S MAGIC will strike the tender parts of your heart and you will never forget the trio of vulnerable, fierce women at its center—Suzette, Maple, and Agnes. This is the real Black South—Shreveport, Louisiana, conjured in both surprising and familiar ways—Black women discovering secrets, reclaiming themselves and leading the way. This book left a lasting impression on me long after the pages were closed. Destiny Birdsong is a powerful storyteller. An impressive debut!"   —Crystal Wilkinson, author of *Perfect Black*

"The region is vividly portrayed, the voices so startlingly real you'll think the characters are sitting right next to you. Sexy, gritty, unapologetic, this one will be talked about all year."

—*Parnassus Musing*

"Birdsong's prose sings with a poet's sensibility, so each story is carried along with pitch-perfect rhythm and nuanced understanding of human foibles. In the end, Agnes, Suzette, and Maple are true to themselves, stepping into their own power and defying predictable solutions."   —*Chapter 16/Humanities Tennessee*

ALSO BY DESTINY O. BIRDSONG

Poetry

Negotiations

NOBODY'S
MAGIC

DESTINY O. BIRDSONG

GRAND
CENTRAL

New York   Boston

Copyright © 2022 by Destiny O. Birdsong
Reading Group Guide Copyright © 2022 by Destiny O. Birdsong and Hachette Book Group, Inc.
Cover design by Tree Abraham. Cover illustration by Adekunle Adeleke. Cover copyright © 2022 by Hachette Book Group, Inc.

Hachette Book Group supports the right to free expression and the value of copyright. The purpose of copyright is to encourage writers and artists to produce the creative works that enrich our culture.

The scanning, uploading, and distribution of this book without permission is a theft of the author's intellectual property. If you would like permission to use material from the book (other than for review purposes), please contact permissions@hbgusa.com. Thank you for your support of the author's rights.

Grand Central Publishing
Hachette Book Group
1290 Avenue of the Americas, New York, NY 10104
grandcentralpublishing.com
twitter.com/grandcentralpub

Originally published in hardcover and ebook by Grand Central Publishing in February 2022.

First Trade Edition: January 2023

Grand Central Publishing is a division of Hachette Book Group, Inc. The Grand Central Publishing name and logo is a trademark of Hachette Book Group, Inc.

The publisher is not responsible for websites (or their content) that are not owned by the publisher.

The Hachette Speakers Bureau provides a wide range of authors for speaking events. To find out more, go to www.hachettespeakersbureau.com or call (866) 376-6591.

Lucille Clifton, excerpt from "defending my tongue" from *The Collected Poems of Lucille Clifton*. Copyright © 1991 by Lucille Clifton. Reprinted with the permission of The Permissions Company, LLC on behalf of BOA Editions, Ltd., boaeditions.org.

Library of Congress Cataloging-in-Publication Data

Names: Birdsong, Destiny O., 1981- author.
Title: Nobody's magic / Destiny O. Birdsong.
Description: First Edition. | New York : Grand Central Publishing, 2022. |
  Summary: "In this glittering triptych novel, Suzette, Maple and Agnes, three Black women with albinism, call Shreveport, Louisiana, home. At the bustling intersection of the American South and Southwest, these three women find themselves at the crossroads of their own lives. Suzette, a pampered twenty-year-old, has been sheltered from the outside world since a dangerous childhood encounter. Now, a budding romance with a sweet mechanic allows Suzette to seek independence, which unleashes dark reactions in those closest to her. In discovering her autonomy, Suzette is forced to decide what she is willing to sacrifice in order to make her own way in the world. Maple is reeling from the unsolved murder of her free-spirited mother. She flees the media circus and her judgmental grandmother by shutting herself off from the world in a spare room of the motel where she works. One night, Maple connects with Chad, someone who may understand her pain more than she realizes, and discovers that the key to her mother's death may be within her reach. Agnes is far from home, working yet another mind-numbing job. She attracts the interest of a lonely security guard and army veteran who's looking for a traditional life for himself and his young son. He's convinced that she wields a certain "magic," but Agnes soon unleashes a power within herself that will shock them both and send her on a trip to confront not only her family and her past, but also herself. This novel, told in three parts, is a searing meditation on grief, female strength, and self-discovery set against a backdrop of complicated social and racial histories. Nobody's Magic is a testament to the power of family-the ones you're born in and the ones you choose. And in these three narratives, among the yearning and loss, each of these women may find a seed of hope for the future"
  -- Provided by publisher.
Identifiers: LCCN 2021041292 | ISBN 9781538721407 (trade pbk.) | ISBN 9781538721414 (ebook)
Classification: LCC PS3602.I739 N63 2022 | DDC 813/.6--dc23
LC record available at https://lccn.loc.gov/2021041292
ISBNs: 9781538721407 (trade pbk.), 9781538721414 (ebook)

Printed in the United States of America

LSC-C

Printing 1, 2022

for my city

CONTENTS

no what i be talking about
the dirt   the tree   the land
scape can only be said
in this language   the words
be hard be bumping out too much
to be contained in one thin tongue

—"defending my tongue," by Lucille Clifton

NOBODY'S MAGIC

DRIVE

I.

I didn't really kick it that much before Doni cause I felt like I had everything I needed right where I was. I still live at home, and my daddy own Elkins Custom Auto, so we do pretty good. Nice cars, of course; nice house. Movie room downstairs; game room upstairs. The sunporch, which I love cause it's just the right amount of shade, and I can sit outside all day playing games on my phone or shopping online and not get burned. My friend Drina would come over and my mama would make us food while we sit and talk. Or if we did go out, it was to shop, like at Mall St. Vincent. That's where the good Dillard's is, the one with the Coach bags. I got my daddy to buy me one awhile back, but then I kinda wanted this other one that was beige with a flower on the buckle, and oooh! It was *flames*. But my daddy said I needed to get tired of the one I had, and when that happened, he'd buy me the other one. Then my mama said, "Careful, Curtis; she gon stop thinking you hung the moon." I swear my mama used to say that every time my daddy said no, and he would just laugh, but when everything started to happen, he'd just look at her like she was crazy. And I mean, I loved my daddy—still do—but I never thought my daddy hung nothing. And if he did hang the moon, I hate to tell him, but he hung it kinda crooked.

Stuff started happening in the fall—I know that cause my daddy had on his light jacket when he left, and my mama made coffee and we was out on the porch with each other under some throws, waiting for Drina. Drina didn't go to college neither, but she do go to school part-time for cosmetology, and she work at MetroPCS and do people's hair on the side. That day, I was paying Drina to redo my braids I had got over the summer. I coulda went down to Tresses, but I didn't wanna sit in a chair all day, especially if the TV I gotta watch ain't even got cable. Plus, Drina needed the money cause all the folks we went to school with had left for college again, but she had spent all their back-to-school hair money on her own tuition. So yeah—it was fall.

Drina do a good job, too, and I begged her to do it on the porch so I could see the birds. I'm always looking for blue jays—they so pretty. Or goldfinches. And then one time me and Mama saw a heron flying. She say it's probably cause of the pond, even though it's way out on the property, even past the other garage. Anyway, I ask Drina if she can do my hair out there.

"But, Suzette. It's kinda cold right now."

"It'll warm up around ten. And I'll get Mama to start up the fireplace till it do."

"But I don't want my hands—"

"And some coffee too. *Mama! Bring Drina some coffee out to the porch!* You hongry? We had cinnamon rolls for breakfast. And I think it's still some sausage left over."

"How I'ma do your hair if I'm eatin all this food?"

When Mama brought out the coffee, she say, "Drina, I don't know why this girl got you out here on this porch tryin to do some hair."

And Drina say, "I treat her like the rest of y'all do, Ms. Elkins. Cain't nobody tell her no except Mr. Curtis."

Then Mama and Drina started laughing.

And I pout, cause Drina supposed to be my friend but she talking bout me like everybody else, and that ain't right. If I really am spoiled rotten, it's cause Mama and Daddy was doing too much when I was little. I couldn't go outside cause I might get sunburn. I couldn't play with the other kids cause they didn't treat me right. I couldn't stay after school or do no kinda activities after the voodoo incident. I couldn't even do debutante ball cause every girl was supposed to host an event for the debs at her house and my daddy say them people just wanted to see how we lived and he wasn't having it. And he didn't want me going off to college cause what if I didn't like it, or what if I got caught up with some no-good nigga cause I wouldn't know no better noway, since I didn't date in high school. Just woulda been a waste of money—that's what Daddy said. And I couldn't have a car cause I didn't have a driver's license and I had to get bioptic glasses to pass the eye test and we had to go to Nacogdoches for that cause the LSU clinic always booked like a year in advance, and Daddy would do it the next time he got time off work. So it was just like a cycle: couldn't do nothing now cause I didn't do nothing then. So the least I could do was sit on the porch and see some birds while I got my hair done. Damn.

Ever since I was little, when my daddy come home from work, I holler "Dadaaaaaaayyyyyyyy!" And wherever I am in the house, he come give me a hug and I get to smell the oil and paint thinner on him and sometimes he bring me something. It's always small, like a candy bar or a keychain. I got bout a hundred keychains and no car key to put on em. So, that day, Drina was mostly done with my hair and it was about six o'clock and I hear my daddy come through the living room saying, "Hey, where my baby girl? Where my hug?" And I holler back, "Come see my hair!" And he walk on the porch with Doni, who nobody told me was even in the house. Doni came cause he and my daddy had been working on this car my mama been wanting since she sold Mary Kay. A pink Cadillac. They restored a old, old one, though, and they did some of it at the house cause my daddy don't like folks all in his business. He didn't tow it to the shop till it was almost time to paint it. So Doni come out and he say hey to everybody except me, so I call him on it.

"Hey, *Doni*."

"Oh, yeah, hey, Suzette. I saw you; you just looked busy, and I wudn't tryna bother you."

I put my magazine down. "I ain't busy. Unless I'm busy bein bored." Drina yanked a little too hard on one of my braids while she was finishing it, and it better not have been cause she copped an attitude. "How you doin?" I asked.

"I cain't complain. Dang, them braids is fire, Drina. I see you mixing the blond and lavender. Tha's cute."

Drina giggled a little and said thank you, but I'm feeling a way cause they *my* braids, and he still acting like I ain't even in the room.

"These was my idea. I saw em on Instagram."

Doni just ignore me and come close to look at Drina's hands. "Man, I need to learn how to do hair. Make me a little extra change."

Drina's ass start kee-keeing again. I'm pissed now.

"Did you come out here for something? Or is you tryna to enroll in beauty school?"

"As a matter of fact, I did," and he had the nerve to turn his back to me and ask my mama if she wanna come look at paint colors cause they gon be ready to do that soon and he think a three-tone job on the trim would look nice. When he leave, he say, "Bye, Miz Elkins; bye, Drina. Take it easy." And I'm so mad I don't say nothing to nobody else for the rest of the day.

"Whatchu think about Doni comin over here like that?" It's Sunday morning, and I just had my coffee. I'm on the phone with Drina cause I wanna go to the mall but I don't wanna go with my mama.

"He didn't mean nuthin by it," she sighed. "I think he kinda sweet."

"Sweet?!"

"Yeah. He said he liked your hair. Men don't never say stuff like that unless they want somethin."

"Well, he didn't say that. What he said was he liked how you was doing it."

"I don't see what the difference is."

So I just change the subject, cause Drina playing stupid and I'm getting mad again.

"You coming?"

"Where?"

"To the mall!"

"Zettie, honey, I'm tired. I got a practical dem at school Monday and I gotta go grocery shopping for Big Mama later. And what they got in the mall that you ain't bought already?"

"I just wanted to get out of the house."

"Shoot, if that's all you want you can come run errands with me. We'll go eat somewhere after. I'll come get you around five. I'm just gon take a quick nap first."

"Man, I guess." And I get off the phone quick cause I don't wanna give her the satisfaction of hearing me give in.

But I still had a whole afternoon to find stuff to do while I waited for Drina. I was tired of Snapchat and looking at makeup tutorials and checking on the stuff that just went on sale at Nordstrom's on-line. And I was tired of lurking, too, looking for folks I went to school with, trying to see what they was doing, especially if they went to college. Everybody I knew wanted to go to Xavier or Southern:

the Black schools. If it was me I woulda picked Xavier cause the campus was prettier. But Daddy said it wasn't worth the tuition, and you know the rest. So instead of being there, I just used to watch folks act a fool online during homecoming and then at Mardi Gras and spring break. Half the time they'd be drunk and the girls' titties would be falling out they tops cause they don't know how to buy clothes that fit right. But real talk, I'd probly be out there doing the same thing if I could. And then I realized I was hating on them girls cause I was jealous and I needed to do better. But I didn't know what doing better looked like, so I put my phone down for a while, and went out to watch Daddy work on Mama's car seats.

The car was already at the shop getting painted, but they had ripped out the seats so Daddy could work on them at home. I don't know as much as my daddy do about restoring cars, but I like this part. I like watching old stuff get made up to look different, even though it's the same. It's how I feel when I put on my makeup in the morning, and I pencil in my eyebrows. Like, it's me, but better. I make my face up every day.

Daddy built this detached garage on the land out back after we bought the house, and he put just about everything he want in it, including a tall stool with a back for me to sit so I can watch him work, since he don't really let us come to the shop like that. Daddy said he coulda sent off for Mama's seats, but he wanted to do them hisself. When I walked in, him and Doni was ripping off the covers and setting them to the side so they could trace them on the new fabric, which was still bundled up on the worktable. Daddy bought two kinds of fabric, and he let me help him pick it out. One was leather, and it kinda reminded me of these boots I bought myself one Christmas, and the other one was like a damask. The color on both of them was called Chateau Mauve, and even while we was picking them out, I knew them seats was gonna be the best ones I ever seen in a car. It was the first time I felt jealous of Mama, cause Daddy gave me the money for them boots, but Mama got a whole damn car.

So I'm already a little irritated, and I'm even more irritated cause Doni there. Even though I figured he might be. I just wasn't ready. But I hop up on the stool and look around.

"Daddy, you gon clean them cushions before you put that new fabric on, right?"

Daddy just keep doing what he doing, like he do when he ignoring me.

Doni looked over at him and smirked. "Mr. Elkins, you didn't tell me the Queen Bee was gon grace us wit her royal presence this early."

"Excuse you, I been up. And I always come out here to watch my daddy."

Doni laughs. "You come out here to watch him, or direct him?"

"Them cushions is nasty."

"Car gon drive just the same."

"Did I say it wouldn't?"

"I guess you didn't. You talking so much, I mighta misheard you. My apologies, madam." And Doni turns and gives me a deep bow while he still holding one of the old covers, looking like a bullfighter. Daddy got the fans on, to bring in some of the cool afternoon air from outside, but it's still hot in here, and Doni sweating a little, just enough for his arms and chest to look wet. He only wearing a wife beater, so you can see it. I'm mad, and he looking back at me, all confident. More comfortable in my house than I am.

For the next couple of hours I watch them work: my daddy doing the stuff he wanna do and letting Doni do the rest. My daddy be barking at folks sometimes, and he was doing a little bit of that with Doni, but Doni stay cool as a cucumber. Daddy got a big sewing machine in there, but he was teaching Doni how to hand-stitch the leather, watching him so he don't make no mistakes. After a while, though, he left him alone. When Doni finish one seat, he take it to show Daddy. Daddy rubbed his thumb across the seams to make sure they wasn't bunched up.

"That look good, boy," he say to Doni, almost like he surprised hisself.

Doni say, "Thank you, Mr. Curtis," and he let Daddy finish with the tracing. But as he was walking away, Doni look back at him again, but Daddy's head is down. Then Doni look up at me and hold up the new seat cover like he making a toast or something, and wink. I smile a little, not cause I'm trying to flirt or nothing, but cause Daddy was sitting right there, and he missed the whole thing.

DRINA CAME TO PICK ME up after six, and I know she think she slick cause she knew I was gon ask if we could just *stop by* the mall, but it was already closed. Doni and Daddy were in the den drinking beer while my mama was making dinner in the kitchen. I'm in my room getting ready while Drina laying across my bed.

"We just running errands, Suzette."

"I know. I don't wanna leave the house looking any kind of way." I'm tugging at a halter top I had just ordered online. It was cute, but the keyhole in the middle wouldn't sit right. Drina got up and came over to the mirror with her face all scrunched up, but she still trying to help. She start adjusting the top from the back, and then moved around to the front to make sure the built-in bra was sitting right. It was a little thin shelf bra, though; it was flimsy and the ones like that sometimes flip down if you big up top. I was already kinda spilling out of it. *And* my nipples was showing through. Drina put her hands over them like they was blinding her.

"Ain'tchu gon be cold? You know it get cool at night now."

"I'll bring a jacket."

She rolled her eyes. "I hope you picked one out already. We runnin late."

"We runnin late cause you didn't show up till a hour after you said you was gon show up."

"And you still ain't ready."

While Drina was fussing with the top, I checked my makeup in the mirror. I always smile, and then I mean-mug to see how it look both ways, and that night I thought it looked all right, but I had to wipe a little lipstick off the dip on my top lip. I always catch a little right there cause my dip is deep, like Mama's. But I swear I got my daddy's whole face for real; both of ours is heart-shaped and we got the same nose: kinda flat but kinda narrow too. Mama say it's like a Barbie doll's, but the kids at school used to say it was like an alien's. I really didn't get nothing else from Mama except the way my eyes set. They far apart, just like hers. But they big, like Daddy's; plus I wear a lot of eye makeup, so sometimes, you can't really tell.

My door was open, and I hear somebody snickering. We both turn around, and it's Doni. Drina take her hands back real quick, and start pulling her T-shirt down like she tryna get the wrinkles out.

"H-hey, Doni. How you doin?"

"Wassup, Drina. I cain't complain."

"Wouldn't do you no good anyway."

"Shole wouldn't. You good?"

I turn around from where I was looking in the mirror and I know I'm standing awkward. "Whatchu all the way up here for?"

"Lookin for a bathroom."

"You passed three of em downstairs."

"I was lookin for a private one if you know what I mean." He turns to Drina and shakes his head. "Why she so nosey?"

And Drina laughs, with her disloyal ass.

"Well, you cain't use mine, so get out of here."

"I wasn't trying to." He turns to leave. "You look nice, though!" he yells from somewhere in the hallway. I felt like he was prolly making fun of me, and I was so embarrassed by that I grabbed a jacket from the pile on my chair and put it on quick. I don't even think it matched.

"Let's go." I start looking around for a purse.

Drina sighs, "Finally."

And I'm already on my way downstairs before she can catch up.

DON'T NOBODY UNDERSTAND WHY I work so hard to look the way I do. People gon stare at me anyway, even though I been living here my whole life. I think there was another albino girl here, but she older, and anyway, she moved. I don't know how people treated her, but everybody my age just as ignorant as they wanna be. I never really got picked on. I mean—I had my share of bullies, but Drina took care of those, especially in high school. She would come ready for em: sneakers on, hair pulled up in a bun. And everybody that wanted to fight me would back down. Drina little, and she quiet, but she don't put up with a lot of mess. People come at her the wrong way, she start circling the room, fists balled up. And if you keep talking, then she'll just start swinging.

So I never got beat up or nothing, but people asked me the same questions for damn near twenty years: "Can you see in the dark?" "Why your eyes move like that?" "You a witch?" "You got special powers, don't you. What's your special powers?" Man, I used to come home from elementary school crying every day, even though Drina and me was friends and I had somebody to sit with me at lunch and play at recess. Mama almost took me out of school a *few* times before the voodoo thing happened, and then she did take me out for a while after. But I didn't get to see Drina cause her mama didn't have a car back then and my mama didn't like going all the way to Cedar Grove, so I started throwing fits and finally she let me go back to school. But I couldn't ride the bus or stay after or have sleepovers with nobody except Drina, and most of the time she came over here. And if Drina hadn't been the one to tell my mama what the Moutons was trying to do to me, she might not have been able to come over either.

WHEN I WAS ABOUT SEVEN, me and Drina met this new girl named MarLisha. MarLisha was from Slidell, but her grandmama's family was from some part of Africa. Nigeria? Tanzania? I can't remember. MarLisha grandmama came here and married a Creole dude Down South and that's where they all lived until Katrina hit, right when we started the third grade. The first time MarLisha saw me she said, "Oh, you the same color as my pit. Her name Biscuit."

Then she started playing with us during recess. I liked her. I thought she was pretty, with them thick eyebrows like all the Creoles got, and that long hair she would let us play in if we went out past the monkey bars so nobody else would ask to do it too. But Drina thought she was stuck up: she didn't understand why MarLisha only wanted to play with us. Me and Drina hung only with each other cause we ain't have no choice. Nobody else really fooled with us. I guess Drina thought anybody that had other options and wouldn't take em was up to something. And after what happened, maybe she was right.

MarLisha was too nice. She started bringing candy and stuff to school and she would only share with us, so we'd go off to our little edge of the playground to eat and talk. When Lisha's mama came to school to work as a parent aide, she would give me and Drina rides home, even though I lived on the opposite side of the city. Lisha and Drina lived up the street from each other. Sometimes, Ms. Mouton would take us all the way to the McDonald's on Airline so we could play at the PlayPlace before we went home. We could get there and back by four o'clock, which was when my mama was supposed to be home from the shop. I used to come back telling Mama and Daddy how Ms. Mouton would always let us get chocolate syrup on our dollar cones and how she said we had to make a wish every time we crossed over the Red River to get into Bossier.

Mama said, "Well, I'm glad you got you a little group of friends."

My daddy wasn't all that impressed. He looked at Mama. "Did this woman ask you if she could bring Suzette home?"

Back then, Mama was still working part-time at the shop, doing the books, and selling Mary Kay on the side. Sometimes they got into it cause Daddy didn't trust nobody else with the books, but he also wanted her to be at home when I got back from school, and have dinner ready by the time he got back, which was usually around six when he let his GM close the place down. Mama didn't always do that, though. A couple times I got home before she did, and I would go sit on the sunporch till she pulled up. When Ms. Mouton brought me, she would pull in the driveway and we'd all wait on Mama. That was before the gate. Mama bribed me with a singing Hannah Montana doll so I wouldn't tell Daddy about it, but she got nervous every time he asked me questions.

When he asked about Ms. Mouton, Mama looked at me hard, probably to remind me we had a deal. Then she looked at him. "The first time she brought her home, she did, yeah. And now, if she work at the school, she'll let me know she doin it and what time they gon be home."

"Oh, okay, tell *me* something. Cause you know I don't like her out there with folks we don't know."

"I know her."

"I guess that's all right for now. Next time she come to my house, though, I want to meet her."

"You get off work at a reasonable hour, you can."

Daddy stroked his beard a little bit, like he do when he about to go off on you, but he didn't say nothing after that, just put some gravy on his mashed potatoes and ate em.

ONE DAY, LISHA ASKED IF I wanted to sleep over her house one Friday night. Her mama wanted to take us to Pecanland Mall in the morning, and we would have to wake up early to drive to Monroe. Drina could come, too, but since she stayed so close, she didn't need to spend the night. That's what Ms. Mouton said. And Ms. Mouton would ask my mama, too, so all I had to do was ride home with them after school that day. Same as always.

I didn't think nothing of it until that Friday morning, when the principal came to our room and asked if me, Drina, and Lisha could come to the office, and we should bring all our stuff. The whole room went quiet. Usually, if you got called for checkout or something, like your parents were bringing you your lunch or surprising you with a doctor's appointment, they just called you over the intercom. Principal didn't show up unless something bad had happened. But why they would want me, Lisha, *and* Drina? Even Ms. Haskell looked confused. I looked over at Drina when we got to our little lockers to get our backpacks. But she didn't say a word. She just looked scared.

When we made it to the office, the principal had me and Drina wait up front with Ms. Bradberry, the secretary, while she took Lisha to one of the sickrooms. When she came back, she took us to a part of the office I'd never seen. It was a big room with a big table, and a bunch of people was already in it: my mama, Daddy, Drina's mama Miss Tonya, a police officer who looked like he didn't wanna be there, and a redheaded white woman wearing a navy-blue suit. She was pale, like me, but covered in freckles, even her hands. The only person who wasn't there was Ms. Mouton, and I didn't know why, but that seemed important. When we got there, the principal sat us down and the white woman got up. She walked over and shook our hands.

"Hello! My name is Miss Siobhan McCrary. But you can call me Miss Siobhan." I liked that. Her name sounded like Chavonne, one of my older cousins. "I'm a social worker. Do you know what that is?"

We just stared.

"Well, I help make sure little girls like you are okay, and that no one hurts them, and that's why I'm here today." She walked back over to her chair, pulled out a recorder, and set it next to the notepad sitting in front of her. "I'm gonna ask you each some questions about something we think might have happened. Is that okay?"

Me and Drina both nodded, cause we was too scared to do anything else. Miss Siobhan sat back down.

"Okay. Well, first, I want to talk a little bit to Fredrina. Fredrina, can you tell us what you told your mom last night about something you heard Ms. Mouton say?"

"Tell the truth, Drina." Miss Tonya's voice sounded meaner than I ever heard it. Her big orange earrings twisted back and forth while she talked, and her matching headscarf was bobbing so hard I thought she might undo it if she kept talking.

"Yes, ma'am," said Drina, lowering her head.

"What happened yesterday when you were riding home with Ms. Mouton and MarLisha?" asked Miss Siobhan. She pressed the record button, and when she did, my daddy walked over and picked me up out of my chair. He took me across the table, where him and Mama was sitting. I sat in his lap. Drina started crying.

"It's okay, Fredrina. You're not going to get in trouble with anyone today." Miss Siobhan leaned back in her chair, but then almost like she forgot, moved the box of Kleenex over to Drina's side of the table.

"Except with me, if she don't start talking." That was Miss Tonya.

Drina put the Kleenex over her face so she could cry into it. She was trying to keep quiet, before her mama gave her something to cry about.

"Take your time," said Miss Siobhan.

Drina pulled away the Kleenex and wiped her face with her hands. "I fell asleep. On the way home. And when I woke up, they was talking."

"Who was talking?" asked Miss Siobhan.

"Lisha. And Ms. Mouton."

"And what were they talking about, Fredrina?"

Drina pointed at me and started sobbing again. Miss Tonya shook her head like it was a shame.

"Lisha…Lisha asked her mama if they was really gon cut her eyes out. And her mama said hush cause I might not be sleep. And then Lisha said, 'Mama, you gon let me watch?' And then Ms. Mouton said she talked too much and she needed to keep her mouth shut cause she wasn't s'posed to hear that noway. They was just gon play a game with Suzette. Nothing bad was really gon happen."

Miss Siobhan leaned forward again, her hand across the table in front of Drina. "So, Ms. Mouton said that it wasn't true, that she wasn't going to hurt Suzette?"

"No. She jus said nothing bad was gon happen."

"Did you believe her?"

Drina wiped her face again and shook her head.

"And why didn't you believe her? Was she laughing? Was she angry? How did she sound?"

"She sounded mad."

"And why do you think she was angry? What do you think made her angry?"

"Lisha. Cause she kept talking."

"So she didn't sound angry because MarLisha was telling a fib?"

"No, ma'am. I didn't think that."

"And what did you do when you heard them talking?"

"I just played sleep. Till I got home."

"And then what happened?"

"I told my grandmama. And then, when my mama got home from work, she told her what happened."

"Is there anything else, Fredrina? Anything else you remember from the car ride home?"

Drina nodded. "Ms. Mouton said, 'It's not like we was gon kill her. We just need her eyes. She probably can't see too good anyway.' But that's a lie. I play with Suzie all the time. I know she can see."

Miss Siobhan leaned back from the table and was quiet for a minute. All the adults too. Nobody said nothing. Then, Miss Siobhan:

"Fredrina, I'm just going to ask this to be sure, but are you absolutely positive about what you heard? You're sure you were awake, and not dreaming?"

Drina looked up for the first time. "Yes, ma'am. I heard it."

"And you're sure you're telling the truth? Because this is really important. We wouldn't want Ms. Mouton to get in trouble for something that didn't happen."

"No, ma'am," said Drina. "I ain't lying about this."

Miss Tonya chimed in. "She a good child. She don't make up stories, Miss McCrary."

Miss Siobhan nodded, then turned to me. "Suzette, I need to ask you if you've ever heard any conversations like this before, with Ms. Mouton or MarLisha?"

Mama told me to tell the truth, just like Miss Tonya did, but she wasn't as convincing. Plus, she didn't have to be. I didn't know nothing, so that's what I said. My daddy kissed the top of my head and bounced me a little. He was holding on to me tight. Mama looked scared. She tried to reach for one of my feet and wiggle it, but Daddy moved me to the other side of his lap.

"Suzette." Miss Siobhan picked up her pen for the first time. "Has Ms. Mouton ever touched you in a way that hurt you, or made you feel like you weren't safe?"

I swear I tried to think of something, but Ms. Mouton was always so nice. She ain't never even talk about my color, or looked at me funny, even though some grown folks had. She ain't do none of that from the first time I met her till then. I shook my head.

"No, ma'am."

"How about anyone else? Anyone in the car with Ms. Mouton or anyone she introduced you to? Has anyone who knows MarLisha or Ms. Mouton ever done anything to you that you didn't like or that made you feel uncomfortable?"

I shook my head. "I met her grandmama, though. Miss Adimu."

"And who is Miss Adimu? Is she Ms. Mouton's grandmother?"

"No, ma'am. She MarLisha's grandmama. The one know voodoo."

"Voodoo?"

"Yeah. That's what MarLisha say."

"Oh, so what kind of voodoo does she know? What does that mean when someone says they know voodoo?"

All of a sudden I felt scared, too, and I grabbed the collar on my daddy's work uniform. "I thought it mean she cast spells on people. Stuff like that."

"Oh yeah. I see. Like a witch or something?"

"Yes, ma'am."

"Okay. I understand that. And did she ever talk to you about her spells?"

"No, ma'am. Not to me. I just heard that from MarLisha."

"Ah, okay. But you said you met her? How many times did you meet her? Do you remember?"

"Maybe just once or twice, if Ms. Mouton picked her up from somewhere."

"I see. Did she ever talk to you? What did she say to you when you met her?"

"She said I had real pretty eyes."

My parents—they was never lovey-dovey like that; they would joke and play with each other when I was younger, but I never caught em hugged up or kissing or nothing. They old, so they old-school. My daddy one of them dudes that do stuff for you behind your back to show you how he feel about you. He used to wake up early to detail my mama car while she was still sleep, or go get us all breakfast from Southfield Grill, or buy me a bag and leave it on my bed next to me, propped up on all my pillows while I was sleep. And sometimes he would take us to the Shreveport Club for fancy dinners or him and Mama would go for drives in some of the cars he was working on if my cousins were at home and could watch me. Or we would all ride over to Texas for his car shows. He still did stuff like that after the voodoo incident, but him and my mama didn't really vibe like they used to. Still, I only heard my parents argue twice in my life, and I only seen it once, and the time I seen it was when we got home from school that day after talking with Miss Siobhan. Daddy didn't go back to the shop; he went and got me some McDonald's with a dollar cone and we sat in the movie room and watched cartoons. My mama stayed out of sight for a while, but then she came in to see if I was all right after what I heard. Daddy went off.

"Oh, so all of a sudden you concerned, after you let her go wherever with whoever while you runnin round the city sellin makeup."

Mama shot back, "Oh, that's a *bald-face* lie. When that woman was bringing her home from school I was comin from *yo* shop doing *yo* books."

"Well, we don't need them services no mo, ma'am. I'll find somebody else do that. You need to be at home with this child."

"Yeah, cause she do only got one parent."

"That's what it feel like to me, Miss Mary Kay."

"Go to hell, Curtis."

"Did you really think somebody in this city was gon mean her any good? Them people said all kinda stuff when we brought my baby home. It was my fault working on cars all the time. Inhellin paint. It's your fault for being too old callin yo'self gettin pregnant. We shoulda left her at the hospital. We shoulda gave her away. They said all kinda stuff."

"*Everybody ain't evil, Curtis!* Everybody don't think like that!"

"Yeah, and you happen to find the one person in the whole damn city who don't. Naw, she just wanna pluck out my baby eyes for some crazy— Hell, I don't even know."

"I made a mistake. I'd'n admitted that already. Ain't nuthin else I can do."

"I never wanted no working woman noway. You always s'posed to stay home with the chuldren. I never believed in all that runnin the streets, goin in folks' houses sellin stuff. You don't even know them people. Ain't no tellin what they might do to you once you passed the front do'. Might mess around and do to you what they tried to do to my baby girl."

Mama beckoned for me and asked if I wanted to come help her make spaghetti, but Daddy told me to finish my cone and then we was gon watch *The Little Mermaid* and he just pretended like Mama wasn't even standing there. Finally, she left, and the following Monday, she let me sleep till ten and told me we was gon do things a little different from now on.

"I'm not going to school today?" I asked, thinking bout Drina.

"Not today, baby. Just wanna make sure you safe."

"What, Ms. Mouton grading papers for Ms. Haskell again?"

"I don't think so, baby, but you know what? We ain't never gotta think about, worry bout, or talk about them folks ever again. MarLisha gone to stay with some other folks and I don't know what they gon do to Ms. Mouton, but we'll cross that bridge when we get to it. From now on, it's just me and you. Now get up. Just cause you gettin homeschooled don't mean you ain't gotta put no clothes on."

And for a long time, it was just like that, me and Mama in the house all day, Daddy at work. Even when I went back to school, it was me and her in the morning, and she would dress me up and when I turned twelve, do my makeup. That's really how I got into all that stuff. Then it'd be me and her again soon as I got out, and we would cook dinner together or run errands. I didn't mind it necessarily— my mama good company most of the time—and I guess neither did she. She never seemed too sad about it. But she never seemed too happy either.

THE SATURDAY AFTER I WATCHED Daddy and Doni do Mama's seat covers, I heard something else happening in the garage out back, so I went out there. It was Doni, sandblasting the seat frames so they could seal them before they put the cushions back on. When he saw me, he turned off the blaster and took his mask off, but then he just nodded wassup, like we was passing each other on the street.

"Oh. I thought my daddy was out here."

"He was, but he ran to check on the shop, so it's just me. And no, I ain't got no money for you to go to no mall." Then he chuckled at his own joke. I hate when niggas do that.

"Why you always so mean to me?"

Doni stared at me for a moment, like he didn't understand what I was saying at first, and then he got up and walked back into the garage. When he found what he was looking for, he walked back and handed me another respirator. "Put this on if you gon be out here." Then he sat down on the ground, but didn't pick up the blaster again. He just pulled a rag out of his back pocket and wiped his face. He kinda skinny, but he wiry, and a pretty brown. Kinda reddish, like my mama's teakettle. He had a fresh fade too; probably hit the barbershop the day before since it was payday. He got a gap in his front teeth, one you can only see if you really looking at him. After he wiped his face, he started talking.

"I ain't mean to you. I treat you like I treat all my friends. Plus, I treat you like you treat all *your* friends."

"Wha's that supposed to mean?"

"It mean we friends."

"No it don't, cause if it do, then you ain't got no friends."

He laughed, maybe at me. "Naw, I still got a couple left." He looked down at the rust and stuff come off the frames and nodded again. Then he turned back to me. "Why'on't you come out and meet some of my friends. One of em is having a cookout tonight. You can ride wit me if you ain't got plans."

I don't know exactly what he trying to do, so I just try to play like I'm busy. "I was planning on doing something with Drina, but I'll think about it."

"Oh, word? Cause I heard Drina was coming to the cookout."

I don't know how he knew that. And I couldn't help but look surprised. "Really?"

"Yeah, so y'all can still hang out, but you can ride there wit me if you want. I'll come back and get you round eight."

I was gon say something else, but then he turned on the blaster again and put on his mask. I left, and when I got back upstairs, I realized I still had the one he gave me in my hand. I told myself I'd take it back down later. Real quick, I put it on, and I could smell my daddy's snuff breath in it, so I snatched it off. I didn't know what I was doing.

"Now, where y'all goin again?" My daddy was drinking a beer in the kitchen, and my mama was soaking collards in the sink.

"Somebody birthday party," I said. I was already dressed, sitting at the kitchen bar, and it was only 7:15. I had on a new pair of jeans with this off-the-shoulder shirt. It was long sleeved, and lavender, like my hair. I think lavender is a good fall color, even though everybody swear it's just for spring. I like it cause it sets off my skin.

"Oh, probably Jaydell's. You know, one work at the shop." Daddy turned to my mama and she dunked both her hands in the water and didn't say nothing. "Well, y'all be careful. I don't know why you wanna go out this late by yourself, but since Fredrina gon be there I guess it's not a problem."

"Daddy, I go out this late sometimes. And I'm not going by myself. Doni say he coming to pick me up in a few minutes."

"Well…" And Daddy didn't say nothing after that—just put his empty bottle on the counter and left the kitchen. When he left, my mama turned around to get a good look at me, hands still in the water.

"You look cute with your purple lipstick."

I mean, it's actually called Plum Vamperiwinkle, but it's okay. I thanked her anyway.

DONI GOT A NICE CAR. It's an Eclipse, but it's fixed up: blue and black interior—even the dashboard—plus underglows. Those were purple. I was wondering if Daddy helped him do it, and maybe he was reading my mind, cause he say: "Yeah, me and your dad worked on this car for months. Soon as I got the engine straight, he had me bring it in, and we'd mess around wit it when it was slow."

"That's good. It look nice."

"Thank ya," he said. "And so do you. Matching my lights."

That made me a little nervous, cause I didn't want him thinking I did it on purpose. "I didn't even know all your lights was purple. I guess I only see this car in the daytime."

"If you came out more, you could see it."

By this time, he'd pulled up to our gate, which is right off Highway 79. The house is way back from the road; you gotta know where you going to even know it's back there. And quiet as it's kept that's probly why Daddy bought it. People think we live in Shreveport city limits, but we really live in Greenwood, and we way closer to the shop than most folks realize. But Doni the only person work there that Daddy ever let come to the house. Doni had to get on the gate's white list so it could read his license plate, and then my daddy had to tell the state troopers that be posted all up through here that Doni worked for him so they'd leave him alone. He mighta said something to the neighbors, too, but all the houses round here so tucked off in the woods we don't hardly ever see each other. This really don't even feel like a neighborhood like Queensborough or Sunset Acres where they got a lot of shooting but they also got block parties and folks come over to your house to get a plate if you cook out for the Fourth. But us being tucked off over here might be a good thing cause Daddy say white folks don't want us living near them noway, so the less they see of us, the better. So we just a bunch of properties with nothing but trees and water in between us. In high school, I used to be bored in classrooms full of people. Now I be bored and don't even have nobody to look at, except Mama and the birds.

You don't really hit civilization till you get to Pines Road. That's where Doni stopped at the Shell station to get some cigarettes before we hit the highway. I like this part of the city all right, but it still feel kinda country. The biggest attraction is the Walmart and it always be cluttered and the parking lot look like a landfill. People just throw they whole fast-food bag out the window and keep going. I wish Daddy had bought a house in Long Lake or off Ellerbe. Those houses be just as nice, and a lot of them be having pools and jacuzzis or be backed up to the water. It's a Walmart out that way, too, but they got the Target (which be way cleaner); a Kirkland's and an Ulta, where I be getting some of my makeup; a Carrabba's, and some local eateries, too, like that new seafood place whose name I can't think of. But Daddy say them new neighborhoods put the houses too close together, and they ain't big as ours but they cost more money. I mean, we do got a lot of rooms, but we coulda moved to a big house out in Spring Lake, too, so I could get to Line Avenue and Pierremont easier, where they got the boutiques run by the little old white women. They be nice to you most of the time, but sometimes they swear they the only people who know bout fashion. Sometimes

I take Drina in there just to put a outfit together so I can argue wit em. Really it just be me arguing; Drina don't never say nothing. She ain't as comfortable being around white people as I am. And hell, half the reason I am prolly got something to do with money. But money don't make you comfortable everywhere. I realized I hadn't really been saying nothing to Doni, so I tried to think, but when we got on the freeway, he started talking bout his car again.

"Yeah, I be out wit it sometimes. Take it to car meets and stuff like that. But these fools out here be doing too much. They'll take a '85 Cutlass and try to make it look like a Maserati. See, me? When I finish wit a car, I want it to look good as it did the year it came off the line. I'm sayin, it can be tricked out and all that. Crazy colors and lights. I love that shit. But it need to look like what it is. That's what I like about Mr. Curtis. He'll do something by hand to make sure it's done right, and not like it's just been pieced together from whatever you last saw in a car magazine."

I thought about my makeup, and I said, "Yeah, I can understand that. Gotta take your time. Otherwise, you be looking throwed."

"Yep."

Doni looked over at me, hand on the clutch. He smiled and I could see his gap. "When we gon start working on your car?" He shook his head. "Oh, man. Your daddy prolly won't even let none of us *touch* yo car. He'll prolly buy you a brand-new one and then do whatever he wanna do to it by hisself. What kind you want?"

"I don't drive," I told him. "Well…I do, a little. I'm still learning how."

"Really? How old are you, bout twenty?"

"Yeah. I mean, I know how to do it, but I ain't never been taught. I never had classes or nothing like that."

"Why not?"

"I don't know."

I didn't wanna tell him about the eye stuff, but there he go, mindreading again.

"Oh yeah, well your daddy said you might need some custom glasses or something like that."

"Yeah. They would just be for driving, though. So I can see the street signs."

"Oh, okay, I guess that make sense. Like if the sun is out or something."

"No, not like that." I stuck my hands between my thighs, which is what I do when I'm nervous. "So, like, I can see everything, just not, like, make out small stuff, like the letters on street signs and stuff."

"Oh, okay." Doni nodded as he checked his blind spot. "Now see? That make sense to me, cause you can see everything as far as I can tell. You see everything in that lil garage out back of the house." His voice went up to mimic mine. "Daddy, them seats is *nasty*. Whatchu gon do bout them seats?" I reached over to push him a little and he let go of the clutch so he could block my hand. "See? If you can see to hit, you can see everything."

JAYDELL LIVE IN MOORETOWN, WHICH is the hood, but it's some decent houses over here too. They not that big, but some people keep up the exteriors and they lawns. Especially the older folks, who moved over here back when it was still a neighborhood for the schoolteacher-type Black folks. And people over here definitely be having nice cars. But the folks at Jaydell's house was outshining all the neighbors that night. I'm telling you, we had to park halfway up the block and walk, and all the way there I was looking at cars that been through my daddy shop. Or cars that been worked on by the dudes that been through my daddy shop. There was suicide doors.

Candy paint. Somebody even had a dually—them big-ass trucks. Some folks that came out for the party was still outside looking at each other's cars, and this one dude with a Camaro had his hood up showing off a painting of a woman in a two-piece thong. I looked, and it was Foxy Brown. The one from Daddy's movies.

"Damn, that's flames," I said.

"Oh, you like that?" Doni asked. "Man, you prolly think my car ain't shit then."

"Naw—like I said, yours is nice too. And you be keeping it classy, like you said."

"Yes, ma'am. Be trying to anyway. I did like that yellow Karmann we just passed, though. I said if I ever buy a house and I got space enough to fix up cars like your daddy be doin out back of his, I'd get me a Model T. Redo everything on it."

"Yeah, that'd be nice."

"Wouldn't it though?"

As soon as we came up to the house, I got nervous. It was too many people out front *and* on the inside, yelling, slappin dominoes, sliding past each other with drinks, trying not to spill nothing on the furniture. I had to say "excuse me" too many times. And people were looking me up and down as usual, or stopping what they was doing as we passed by, Doni in front, leading me by the hand. Man, it felt like being on a runway—everybody got a good look. I was so glad I don't be going nowhere dressed any kind of way. When we passed by one group, somebody said, "I see dead people," and everybody started laughing and yelling, "You wrong," but Doni act like he didn't hear them, so neither did I. Plus, I knew I looked good. My braids still looked fresh, and even my mama said I looked pretty. She don't say that to everybody.

When Doni found Jaydell in the kitchen, they dapped each other up and I thought I saw Doni pass him some money.

"'Sup, birthday boy!"

"You already know." Then Jaydell turned to me. "Oh, okay, Donno. I see you done took a walk on the wild side. How you doin? Your name Suzette, right?" And he leaned in, like most people do cause they think I can't see them. Or they trying to see me better, cause maybe it's they first time. I took a step back cause he was too close. Plus, his breath smelled like Waste Management.

"Yeah. I'm Suzette."

He held out the hand that wasn't holding a drink. "I'm Jay. I work at your daddy's shop. Welcome to my lil kickback." It was way too many people over there to call it no kickback, but he knew that. I got what Doni meant when he said some niggas be doin too much.

"How you doin? Oh, and happy birthday."

"Thank you. I cain't complain. Made it another year without twelve or the jackboys gettin me. And now I'd'n got to meet you too. So you'd'n finally decided to come out of…what…Long Lake? With them million-dollar houses? Tha's where y'all stay?"

Doni broke in. "Mane, don't be askin her all that. You know Mr. Curtis don't play that shit."

"Mane, I'm just tryna find out if the nigga live in Shreveport at all. We know yo understudyin ass ain't gon tell nobody."

"If he wanted you to know, he'da told the rest of y'all by now. How long you been working there—ten years?"

"Yep. Came on right after you, right before what happened with Dolo."

By the time he said that, Doni was standing behind me, and I felt him shift a little, like he had raised his hand or something, and Jaydell changed the subject like *that*. He took another sip from his cup.

"A'ight. Well, come on, let me getch'all sum'n to eat."

He led us out to the backyard, where there was even more people sitting on lawn chairs and on top of coolers. It was some kids running around with little water guns too. They stopped short when they saw me, but I'm used to getting that with little kids. I just tried to ignore them, but the adults wasn't no better. They stared too. All except for this group off to one side, sitting in a half circle facing away from everybody, in the kinda lawn chairs you can prop your feet up on. They wasn't really paying other folks attention; just talking. A couple of the girls was sitting on the other girls' laps, and one of them had on a tight mini-sundress and some nice sneakers, legs crossed, drinking a beer and leaning over to shake somebody's arm while telling a story. She had on a blond lace front, and it was half covering her face, but I bout fell out when I saw who it was.

"Drina?"

Doni had already told me that she'd be there, but she just looked…different. She even had on eye makeup. She sat up real quick and pulled her dress down.

"Heyyyyyy, Suzette. Whatchu doin here?" And finally, everybody turned around to look at me, Jaydell, and Doni. I didn't know what to say, so I just pointed at Doni.

"Oh. Okay." She smiled like she was in on a secret.

Then we just stood there for a minute, till Jaydell said, "Aye, let's go get them some plates."

So we walked off, and I tried not to look back at Drina cause I didn't want her to think I was worried bout her being there and not telling me she was coming. Instead, I let Jaydell uncover the trays to show us what all they had: leg quarters; beef ribs, cause he say the swine'll kill you; hot dogs (also beef); hamburgers; corn on the cob and some vegetable skewers; potato salad and baked beans; some chips and cookies, stuff like that; fruit salad; some macaroni salad too; and then some plain baked potatoes somebody had wrapped up and threw on the grill. "I try to keep it healthy, you know?" he said. It wasn't really no toppings for them, though, just some Country

Crock in a bowl of ice next to some salt and pepper. Somebody had
even brought some crawfish, and it was still a lot of them left cause
they were out of season, so folks probably thought they was too small
to even mess with. I put a few on my plate anyway. When me and
Doni set our plates down at a little foldout table, I looked at what all
I got. "Man, I think I'ma need some napkins."

Doni licked some potato salad off his finger. "I'll get em for you.
Oh, and we forgot drinks. You drinkin?"

"What they got?"

When we was making our plates, Jaydell's girlfriend had come
over and they made plates, too, and Jaydell left us at the table so
he could show Doni where the coolers were. I was watching Doni
say hey to everybody, and then everybody pointing at me, and Doni
saying something and then dapping them up and walking off, but
then Jaydell's girlfriend started talking, and she distracted me.

"Hey, I didn't even introduce myself. I'm Lexi. You're Suzette,
right?"

"Yeah," I said, cause I don't really like a lot of females, and I tried
to keep it short, but Lexi kept talking.

"I like your lipstick, girl. And your hair. Who did it?"

"My friend Drina." I was about to point over to her, but I didn't
want her to think I was talking bad about her. Cause I felt like her
eyes was on me the whole time.

"Okay! See, I like you. Some women won't even tell you cause
they don't want you getting the same style, or they don't want your
hair to look as good as theirs." She chuckled a little and picked up
the Styrofoam cup she was sitting next to.

"No, she my friend. And she good! It wouldn't make sense for her
to lose business cause I was tryin to be petty."

Lexi swallowed and smiled. "That's what I be saying."

It took awhile for them to come back with the drinks, and, usually, that make me nervous too: when I go somewhere I don't know nobody and the person I'm with just disappear. But Lexi seemed all right; she was talking about hair, and I like to talk about that, too, so we did that while I was trying to keep the gnats away from our food. It wasn't that many mosquitoes since it was getting cooler, or flies neither, but gnats be here damn near year-round till it start getting cold for real; then they die off.

When Doni came back, him and Jaydell handed us our drinks, and Jaydell went off for a minute to help some other folks fix plates, but Doni stayed and talked to Lexi till he came back. I liked that; how he didn't leave me by myself again. And them talking kept me busy listening, so I wasn't trying to see what people were looking at, or what Drina was doing. I found out Doni and Lexi went to school together, and Lexi was in nursing school with one of Doni's sisters. While they was talking, Lexi asked me if I was home from college for the weekend. I was kinda impressed she thought I looked like a college girl, but then I thought about Xavier and how my daddy clitblocked me and that made me tense up again.

"I'm not in school yet. I'm still tryna figure out what I wanna do." Lexi nodded, and Doni popped a deviled egg in his mouth.

"That's all right," he said while he was still chewing. "You young. You got plenty of time to figure it out."

But I felt bad cause it sounded like I wasn't doing nothing, so I busted out, "I like fashion, though. Clothes, makeup, hair, like what me and Lexi was talking about. That kind of stuff."

"Yeah, a stylist! That's good," Lexi said. "One of my friends just opened a boutique on Line Avenue and she offer personal styling services out of it. I think it's doing pretty good."

And I hadn't never thought about that, but yeah, maybe that is what I wanna do.

Anyway, while Doni and Lexi were catching up, people would

come by and speak, and Doni would introduce me. Or they would wave at him from across the yard and he would wave back and tell me who they was, if they was kin to him. It's a lot of Taylors in Shreveport, so Doni got a gang of cousins. Jaydell came back eventually, and him and Doni got loud, laughing about crazy customers who wrecked their cars doing dumb shit, and how my daddy would talk to people.

"He don't care, man," Jaydell said, "Black, white. If you tryin to get over, he'll put you out."

Doni was like, "Yessir, but that's how you know he got clout. He earned it, though. And he fair too. He don't do folks dirty; you get good work for your money. But he don't play neither."

And I never thought about my daddy like that, but that made me proud, you know? And it also made me think about how, if I ever opened a boutique, I would want people to say that about me.

After a while I enjoyed being there, over Jaydell's. After he stopped acting like I'd just crawled out of a dungeon, he seemed okay. And Lexi was nice. She didn't ask me stupid stuff, and she didn't treat me like I was uppity cause of my daddy. She just talked to me like I was anybody else. Plus, she said we could maybe go to her friend's boutique one Saturday when she was free. I wanted to do that just to see what it was like, so I gave her my number, and had almost forgot Drina was there till she stopped by the table to say bye. She was kinda drunk, so she was even louder than when we came in, and I ain't used to that Drina at all. And that little dress? She did look cute, though, with her legs out. And I mean *all* her legs, cause that dress was short. It was strapless and had a corset top, but it was floral print and flared at the waist. It looked like something I woulda picked out, but I woulda told her to leave them Reeboks at home. When her friends was saying bye to Jaydell, she pulled me to the side real quick and kissed me on the cheek. Her lips were cold, like she had just turned up a bottle.

"I love you, Zettie."

"Um, okay. Love you too." I didn't know why she was saying that. I wonder if she thought I was jealous or sad cause she was there with all these people I didn't even know she was cool with, and she seemed like this was her crowd, but everybody was looking at me like I walked off the moon. She put her arm around my shoulder, and looked at me for a minute before she leaned in, breath smelling like malt liquor.

"I see you out here on your date."

"Whatchu mean? I ain't on no date."

"Who was that fixing your drink then? And getting you some mo of them little bitty crawfish?" I hadn't even known Doni did that. I looked over at him and sure enough he had a cup in his hand with some foil on top, probably cause all the to-go plates was gone. I looked back at Drina.

"Mane, come on. That's just how Doni is. I think he just wanted somebody to be here wit him. Keep him company."

Drina looked at me like I should know better. "Okay, but he work wit all these people. He *got* company."

I changed the subject. "And look at you out here all dolled up. When you start dressing like this? I ain't never seen this dress before."

"I switch it up sometimes. You like it?"

"It's cute."

"Thank you, girl." She shrugged her shoulders and then wrapped her hands around them, like she was cold.

Doni looked over at us and held up his keys. "Hey, Suzette, you bout ready to go?"

"Yeah, I'm ready."

Drina looked at both of us, then gave me a hug. Before she pulled away, she whispered in my ear again, "I love you, Zettie."

And I was about to say something back, but she hopped on over to Doni and hugged him. She said something to him, too, but I couldn't hear it.

"YOU WANNA PRACTICE DRIVING? CAIN'T tell your dad, though."

This was about a week later. Doni had asked if I wanted to go see *The Predator* at the Regal in Bossier, and I hadn't wanted to see it when it first came out, but I guess I said yes cause there was this new outfit I wanted to wear, and I hadn't been out in a while. It was a neon-green catsuit, but it was black lace from the elbow down and the knee down. It reminded me of a race car suit—that's why I got it. And a blue one too. I thought maybe if we went to another party together or a car meetup I could wear one of them. But he had asked about the movies first.

Drina wasn't going nowhere at the time cause she said she was broke. I offered her some gas money, but then she said she was tired. She'd been full of excuses lately. Prolly so she could go out with her other friends. Who knows? So when Doni asked, I said yeah. My daddy screwed his face up when I told him, and right before I left, I heard him talking to Mama in the kitchen while I was in the half bathroom between the kitchen and the dining room, checking on my makeup.

"I wonder what's going on with that." Daddy was rapping his knuckles on the counter while he was talking.

"Nothing. You know Doni a responsible young man."

"I need to know what his intentions are, though."

"Then why don't you ask him?"

I heard somebody set something in the sink. Then my mama started talking again.

"You cain't keep her in this house forever, Curtis. Doni and Drina bout the only folks she know cause she don't go nowhere."

"You know how them people are."

"But 'them people' ain't Doni or Drina. Plus, them people ain't gon change. So what we gon do? Keep her holed up forever?"

More silence. Then my mama laughed. "I don't know why they named that boy Hedonis. But he ain't gon do nothing to Suzie. He respect you too much, if nuthin else. All you done did for that boy? Leave em alone."

And it pissed me off cause Daddy always do this: act like Drina the only person in the world ain't trying to kill me. And usually I didn't care about it but Drina had been MIA and I'd been in the house for damn near seven days looking him and Mama upside the head and not doing a damn thing else. I was bout to come out and say something, but Daddy left and went back into the movie room.

Me and Doni was done watching *Predator* and that had been cool, but I didn't know about driving Doni's car. I drove my mama's car sometimes, when Daddy wasn't home, but just to do little stuff like go to the corner store or the hairdresser up on Pines, and never at night. Too much stuff happening, my mama say; plus, Daddy be home at night. But I didn't know where I would be driving in Doni's car—like, on the highway or over bridges or what. I guess all that made me embarrassed.

"I ain't got the glasses," I told Doni. We were cutting through a empty parking lot at Pierre Bossier, back behind Dillard's, which was closed like the rest of the mall, but the lights was on. I checked out the mannequins near the doors, and they were already done up for the winter: scarves and red coats and furry boots, hot as it is down here year-round.

"Bet," said Doni. "Welp. I'm ready when you are."

"My daddy say he gon teach me anyway."

Doni shrugged as he pulled out the lot, turning the wheel slow with one hand. "Yeah, he prolly will."

First he stopped to get some cigarettes; then we drove through a couple neighborhoods before we ended up in South Highland, where they got a few nice houses, and don't nobody believe in curtains. We saw some flatscreens on through the windows, but wasn't nobody in front of em. I guess even white folks gotta get out the house on the weekends. Doni pointed out the ones he liked, and after a while I figured out the bigger they were, the faster he'd tell me he liked em. I didn't think none of them was all that special. A lot of em was older houses; this supposed to be a historic district now, but just cause a house been up a hundred years don't mean it need to stay up, you know what I'm sayin? And anyway, one thing Daddy was right about when he said he didn't wanna live in the city is that you get more house for your buck. Our house twice the size of some of these. Me *and* my parents got separate balconies attached to our rooms. And our foyer the size of its own room. The only thing is that our furniture is kinda dated—I been trying to get Mama to let me get the living room set reupholstered for months. But it *is* better made, so we ain't been having to replace it every two years. Folks'll buy a house and fill it up with cheap shit that look good for now, but don't really last. My mama call that "new money behavior." I mean, we new money, too, but we try not to act like it.

"Man, this city stay changin on me," Doni said as he turned onto Erie. "We use to call some parts of Highland the *Low*land. Always some shit going down. Always niggas out in the streets up to no good. Now look. Folks buyin this shit up. And watch: before you know it they gon flip Wilkerson Terrace, too, and turn them Section Eights into condos. Cause they already gettin the garages, convertin em into little bougie brunch places. Now I hear talk of somebody putting a auto shop out here. That shit ain't gon do nuthin tho. Elkins still the best place to go, hands down. Folks even come from

Oklahoma to bring us they cars. Oh, shit, look at this one over on your side." Doni pointed to my window so I could look out. It was one of the newer houses, and it was all glass up front, floor to ceiling, and all the lights was on so you could see everything. It was beautiful, but I didn't want him to know I agreed with him.

"These is a'ight, but I like my daddy's house better. Maybe my uncle's. His got the wraparound porch. And they kitchen got better appliances than ours. They upgraded it awhile back. But ours is still bigger. And we got the movie room with the recliners and all that."

Doni blew smoke out the crack in the window like he'd been doing, but this time, he turned to me and a little was still coming out of his mouth. "'Ours.' You think your daddy hung the moon, huh?"

"Why everybody keep saying that?"

"Prolly cause we all see it." I didn't say nothing after that, but then, a few blocks up, he was like, "You wanna stay there forever? Is that where you wanna live?"

"Say what now?" I was on Instagram checking likes for my picture of what I had on and I had got like two hundred while we was in the movie, so I'd kinda forgot what we was talking about.

"Live at your daddy's. Is that what you want?" he asked again.

And I don't know. Something bout the way he said that; I don't think he was asking what I think he was asking. It felt like he had twisted something in me, and I wasn't hurt or nothing, just bothered.

"Why you say it like that?"

"I didn't say it like nuthin. Just askin a question to see where your head at."

"Why you worried bout it, though?"

He took another drag, and blew out the crack. "I'm not worried. I just wanted to know what you wanted. Like, you gon move out? You want a family? Or something else? Move in with Drina? Some other kind of…I don't know."

"Some other kind of what?"

Doni looked over at me quickly. "Naw…I mean, like, take my oldest sister, Reen. She gon stay at my mama's house forever cause that's how she is. She take care of everybody and that's, like, what she *do*. That's what she wanna do and that's *all* she wanna do."

"Well, I'm not that," I said quickly so he didn't get nothing confused.

"Well, we *know* that."

"And what that mean?"

"I mean, you ain't taking care of your parents. You're like— It's like the other way around. Naw, that's not what— Okay, I'm sayin, you like living there wit em, right? Y'all get along and everybody happy. Like, that's where you wanna be, like Reen."

And he looked over at me because I guess I was supposed to say yeah, but I didn't. Instead, I say, "Why you riding around these white folks' neighborhoods looking at houses? We liable to get pulled over. Or I'ma choke cause you blowing them cancer sticks in my face."

He looked over at me again and busted out laughing.

"What's that about?" I asked. I musta been getting on his nerves, cause he was sure getting on mine.

"You mad at me again, Miss Suzette?"

"No. Just tired."

"You wanna go home?" I didn't say nothing. So we rode around for a little more, and then pulled into the little spot in front of the duck pond. He opened the console and pulled out a little package.

"Wha's that?"

"Oatmeal."

"Why?"

"Better for em than bread. You coming?"

It was a couple of other cars in the parking lot, but I didn't see nobody, and I wasn't necessarily trying to look. I know what people come out here for, and I hoped he wasn't trying to do nothing shady. I know what some dudes be thinking about me. One time, me and Drina was out on the Boardwalk and this dude we went to school with named JaQuavian came up behind us and said real loud, "Aye, I heard albino bitches be wilin out in bed. That shit be magical. Like, it can cure AIDS or some shit. You gon take me home?"

I was so shook I didn't know how to respond, but when Drina told him to get the fuck on somewhere, he was like, "What, you must be mad cause y'all fuckin." Then when she put her arm around my waist so she could lead me away, he started yelling even louder: "Aw, shit! That really *is* her girl!"

So I didn't know what Doni had me out here trying to do, but I wasn't with it. Still, I pulled back the door handle anyway.

"Ain't the ducks sleep?"

"Not all of em."

We stood out there for a while before I saw one. He was beautiful. Green, green head. Body like a dirty brown, but soft-looking. I ain't never seen no duck come up *out* the water for no uncooked oatmeal. He act like him and Doni knew each other. But when Doni held out a handful, the duck would take a couple steps, then back up, wings kinda up, then step forward again.

"What he doing?" I whispered just in case I scared him.

"I guess he makin sure this is what he want."

"Ain't he hungry?"

"Probly. But he ain't stupid. Everything taste good to you ain't good for you."

"Oatmeal taste good to him?"

"I'own know, but it keep em healthy. Ducks that get too much table food get fucked-up wings called Angel Wings." He sprinkled some more oatmeal in his hand. "It look cool, cause the wings look backward, kinda like suicide doors, but they can't fly."

"For real?"

"I don't make shit up. But that's deep, ain't it? You feed em too good, they lose they ability to even move around."

It was quiet for a little while. Then Doni said, "I look at houses so I can have a idea of what I want. I gotta know what I want before I go get it, even if I change my mind between Point A and Point B. Otherwise, I'm scared I'm just gon be feeding off other people's scraps for the rest of my life."

"Like the ducks?"

"*Just* like the ducks."

"So we really just out here to feed some ducks." I didn't wanna say what I thought he might be doing, so I just kinda nodded toward the cars in the parking lot.

He busted out laughing again. "Whoa! I'm not sure who you been messin wit, Miss Suzie, but we don't even know each other like that. I gotta see where your head at first."

"What that mean?"

"It mean I'm twenty-seven and I ain't in these streets like that. And I'm lookin for somethin…Sheeeeit, I'own even know. But I been lookin for somethin a little more permanent. A little more real."

"Real like what?"

Doni threw his handful of oatmeal on the ground. "I wish I could tell you, baby. But I'll know it when I see it. And I ain't seen it yet."

"Then why you out here wit me?"

"Cause we just came from the movies, right?" And he winked.

That duck was still scared, maybe of me, so we walked back up from the water and sat on the hood of the car while Doni showed me a couple of constellations. A belt or something like that. The Dipper. He traced out the parts with his finger so I could see them.

Cause sometimes, I do see a thing, but it's kinda jumbled and it take awhile for it to click in my brain. Then out the blue, he said, "You said fashion, right? You wanna do that?"

"Yeah. I mean…I like clothes. Getting made up. Looking nice. Even hair stuff. That's why I love going to Dollar Mania. That's like Disney to me for real; I be going crazy in there. Or I'll see somethin I like and I get it cheaper online. Or better quality, cause them clothes in there be cute but they be knockoffs from China and two sizes too small for anybody. That hair be overpriced too." I remembered how he acted that day I was getting my hair done. "I even picked out this color for Drina to do my braids in."

He picked up one of my braids and held it, like he was inspecting it or something. "Yeah. You must be like your daddy. Or like me wit cars. Take it and make somethin nice out of it. Or get somebody else to do it."

"Yeah, like make it look more like itself. But better." I knew I was echoing something he had said earlier, but I felt like that, too, so I figured it was okay.

"Yep. That's why I love what I do."

"For real?"

"Hell yeah"—and he dropped my braid so he could demonstrate— "I like doin stuff with my hands. Always been like that, since I was little. Takin apart the TV, toaster, shit like that when my mama was at work. But cars was the first thing I could play around with and they still worked. Hell, sometimes they worked better, once I got my uncle to teach me. But when your dad hired me, I told him I would do whatever. I could learn. And I did. I'm still learnin, if I'm gon be real. Your daddy teach me somethin new every day. But yeah. I like that. Takin somethin and puttin it back together, leaving it better than it was before I got my hands on it."

I didn't know what to say about that. It sounded like he was serious, and I didn't even know if I could be serious with Doni. Hell, what if he was out here like JaQuavian, trying to play me? But it didn't seem like that, so I just nodded. I was gon let him talk, and then he said, "You feel that way about fashion?"

"Huh?"

"I said do you feel that way about fashion? Clothes."

"Child, I don't know. I don't know if I feel like that about anything, except maybe shoppin. But I guess maybe that's the same thing. I like putting outfits together, creating a look that don't look like everybody else. I hate being basic. And I'll do research and stuff, too, see what's hot, and sometimes I'll, like, work from that, but then sometimes I'll do the exact opposite."

"So you a game changer."

"Yep. I figure if folks gon be looking, they might as well see somethin interesting."

Doni nodded. "Hell yeah. I know that's right." He looked like he was about to light another cigarette, but then he just folded his arms across his chest and looked up at all the constellations he pointed out. Then he said, "I hope you figure out what it is, the thing you wanna do. Cause you can do it."

"I know I can. I can do anything."

He looked over at me. "I wasn't saying you cain't. I was just saying— Welp, people will tell you that all the time, right? But then sometimes they don't always expect you to *really* do everything. But then, once you start making real moves, moves by yourself, they get nervous. Scared. Jealous. So you gotta pick out what you really wanna do for yourself, you know? Then do that. And don't let these fools out here try and block you. Or make you so mad you do something crazy."

"Okay." I paused for a minute. "I see what you mean." But I really didn't. I felt weird, like maybe he was trying to talk circles around me. Or maybe not like that. Maybe like he was trying to tell me something without saying it. My mama be doing that sometimes and I hate it, but I don't never say nothing cause I figure when it's time for me to know, I'll know. People act like you gotta find out everything going on under the sun, and sometimes it's better if the knowing find you first.

We sat out there for the longest, but I didn't mind. Not being in the house made me feel good. I was out and about, and Drina wasn't driving me around and dropping me off when she got tired of me. That felt good too. But after a while, Doni put his arm around my shoulder and said, "You ready to go, Miss Suzie?" And when I said yeah, he moved my braids back and kissed me a couple times on the cheek. Then he turned my chin toward him and kissed me for real, like, *on* the mouth. But I didn't really know what it meant. We didn't tongue or nothing; it was just a kiss, but it was a *kiss* kiss, and I hadn't had one of those since me and Drina used to practice on each other in the seventh grade. I could taste his cigarettes and the breath mints he kept in a tin in his pocket that jangled around every time he moved. It was a good kiss. I woulda been down to stay, but then he got up and opened my car door, and I knew I was gon have to go home sooner or later.

OH, DADDY WAS BIG MAD at me in the morning, but he wouldn't say nothing about it, just grumping around the house not talking to nobody. He wouldn't even stay in the same room with me when I walked in, so I turned to Mama to see what I could find out, but she wouldn't tell me nothing.

"Don't worry bout him," was all she said. "I'll straighten him out."

It wasn't till the middle of the night I figured out what she meant. I had got up to use the bathroom and I kinda heard them, cause the house was quiet and I'd left my door open. I had to sneak out of my room to the end of my part of the hallway, in the little nook before you get to the catwalk, so they couldn't see me. They was right below me, in the living room. I couldn't see what they was doing, but Daddy was *loud*.

"What she doin comin home that late? I know ain't no movie last that long."

"Curtis, please. That girl twenty years old. You need to be happy she ain't came home high or pregnant."

"Is you crazy? I'll mess around and kill somebody."

"Kill who?"

Daddy ain't say nothing.

Then Mama go, "If I done told you once, I done told you a thousand times, we cain't stop her from living her life. She grown. She *supposed* to wanna go out and meet people. She supposed to wanna go on dates." Before the kiss, I don't believe I had even thought about going to the movies with Doni as a date. But I guess it was. He paid.

"I ain't gon never get over them people not protectin my baby. That woman ain't never go to jail."

"How was we gon put her there with nuthin but a story from a eight-year-old who was half sleep at the time? And then put Suzette through testifyin and all that? Where you think her and Doni be going? To Slidell to see Miss Adimu? Cause Arlinda Mouton been dead. Prolly from sadness. You know MarLisha was her only child, and she ain't never get her back after that. That was punishment enough."

Daddy changed the subject. "Where they go last night? Do he treat her respectfully? Keep her from round people that don't mean her no good? We don't know none of that."

"Is that his job?"

"It is if he taking her places. Wait. You know what? That ain't his job. That's my job."

My mama laughed. "Curtis? Baby? Tha's not your job anymore. She a grown woman."

"She may be grown, but she ain't like everybody else."

"I don't understand you a'tall."

"Why? Did I stutter?"

"You the main one said you wanted her to have a normal life. And after the voodoo stuff you said the best way to do that was to keep her away from every damn body. So, if she done lived a normal life, like you wanted, what make her different?"

My daddy got quiet, but my mama kept talking.

"If we damned cause we did, wonder what woulda happened if we didn't."

"I didn't say we was no 'damned.' You puttin words in my mouth."

"I ain't doin shit cause you not saying nuthin."

"And now you cussin me out."

"Curtis, I'm bout to go to bed, cause you done lost your mind. But lemme tell you this, cause here's what's gon happen. You gon leave that girl alone. She wanna go out, we gon let her go. She old enough to make her own decisions. And I *know* I did my job. I *know* she know right from wrong. And I bet *not* hear talk uh you doin nuthin to Doni, or doin nuthin to her cause then you gon have to deal wit me, hear that? Wife or no wife, I ain't playing with you. That's *my* baby girl, and I been lettin you call the shots for twenty years, but the day of me doin that is over. She grown. Let her go."

It got real quiet after that, and after a while, I went back to my room and tried to shut the door quietly cause I was scared. I ain't seen my mama talk to my daddy like that since the third grade. But what I had *never* seen was my daddy letting her.

And what the hell happened to Ms. Mouton?

I DON'T KNOW—HEARING ALL that made me wonder what my fault was in all this. Like, maybe I played sick too many times as a kid, and after they took me out of school, I made like there was too much stuff I couldn't do so I didn't have to do it, and now I really can't do nothing without my daddy having a problem. Or maybe they both just felt sorry for me cause I was different and they knew life was gon be hard. Harder than getting away from Ms. Mouton, cause them or Drina wasn't always gon be around to stop it. I mean it really made me feel bad, like I had done them dirty or something, and I did myself dirty, too, maybe just for being born. Maybe I did, but I couldn't figure it out by myself. Probably the best person to talk to about it was Doni, cause I felt like maybe that's kinda what he was trying to say at the park, but I didn't wanna do that cause part of Mama and Daddy's fight was about him. Plus, I don't know. I don't really trust dudes like that. So I called Drina, cause maybe she would get it. She's known me almost my whole life, since kindergarten, when the kids made fun of me and she said, "Tha's all right. She just put on too much baby powder this mornin." I was scared about what she was gon think the next day, but she stayed my friend, and she been my best friend ever since—through everything. But I still didn't know how to get the conversation started, so I went the roundabout way, and called to talk about another purse I wanted, and then I was like, "You think I be asking for too much? From my daddy and mama?"

Drina paused for a minute. "Whatchu mean?"

"Like for stuff. You think I'm too spoiled?"

Drina laughed. "Suzie. How I'm s'posed to know? I mean, you a only child. Who else they gon buy for?"

"Yeah. That's true. But I guess that's not what I mean. I'm wonderin if maybe I made them feel like they had to take care of me.

Like a lot. If I made them feel sorry for me." I didn't wanna go further cause I didn't necessarily know if I wanted to talk about all of it.

"Ohhhhh. Okay. Naw, Zettie. You didn't do nothing wrong. Your parents love you. They gon protect you no matter what. They always been like that, prolly since before you knew what it was or who *they* was. You cain't beat yourself up about that."

"But what if I don't want them to do it no more?"

"What, protect you?"

"Well, like, shelter me. I might be missin out on some stuff."

Drina said, "Hmph. Well, I think I see what you're talking about."

"Yeah."

Drina sighed. "Well, I mean, they good people, your parents. I wouldn't cut em out completely, you know? Cause they know stuff you don't. And they can look out for you when you don't see all that's going on. Maybe just take a little space for yourself. Let em know you gon be all right. And let em know you still need em, even if you don't need em for everything."

"How I'm supposed to do all'at?"

"Them your parents. You tell me."

And I really woulda just hung up in her face but she already sounded kinda down, so I just said, "I guess I gotta figure that part out. But what's goin on with you? You sound depressed. And how come we don't do stuff together no more?"

Drina cleared her throat. "I just been tired, I guess. School and work. And home. That's all I do. Plus, what about Doni? You got somebody else to ride you round the city now. Take you to parties. Whatchall do after you left?"

"Nothin. We just friends." For some reason, I didn't wanna say nothing about the movie date or the kiss.

"That's what I meant. He's your new friend." I thought she was gonna make a joke about it or something, but she didn't.

"Oh. Okay. Cause I was bout to say…"

Kiss or no kiss, I didn't think Doni was interested, especially since what he said at the park about wanting somebody who was about something. And that made me a little sad, too, but I wasn't gonna talk about that. I was really bout to go, but then I remembered something I wanted to ask Drina about the party.

"Drina, whatchu whisper to Doni that night, before you left?"

"When, at Jaydell's birthday party?"

"Yep."

"Girl, I was halfway tore up, I don't even know if I can remember."

"Yeah you do. You said 'I love you' to me and then you said something to him."

"Oh, yeah. Okay. I remember that."

"Whatchu say? To him, I mean."

Drina sighed. "What I say…Hmm…What I say…" And just when I was about to hang up in her face for real, she was like, "I told him to be careful with you, cause you ain't like these other ones out here. You younger than you look, and you special. You my whole heart."

FOR ABOUT A MONTH, I didn't see Doni at all. He ain't even come back over to the house, but I told myself that's cause Mama's car was at the shop, and they had finished the seats and took them back up there a few weeks before. But when I texted him to say wassup, check in on him, he said he'd been busy working. Daddy had gave him some extra hours before the holidays and he was just running back and forth, back and forth all day, so I left it alone. I hoped Daddy hadn't scared him away, but I was kinda scared to ask because, if he hadn't, Doni woulda wondered why I thought that was the case and then maybe he would get worried about Daddy when he didn't need to be. And I couldn't check on him online to see what he was doin or nothing like that cause he *old*-school—I mean, Doni ain't even on *Facebook*.

It had got cold for real by the time I saw him again, and I was sick because I always get sick when the weather change. I had also got sick of watching *Real Housewives* and seeing heifers fight all the time. And I couldn't go out on the porch cause it was too cool for my throat, so I was just laying on the couch looking out at it hoping a bird would come by when the doorbell rang. I'd heard the alert on my phone that somebody had come through the gate, but it was the middle of the day, so I figured it was just the mailman. I couldn't hear what the person was saying, but I heard Mama say something, and then I heard footsteps through the foyer. Next thing I know, Doni standing over me in his Carhartt coat and coveralls.

"Suzette! What's good?"

"Hey, Doni. Long time, no see."

"Yeah, Mr. Curtis been keeping me busy." He jammed his hands in his pockets. "I heard you was sick."

"Yeah, I always catch a cold round this time of year."

"For real?" He smiled. "What, you been out gallivantin at night?"

"Galli— Who even say that anymore? You a old man."

He laughed this time, showing his gap, and I missed seeing him like that. "That's all right," he said. "Old man know how not to catch a cold."

"You say that now. Season ain't over yet."

Doni looked down at the couch. "And you rude too. You not gon let me sit down?"

"No. I might be contagious."

"Ain't nothing a little camphor won't fix." Doni sat near my feet. "How's Drina?" he asked, but kinda flat like he already knew the answer.

"She all right, I guess. She say she been busy, so I don't see her like I used to."

"For real? Thought y'all would be out every day, holiday shopping or something. You been keeping busy?"

"Not too busy. Buying clothes. I looked at some classes online for the spring. Fashion design classes."

"Word? Tha's wha's up! You bout to start school?"

"Maybe. Daddy say he gotta see, though. Mama might not be able to do all that running back and forth to get me every day. But I said maybe I can take one class at a time, maybe a couple times a week."

"Yeah." He nodded like he was excited. Maybe it sounded like I was somebody who was about something for a change.

"Yeah. And Mama said she'll teach me how to sew cause she say I might need to know how to do that."

"Yeah, she prolly right." He leaned back a little into the cushions. "I know how to sew too," he said, bending his head so he could scratch his crown.

"Yeah, I know. I remember watching you do the seats."

"Yep. It's easy to learn too. If your mama don't teach you, let me know."

"I thought you was busy at the shop, though."

He looked away for a minute, out onto the porch, maybe even through the screen at the trees. "Yeah," he said shortly. "I been busy. But I can make time."

By that time, my mama had come back through the kitchen from wherever she was, and she said, "Doni, I was just on my way out to get some soup and crackers for Zettie. You wanna stay here with her while I'm gone?"

He paused for a minute, like he didn't know what to say, but then he was like, "Know what? I'll go for you, Miz Elkins. I just gotta pick up a part for Mr. Curtis first, but I'll be right back. Whatchu need?"

Mama gave him her list, and after he left, I wanted to ask her what all that was about, trying to let him stay there while she was gone. But she ran off somewhere in the house, and I kinda dozed off, so I didn't see her again till he got back.

He didn't stay too long after that, said he had to get back to the shop for good before Daddy did. But he did bring me some soup from Olive Garden, so my mama didn't have to make any. He brought some Ritz crackers and ginger ale, too, and he watched me eat while we watched TV. He made like he was gon feed me at first, but he kept playing around, doing the spoon like a airplane and making me have to move my head to eat it cause he say I needed to get my strength up and move the cold out of my chest. Then a couple times he pulled a U-turn with the spoon and ate the soup hisself. I told him I was gon laugh at him when he got sick, cause that's nasty, but he was like, "Don't forget, I'ma old man. I'd'n had everything already. You cain't make me sick." He even had Mama laughing, and then I just gave up and fed myself cause he was really gon mess around and eat all my damn soup.

When he left, he said, "Y'all take it easy." And to me he said, "Know what? I'ma hit you up later," like he had made a decision about something. My mama walked him out, and later that night, he sent me a text message from his old-ass flip phone. It said, it was really good seeing you miss suzette hope you get out from under the weather soon. Pause. & that raggedy quilt.

I said, This my dead great-grandmama quilt! It's a heirloom!

And then he said, that's nice but it's done & she shoulda took it with her. That made me laugh.

Then he was like, maybe once you learn how to sew you can make another one don't forget what i said at the park you gotta do what you wanna do even if other folks is shuffling they feet.

Pause.

ok i'll be seeing you ;-)

I wanted to ask Mama about that, too, but she was in the kitchen washing dishes, and I got tired of watching TV anyway, so I went back to my room to lay down. I stopped by my bathroom on my way there, and when I was washing my hands, I saw myself in the mirror. Braids need redoing. Lips crusty. And my face. Doni did all that, and I ain't even have no makeup on my face. If I had penciled in my eyebrows, they probably woulda been raised.

MAN, IT TOOK ME ALMOST another week to get better, but when I was well enough to put some clothes on, I went out to the garage where Daddy was checking on Mama's car. He had just gave it to her, and she'd been driving it around a little, but he was doing little stuff to it now: checking the lights and stuff. I got up on the stool and watched for a few minutes. I didn't ask nothing about the car. Daddy was fussing with the rearview mirror now, putting on the wide-angle one he'd ordered that had just come in.

"That's big, Daddy. Mama gon be able to see what people playing on the radio if they behind her."

Daddy shined up the mirror before he responded. "She need to. You know how y'all women drive."

"Not me. I don't know. I don't drive."

Daddy didn't say nothing to that.

"Daddy, when I'ma learn how to drive?"

Daddy stopped playing around with the new mirror, and his back was to me when he answered. "You know you need them glasses, Suzette. And I ain't had a chance to take you to Nacogdoches to get fitted for em. I gotta do it when I get a day off." His voice got a little testy, but I kept going.

"Mama could take me. Especially now she got that car."

"I don't want your mama driving to Texas for that."

"Mama go to Waskom all the time. That's Texas."

"That ain't the same thing. Waskom close."

He was doing it again, and I thought about that time Mama went off on him after I came home that night. I didn't wanna start nothing like that, but I always stopped somewhere around this part, and I knew if I did, I wasn't gon get no closer to what I wanted. Whatever it was.

"Okay, so when you gon take off to do it, Daddy? You take off for the Bayou Classic. You take off for the Battle of the Bands and the family reunion. When you gon do this? It prolly won't even take a whole day. We go get fitted for em and then we go back when I gotta pick em up. I already know. I looked into it."

He just kept doing what he was doing, and that made me mad, but I didn't wanna do him like Mama did him. I gave him a little while, and then I was like, "Daddy. You hear me? When you gon take off?"

He got out of the car and shut the door carefully. "You tell me, since you got all the answers."

"You do this all the time, Daddy. When you don't wanna do somethin, you just start telling folks they know everythang. You don't want me to learn how to drive? Why not, Daddy? Cause if you don't, I need to stop asking. I can get Doni or Drina to do it."

Daddy looked over at me like I had lost my mind, but then he just looked kinda thoughtful. "When the last time you seen Doni?"

"He came over last week, and brought me some soup cause I was sick."

"How he know you was sick?"

"He didn't. He was on his way somewhere and stopped by. Then Mama told him and he came in to see about me."

"What he doin up in my house while I ain't here?"

"Nuthin. He just came by. I didn't ask him to, but it was good seein him. You mad about that, too, Daddy?"

"I ain't mad about nuthin but the fact he came to my house without my permission."

"My friends need permission to come over here now? Drina don't need permission."

"I reckon she don't. She respectful."

"Doni respectful too."

"How so?"

"He nice. He take me out and he talk to me about stuff. He encourage me to do stuff, like go to school, or learn how to sew. He even say he'll help me learn to drive if I want."

"Is that so?"

"Yeah. That's what friends is supposed to do. Right, Daddy?"

"So y'all just friends now?"

"We ain't never been nuthin *but* friends, and barely that till recently. You know I couldn't stand Doni."

"But he make you a few promises and now all of a sudden y'all buddies."

"Naw. It ain't like that. I never told him to do none of that stuff. I been waiting on Mama. And I been waitin on you."

Daddy didn't say nothing else, and I tried to wait him out, but he just kept shining up the mirror and then the whole car. I halfway wondered if that's why he fixed cars in the first place: to have something to control like he do everything else. And that made me think of Doni offering to do all that stuff. Maybe he was the same way. Hell, I didn't know.

Finally, I got up to go, but I turned around right before I left and said, "You cain't fix me, Daddy. That's the problem. But it's okay. I got me. You don't have to keep doing whatchu been doin." And I left real quick before he said anything, cause I ain't never talked to

Daddy like that before. And I ain't Mama. Wasn't no telling what he mighta done to me. Plus, if he had asked what the hell I was tryin to say, I wouldn't have been able to tell him.

ON FRIDAY LEXI CALLED ME to say she was sorry she had been so busy, but she wanted to see if I still wanted to go to that store. She say she like shopping on Sundays cause folks don't really clothes shop on Sundays. They like to go on Friday and Saturday so everybody can see them, or so they can get outfits for the club. I said, "That's really what's up; that's why I like Sunday shopping too," and I told her we could go whenever. And I didn't say it, but it wasn't like I had nothing to do noway, cause it had been a smooth two months since me and Drina went *anywhere*. She ain't even call to catch up or say she was sorry for being busy like she usually do.

SEEM LIKE EVERYBODY WHO WORK for my daddy and they kinfolk got the hookup on cars. Lexi got a Nissan SUV—I think it's a Rogue—and it's pretty nice inside; it's got swivel seats in the front that look kinda like little couches. I ain't never seen seats like that, and I wondered what Doni woulda thought, since he said sometimes folks be doing too much with they cars. I pointed to the camera, which had front, rear, and bird's-eye view. "I'ma need one of those when I get my car."

"Girl, you don't know how many accidents this camera saved me from." Lexi the only person I know ain't never asked me why I don't already have a car. She just told the radio to play her mix, and we knocked all the way to the boutique, dudes looking the whole time, trying to see who was driving cause Lexi's car got rims and ChromaFlair paint.

When we got to the store, it was pretty empty. Lexi's friend's name was Trishelle, and the new retail side of the store was named Belinda's Closet, after her mama. The other part where she sold vintage stuff and did custom orders was called Might Be the Thredz. Trishelle told me to look around both sides and let her know what I thought, and when I say I fell in love, I fell in *love*. I was putting together outfits left and right in there; for me mostly, but then I saw this coatdress for my mama that look just like the seats in her Cadillac. I had to get that, and I was looking at some retro jewelry when Lexi and Trishelle came back. When they saw me, they started laughing.

"You trying to buy up the whole store, huh?" Lexi said, but Trishelle stopped her.

"Girl, don't be blocking my blessing. Let her get whatever she want."

While Trishelle was ringing me up, she told me the most important part of having a good store is knowing what to buy so you can sell it. "But you look like you already figured out what your aesthetic is," she said, looking through what I'd picked out. "You got good taste." I said thank you, and then I realized ain't nobody I just met ever said that to me. But that may be cause I don't talk to too many people.

Right before we left, she was like, "Suzette, let me know if you wanna work here a little bit during the holidays. Shayla go to LSUS, but she live in Arkansas, so when she go home for break I might need some help."

I never worked before, but before I even knew what I was saying, I was like, "Hell yeah, I'll work here. I wanna open a place like this one."

"Well, long as you ain't tryin to take mine, we good."

We both laughed, but I didn't want her to get it twisted, so I said,

"Well, I know I gotta go to school first. It might take awhile." And Trishelle said yeah, it do take awhile, but it's worth it to own your own business. Plus, she said to take some accounting classes, cause I need to know how to count my own money. I ain't never been so excited to come home from shopping in my life. Just the idea of owning a place like that. Coming in when you want; deciding what you want in it. I already do that for my closet, but I could have a whole store. Even working in one would be cool; I was damn near dressing the mannequins in there before I left. And if Trishelle want some feedback about stuff to buy…now that's something I could do. I fell asleep thinking about locations and names. Line Avenue was a good place, cause it's the middle of town: you got the hood down the street, and the old money coming from a little farther away, out of Spring Lake and Ellerbe. But Trishelle already got that spot. Maybe I could do over on Seventieth, or somewhere on the Loop. It stay busy over there.

And I *might* name a store after my mama, too, but I don't know how I feel about Delphine's.

"MAMA, CAN I ASK YOU something?" My mama was on the couch, hand-sewing something. Look like letters on a baby blanket.

"Yeah, baby. If it's about sewing, though"—and she paused while she checked a stitch—"I haven't forgotten about you. I just been busy helping Mrs. McShan with her granddaughter's baby shower." Mrs. McShan and Mama was in this quilting group, but Mrs. McShan stopped cause her diabetes started making her finger joints hurt.

"No, it's not about that. It's about a job."

She pushed up her glasses and kept sewing, so I said, "A job for me. Somebody offered me a job."

That made her look up real quick. I don't know who she thought I'd been talking about a job for. "Huh! Where bout?"

"At a store. A boutique. For clothes."

Mama kept sewing, but she started nodding once she pulled the needle through. "Okay, now you making a little more sense. But who offered you a job?"

"This woman named Trishelle. She own that boutique me and Lexi went to yesterday. She real nice. And I told her I might wanna open a store like hers. After I finish school. She was real helpful too. She told me to take some business classes, so I can handle my own money. Like you did for Daddy." I added that last part in myself.

Mama put the blanket down. "Your own store. Well, I didn't know you wanted that."

"Well, I didn't think about it till I saw the store, and, Mama, I loved it. You already know I know clothes. But I could learn more stuff too. Oh, and it's just part-time. Like a couple hours a week."

"A couple hours a week? How you know she only gon need you a couple hours? Christmas coming up. What if you have to work more than that? And jobs ain't like boots, Suzie. You cain't send em back just cause you changed your mind."

Any other time, I woulda clapped back, cause my mama really did try to play me with that line, but I didn't. I just said, "I won't mind. What else I'ma be doing? Even if Daddy was gon let me go to school, I cain't enroll till the spring."

"And what about that? What if you do wanna enroll? She gon work with your schedule come January?"

"I don't see why not. If I work over Christmas, I'll be covering for a girl on break from LSUS. When she come back, she can take back some of my hours." I didn't wanna say "all," cause that meant I might be planning to quit, and then Mama woulda thought it was a waste of time.

She looked at me hard. "And who gon be doing all that driving, Suzette? Back and forth to work, and then school? I'm gettin too old for that."

"Ain't I been trying to get Daddy to go to Nacogdoches? For my glasses? Ain't I been trying?"

Mama didn't have nothing to say about that, so she looked over at the TV for a while. I waited, and then I asked again, "What else I'ma be doing?"

Mama sighed and picked up the blanket again; then she hit me with what I knew was a delayed no: "Well, let me think about it, Suzette. Then I'll see what I can do." And then I just went up to my room, cause I didn't wanna watch her make somebody else a baby blanket if she wasn't gon do nothing to help me.

COUPLE DAYS LATER, I'M STILL sleep cause it's 6:30 in the morning, but my phone starts buzzing. I ignore it, but it start buzzing again.

It's Doni.

"Morning! You sound sleep."

"I was. What's going on?"

"I cain't tell you all that, but you need to get up and get dressed. Your mama been tryna call you downstairs for fifteen minutes, but she rushing too. We gotta get on the road in the next hour."

"On the road?!"

"Yes, ma'am. Your mama'll tell you about it, but you better get dressed quick. We got in at the last minute and we cain't be late."

I was starting to wake up, and I don't know why, but I started getting nervous.

"Whatchu talking about, Doni? Where you tryna take me? And why Mama didn't call my phone?"

"Cain't talk about that right now, but don't worry. I'm not gon kidnap you. Your mama comin too."

"Doni—"

"Twenty minutes, Miss Suzie. I'm serious. And don't try to dress up neither. This ain't that kinda party, and we ain't got that kinda time." *Click.*

Usually, that woulda made me take twice as long, but I didn't know what I couldn't be late for, so I just threw on a matching sweaterdress and hat (cause I had started taking down my braids) and grabbed my new purse—the Coach one I wanted. Daddy left it outside my bedroom door one day, I guess as a way to make up, but I just took it and didn't say nothing about it. A bag wasn't gon fix what was going on between us; plus, like I said, Mama got a whole Cadillac, and all I got was something I still can't put a set of car keys in. Apples ain't oranges.

When I get downstairs, I'm halfway expecting to have to explain to Mama why I'm dressed when I don't even know, but as soon as she see me, she grab her purse and start looking for her keys. "Come on, we gotta go get Doni, and then we gotta get on the road. Go grab you some of them granola bars. We'll get something to eat on the way back."

"Can I make some coffee?"

"No. We ain't got enough time. See if Doni can't make you some while we on our way."

"Mama, where we goin?"

"I'll let Doni tell you once we get him. It was his idea. But right now we gotta leave. I don't wanna be rushin on no highway."

I grab some bars and by the time I get to the garage, the garage door is already all the way up. I figured since we were on our way to get Doni, and everybody in a hurry, I'll find out what's up soon enough. Plus, if it was for something like we was going to get my daddy a Christmas gift, I didn't wanna know just yet; I'd rather just be excited about the possibilities for a minute, and then get disappointed when we pull up to the boat shop or whatever. Then, too, I was kinda excited to spend some more time with Doni. And I wanted to feel that feeling without thinking about my daddy.

So I just kept my mouth shut and tried to wake up without my coffee, but man, I was glad when Doni came out of his front door with a Yeti. I had never been to his apartments before, even though they right off Pines Road, in La Tierra. They was all brown two-story buildings, shaped like Monopoly hotels, with no grass around em. Looked like nothing *but* single niggas lived over there. But I also get why he liked those houses in South Highland. More room, looked like. Everybody not all over top of each other. And them houses was built more interesting than this. And they had nice grass.

When he got in the car, Doni ain't really even speak, just looked at my mama and said, "I been waiting to ride in this one for a minute! Guess that's the next-best thing to driving it, huh, Miz Elkins?" Mama laughed like she always do around Doni. I swear they got a crush on each other.

"Hey, can I have some of that coffee?" I turned around from the front seat.

"It's for you anyway," he said, and I almost didn't believe him, cause I never texted him to ask for it. "I put some cream and sugar in it, but if it's not enough, my bad."

"It's not even gon matter," I said, but I knew I sounded ungrateful, so I said, "But for real, thank you. I appreciate it."

"My pleasure, Miss Lady. With the *white* boots on, matching the purse. *And* the furry hat. You got the snowbunny vibe today. I like it."

I started smiling, but I tried to hide it by drinking out the cup.

"Don't spill nuthin in my new car, Suzette," said my mama.

"*Okay*, Mama. Like I don't know better. I'm the one picked out this upholstery. Anyway, where we goin?" Doni handed me some paper towels and I spread them on my lap. And, almost at the same time, my mama and Doni both said, "Nacogdoches."

I bout fell out.

"*Nacogdoches? For what?*" But I already knew.

"The glasses," Doni said.

I looked at Mama. "Where Daddy at? Do he know?"

Doni let Mama answer that one. "Your daddy at work and I'm grown. I go where I wanna go."

"And how Doni get off work?"

"Personal day," Doni said. He patted the seat next to him. "And I might mess around and catch up on a little sleep while I'm back here."

"Daddy let you off work for this?"

"Like I said, personal day. And we ain't doin nuthin but test-driving this car anyway, making sure it run good."

I turn back to the front. "But Mama, you *been* driving this car around the city. You already know it drive good."

Mama was merging with the dwindling traffic of folk who work in Texas, and folks going home from gambling on the riverboats all weekend. "Well, this is highway driving, sweetie, and there's a difference. You gon have to know that soon."

"And who gon finish teaching me how to drive? You?"

"No, ma'am. And shole not in this car. You got Doni for that."

"That's right, Miz Elkins. I'm a expert. I taught all four of my sisters, even before I was old enough to get a license."

I shut up then, cause I didn't know what else to say. I kinda wanted to know whose idea it was, and I guess I coulda said thank you, but we wasn't there yet. Plus, it felt weird to have Doni with us, and if I started talking…I didn't know. I was feeling a lot of stuff right then.

II.

Nacogdoches. Lord, what we do that for? When we got home, Daddy wasn't there, but you could tell he had been, cause stuff didn't look like it did when we left. It was a half-full cup of coffee in the sink, and grounds was all over the kitchen counter and the floor. He had left all the cabinets open and put plates and cups out, like he was about to reline the shelves. Trash can kicked over. All that. Oh, and one of the dinette chairs was turned around, pointed toward the garage door like he had been sitting in it, waiting for us to come back. He musta been there for a while. We had dropped Doni off already, but I texted him as soon as we saw the empty chair: i think daddy know something was up today. He texted back: i already know. he came by here bout ten minutes ago lucky I was back so i'm straight. hope y'all alright.

I told him we was but I'd keep him posted.

Mama played it cool, though. She just put our to-go plates in the fridge, turned the chair around, wiped up the grounds, then put on a pot roast for dinner after she put all the dinnerware back up on the shelves. It was barely two in the afternoon. I watched her for a little bit—well, I was watching her while I was pretending to watch *The Real*—but then I just got up and went in my room. I felt tired, like somebody had tried to pull apart my bones while spinning me around, but when I laid down I couldn't fall asleep. I propped myself up on one elbow and looked around my room. It looked like it always did, but I didn't feel like it was mine anymore. Like, let's say I learned how to drive. And I got my own car. That would be the most important thing I had. Not my clothes, or the boots in boxes with photos on the front so I could see what's what. Not my purses in the skinny bookcases I use like cubbyhole stands. Not my tall bed with the steps on the sides, or the canopy with the curtain. Naw, if I ever got a car, *that* would be the most important thing I had. Even if it was old and not fixed up. I didn't even care. And the thought of that made me scared, because I had never wanted nothing bad enough or long enough to be willing to take whatever, even if it wasn't the best version of it. Even if it wasn't new. And I was nervous, too, cause the way Daddy acted while we was gone meant getting a car wasn't gon come as easy as all this other stuff. I felt like it was worth it, though.

While I was trying to fall asleep, I messaged Drina to tell her I finally went to get my glasses. I figured she was in class, but she would text me back later. My phone buzzed almost as soon as I put it down.

That's good Zettie your mama took you?

Yeah. My mama and Doni.

Oh. How Doni come?

He took a day off work. It was his idea too. He asked my mama if he could take me but she said she would do it but she let him be the one to wake me up. I don't know why they did it like that. Prolly so if my daddy go off he can't be madder at one of them than the other.

Oh. That's so sweet of him.

Yeah. He trying to act right.

That's good.

When we gon go to the mall again?

I don't know Zettie I been busy with school and stuff.

You stay busy with that but you used to come by at least.

Yeah but you got Doni and your mama and you gon be driving yourself places soon.

OK. Then: I don't be asking you to come over just to take me places.

I know. That's not why I came neither.

Well? What changed?

Nothing. I gotta go Zet. HYU later ok?

But she never did.

I SLEPT FOR A LONG time, and for a long time after that, I just laid in bed thinking about the day and whatever was gon happen next. When we was at the doctor's, Doni did a lot of the talking. Mama stayed in the waiting room working on a throw or something, but when they called me back, he said, "You want me to come keep you company?"

The assistants loved him cause he would smile at them and ask questions about how they was doing and stuff. When the doctor came in to test me and started talking about the glasses, he turned to Doni instead of me, and then before he left he shook Doni's hand and said, "We'll get her on the road soon, so you won't have to drive her everywhere."

And Doni laughed and said, "Oh, I don't mind doin that at all. But this bout her, not me."

And the doctor smiled and then *finally* turned to me and said, "Oh, he's a keeper."

I just smiled back cause I didn't know why Doni didn't tell him we ain't together. And if anybody's been taking me everywhere, it would probably be Mama. Or Drina. And I felt kinda bad cause Drina wasn't there, but I didn't know why that mattered all of a sudden. Maybe cause I missed her. But she was acting like she ain't miss me at all. And I can't force people. And then Doni—he didn't really like me like that, did he? He ain't mentioned the kiss at the park since.

After we dropped him off, I asked Mama why she let him come to the back when she didn't even bother to get up. She said, "You didn't really need nobody, but if you let him come, you musta wanted him to. Wouldn'ta mattered what I wanted if you didn't want the same thing."

"But if you didn't think it was right, you shoulda said something."

"I didn't think nuthin bout it. And *that* cain't be my job forever anyway. You want something to happen a certain way? Then you got to speak up for yourself."

I ATE IN MY ROOM that night and watched some reruns and a little crime TV, but I don't like that the way I used to. Seem like it just ain't fair for people to die too young, or before they finish school, or just after they have a baby. So after a while I turned everything off and took my plate downstairs. The house was too quiet. I guess Mama and Daddy was gon save their shots for in the morning.

But when I came down the next morning around nine, Mama was in the kitchen by herself, talking on the phone and brewing coffee. It sounded like she was making an appointment with somebody. When she got off the phone, I asked her what was the matter.

"I'm going to look at cars."

"A car for me?"

"For me. Curtis took my goddamn Cadillac."

"What?!"

"You heard me. Woke up today, went through the garage to get somethin out the deep freezer, and it's gone."

"Was somethin wrong wit it?"

"Hell naw, Suzette! Didn't we just come back from out of town in it? Wudn't shit wrong with that car."

"You call him? What he say?"

"That somethin been recalled. But that's a damn lie."

When Mama get mad like that, I like to back off, cause, if she talk too crazy, I'ma say something back and before you know it, we arguing. So I just put my hand up and nodded like, *Yeah, you right*, and went for the coffeepot, but Mama snatched it and poured herself a cup first before she stomped back to her room to get dressed. "If you comin wit me, you need to be ready by ten. We can take the old truck." That was Daddy's, but I didn't point out nothing, just said okay and went to get dressed. I had to see what was gon happen with this. And I couldn't let Mama pick out no trash.

I DIDN'T REALIZE I WAS supposed to come so I could drive the truck home once Mama picked out a car. I thought it was funny cause I always thought Mama liked big cars: Caddies, Suburbans, stuff like that. But she got a little one this time. It was a Corolla. My mama don't do cars like that, though. If she get a Chevy, it's gon be a Lac. She go to Toyota, it's gon be a Lexus. She didn't say nothing when the salesman asked about Daddy, and whether this was a car he was planning to customize or something. That woulda been good promo for the dealership. But Mama was tough. She didn't do no small talk and she didn't look at that sticker price. She had a number in her head, and almost walked out three times before he agreed with her. Then we waited for another three hours after she signed the paperwork so they could update the navigation system and put a better radio in or something. I was back and forth on Instagram, checking the likes on a picture I had put up of me and Doni at Jethreaux's, on the way back from Nacogdoches. I really used to live my whole life online, having whole-ass conversations with people I wasn't never gon meet in real life. And posting selfies, too, when I was bored, but I wanted to try a new look and see if people liked it. And I used to get play sometimes. A few dudes even slid in my DMs, but some of em just wanted clit pics and the ones that wanted to meet made me nervous. So it never was really nothing going on. And I guess that's why I hadn't checked my notifications in so long; I'd just been play-living on there anyway.

"He aint online so y'all can talk about him all you want." That's how I'd captioned the picture. This makeup girl I follow who live in Virginia said, "Y'all make a cute couple y'all need to go out on the town so I can c him dressed up & u with ur face beat." I was also checking to see if anybody was trying to claim him, cause my Insta is public. But no one did, so I guessed that meant he was officially single.

Mama hadn't bothered to ask how I felt about driving that long way from Industrial Loop, and if I was scared. She just got in front of me on the road, and just told me to do what she did, right after she told me not to hit her brand-new car. We took the streets, of course, and after a while, it felt easy, but somebody gon have to teach me not to be nervous when other cars get close to me, and how to drive on the freeway.

On the way back, Mama cut through University Terrace, one of the neighborhoods me and Doni drove through after the movies, and once I stopped being terrified, I started looking around at the houses. I still thought ours was better, but I think it's cool to have something to dream about—something you can see. I thought about what Doni might look like pulling up to one of those houses in the Eclipse, blowing smoke out the window. Or waxing the car in the driveway on the weekends. I could make his coffee or breakfast or whatever. But naw, I didn't want him like that, did I? On some picket-fence stuff? I was thinking about that so hard I almost ran in back of Mama at a stop sign.

LATER THAT NIGHT, I WAS sitting on my floor cause I had finally taken out the rest of my braids. I was doing a pre-poo treatment and rebraiding my hair up in plaits before I washed it. I still didn't know what I wanted to do with it for the winter. I was scratching dirt out my scalp, then putting aloe on it, and thinking I guess. When we got back from the dealership, I asked Mama why she bought that little car, and she said Daddy wasn't gon keep her Cadillac for long; he'd give it back and maybe the new car could go to me if I acted right. I had kinda seen that coming, but it still surprised me. Mama rarely ever gave me stuff. It was usually Daddy. But even this gift had his hand on it. He the one took the Caddy. And she might not wanna admit it, but wasn't no salesman in the city gon let a customer married to the most famous custom car dealer in the Ark-La-Tex walk off the lot without buying, especially if they didn't know what was going on between them at home. But the comb's teeth caught the top of my ear as I was thinking: lil dude at the dealership might have to pay for that sale later on.

I was on the other side of my bed, so I couldn't see, but I heard my door open. No knocking, no nothing, so I crawled around the bed on my hands and knees and saw his work boots and the bottoms of his coveralls first before I looked up at his face. Daddy was holding a little box, like what earrings come in. He got to the other side of my bed and looked around.

"You ain't got no clean place to sit in here?" he asked. The only place didn't have stuff thrown on it was my bed, but he had just came from the shop and he was filthy. I started to get up.

"Naw, don't worry bout it." Daddy took my vanity stool, grabbed a towel from on top of my pile of clothes on the chaise lounge, and sat down. It felt funny to be on the floor like that with him there, but I stayed.

"Whatchu doin?" Daddy balanced the box on his left knee. I tried to act like I didn't see it and, if I did, I wasn't concerned about it.

"My hair."

"Ain't seen you in a while."

"Been busy, Daddy. Tryna get in school, learn how to drive. I'ma try to start working soon too."

Daddy leaned back on the stool a little. "Working?! Huh. Well. You gon be doing a lot of runnin around if you tryna do all that."

"Yessir," I said, and that made me think of Doni, how he say that all the time. "That's why I wanna learn how to drive. Mama let me drive a little today, and I was okay on the streets. So I know a little bit." I didn't tell him what we was doing at the time. He had to have seen that new car in the driveway, though.

"Huh. Well, that's good."

"I know, Daddy." I was undoing and redoing a plait I just finished. "I just wanna be independent, so you and Mama won't have to do everything for me for the rest of my life. I wanna work and start a business. I wanna be like you."

Daddy put his hands on his knees, and one hand covered the box. It jangled a little. It was empty except for something loose in it. Some kinda metal. I kept it cool, though.

"Like me, huh," he said, like I've heard him talk to his customers on the streets when they ask to bring their cars in for something crazy.

"Yeah. People always talking about how you do right by your customers and you do good work. That's what I want, Daddy. I want to own stores and have people talk about my clothes and stuff just like that."

"Who been talking bout me and my shop?"

"Nobody, Daddy. That was months ago, at Jaydell's party."

Daddy took off his cap and rubbed his head. "Oh. Yeah. Okay. Speaking of which, you done seen Doni lately? He ain't been back over my house when I'm not here, has he?"

"No, sir." And that wasn't a complete lie. I dipped my head to start a plait in the back.

"Good, cause you gotta learn how to watch people. You don't know everything you need to know bout that boy."

"Wha's there to know? He a good dude. I mean, you trust him. He work for you, don't he?"

"Just cause he work for me don't mean he a good dude."

"Whatchu tryna say, Daddy?"

"Ask him bout what he do to Dolo."

"Who is Dolo?"

"Man used to work at the shop. Say his name and see how he respond. Then you'll understand what I'm talking bout."

I finished my plait, and a little tangle of hair came out at the end. I was hoping it was just more shedding coming out from the braids. I looked at it, and then I looked at him.

"Daddy, why you come in here if you ain't gon tell me nothing?"

"Welp, I came in here to make you a deal." And he handed me the box. When I opened it, I saw the jeweled Cadillac keychain. Mama's keys. I gasped.

"Look here, let me explain." He leaned back and put his hands on his knees again, and when he gripped them I could see the dirt under his fingernails.

"You really the one that helped make that car. You picked out the seats, and you came and watched us while we worked on it. But your mama didn't know how to appreciate it. Soon as she got her hands on it good, she ran it out of town, putting highway miles on it, and you might not know it, but that's not too good for a old car. But them kinda cars is still built to last better than that little Corolla. They not all that plastic and fiberglass. You learn how to drive in the Caddy and it'll keep up wit you. I wouldn't recommend goin nowhere too far away, though. Keep it in the neighborhood, maybe go up to the school, but we'll talk about that at a later date, maybe for the summer. Not right now. And then, once you learn, maybe we can get you something a little smaller, a little newer, but better than that little piece of somethin your mama ran out and bought."

So he had seen the car. I looped the key ring around one of my fingers. Mama had bought a custom-made jeweled phone case to go with that key ring. It had all her favorite things on it: a high heel and a wineglass. A little oven mitt and the Cadillac emblem with pink crystals, just like this keychain.

"Daddy, why you tryna give me Mama's car? That's her baby."

"She done got another new car now."

"But that one's supposed to be for me."

"Don't have to be."

"Daddy."

"Listen, I'm tryna keep you out of trouble. You get a nice, sturdy car, you and Drina can tear up the city in it. Hell, you could even try to tear it up if you wanted to. I'll fix it for you. And you ain't gotta worry about using no nigga for rides. And I really might try to take that other car back, cause Action Toyota don't sell nothing but lemons noway."

"That's a new car, though, Daddy. You can't do that."

"I can if it's a lemon. Prolly ain't no good and she prolly didn't haggle enough to bring down the price."

"We haggled."

"Whatchall know bout haggling?"

I tried to hand him back the keys. "Daddy, I can't take this. You already know I can't."

"Yeah you can. You just done started thinkin you and your mama buddies when you ain't. You see, she made sure she got this car. She didn't bother to ask if you even wanted one. Now she tryna say that new one yourn? She still got the Escalade down at the shop that we ain't even sold yet. She gon keep that one too. She tell you that?"

I started getting confused, but I knew something about what my daddy was saying wasn't right. It felt like he was tryna brainwash me and I couldn't figure out if it was against Mama or Doni or both. But he wouldn't do nuthin crazy like that, would he? He was my daddy.

"No—she didn't tell me that."

"I reckon she wouldn't unless she wanted you to know." Daddy leaned toward me. I was still on the ground. He was never a real big man, but from where I was sitting, he looked huge. He smiled at me and shook his head.

"See, she really don't even *need* that car, but she selfish. Why'on't you go on take it, and we figure out everything else later? I'll take you to the shop to go get it right now, and you can bring it back here, just like you did the truck. You did real good on the roads. No speeding. No sudden stops except one."

That got me scared. "Daddy, how you know how I got it back here?"

"Sugar, I got eyes. And I got eyes everywhere."

Mama was somewhere in the house when we left, and I would have texted her, but I didn't want them to start arguing, so I just slapped on a headwrap and left. I mean, I wasn't gon keep the car. I just wanted to drive around in it, and, real talk, I wanted to see what Daddy was trying to do. When we got to the shop, a couple of the men were still there, working on a orange Mustang with an electric blue racing stripe down the front. That shit looked dope. The men kept their heads down when we walked through to the back, waving a hand over their shoulders or nodding without actually looking at us. I mean, I know he run a tight ship, but it felt like they was scared of me. Doni wasn't nowhere to be found.

Mama's car was out back in one of the pods, locked up in the holding area, where they keep the stuff they were either done working on, or hadn't started working on yet. Even in the dark that Caddy was *clean*—that orange car in the shop ain't have nothing on it. Daddy handed me the keys and motioned for me to get in on the driver's side while he opened the passenger door. We had been quiet the whole ride over, Daddy playing oldies and me on my phone. When I thought he wasn't looking, I typed a few words to Doni, but he always looked back over at me before I could hit send.

Daddy opened the driver's-side door of the Lac and waved his hand for me to get in.

"Why you letting me drive without the glasses?"

Daddy went around to the passenger side and got in before he answered. "You'll be all right long as you stay on the surface streets. And you ain't doin nuthin but driving home anyway."

"Yeah. But it's crazy if I went through all that trouble to get em and you was gon let me drive wit'out em."

He was looking through the glove compartment for something, so he didn't answer at first, but after a while, he just grunted. "Well, that was mostly your mama anyway, who was worried. She even go over basic driving rules with you?"

"Naw, but I been studying the book. I know how to do just about everything." I didn't tell him how she'd been letting me drive before.

"Well, I'ma make you back outtuh here and take me around the block a few times just to make sure." As I shifted into reverse, he mumbled, almost under his breath, "I guess she just a baby doll to dress up and carry around." He didn't know what a hypocrite he sounded like.

When I dropped him back off at the shop, he said, "I'ma check on a couple jobs before I send these fools home. I'll see you back at the house in a minute."

"Yessir," I said, just like Doni, and sped off.

HE WAS EATING A BOWL of cereal when he answered the door. He'd taken off the top of his coveralls and just had on a wife beater up top. The sleeves of the coveralls hung loose down his thighs. He tried to hitch everything up real quick when he realized it was me.

"Damn, Suzette. Whatchu doin here?" He moved by so I could step in, but stayed at the door like I wasn't supposed to be there for long. "Didn't you just text me bout ten minutes ago?"

"I did, but I figured I'd just come on anyway, see if you was here." I didn't mention the fact that he didn't respond right away. We ain't together, so I couldn't really get mad.

"How you get here, though?" He went to the doorway, peeking out. "Is that your mama?" he asked when he saw the Cadillac. "She picked the car up from the shop?"

"Naw. It's just me."

"What?!" Doni dropped the spoon back in the bowl fast—so fast a little milk splashed up on his wrist. "Suzette. How the hell you get that car?"

"Daddy. He gave it to me. He said I could have it if I wanted to."

"In exchange for what? Cause if it's got anythang to do with me, you got to leave *right* now. He know you here?"

"Naw. He think I'm on my way home. He still at the shop, I think. He mighta left by now, though."

"Suzette, whatchu tell him to get that car? You told him somethin bout me and you?"

"Naw! I don't know why he gave it to me. I think it's to turn me against Mama. Maybe you, too, even though we didn't talk about you. But he don't know I would never do that. He did say you need to tell me something bout some dude used to work at the shop, though."

Doni backed up from me real fast and put the bowl down on the coffee table. "I bet he did." He took me by the arm. "Su, you gotta get home before he do. Cause he ain't give you that car for nuthin, and if he find out where you'd'n took it, it's gon be trouble for at least one of us. Probly me." He shuffled me outside, and when we got close to the Cadillac, he started shaking his head. "I still can't believe he took your mama car. And now you done let him give it to you. This shit is crazy."

"No. Wait—no." We was walking fast so I felt like I had to talk fast. "I wouldn't do my mama like that. I'ma give her the keys soon as I get home."

"You better, cuz. Cause this is wrong. I'own know what he got up his sleeve. Shit prolly got a tracker on it or something."

"You think he would do that?"

"I *know* he would do it." Doni sat me in the driver's seat and tried to kiss me away, but I moved my head.

"Tell me bout that dude used to work in the shop."

"Suzette. You need to go."

"No."

"Suzette!"

"What!"

"This ain't no game. You need to go home, give your mama back her car, and I'll call you later."

"That's a lie. You not gon call me. If you scared enough of my daddy right now, and we face-to-face, what you gon do on your phone? You gon curve me like you do whenever he scare you into leaving me alone." Doni looked at me hard. I guess cause this was the first time I talked like that. I kept going.

"All y'all treat me like I'm stupid. Like it's stuff I'm just too slow to figure out, but I feel like don't nobody tell me nuthin cause y'all want me to be stupid. Everybody. Even Drina. I'm sick of this shit." I was getting loud, and I forgot we was in a complex. Doni looked around like he was nervous.

"Naw, not me. That's some bullshit right there. I ain't never treated you like that."

"But you know what I'm talkin bout."

"I do know, but now ain't the time for all this."

"It won't take you five minutes to tell me this story. You tell me and I'ma bounce. I'll go home. I'll do just what you told me to do. But you gotta tell me what's up first."

Doni shook his head.

"You betta start talkin or I'ma start blowin this horn."

He was leaned down in front of the driver's-side window, and when I said that, he slapped his hands on his knees cause he was mad. But then he stood up, went around the car, and got in, closing the car door gently, like my daddy do cause he say you ain't gotta slam no car door to close it. When he got in, he started patting his pockets for his cigarettes, but they was back in the apartment somewhere. He hit his knee again, but then said, "I don't need em noway. If I smoke in here they'll *know* where you been." I just looked at him. I was waiting for him to start.

Doni wiped his face with his bare hand, and it stopped at his mouth for a minute, like he was trying to hold something in. Then he leaned back in his seat and stared straight ahead. "Mane, I cain't be going against yo daddy wit you like this. You don't understand. He saved me. That's what he was tryna snitch on."

"Saved you from what?"

"Myself."

I turned in the seat so I could face him, even though he wouldn't look at me. "You gon have to explain to me whatchu talkin about."

Doni scratched the back of his head and then inspected his fingernails before he spoke. "Mane, you was so young when it happened. You prolly wasn't even watching the news then."

I sighed. "So, we gon keep doing this back-and-forth, or you gon tell me what the fuck happened?"

Doni sat up straight again, balled one hand into a fist, and hit his other hand. "That's not me no mo, though. I'm different. I don't do shit like that no mo. That person died. A long time ago."

"Wait, what? You *killed* somebody?"

Doni waved his hand real quick. "Naw, naw. Nuthin like that. I just mean that person I was. He died."

"Who was he?"

"Angry. Real angry, all the time. At everybody."

And you know what? I just leaned back and stopped asking questions, because every time I asked, he would figure out how to answer the question but not really say nothing. So I let him get uncomfortable. Just sat there quiet until he started talking.

He took a deep breath. "It was probly late '09. I had just finished high school. And I wanted to go to the army and be a engineer cause I'm good with my hands, you know? But they said I had some kind of heart thang—arrhythmia—so they sent me home from the physical and told me to follow up with a doctor and see what it was. I didn't have no doctor, so I never went back. But man I was, like, devastated. I didn't wanna stay here cause really wasn't nuthin here I wanted to do. Didn't wanna work at no casino. Didn't want to drive trucks in and out the oil field, cause that shit just *look* boring. And I knew I wasn't going to college wit'out no army money, so I wasn't gon do nursing or PT or nothing like that. Cleaning up mess and watching folks die. Then you gotta watch the family fight over the body. I know what that's about. Reen and Peanut tell me about it all the time where they work. So I just felt trapped."

I listened.

"And then I saw your dad shop was hiring. And I knew I could do that cause I worked on cars all the time. So I went in for a interview and I got the job. And it was straight. I just worked the mechanic side at first, though. But I would watch the dudes paint and do bodywork and I was like, 'Bet. One day, I'ma learn how to do that.' Cause they made the most money in the shop anyway. And your daddy, he was cool with me once he figured out I knew what I was doin under the hood, you know? So he started letting me do a little bodywork here and there, when the shop was closed, or when it was slow. Man, I was so excited. Too excited. That's all I wanted to do.

"But there was this one nigga. Dolomite. They called him that cause he had a Triumph Dolomite. Car was old as shit. But he restored it. Shit, his ass was old too. In his fifties, maybe. They used to say he ran women back in the day, too, but I ain't really have no problem with him. He was the head of the paint crew. Or he thought he was. And when I started learning how to paint, he act like he had a problem wit it. Started talking shit about how we didn't need no mo paint or body techs. Talkin about my practice jobs, you know. Little petty shit. And he wouldn't never say shit around your daddy. He was one of them kinda niggas. He would do it when your daddy was out, when it was just the crew. And I couldn't stand his ass. I started getting into it with that nigga *every day*.

"And then, he just…ran up on me at the wrong time. All kind of shit was happening. My baby sister Talitha had got pregnant. I thought *my* girl might be pregnant. My mama was so worried about everybody else she started getting sick. Shit was just…Everything was wrong. And I come in the shop wit all that, and then Dolo start in on me. It was like he sensed I was down, and that nigga was gon kick my guts out before the day was over. So he start talking. And your dad was off doin something, but we was trying out this new paint technique and he had told me I could do one of the doors on this car. I wasn't even finished and Dolo was all over it, roasting the paint job, roasting me. And he *kept* sayin under-the-hood niggas needed to stay under the hood.

"And for real, Suzette, I wasn't never tryin to take nobody's nuthin. Ain't nothing wrong wit wanting to do something else, you know. Really, I just wanted to have a few more skills, in case I needed to make more money. Tha's why I be tellin you to go to school. Get yours. Cause I been that dude. Just waiting for stuff to get better but it ain't. So you just gotta make a move. Try something. That's all I be tryna tell you."

"Yeah, you do be doing that." I tried to let him know I appreciated it, but I was impatient. "So what happened wit you and Dolo?"

It took him awhile. He put his hand up to his mouth again. After a minute, he put his hand on the back of his neck.

"He got burned."

"How?"

"We got in a fight."

"How he get burned, though?"

"I set him on fire."

I was so shocked my ears started ringing. Like, I literally heard sirens in my head. Doni, the dude who could sew and feed ducks, set somebody *on fire*?

"Stop playing wit me."

"You wanted to know. Now you know."

"So, what…what happened to him? Is he okay?"

"I don't know. He live upstate somewhere wit his sister. He all right I guess. He went to rehab and all that. He got some scars, tho. I mean, that's what I heard. By time I got out, he was gone."

"Where his scars at?" I wanted to know if he could cover them up. If he could walk around without people staring at him like they stare at me.

"His arms and stuff. Maybe a little on his chest and neck. I ain't seen him. Some dudes at the shop keep up wit him."

"Can he move around? Take care of himself?"

"I think so. I mean, I *really* don't keep in touch wit'im, Suzette."

"Why you do that, though? And how?"

"Paint thinner. A lighter. Whatchu think?" Doni cracked the window and started patting his pockets. "Mane, I might have to run get my squares."

"Can't smoke in here, remember? Especially if you don't want Daddy to know we was together."

"I know, man. I know." He laughed a little and shook his head. "But now you see what we be having to do around the shop to handle him. You gotta get good at that if you want him to let you do anything."

"I'm a grown-ass woman."

"Shit, I didn't say you wasn't. I'm sayin you need to learn how to handle him."

I sighed. "Maybe you right. I still cain't figure out this shit with the car. It's crazy. You know him *and* my mama done let me drive in the past twenty-four hours? And they both doin it to get back at each other, when two weeks ago they was scared to let me out the house. Well, at least Daddy was. It just don't make no sense. I mean, it do, but it make me wonder what they been sheltering me from my whole life? Was I really in that much danger, goin out, goin to school? Daddy mighta been selling me a bill of goods the whole time."

Doni snapped his finger in my direction. "Now you startin to learn how he work. Keep it up, you might become a expert at it."

"Shit, I still got stuff to learn. I came all the way over here when he told me to go straight home. He gon be mad if he get home first."

"He sure will." Doni made a motion like he was about to open the door.

"Wait! But what made you do that? Set Dolo on fire?"

He paused and let out a half whistle. "I don't know, baby. Rage. I was mad. We was fistfighting, and I was already winning, cause the nigga was old. Then I just lost it, I guess. I started hitting him and I hitting everything I was mad at: Talitha boyfriend. The army doctor. Me. And then I saw the jug of thinner. And dude was already on the floor. I just snapped. But soon as the flames went up, I panicked and put him out. On God: I started it, and I finished it. I found this big piece of foam we had laying around and started hitting him. But he was still burned pretty bad. Even I got burned a little bit. On my hands." He rubbed them together.

"And you went to jail?"

"Sure did. Eleven months. Mane, you know how this state is. They tried to throw all kinda shit at me. Attempted murder, arson, destruction of property. All that. But your daddy stepped in. He got me a lawyer. And he did something with the DA, too, so they bumped it down to aggravated assault. Mr. Curtis wouldn't let em charge me with nothing have to do with the shop. He said wasn't nuthin damaged anyway."

"My daddy know the DA?"

"Yeah. He said he knew him from way back; something happened and dude owed him a favor. I don't know." Doni had sat back in his seat again, but he was getting restless cause he couldn't smoke, so he started playing around with his hands again, clenching and unclenching his fists.

"Favor for what?"

"A woman. Some woman did something to him, but they couldn't prosecute her cause they didn't have enough on her. And I'own even know if that part is the truth. A CO told me that one day while we was shootin the shit."

"Damn. That was prolly Ms. Mouton."

"Who is that?"

"This woman that tried to pluck out my eyes in the third grade."

Doni did a double take. "What?"

"It's a long story, and if you want me to go home soon I can't tell it to you right now."

"Mane, this shit is crazy." Doni started patting himself down for cigarettes again.

"Did the CO say anything about how she died?"

"Wait, that woman *died*?"

"Ms. Mouton? Yeah. That's what I heard my mama say a couple months ago."

Doni put both hands on his face and leaned back in the car seat. Then he shook his head real hard.

"Naw. Naw, he wouldn't do no shit like that," he said, sounding like he was trying to convince himself. "If something like that happened, Trahan or Slaughter or one of them fools woulda known. Shit, all they did was gossip on they shifts. And they knew all kinda shit, about politicians, all that. But, fam. Yo daddy…he really is that powerful."

"Yeah, but like you said, he wouldn't do that." I said it real quiet, though, cause I didn't know if I still believed it. Plus, five minutes before, I wouldn't have believed Doni could try to burn somebody up. And I still had questions about that.

"So what about the dude? That you set on fire. Where he at again?"

Doni looked back. "Upstate somewhere, like I said. Detroit, I think. Mane, your daddy mighta even gave him money to leave."

"Why would he do all that for you—my daddy?"

Doni sighed again and tapped the dashboard with his knuckles. "Man, Suzette, if I knew that I'd know what to do bout all this right here. He ain't never really talk about it. When I got out of jail he called and asked me when I was comin back to work and I ain't even know what to say. And when I came back ain't nobody say shit about what happened. Not even Jaydell, even though he messier than a snitch. And when I tried to thank Mr. Curtis, he said, 'You only got to do that one time, and we ain't never gotta bring this up again.' But ever since, I been working to pay him back. I don't never ask for nothing, Suzie. Not my raises. Not vacation time. I get what he give me. Cause I know it could be worse. A lot worse."

"So he get to do to you what you let him. Cause he know he saved you and you know if he hadn't…" I couldn't finish cause I was thinking about myself, but Doni got it.

"Yeah," he said. "Just like that. You already know."

"Why you think he like that, though?"

Doni huffed and looked out the passenger window again. "Mane, you tryna keep me out here all night. He prolly on his way over here *right now*."

"It shouldn't take that long to answer one question."

"That's the thing. I ain't got no answer. I don't *know*." He got quiet for a few seconds. "But you know what, though? When I was locked up, looking at Slaughter 'n'em strutting around that bitch, I was like, 'You know what? Sometimes, the only thing life really about is having the most power in the room.' I mean, we can say a lot about your daddy, but he a hardworking dude. And he a *good* dude. And that's part of how he got so much power. Man, he done bought so many cars for people, so many toys for niggas' kids that work at the shop. He done paid light bills and put folks through school. Paid for funerals. I mean, he really done helped the whole community if I'm bein honest about it. But everybody around the shop—and I mean everybody, Suzette—we owe him something. Money. Time. Freedom. Other legal shit. Back child support and custody bullshit. And I feel like that's the way he want it. Like he don't feel comfortable wit you around him if you don't owe him some kind of debt. Cause when you owe him, he got more power. But I get why he like that. Shit, a Black man a hunnit fithy, two hunnit years ago? This whole damn state was a plantation and it owned you. Now they got new ways of doin that. Look at Angola. You get locked up they put you right back in the field. Or the damn chicken plant over in Bastrop. If you a Black man out here, you gotta protect what you got, and power is the best way to do it. Otherwise, somebody'll take what's yours. White folks. Trifling niggas. I ain't sayin it's right. But I'm sayin I get the logic."

"No it *ain't* right," I said. "Plus, not every man gotta be like that. You ain't like that. Are you?"

Doni looked over at me and shrugged. "I was wit Dolo. And shit, if we bein real I still got my vices. But the truth is, I ain't never had nuthin worth losin." He turned from me and looked out the passenger window. The streetlights glinted off the little crucifix he wore around his neck and lit up his face. Doni got a face like a little boy, which is why I don't even think I knew how old he really was till he said it at the duck pond. But he got a hard face too. The way his jaw set. The little lines in his forehead when he thinking hard, or trying to figure out what he gon tell you. I hadn't noticed none of that before. My mama say if people have a hard life, you can tell it in their face. And I saw it, right then. I don't necessarily think she meant it as a compliment, but it made Doni more handsome, I think. More real. That's what everybody online be trying to create with filters and makeup and angles. Something that look authentic, like what people see is what you really are. He had it right there. And it was from the lines. It was like the opposite of everything I thought was supposed to make you beautiful.

We sat like that for a few minutes; me looking at Doni and Doni looking outside. It had been a long time since I had to process something this big. I looked down at the steering wheel. All I could think to say was, "Doni, would you ever do that again? What you did to Dolo?"

He looked over at me, but I wasn't looking at him, so he waited until I looked up. When I didn't, he took my face by the chin and turned it toward him.

"Suzette. Hear me good. I would never do that again to another human being in my life. And I know that don't mean nuthin to you cause you ain't me and you ain't even know that part of me till just now. But all I can say is I wouldn't do it. And all you can do is believe me or not believe me. It's as simple as that." He opened the door and leaned back like he was gonna kiss me, but then changed his mind. "Naw. I need to leave and you do too. Get this car home in one piece and hit me up later."

I GOT HOME, AND DADDY was on the front porch in one of the rocking chairs. When I pulled in, he jumped up so fast the chair rocked back and hit the wall. I saw Mama peek out one of the windows, and I braced myself. I had hoped she wouldn't find out before I could hand her keys back, but it was what it was.

Daddy ran up to the driver's side of the car and jerked it open. "Where the hell you been? You left the shop two hours ago and it don't take that long to get from there to here. What the hell you been doing?" He was so close to me I was grateful Doni didn't smoke while I was there cause he woulda smelled it on my clothes. When I didn't answer, Daddy balled up one of his fists.

Mama came waddling out fast in her house shoes. *Slap, slap, slap.* "Leave her alone, Curtis. And you"—she pointed at me—"you get in this house." I just looked at them. I don't know why, but I suddenly realized how old they were. I coulda been a grandkid for both of them, but they had me late. I grew up late too. We shouldn't have been fighting about something as basic as this.

I didn't want to go in the house just cause somebody told me to, but it didn't really make sense to stay out there, so I started walking toward the front door slow. I hugged my purse close, just in case. While I was walking, I felt somebody shove me forward. Then my mama said, "Keep your hands off her."

"Yeah," I snapped. "Unless you wanna go to the chicken farm."

"Whatchu say to me?"

"You heard me the first time." And I meant it, but I walked faster to get out of his reach.

When I got in the house, wasn't nowhere else to go but my room, which, all of a sudden, felt like a refuge. I shut the door and threw my purse down in the chair on top of my clothes. I was halfway out of my top when the door burst open. I covered myself quick, but I could see in the mirror it was Mama. She stopped short of the little rug I was standing on and glared at me in the mirror.

"You red-faced heifer. After everything I done did for you—*over* that fool—and this is how you wanna pay me back? You really think he just gon let you have that car without a price? Don't nothing that nigga give be for free. I can tell you that from personal experience."

"I already know that. I ain't never wanted the car to keep. I just wanted to drive it." I finished taking off my shirt. Maybe she would feel uncomfortable enough to leave.

"You a lie. You always wanted it. Ever since you picked out the color for them seats you wanted it. And now you got it. So what you gon do with it? Drive it to pick up your glasses? If you think that's gon happen you gon have to fight me first."

I looked her dead-on in the mirror. "I ain't no lie. I never wanted that car. Daddy said something bout Doni and I went to go see him, to see if it was true. I was gon hand your keys right back to you, since your husband wouldn't."

Mama looked like she was about to hit me. I'm saying, I think I saw her hand move a little, but she turned her head to the side real quick like she was trying to get the thought out of her mind. Then she said real calm-like, "Then why ain'tchu tell me that, Suzette? You couldn'ta texted me? And you couldn'ta waited till I got things situated and gave you the other car?"

"Daddy said he was gon take that other car back."

"You cain't take back no damn car. That was a lie and you shoulda known it was from the jump."

"Should I? Because y'all don't really want me to know nuthin. You keep me in this house, you keep me in the dark about everything. What I'm supposed to know other than what both of y'all tell me?"

"You should know to believe me over him."

"Why? Both of y'all been fighting and using me like bait since the third grade. You bribe me to do one thing and then he bribe me to do somethin else. I really don't want nuthin from neither one of y'all, but to just be my parents. Like, normal parents. You can figure out what you wanna do with your husband on your own time. I'm over this shit."

"Watch your goddamn mouth. Where my keys?"

"You get em when you give me keys to the Toyota."

Mama stood there for a minute like I was gonna change my mind, but then I just started playing with my hair and modeling for myself until she figured out I wasn't playing. When she started walking away, I reached for my purse and was opening it, but I wasn't quick enough, I guess. She threw them shits at my face, but they missed and hit me on the shoulder. I just stayed calm. I picked them up off the ground and put them on my bed. Then I walked over to her and gave her back her keys.

"You should be glad I won't do you like you do me," I said. As she was walking out, I said, "Nice doing business witcha."

THE NEXT DAY, FIRST THING I did was take the Toyota up to Belinda's to see if Trishelle still wanted me to work there. It was late November, so I figured it might be a good time to check. I also thought it would be good to just go on my own so she would know I had transportation. I made sure I had a garage door opener so I could get back in the house. Mama always kept the door into the kitchen unlocked, and I didn't know what they was gon try to do to me for talking back to both of them last night. But they was bugging. This shit felt so stupid. Girls my age was married, pregnant, and these fools didn't even wanna let me drive. I guess I was supposed to just sit around and wait for somebody to give me permission to live my life.

When I walked in, the girl I think I was supposed to replace was there, folding some camis to put on display tables. Trishelle was up front this time, watching the door from the register. I felt weird asking about the job when ole girl was standing right there, but Trishelle beat me to it.

"Hey, girl! You still tryna work for me?" She smiled and she had on one of the prettiest lace fronts I've ever seen. Dark and wavy, which is good for the holidays. Folks always wanna take holiday pics that look like they out in the snow, and dark hair is a good contrast.

"If you want me to," I said, and Trishelle motioned for me to go with her to the back, in her office. She closed the door and sat across from me at the desk.

"Sheena might be leaving for good," she said, looking serious. "She missing her boyfriend, and she don't like school. I done seen this before; my guess is she either gonna go home for break and get engaged, pregnant, or both. Either way I don't think she gon be here too much longer."

"Oh. That's messed up." I wondered if me and Doni was *together* together, would I do the same thing? I didn't know.

Trishelle shrugged. "It is what it is. So, if you wanna come on, I might need you full-time."

"Really?"

"Yeah, I mean, definitely in a few weeks for the holidays, and that's what I had originally said anyway, but maybe for the New Year too."

I tugged my purse strap a little and shifted around in my seat. "Well, I had thought about school for the spring." Mama had warned me about this. Maybe me working here was too good to be true.

"Well, I could still use you. And we can work with your schedule, if you can work with ours. You got kids?"

"No."

"Good. I love em but they take up all your time. I think we could make this work, then."

"Really? Man, that's dope, but I prolly need to talk to my parents about it, cause…"

"How old are you?" Trishelle squinted a little bit, like she was trying to guess, but it made me tense up a little. I knew I sounded like I was still in high school, but I really did at least wanna talk to Mama about it. She would know what to do—if she was speaking to me again when I got home.

"Twenty."

"Okay, okay." Trishelle leaned back in her chair and crossed her legs. She was wearing this beige catsuit that was so fire. And these thigh-high boots with a mink ring around the shaft. A little bit of the fur peeked up over the top of the desk. "Lexi told me your dad was a little strict. Y'all religious?"

"No, they just protective, cause I'm albino I guess."

"Huh. I guess I can understand that. Well, how bout this? Take a little time to think about it, and maybe talk to your parents about it and then let me know? Sheena don't leave for Magnolia till the tenth."

"Yeah, I can do that," I said, and she looked at me for a minute, and then took a business card out of a holder and scribbled her number on it.

"That's my cell," she said. "You can call whenever." She squinted at me again. "Hey, don't you run with Drina? From Cedar Grove? Live over off Eighty-Fourth?"

"Yeah, you know her?" I got a little excited about that.

"I do. Haven't seen her in a while. Tell her to hit me up." And she said it in a way I didn't understand, but I thought about it as I drove away.

THE WHOLE DAY. THE WHOLE *day* of me picking up my glasses was just...wild. And I shoulda known it would be the day before. It was a whole week after me, Mama, and Daddy got into it. I know my daddy hold grudges, but I thought Mama woulda got over it by then. That's why I went to tell her the glasses was ready for us to go pick up. She was sitting in the living room, looking out the big front window, drinking coffee. When I asked her when she wanted to go get em, she didn't even turn around.

"You find somebody else to go witchu. And if you try and take *either* of my cars—to Texas? You gon have to fight me comin and goin. So you not gon get too far."

"Really? You still on that."

"I sure am. And you betta get out of my face fore I be on something else."

And when I just stood there, she picked up her coffee cup and walked past me out onto the sunporch. So I went up to my room and hoped she got sick tryna sit out there in forty-degree weather like she was doing something.

But when it got later, I knew she wasn't playing. So I tried to text Drina, but she wouldn't answer. Then I hit up Doni and asked him if I gave him gas money, would he go.

Dunno. Your daddy been on me hard at work might not get to take time off

Then about an hour later:

Wait i might be able to finesse it my youngest sis pregnant again i can say i need to take her to the dr and i just need half a day.

Then, an hour later:

Its set. we gotta go and come back tho. no stopping for crab legs

So the next day, Doni waited until he knew my daddy was at the shop, then picked me up from outside the gate. I was in the waiting room at the doctor's freaking out, cause I didn't even ask if I needed my mama there for nothing; I just showed up. I had worn a navy quarter-sleeve shirtdress with some tan boots, and I kept wiping my hands on my skirt cause they was clammy. Doni was reading a magazine, but the last time I did that, he put it down and put his hands on top of my hands.

"It's gon be all right. They comin."

"They said they wasn't busy today." I said it loud enough for the receptionist to hear.

"That don't mean they ain't got other stuff to do," he whispered.

"Then they shoulda did it fore I got here."

Doni was about to say something else, but the assistant came out and said we could come on back.

But then I got mad again when the doctor was adjusting the telescopes and he wouldn't stop talking bout how in a few years I might get some lenses that work like no-line bifocals. Then he started talking about driving, and how my eyesight with my contacts was almost good enough to get the daylight restriction taken off my license after a year. I didn't know nothing about that.

"Whatchu mean?"

"Well, over in Louisiana, you have to drive for a year with a daytime-only restriction on your license if you get a Class E with bioptic lenses."

"Can I get a different class then?"

The doctor laughed a little while he was putting the glasses on me for the umpteenth time trying to adjust the scopes.

"No, it doesn't work like that. But don't worry. That year will pass right on by, and you'll probably be a more confident driver for it. Then you and your sweetheart can go back up to the DMV and get it all taken care of. Most of my patients are happy to be able to drive at all, so they don't mind."

I looked over at Doni, but the doctor moved my head back toward him.

"I thought I could just go get my license."

"Well, not exactly. You gotta take a driving class, too, at a school with instructors who specialize in low-vision, and then they have to sign off on a driving test at the school before you take the one at the DMV."

I had vaguely remembered seeing that when I looked all this up, but in all my excitement I forgot, and I was mad about forgetting cause it made me look stupid in front of Doni. So when Dr. Ruskin said I needed to do a brief training with the bioptics before he could sign off on my form, I bout flipped out. But Doni jumped in.

"We appreciate this, Doc, getting us in on short notice and everything. How long is the training?"

"Oh, not more than an hour. I just need to say we did something to sign off on my part of all this. When she takes the driving class, the special instructor will have her do field tests using the lenses on the road. The one we do here is testing her ability to use the glasses, just so she knows the basics. I'll play a short video, and then one of the assistants will take her outside, around the block, and ask her to identify a few things. It's pretty simple."

Doni started talking to me. "That don't sound too bad, do it?"

I wouldn't look back at him this time. "Would it matter if it did?"

The doctor adjusted the glasses on my face and turned my chair toward Doni.

"How does she look, champ? You tell her she's beautiful and I'll throw in a free eyewear case for you." And I let him laugh at himself by himself.

Doni raised one eyebrow and nodded. "It— They look all right."

I looked down at the mirror on the table behind him. I looked like a freak, with a big-ass camera-looking thing stuck to some glasses look like even my daddy was too young to pick out.

"Y'all ain't have no styles other than this?"

"Well, this is the very basic style because you don't typically wear glasses. You wear contacts, and you see best with contacts, so we want you to always wear those, especially when you're driving. Since you didn't need prescription glasses, we didn't order anything special. But you can change these up later, if you want. And remember, you only have to wear them when you're driving. You get to where you're going, pop em off, and you can even leave them in the car, as long as you keep them in a cool place out of direct sunlight. Heat can warp the scopes."

I exhaled loudly, and he just kept fiddling with them like he didn't hear me at all.

When he left to go get the assistant, Doni walked over to my chair, bent down in front of me, and put a hand on my shoulder like he was a coach.

"You doin all right, Miss Lady?"

"I'm fine," I said, the way my mama say it to my daddy when she got an attitude.

"Listen." Doni looked over at the door cause someone passed by it. "Things not always gon turn out exactly how you want em to. And folks not always gon do what you want em to do. That's…that's life, baby. But you gotta stay focused on your goal. On whatchu want. You been talking bout this since the day we started talking, really. And you this close"—he put up his fingers to show me—"but you bout to piss these people off. And then whatchu gon do? Be out here looking like Boo Boo the Fool with an expensive pair of glasses ain't no doctor signed off on for you to drive in? You gotta learn how to work the system, baby. It ain't built in your favor right now, but you gotta figure out how to slide on em to get what you need."

I rolled my eyes.

"Look." He put my face in his hands. "I been heated before; I done flashed out on people. You *know* that. That shit ain't productive at all. You got to look at the bigger picture. Year from now, you on Easy Street. Daddy'll come around, probably get you a new car. Hell, I'll fix you up a car if you want me to. And even before that, you do the class, get your license, and you'll at least be able to do stuff during the day. School. Work. That's the most important two things anyway. You need to go somewhere at night? I got you. I mean, you might have to keep walking to the gate so I can pick you up. But I gotchu."

I had to laugh at that, and he did too.

He took his hands off my cheeks right before the tech came in, and I had to wipe my face real quick cause I was crying.

WE HAD STOPPED AT A gas station in De Berry cause Doni said he needed to use the bathroom. He was only in there a minute and came out with all kinda stuff: Fanta and some Hot Fries and a pack of cookies. I was still sitting in the passenger seat, and he came up to my side like dudes who be in the parking lot, tryna talk to girls.

"Welp. You got your glasses now, Miss Daisy, and I'm not gon have to drive you nowhere after a while. You wanna go'on head and practice? We ain't gotta tell nobody."

Before I could say something, Doni snatched the case out of my lap and opened it. He took the glasses out and wiped them with his shirt.

"Highway driving easier than people make it out to be. Once you get in a rhythm, it's kinda like playing *Tetris*. If you gotta get away from folks, you fit yourself around them and keep it moving. Plus, no stoplights."

"How long you expect me to drive?"

"We only bout twenty minutes from your house, if that. So twenty minutes."

"I'm kinda nervous. You gon kill me if I do something to your car."

"Naw, I wouldn't do nothing like that. And if you get too scared we can pull over and I'll take back over. We got a deal, Miss Suzie?"

Man, my hands was sweaty when we switched places and Doni was showing me where all the stuff was: turn signal and all that. But I made it out and onto the highway all right. When I got more comfortable, Doni stopped talking and started pulling up music for the stereo. It had Wi-Fi, so he could play iTunes, Amazon, whatever. He was so funny sometimes. Old-ass phone. Top-of-the-line sound system.

"I got a rule in my car that whoever driving get to call it," he said while he was searching. "That's usually cause I'm the one driving, but I'll let you choose, since you doing so good. Whatchu like to listen to?" I waited until I passed a truck and got back in the slow lane.

"I like Rico Nasty. Flo Milli." He nodded like my daddy do when he think something all right.

"Oh. And Megan."

"Thee Stallion?" Doni rared back against the passenger door and looked me up and down.

"Hell yeah. She good."

"Well, you right about that. Ain't nuthin wrong wit that at all."

I looked over at him quick, through the telescope part. All I could see was red. It was his mouth cause he'd been drinking that Fanta. He was snickering.

"What's funny?"

"You."

"Why I gotta be funny?"

"Cause I been thinking you was straitlaced, and it look like I been sadly mistaken."

"I guess you was." I'm not gon lie. I was feeling good cause I was driving on the freeway, and I don't even know if I had planned to do that when I first started wanting to get my license. I had just wanted to be able to get around the city.

"Ohhhh, okay." Doni nodded his head and snickered again while he took another swallow of pop. "So soon enough, you gon be running these streets, and running these niggas like your favorite rappers."

"Something like that."

"You mighta been doing that already."

"Now you right about that. I might have."

"Okay, then. Well, let me put on some riding music for you." He started playing *Tina Snow* on shuffle, and "Hot Girl" came on.

"That's a bop right there." And I started rapping with the lyrics.

He acted like he was impressed. "You know what? You remind me of this girl I used to mess with. She came off, like, kinda like, goofy, but when you got her by herself, she knew how to come wit it."

"Did you just call me goofy?"

Doni laughed. "Naw, naw. I mean, she was real quiet. Church girl."

"What happened to her?"

"Whatchu think? Didn't work out."

"Were you sad about it?"

"Not after a while. I don't let my feelings stay in one place if the other person don't want em." He looked at me and smiled. "But I shole preciate the memories."

"What memories?"

"Aw, Miss Suzie, you might not be old enough for them stories."

"Try me."

Doni adjusted himself in the seat and scratched behind one of his ears. "Sheeeeeitttt. We used to drive around and do shit in the car."

"Like what?"

"Whatever she felt like doing to me. Or vice versa."

"Y'all was having sex while you was driving?"

Doni laughed. "We...used to help each other out from time to time. Make the driving experience more enjoyable. Like I said, Liza was a church girl. She wore a lot of skirts. And no draws." He chuckled again.

"Y'all didn't never get pulled over?"

"Naw. We wasn't doing stuff you could see. Unless you was a trucker."

I was speechless. I ain't never heard of no shit like that. Then here go Doni being psychic again.

"I was wild then, though. I ain't really into all that nowadays."

"What happened?"

"I got old, I guess."

"Why you always talk about yourself like you old?"

"Cause I'd'n seen too much. And I outlived some folks that was smarter and faster than me. Few of em." He leaned back in the seat again and grabbed the remote so he could let it back a little. "You doin all right now, so I can relax."

"I wanna hear more about you and this girl."

"Awwwww, whatchu trying to do, Miss Suzie? Find out how to turn me out?"

"Naw. I'm just nosy."

"We used to make each other happy. That's all."

"How?" I kept my eyes on the road cause I was getting a little jealous about what he was gonna tell me, but I didn't want him to see that on my face.

"Well, okay, I won't go into all the stuff she did cause that's her business. But *I* used to play wit her while she was driving."

"But like, how?"

Doni sighed; then he put two fingers in my lap. "Well, this was one way…" And he curled them, like he was reaching for something between the buttons, under my dress. "You see what I'm saying?"

"Didn't she get distracted?"

"She wasn't supposed to. It was part of her driving test."

I was feeling real grown then. And jealous. "You gon give me a test like that?"

Doni busted out laughing. "Mane, you must be outcho mind. You tryna get me killed."

"I'm serious." I took my eyes off the road and looked at him for a few seconds longer than the last time. And I made sure I didn't swerve or nothing, so he knew I wasn't playing. But then I had to turn back around to make sure I didn't run off the road.

"You not gon have Mr. Curtis choppin me up and puttin me in the trunk of a car going to the junkyard."

"You scared of him? He in a whole nother state and you not even gon put your hand on it? I'm tryna see if you as good as you say you was."

Doni took another sip of pop and shook his head. "Be careful what you ask for."

"Try me," I said again, cause that's what Megan woulda said, I think.

Doni put his hand back on my knee and started playing chicken: he would move it up my leg a few inches, then stop. "You sure?"

And I would nod, so he would do it again, and again, until his hand was up my skirt, and he took a single finger and started tracing my pantyline. His fingers were cold from the bottle.

Something clicked, like, in my body, and in my back, and my face got hot. I shifted a little, so I could open my legs a little. Man, my mama woulda called me all kinds of loose if she knew about this. He took his two fingers and pulled my panties to the side, and just kinda grazed my lips. I started tingling. He was looking out the windshield, though, and I figured he was trying to make sure he wasn't distracting me too much, so that's what I did too. I stayed focused on the road, but I felt…good. Like even calmer than when we first started. We came up on a eighteen-wheeler, and I zipped around him like that. No problem.

Doni chuckled. "Must notta wanted him to see us from up there."

"Oh, I wasn't even thinking about that."

"You doin good," he said quietly, moving his fingers faster.

"That's all you gon do, though?" I thought maybe he was gon slide em in or something.

"Mane, I already told you at the doctor's office. Thangs ain't always gon go the way you want em to. You ain't ready for all that anyway."

"So you know what I'm ready for? You sound like Curtis."

"You keep sweet-talkin me, I'ma take my hand back and start eating my chips."

I stayed quiet after that.

I didn't know what coming felt like then, but from what I'd heard, I knew it didn't happen in the car. I did get real wet after a while, but then we got close to Greenwood and Doni stopped cause I had to start paying attention. We was coming up to my exit. He kept his hand on my thigh, though, and told me how to get in the exit lane and slow down as I got to the light. And then the rest of it was easy cause it was all streets I knew, but I felt better on them now. I didn't get nervous about people getting too close up on the car, and I wasn't making all them wide turns like I usually do. I came up to the gate and parked. Wasn't nobody home, not even Mama.

"We done did enough for today, Miss Suzie, and I gotta get to work by one. But I'ma see you later, all right?"

"Yeah." But I didn't really move.

He came around to the driver's side and opened the door. Then he bent down and gave me a kiss on the mouth. When he finished, he touched my nose with his wet finger and said, "Tag. Love's on your face." His hands still smelled like me.

"No you *didn't*."

"What, so I can have it on my hands, but you not supposed to touch it? It's yours."

"That's nasty."

"Then it's your nasty." Then he opened the door and chucked me the deuces.

I WENT IN AND LAID across my bed, still wearing my clothes. My skirt had a wet spot on the back, but I wouldn't take it off cause it reminded me of being in the car, and that made me happy. I rolled to one side and put one hand between my legs, where his hands had been not even twenty minutes ago. I didn't do what he did, but I did reach in my panties and put two of my fingers on my lips. They was still wet. Then I held my fingers up so I could look at the stuff on them. It looked like snot, but clear. Clean. I touched one finger to my face. Then I put one to my mouth and licked it. It was a little salty, like contact solution. That made sense. And I thought, *Girl, you acting crazy*, but then I remembered what Doni said. It was my nasty, so it was all right.

I turned my hands over. I got Mama's eyes and her hands too: You know, the way they wrinkle up at the knuckles. The way my cuticles be in a straight line if I don't push them back. All Mama. I wonder what she felt like the first time she did something with Daddy. Did she feel like this? Like the fabric over her head had ripped a little, and she was seeing there was something outside it for the first time? Something she wanted to get to? I knew Doni and Daddy was two different people. Doni been to jail. I hadn't forgot that either. But was I supposed to care? And when he said he would never do that to nobody again, didn't I believe him? And since I did, didn't that mean that whatever I felt about him was safe too?

I wiped my fingers with my other hand and just laid there, looking up at my canopy. I was glad I was at home by myself. I didn't have to talk to nobody, or explain why I was just sitting there in the quiet, not watching TV or nothing. Just staring off into space. I could just be. So all I did for the rest of the day was count and recount the little scallops on my canopy. There was patterns and little color flecks in the lace I hadn't even seen before, and I thought that might be cause I hadn't really been paying attention.

I SPENT THE REST OF the week playing it cool in front of my folks, which was easy cause they weren't talking to each other or me. The gag was that that didn't make life all that different. Daddy came home from work and went in the movie room. Mama stayed under the lamp in the living room, knitting stuff for Mrs. McShan, and I watched TV in my room. If I got hungry, I'd go down and get me a plate of whatever Mama left on the stove, and tried to be as quiet as possible. I needed to be by myself for a little while. And I guess I also needed to listen to Chrisette Michele's "A Couple of Forevers" on repeat until even I got tired of it. It's kinda old, but Mama used to play it all the time back in the day. I'd come home from school and she'd be blasting it in the kitchen and cleaning chitlins, which only Daddy ate. She never played it for him while he was there, but when he came home, the chitlins and whatever she made for us would be done. I kinda wished they could go back to the way they were then, but I knew going back meant I would have to go back to what I was doing then, which was not a damn thing.

I had to talk to somebody about everything, though, so I called Drina that Friday to see if she wanted to get something to eat. Somebody said this new place off Youree had good fried oyster po'boys, and I wanted one. It was the first time in forever Drina actually answered, and she said she wanted to go too.

She came to pick me up and we rode over there like normal, talking about school and her big mama and what she be finding out while doing people hair. I kept it cute and just talked about that stuff cause I didn't wanna say nothing about what happened till we had got in the place and sat down, cause then the conversation wouldn't be interrupted. Drina had just got back from getting some sweet tea and I was putting some ketchup in a bowl so it wouldn't touch my fries before I started eating them. When she sat down I started talking.

"Girl, I gotta tell you what happened with Doni."

"Okay."

"He took me to Nacogdoches, to pick up my glasses. Mama and Daddy been trippin."

"And what—they wouldn't take you back? That's messed up."

"Yeah, but something happened on the way home."

Drina put her cup down. "Like what." She looked concerned.

"Naw, nothing bad. But he—" And I held up my two fingers.

"Ohhhh. Okay." Drina bucked her eyes and picked up her drink again. "In the parking lot at the eye doctor? That's…different."

"Naw, girl. While I was driving."

"Well, damn." She looked like she was bout to say something, but shrugged it off. "How was it?"

"I don't know. It felt good to me."

She rolled her eyes at that one. "I forgot you ain't got nobody to compare it to, so he prolly trash. Niggas don't never know what they doin when they finger pop."

"Well, like I said, it felt good to me."

"You nut?"

"No, but when I got home—"

She laughed again, like she just heard a nasty joke. "So the answer is no, you don't know how it's s'posed to feel." She rolled her eyes. "You know what, though? Good for you. So what's next: y'all go together now?" She said it real sarcastic.

"Naw. I kinda like him, though."

"You tell him?"

"I mean, I let him do all that. Ain't he supposed to know?"

"You know what? You right. He might know. And he mighta done that and some mo stuff to somebody else right after he dropped you off." She laughed her nasty little laugh again.

I didn't want her to know I felt any kinda way about what she said, but maybe she had some information I needed.

"Wait. Is he messin wit somebody else?"

"Prolly."

"Who is it?"

"I mean, I'm not sayin I know, but these niggas out here ain't shit. And just cause he fingered you don't mean he interested."

She started eating her sandwich again and I didn't wanna just sit there and let her have the last word, so after I ate a few fries I said, "Oh yeah. I meant to tell you I might be getting a job."

"A job? Where bout?"

"Belinda's. That double shop on Line. I went in for a interview last week. And I drove myself too. All the way to Line. I took the Toyota."

"Belinda's. You mean Trishelle Timmons's shop?"

"Yeah. That's her name. You know her?" I said it before I remembered I already knew that, cause Trishelle told me.

"I know *of* her. How you meet her?"

"Through Lexi, this girl who date a dude work at Daddy shop. Lexi took me over there couple months ago and I met Trishelle. That's how I found out about the opening."

"Huh. Okay, then."

"Is she cool? Do she seem like somebody I'd wanna work for?"

"I guess so."

"But what do that *mean*, Drina." I was tired of the innuendos.

"It mean I'm not gon piss on your little parade of shiny new friends, girl. They cool if they cool wit you. And that's all I got to say about that."

I was starting to get irritated; plus she was distracting me from my po'boy, which really was as good as folks said. They put a rémoulade on it instead of mayonnaise, and that shit was the truth.

"Why you keep acting like you got the tea on all these folks but you not tellin me?"

"Zettie, you putting words in my mouth. I ain't say nuthin bout none of them people."

"Well, you insinuatin a whole lot."

"Whooooa, look at you, hittin me with them *five*-dollar words. I see you. Musta got that from Doni."

"Just answer the fuckin question and stop playin."

"Zettie, stop putting words in my mouth. Everything's fine. Those people are *fine*. How's your sandwich? Is it good? Mine's good. Just the right amount of pickle."

And she started eating like that was the only reason she was sitting at the table, so I just got up and went to get some more sauce, even though I really didn't even feel like eating anymore. Maybe I could ask for a to-go box, too, while I was up. I hoped everything tasted the same when I got home.

I didn't feel like waiting in line, so I waved at one of the line cooks from the side of the counter to see if he could help me out. He was one of those old heads, and he grinned at me when he looked up. "Oh, it's the bombshell coming back. Va-va-va-voom! What can I help you with, Miss Lady?"

I don't know if it's cause I got old parents, but paw-paws stay loving the vibe. I tried not to roll my eyes.

"Can I please have some more rémoulade to go? And can you show me where the boxes are?"

"I sure can. Right behind you over against the wall. And I'll have that sauce right out for you." I walked over to get a box, and I was gonna get Drina one, but I didn't. I didn't know what was wrong with her, but how she treated me made me feel bad. Before that day, Drina ain't never made fun of me in my life. We was best friends for that exact reason: cause she ain't never talked down to me or made me feel different or less than. Well, that was one reason why. But I didn't understand why she wasn't happy for me. Shit, she act like *she* had a thing for Doni.

Everybody was acting a fool, and I didn't know what I was supposed to do aside from going off on folks. But I was tired of all that. They just needed to let me live. Didn't nothing else have to change. I don't know why they was acting like it did.

When I came back to the counter to pick up my sauce, old dude winked at me and made sure his fingers touched my hand when he gave me my to-go ramekins. I said thank you, and just as I was about to turn away, he said, "All right, sistagirl, you take it easy."

"Yes, sir. You too." So he would remember how old he was.

"All right then. And smile! You look like you done lost your best friend."

A COUPLE NIGHTS AFTER THAT wack-ass lunch with Drina, Mama and Daddy went to do something; I think go visit one of Daddy's sick relatives up in Rodessa. Mama still wasn't speaking to him and she wasn't too friendly with me neither so I knew it was gonna be a long ride up there. So I told them I had cramps and didn't want to go. Of course that meant Daddy was gonna try to do a hi and bye cause he probably thought I was gonna sneak somebody over, but them country relatives is long-winded. And they *always* gotta feed you before you go, so he wasn't gon get out of it as fast as he wanted. And his hovering ass didn't know I didn't need to invite nobody over cause I still had a set of Toyota keys.

It took me awhile to get to Cedar Grove cause it was nighttime, so I was slower, and I only took the surface streets I knew, which meant I was slow as hell: West Seventieth to St. Vincent, almost to the mall, then down into the neighborhood on Range Lane, past the Metro PCS where Drina work, and Evergreen Missionary Baptist, where Mama and Daddy got me baptized when I was little. We ain't never lived over here, but it always feel like home when I come through. The little square houses with the carports and the patchy grass on these little bald-headed lawns. Everybody I love come from here: Mama and Daddy. Drina. Even Doni grew up over here, on Seventy-Ninth, close to A. B. Palmer Park. He older than me, but he don't remember when they killed the dude at the Pack and Sack either, or the riots, or when Dick Gregory and them came and called themselves cleaning up the park. And they did, for a while, but now we kinda back on the same shit. It's sad, too, cause Daddy say Cedar Grove used to be its own little town, where you could shop and raise kids. Folks helped each other out. Bought property. Now we don't really own nothing and don't nobody trust nobody.

When I pulled up to Drina's house, her car was under the carport. Miss Tonya's car was gone, and I was glad. Drina's grandmamma was bedridden by then, usually in her little room at the back of the house. So we'd be by ourselves.

I didn't see Drina on the porch until I got out of the car. She was outside in a jacket, sweats, and some house shoes, smoking a blunt. I sat in the other plastic chair but she wouldn't look at me, just watched the street for a few seconds, holding in the smoke before turning her head and blowing it out. I'm used to that, though. I spend half the time looking at the back of Doni head.

"Whatchu doing here?" she asked, trying to stifle a cough. She didn't even sound like she was asking me a question; it was more like she was telling me what time it was.

"Come to see you."

"How you know I was here? You didn't call."

"If I called, you woulda told me you was busy. Like you been doing."

Drina nodded cause she knew she couldn't argue with that. She looked down at the blunt. "Well, you caught me. Long time, no see." She was on that sarcastic shit again cause we was just together two days ago. I tried to start with the simple stuff.

"You never come by no more. And you never wanna go nowhere wit me. And when you do, you mean."

Drina cut her eyes at me. "Ain'tchu busy, though? You got Doni and a car now and school and a job from your new friend. Whatever her name is. Why you even call me the other day? If you can drive here, you can drive over to Youree for a po'boy."

"Because you my friend. I miss spending time wit you. I miss seein you. Mane, there's so much tea I didn't even get into."

"I don't care."

"What?"

"You heard me. I don't care."

"Why you acting like that?"

Drina looked at me for a long time, not blinking. Almost not even moving. For a minute, I thought she was holding in smoke before she blew it out, but she wasn't. She was just looking at me. Then she moved in close, so we was staring each other right in the eyes. Her pupils was big. Guess she was real high. Either that or the blunt was laced. Maybe that's why she was talking crazy. She started speaking slow like she thought something was wrong with me.

"Everything that's ever happened to you, Zettie—your car; your job; hell, Doni—is cause I saved you. I saved you from the Bottoms girls who tried to fight you. I saved you from the niggas in high school that wanted to run trains on you just to see what it was like. I saved your eyes too. You sittin here lookin at me cause I saved your eyes. Whatchu gon give me for that, Zettie? Whatchu *ever* gave me, to make up for that?"

"I never asked you for none of that."

"You didn't have to. You were my friend. And I loved you."

"That should be enough then. If that's the only reason why you did it."

Drina clenched her jaw and looked away like she was losing her patience. Then she turned back to me. "It should have been enough, shouldn't it."

She said it just like that. Real flat.

"Then whatchu want, Drina? It's whatever. I just want us to be friends again."

"What does it matter?"

And I didn't know what she was asking: whether it mattered that she got whatever she wanted, or that we stayed friends, but I screamed, "*Everything about it matter!* You my best friend, Drina, and you saved me. But you actin like I'on't care bout you when I do. And you actin like I'm not grateful for what you did with Ms. Mouton. Or any of em. I don't even know the whole story. But I'm grateful."

I paused for a minute, cause I wanted to calm myself down, but then Drina narrowed her eyes.

"What did you just say to me?"

"Wait—whatchu mean?"

"You 'don't know the whole story.' Is that what the fuck you said?"

And I thought, *Oh, shit, she really bout to get mad.* But if she was gon hit me, I'd try to stay calm enough to see it coming and at least duck. I took another deep breath.

"You never told me to my face what happened with the voodoo thing. Only in that room. Then I heard Ms. Mouton died. Did you know that? How did she die?"

"Fuck am I s'posed to know? Why'on't you go find MarLisha and ask her? And ask her what they said in the car, too, since you'on't believe me."

"I never said I didn't believe you, Drina. I just said I didn't kn—"

"You know what? Fuck you, Suzette. Cause you done got a little dick now and you can't tell whether you comin or goin. You talking bout you don't know what happened but you still *owe* me? What, is this friendship a car note you tryin to pay off? Cool. What you gon pay me? Or, wait, cause you ain't got that job yet, whatchu gon *give* me?" She laughed. "Nuthin. That's what. Cause everything you got belong to somebody else. Mr. Curtis. Ms. Delphine. Even me. I gave you everything I had. Whatever happen to you in *this* life: with work, or with school, or with Doni? Ain't none of that yours. If you go over there *tonight*, and he take your clothes off, they clothes I took you to get. Clothes you bought with Mr. Curtis money." She put her hand up to my head, and wound some of my hair around her finger. "He play in your hair? I do your hair. He fuck you? And you know to spread for him? You know how to fuck him back? You not scared of him cause somebody else took it without asking? I did that. But just what I get back? Nothing. And what I got left with?"

She stared at me for a long time, her hand still in my hair, the blunt in her other hand that she held out of the way, like we was gon fight and she didn't want it to get smushed or put out. I hadn't never seen Drina like this toward me, and I was so confused and so scared I felt like I was bout to cry, but I thought if I did, she might Hulk out on me for real. Or worse, laugh in my face. She was that kinda mad, like she used to get with the bullies at school. I'd only ever seen her get like that when she was protecting me. Maybe I was doing something wrong. I tried to start over with what I knew.

"Drina, you always been my friend. Like my *friend* friend. I ain't never tried to use you or nothing like th—"

"I never said you did."

"I ain't sayin you said it. I'm saying I don't want you to think that. Drina, you the only person I ain't kin to that treated me like somebody from the beginning. Even Doni useta act funny—"

"Doni loves you."

"What?"

"Doni loves you." She said it carefully this time. "Doni is in love with you."

"How you know that?"

Drina laughed and turned away from me, ashing the blunt by tapping it on the porch railing. The sleeve on her hoodie slipped down her hand, and when she looked over to pull it up, she shook her head.

"You think he runnin cross the state line, taking you places, letting people talk about him and why he wanna date you? All that just cuz? Who would do all that for nuthin?"

"Dudes don't like me like that. Not, like, boyfriend-girlfriend."

"Yeah they do. Plenty people do, quiet as it's kept. Tha's how you get people to do so much. They fall for you, and you got em. People talking bout Doni like, 'That shit must be magic for real.' But they don't know you gotta be *in* it to understand it. That's what they don't get."

"Whatchu talkin bout, Drina? You not making no sense."

"Listen, if you really tryna grow up—if you *really* tryna be a functioning adult—you got to understand that don't nobody do nuthin for free. Everybody want somethin. And you gotta figure out what you wanna give em. You can't be boppin around the world thinkin everybody operate out of the kindness of they hearts. Ain't nobody like that. Nobody. And it ain't bad to want nuthin neither. It's not what you want that's the bad thing anyway. It's what you willin to do to get it."

She was talking to me like I was stupid, so I stopped being scared for a minute and started snapping back. I rolled my eyes. "Fine. So, when you did all that shit for me back when we was kids, what did you want, Drina?"

She smirked again and tapped the blunt. "If you gotta ask me to name it, you cain't give it to me." Then she got close to me again. The zipper bottom on her jacket brushed my leg. She got real close, but then she backed away, and went in the house.

But just when she was about to lock the burglar bar door, she said to me, in a low voice, I guess cause her grandmama was inside, "Ain't nothing really changed with us, Zettie. The circumstances different, but I still love you. That ain't gon change. But you grown now. We gotta figure out where I fit, that's all." And then she shut the door, and I hurried up and got in the car cause I didn't want to start crying in the middle of the hood.

"MOVE OUT THE WAY. I'M comin all the way in this time." Doni was blocking the door like he usually do when he answer it, but when he saw my face, he backed up quick, and I took that as a invitation to walk right in.

"Wha's wrong witcho face?"

"Me and Drina got in a fight."

"A fistfight?"

"Naw. A argument."

"Oh. My bad. Your face real red."

"I was cryin."

"About what?"

"I don't even know. She said something bout me taking from her and not givin nuthin back and everybody do that for me but I don't see it and—" My face crumpled up again. Doni led me to the couch and sat me down. He disappeared for a minute, then came back with a roll of toilet tissue. He wound it a few times around his hand and then handed what he tore off to me in his palm, like a bird's nest. I mopped my face with it. He sat down and sighed.

"Y'all shouldn't be fightin like that. Tha's not right."

"You tellin *me* not to fight? I didn't start nuthin!"

"I didn't say you did. I'm just sayin y'all been friends too long for all that. And I hope y'all ain't arguin over nothing stupid, like no nigga."

"What if I said we was?"

"Come on. Both of y'all too smart for that. These niggas out here ain't about nuthin. And anyway, Drina—"

I leaned back so I could get a good look at him. "What if it was about you? What if you was the nigga?"

He looked surprised at first, but then he shook his head. "You lying. Cause if Drina gon fight over anybody—"

"I didn't say she want you. I'm sayin we fought *about* you."

"Say more."

"She say I'm running round wit you and I ain't grateful enough for all she done did for me or something, I cain't remember." I cleaned my nose again, and reached for another wad of tissue, cause I wasn't sure if I wanted to say what was next. I was stalling.

"And she said you in love wit me."

"Say whaaaaat?"

"Yeah. She say she know what it look like."

"I think she need to stay out my business."

"That's what I said. You lookin for somethin else, right? Somebody who about somethin." I know I sounded bitter as hell, but them words had been in the back of my head since the pond.

Doni looked at me a little weird, like he was trying to figure out where he'd heard what I just repeated. His brow wrinkled up. "Who told you I was lookin for somebody that was about somethin?"

"You did. At the duck pond. You said you were lookin for somebody who was about somethin. And you couldn't say what else but you'd know it when you seen it and that hadn't happened yet. So naw, you ain't in love wit me."

Doni leaned back into the cushions and rolled his head over to one side. "Mane, if y'all don't quit putting words in my mouth. I ain't say that. I ain't say what you said I said in the park. I ain't never told Drina nuthin bout how I feel about you. None of it."

"Okay, then, how bout you tell *me* how you feel then? Right now. I'm here. Go'n tell me."

"You come over here. You Debo your way up in my house and now you sittin on my couch. And I let you. You gotta know I have some kinda feelings. You ain't that naïve."

He was talking in circles again, and all I really wanted was for him to say he wanted to be my boyfriend. Or that he didn't, so I wouldn't have to wonder. So I got blunt.

"Okay, word to all that, but do you love me?"

Doni leaned back and looked me up and down. "Damn, do I have to? After we been on three dates? And your mama was wit us on one of em, at Jethreaux's? And then that stuff in the car? That's all it's supposed to take?"

I couldn't say nuthin about that cause I really hadn't been on no dates and I didn't know exactly when you was supposed to fall in love, let alone say it. But maybe I just wanted him to say it cause then everything would be easier to figure out. I would just *know*. But I couldn't say all that, so I tried to think of something else to ask. He kept talking.

"I mean, you my homie." He stretched one arm out behind me on the couch cushion, like he was trying to look comfortable. Nonchalant.

And *that* felt like a diss, so I kinda snapped back, "And tha's all you want?"

"Tha's all I want for now."

"So you just looking for somebody to pass the time."

"Hell, I should be asking you that. I wasn't the one beggin to get finger-fucked on the ride home."

Dammit, I knew it. Drina was right about what she said at lunch. Maybe that's why she was so mad earlier. Cause I was being stupid, and when I let him do that in the car, I let him know I was down for whatever, no strings attached. And I felt played. Which means I got pissed.

"So your bitch ass only did it cause you thought I was *beggin* you, and cause my daddy wasn't nowhere around to scare you off?"

"I would appreciate you watching how you talk to me in my house, Miss Suzie; otherwise, you can go *back* to ya daddy right now." He looked around the room. "I ain't been tryna do nuthin but get to know you. Maybe see what you about. See where your head at. Uppp!" He snapped his fingers and pointed at me. "*That's* what I said at the park, but don't nobody remember that."

He was right; that was what he said. I don't know why I remembered it any different. I think...Hell, I don't know. This shit is hard. Trying to read people and figure out what they about. Meanwhile, every voice in my head sound like my daddy, telling me everybody is bad news.

Doni reached for a half-smoked cigarette in the ashtray, put it in the corner of his mouth, and relit it. "And while we at it, let's talk about Drina for a minute. So, if Drina say I'm in love wit you, and then y'all start fightin about me, wha's that about? Finish that story, since you wanna talk about the truth."

"I'own know why she mad."

"You sure bout that?"

"Nigga, that's why I'm confused. Tha's why I'm cryin." I waved around the tissue. And I looked at him, and he just looked right back at me like I was supposed to know why he asked. But I really didn't. Drina was my best friend. She was supposed to look out for me, especially since I didn't know what I was doing. But saying that made Drina sound like she was my daddy, so I kept quiet.

"For real, though. Drina the one in love with you," Doni said after he took a hit. "Tha's why she said that stuff about me. Deflectin attention."

"No she ain't."

"Then why she tell me that?"

"She did what?!"

"Yes, ma'am. At Jaydell birthday party. She told me to be careful cause she was in love witchu."

"She told me she said something else."

"You can believe whoever you wanna believe, Miss Suzie. But don't be comin over here actin brand-new if you already fuckin around wit somebody else. Cause tha's *not* what I'm looking for, in case you was wonderin. But you prolly gon turn that against me, too, and a week from now tell me I said I didn't want your ass."

There was something about the way he said it that let me know he wasn't lying about Drina. But if that was true, didn't nothing make sense, not even me being there. I needed to go home and figure some stuff out, then talk to her again. I'd been sitting there defending her as my best friend, but I was missing half the damn story. It felt like I'd walked out the house half dressed, trying to clown other people's clothes. I stood up to leave.

"You know what? This some bullshit. Everybody playin games."

Doni shook his head. "Ain't no games being played over here, Miss Suzie. This the real world. People got real secrets. They got real shit they dealin wit. I mean, I really shouldn'ta said nuthin, but I thought you knew. And if you really hearin it for the first time? That shit must feel crazy. So I understand why you wanna leave."

I was mad that he knew so much about me. That he kept hitting every nail on the head. "You'on know nuthin bout how I feel. Or give a damn about me for that matter."

"I do, Miss Suzie. I do. You just maybe ain't ready for how I care."

"What the fuck is that s'posed to mean, Doni?" I was yelling again.

He stood up and hitched up his pants, since he wasn't wearing a belt. "It mean if I want something, I ain't shy about that. But when it's other stuff at stake, or people could get hurt, I think about that shit too. I ain't tryna put hurt out in the world. I done that already. Mane, I set a motherfucker on fire. What I look like only tryna look out for me? What I even look like bein happy, gettin what I want? I can want a whole bunch of shit, but if I don't deserve it, what I look like getting it?"

I was already at the door, with my hand on the knob, but that stopped me in my tracks. I half turned around.

"Who's to say you don't deserve what you want? I mean…if you really want it."

Doni didn't catch my drift. He just sucked his teeth and shrugged. "The world, Suzette. The world tell me that. Every day. And I'm not sayin you naïve, but you ain't been through enough to even understand that." He hit the butt of the cigarette and put it out.

"You don't know me like that. I do understand. The world tell me I don't deserve shit neither. I'm too different. Who gon want me?"

"Not everybody think like that. But you know that already."

"No I don't."

"But you do, man. You already know what it is."

"What is it?" I asked.

"You know what it is."

And I realized that might be the best answer I got that night, but it was better than anything I'd ever got from a dude. And I was still confused—mostly about Drina—but I figured if he had taken it this far, I might as well take a step forward too. So I started walking back toward him, and when we got face-to-face, we just looked at each other. Doni didn't flinch, and neither did I, but I could see that little muscle in his jaw jumping. He turned his head to blow out a last little bit of smoke. When he did, I stepped closer, cause if I ain't learn nothing from people talking about my daddy, it's that talk don't pay the damn bills. You gotta put in the work to let people know who you are, and what you will or won't do. I let my purse fall to the floor.

"Prove it," I said. "Prove to me what it is."

DONI LED ME TO THE back of the apartment, to a room with a low bed, and turned on the lamp. There wasn't nothing else in that room but a chest of drawers and a nightstand. No TV, no nothing. Wasn't even no cologne or nothing on top of the dresser. It was clean as a pin. I wondered what he thought about my room. It always looked like a tornado had run through it. I got a good look around before I spoke.

"You don't wanna keep the lights off?"

"Why would I do that?"

I wanted to say cause people have sex in the dark, but I didn't know. It just felt like it was too bright. He might have figured out what I was thinking, so he said hold on and went to the bathroom. He came back with a wet face towel, and put it over the top of the lamp. It dimmed it a little.

"That better?"

"Yeah. Thank you."

"No need to be shy now. You the one asked to come back here."

"You right." We laughed, but he left the towel up there.

He sat me down on the bed and held my face by the chin while he kissed me. Deep. His mouth tasted like it had in the park and when I laid back on the bed with him on top of me, he put his hands down on the mattress by my shoulders, and his underarms smelled like a man's deodorant. I don't know if it was all those things, or how heavy he felt, or his biceps flexed on either side of me, but I wanted to jump right out of my clothes. This was only my first time, though. But I was ready. I was wet again; my underwear felt tight and uncomfortable. I reached down to see if I could take my pants off. I understood why it felt good to be fast.

Doni stopped my hands and looked at me. Then he put one hand on my face and rubbed his thumb on my cheek.

"You so young," he said.

"I'm not that young. And you not that old. We know what we

doin." I hadn't really thought about the age difference till then. Seven years is a lot when you only twenty. But my parents like fifteen years apart, so I figured it was all right.

"But you ain't been out here like people your age," he said. "I'own know if you ready."

"Ain't no way I can make myself more ready for you now. At least not without doin something I ain't never done."

Doni nodded a little with his mouth parted. You could see just the bottom of his top teeth and the beginning of the little space. His lips looked a little dry, and right when I thought that, he licked em. That shit was sexy.

He nodded again, and started kissing me while he was doing it. His body lowered a little more on me. He was hard, and heavier than I expected, but that's what I liked. I liked the way his weight felt. I liked not knowing what could happen to me next.

Between kisses, he kept talking with his mouth so close to mine I could feel his lips move.

"You somethin else. Like"—and I know he wanted to say *different*, but instead he looked over my face like he was checking it for something—"like a doll. Like a baby doll."

I didn't know what to say about that. I know he meant *pretty*, but I ain't wanna thank him for that.

"You fine too," I said.

That made him pause for a minute. He looked over my head and grinned, almost like he was looking out the window. He bit his bottom lip before he spoke.

"You ain't gotta gas me."

"I'm not."

Doni sighed, then rubbed the side of his face while he was thinking. "Naw. I'own think we can do this. You too inexperienced."

I mean, I knew stuff, but I hadn't done nothing, so he wasn't wrong, but I didn't want him to know I agreed with him, cause he might stop. So I didn't say nothing, and he didn't either, just leaned back and looked at me like he was trying to make sure I was me. I looked right back at him cause I wanted him to know I was serious. Then I said, "Listen, I'm bout to take off the rest of my clothes."

I stood up and pulled off my sweater; then I took off my pants. And then I slowed down a little cause I don't think nobody outside my mama and maybe Drina ever seen me all the way naked. Not as an adult anyway. And of course there was a mirror on the back of the door, so I had to look at everything I was doing. But I'd already committed to it. I don't know what he thought when I took off my bra and panties, but when I saw myself, I was thinking, *You not half-way bad.* I got a pretty good shape, a little bit curvy. I like the way my thighs come together, which ain't the move for like Instagram or nothing, but I think it's cute. I raised my arms to lift my breasts like folks do in posts, and I wondered what he thought about my areolas. They pretty light, but they looked darker under the covered-up lamp, so you could see the contrast a little better. And I almost got lost thinking about that till I turned around, and Doni was staring at me. We looked at each other, and he put his hand down his pants. I put one of my hands down and started rubbing myself too. We was just looking at each other for a long time while we were doing that, and then maybe I hit a nerve or something because I felt like a jolt, and I stopped real quick cause I didn't know what was happening. He saw it, too, cause then he got up and led me to the bed again. And finally he took his clothes off.

His shoulders looked like a sculpture or something, like somebody molded them and then smoothed them down and bronzed everything out. I like his chest too. I like how he kinda skinny, but still built. He even got a six-pack. It had a big tattoo on it, but I couldn't see what it was.

He kissed me, and I put my arms around him. The hard muscles in his back flexed when he moved his body on top of me. He started pulling his boxers down and I helped him get his feet out of them, and then I saw it. A little darker than the rest of him, looking like the air in the room had woke it up, and it was bobbing in it, trying to find a breeze. I touched the tip, and it was wet. Then I wrapped my fingers around it, so I could feel it pulse. I wanted to put my mouth on it, but he stopped me and reached over for something in his nightstand. A condom. And when he put it on, I tried to put him up to my lips, but the condom smelled funny. A little like vinegar. I think it was the rubber.

"Can you take this off until we start?"

"No. Not this time, baby." So I changed my mind about that, and just kissed him again.

I asked myself one last time if I really wanted to do this. And I did, and I knew exactly why. Not for none of the reasons we'd talked about earlier: going against Daddy or making Drina mad or proving I was grown. I wanted to do it because, for once, I wanted to experience something nobody could save me from. I held him for a minute, moving my hand with a rhythm like he had with me in the car: up and down. We kissed harder and harder, but after a while, he stopped and looked me dead in the eyes, like he was giving me one more chance to change my mind. But I just nodded, and I lay all the way down. And I let him spread me, just like Drina said he would.

IT WAS REAL LATE, AND I could already see the missed calls on my phone, but I knew I wasn't going home without seeing Drina again. This time, though, I texted her, but all I said was, You said next time to let you know when i'm coming.

I don't know if it was there the first time I came by, but when I pulled up I saw a orange car next door at the vacant lot. A Mustang, just like the one I saw a few weeks ago at the shop. As I got closer, I could see it had the blue stripe. Drina was inside the house this time, so I knocked, low cause I wasn't sure if her grandmama was up.

"You got a visitor?" I asked, nodding back at the car when she answered the door.

"Naw."

"Then whose car is that?"

"Why?"

"Cause I saw one look like it awhile back."

Drina didn't answer that, but she did open the door and let me in.

"Where everybody at?"

"Gone."

"Your grandmama too?"

"Yep. Down in Mansfield with my uncle and his kids. Me and Mama took her earlier today. Mama at work."

Drina didn't offer me a seat, just sat on the couch and kept watching TV. I sat on the opposite end and tugged at my sweater a little. I still felt naked, even now, in a different house.

"Drina, why you mad at me? What I do?"

Drina wouldn't look at me, just kept watching TV. "You didn't do nuthin."

"Then what you mad about?"

"You wouldn't understand."

"Explain it to me."

Drina picked up the remote and started flipping channels. We sat like that for a minute, watching little clips of folks that lasted a few seconds till she pressed the button. After a few minutes, she reached up to scratch her nose. I took it as an opportunity.

"You get that car from Daddy?"

She looked at me like she was mad I figured it out, then said, "It's just a loan. My car ain't been acting right. That's why it's up under the porch."

"Why he loan it to you?"

"Why you need to know?" Her voice went back to what it sounded like earlier when we were arguing. But I wasn't scared this time, cause I knew something she didn't know I knew.

"I feel like everything that's happenin around me is about me," I said slowly. "But don't nobody wanna tell me wha's goin on. Y'all keep saying I don't need to know, or I don't know enough to get it, but when is somebody gon tell me what I need to know before I can know more? When are y'all gon stop playin me?" My eyes started burning and I knew I was gonna cry, so I looked down so I could squeeze them shut and try to stop the tears. I couldn't be crying in a conversation where I was complaining bout why everybody treated me like a baby. Drina sighed and let her head fall to one side like she was tired of me.

"You know what, though?" I said. "You ain't gotta make me feel like I'm stupid for asking questions, neither. I thought we was better than that, Drina. I ain't never stopped being your best friend. I'own know when you stopped bein mine."

Drina looked down and started examining her acrylics. "Mr. Curtis lent me the car cause he want me to keep tabs on you."

I'd been leaning back on the couch cushions, but I sat up real quick. "Wait, what?"

She nodded, not looking up.

"You mean follow me?"

She put her hand up. "Nawww. Well…somethin like that. Just come around more. Spend more time with you. Keep you busy."

"Why? Cause of Doni?"

"I guess. He don't want y'all together."

"Cause of the jail stuff? Doni already told me what happened. And how is Daddy gon get him out, let him work in the shop *and* come to the house, but we cain't talk to each other?"

Drina rubbed her temples. "I don't know, Zettie. I don't even know how I got caught up in this shit."

I folded my arms, sat back, and crossed my legs. "Well, if he tryna keep something from happenin, he too late."

"I been knew that. I wasn't gon be the one to tell him, though."

"You woulda been lying anyway, cause it just happened."

"Whaaaat? That shit just happened tonight? For real?"

"For real." And I smiled, cause yeah, I was proud of it. But I didn't wanna give too many details right away.

Drina reached back for her ponytail and ran her hands through it. "Damn. Well, tell yo daddy it sure as hell ain't my fault. I didn't even know that's where you was goin when you left here."

"I ain't gotta tell him shit cause I'm grown. And our argument ain't have nuthin to do wit it, so don't feel guilty."

Drina shrugged. "I didn't feel guilty."

Then a few seconds later, she asked quietly, "So how was it?"

"He good at what he do."

Drina laughed. "How would you know?"

"Cause we felt good together."

"Compared to what, though?"

"Everything. My whole life."

"Oh." She laughed. "You must have came then."

I hesitated. For some reason, I didn't want her to know all that.

"I think so."

Drina rolled her eyes. "Zettie. I'ma need you to stop having sex with people if you don't know what's supposed to happen when you do it."

I huffed. "I do know what's supposed to happen."

"If you did, you'da known when you came."

"I did know. And it happened more than once too. First time it was from me, messing around in the mirror. Next time, it was from him, on the bed. Then the third time it felt like I had to pee, and something happened. Like, I felt it, and he felt it, and he told me to just let it go so I did."

"It's okay to say that, then. That it happened."

I didn't say anything. She reached over and shook my thigh.

"Congratulations, girl. It sounds like you a squirter. When you came, did it come out fast?"

"Felt like it. I didn't see it, though."

"Yeah. That's what it was. You a squirter."

"What that mean, though?"

"It's the female version of ejaculation. It's like…So not everybody do it, but it's normal."

"I thought that's what coming was?"

"Yeah, but squirting skeets. Like sperm."

"Oh. Do you do it?"

"No. But I know some women that do."

"Y'all talk about that stuff?" I hadn't even talked about sex with my mama.

"Something like that." Drina leaned back on the couch and picked up the remote, but then thought better and put it on the end table. "Did he do anything you didn't want to do?"

"No. I wanted everything we did. I started it."

"Well, all right then." Drina smiled a little. Then she said, "I'm relieved. He seem like a okay dude, but you never know."

"Yeah."

"So he like you too? Y'all a couple?"

"I like him, but I don't know about all that. I mean…we ain't gotta be together just cause we did somethin." Those were his words more than mine, but I didn't tell her that cause she seemed happy again, like we were back being friends.

"That's right," said Drina, almost like she was talking to a little girl. "And he need to respect whatever you want, no matter what he want instead. You should—"

"Drina. I know that already. You ain't gotta worry. I'm good."

"Okay," she said. "Okay." Then we both looked at the TV. It was a local channel, and a commercial for Belinda's came on. I remembered something, and I pointed to Trishelle helping a woman into a blazer.

"You know Trishelle told me to tell you hey when I was up there asking about the job. She say she ain't seen you lately. I didn't even realize y'all knew each other like that."

Drina tensed a little. "Yeah, we do."

"Oh? Cause you acted like you didn't. How you know her?"

"Why you wanna know?"

"Cause if I'm passing messages between y'all, I need to know what they about."

Drina sighed again, and I glared at her till she spoke. "I used to date her."

"What?"

"Yeah. For a minute."

Of course I was still thinking about what Doni said Drina told him at the party, but I didn't wanna go there just yet cause shit was getting complicated. I wanted to make sure I didn't miss nothing. So, instead, I asked, "Why y'all break up?"

Drina shrugged and looked down at her nails again. "Me acting a fool. Heart wasn't in it."

I just nodded, and suddenly, something from way back made sense. "That's why JaQuavian said that stuff to us on the Boardwalk. Cause he knew you messed with other girls."

"Probly. I don't know dumb-ass-nigga logic, so…" And she shrugged.

Man, finding out all this stuff in one night was making me tired. I really just wanted to get up and leave, but I had to ask. "Drina, if we been friends this long, why you ain't tell me?"

Drina paused for a minute, then looked directly at me. "I didn't really think you wanted to know."

"Of course I woulda wanted to know."

"Now you do."

I took a deep breath. "Doni told me what you said to him at Jaydell party too."

"Doni talk too much."

"He said the same thing about you. Why you ain't want me to know what you said?"

Drina started playing with her ponytail again. "I love you first and foremost cause you my friend. That ain't never gon change."

"Yeah, same wit me." I nodded when I said it, so she knew I wasn't lying.

She nodded, too, like she was finally understanding what I was trying to say on the porch. She kept going. "But I ain't never tried to force it. Even though you driving now and you and Doni doing all this stuff together, and I don't know wha's gon happen to us. Even though your daddy *been* came to me to say he know how I feel and he'd feel better if you did whatever with me, cause he know me and of course you probably got urges cause you grown. But it'd be safer wit me. And part of the reason I didn't say nuthin was cause I didn't even wanna chance it bein somethin you didn't want. Not even tonight, when he said hold on to the car for a little bit cause he was gon talk to you when you got home—"

"Wait. My daddy said *what*?"

Drina stopped talking.

"*I can't believe this shit*!" I screamed, and I was glad her big mama wasn't home. "Why everybody in the world act like they done lost they damn mind?" But then I thought about Mama's Cadillac. Daddy did the exact same thing with me.

Drina looked over at the TV. "But I wouldn't do that to you. I didn't even know if you did that."

And I didn't answer that, cause, shit, I didn't know either. This was my first night doing whatever, and I was late for everything. Looked like everybody already knew what they wanted, but I didn't even know what all there was to want. I looked over at Drina in her sweats and ponytail and no makeup. Tell you the truth, I thought she looked better when she was dolled up. I stared at her till she looked up, and her eyelashes was wet.

"I'm sorry, Zettie. I didn't want no parts of that, but I'm still sorry."

All I could do was shake my head. "That's fucked up. But Daddy been on one lately. I shouldn't be surprised. He been that way wit damn near everybody."

"Yeah." She put her hands up to her face like she did when we was little and she didn't want folks to see her cry. And I just had this moment, like, when I realized even though Drina was family, she wasn't necessarily like Mama and Daddy. She didn't treat me how she treated me and tried to protect me cause she was supposed to. Or, in Daddy's case, cause she felt like I belonged to her. She'd done it because she wanted to, and there's a difference. It's just that I hadn't really thought about that difference before.

I reached over and put my arm around her, then grabbed one of her wrists. "You know what, Drina? I never said thank you for all the stuff you done for me. With MarLisha, and all them girls at school. All that. But I was never your friend just for that stuff. I prolly ain't make you feel like that, though. And I'm sorry. I'm sorry for that, that it didn't look like what it was."

And I took my hand off her wrist to hug her and she hugged me back, tight, and we just sat like that for a few minutes. When we pulled away, I tried to kiss her on the cheek, but I caught her mouth instead. She jumped back a little, and we looked at each other. After a few seconds, she shook her head and smiled.

"You smell like him."

"Like who?"

"Doni."

"Well, you gon have to get used to that."

And she nodded. We sat like that for a while, but then I got up to leave, cause Mama and Daddy didn't know where I was and one of em was liable to either show up or flip out when I got home. I went in to hug Drina one more time, and this time, we kissed on purpose. Her mouth didn't taste or feel like Doni's. It was soft, and slick cause she had on lip gloss. She tasted the same way she did in the seventh grade. She parted my lips and sneaked her tongue in, real quick at first, and then flicked it, so my mouth quivered, and opened wider. And when it did, she stuck her tongue in farther and pushed her breasts against mine. My nipples were still sore from Doni's mouth, and they chafed up against my sweater even though it was angora. I'd forgot to put my bra back on.

I wish I could tell you I kissed her cause I was glad I got my friend back, but that wasn't it. I did it to see how it felt, and while we kissed, I thought about the fact that all the men arguing over my body—like JaQuavian and Daddy and hell, maybe even Doni, cause who knows?—thought it had happened anyway, so we wasn't really doing nuthin that hadn't been imagined. I moved my hand down the front of Drina's shirt and she reached over and grabbed one of my breasts. When she squeezed it, she moaned a little, and I wanted to keep going, but I stopped. I still needed to find out the rest of the story. About Daddy. About MarLisha and Ms. Mouton. I was tired of trusting people with everything when they couldn't even trust me with the truth.

My daddy wasn't as smart as he thought he was. He focused on controlling everything but my feelings. And if he couldn't control my feelings, he couldn't control my body. I almost laughed, thinking about how hard he'd been trying to do that. But here I was tonight, loose as a goose. The gag, though, was that, when me and Drina kissed, it didn't feel like the substitute he wanted it to be. It felt like something else, like something on top of everything else. Wonder what he woulda thought about that.

MAMA WAS SITTING UP IN the kitchen when I got home. We looked at each other, but didn't really speak. I went to the refrigerator for some water to wash everybody else's taste out my mouth. I was tired, too, and didn't necessarily want to have to deal with her. I was about to pass through to the living room when she said, kinda offhandedly, "I don't know where your father is."

"He gone this time of night?" I tried to act surprised.

"Yep. Left a little while ago."

"Oh, he probly looking for me. I hope he don't go to Doni's. And if he do, I hope Doni try to kill him."

"Don't say that," she said, but it sounded like she didn't mean it.

"He crazy."

"He not crazy. Just convinced he know best. Been like that since the day I met him."

Mama and Daddy met at the DMV. I knew that much. Mama had a boyfriend, another older dude who bought her a car, but he was real abusive. He got mad at her one day and beat her up so bad she left, but then he canceled the insurance on the car, which she didn't know till she got pulled over by twelve one night for speeding. They had already suspended her license, and when she went to the DMV, she didn't have enough money for the reinstatement fee. But Daddy was in there getting plates for one of his show cars. He paid her balance and then asked her out on a date. Man, I'd known that story for years, but I never realized Daddy got hold of Mama the same way he got hold of all of us: when we were down and out. I wondered how she felt about Daddy after they got married, when he started doing sneak shit and controlling her just like that dude, but in a different way. I felt bad about the way he used me as part of that, but I also felt like the blame was on them, cause they used me against each other too many times over the years. And when I got a chance to get from under they thumbs, I took it.

I started talking to Mama like she could hear what I'd been thinking. "But y'all gotta let me live, though. Y'all steady tryna control me like I'm y'all's spouse and y'all not each other's. It don't feel right no more. It used to. But it don't now. I ain't tryna live under y'all forever."

Mama looked at me and nodded. "I can understand that. And that was never my intention. I cain't speak for nobody else, though."

"Good, cause Trishelle been offered me a job."

"What job?"

"The one at the store. Full-time too."

"And what about school?"

"You think Daddy gon pay for school after all this?"

"Do you wanna go?"

"I don't know."

"Well, you need to decide what you want."

"I can decide all I want, but what's Daddy gon do? I feel like one of these days he just gon snap cause he ain't callin the shots no more. Wha's gon happen to us then?"

"Suzette, if I had a crystal ball I would tell you exactly wha's gon happen. But I don't. But I do know that you grown and I'ma do my best to respect that as long as you respect me."

"Mama, I wasn't never gon take your Cadillac."

"Good, cause I wasn't gon let you have it."

"Fine, then. Let's move on."

Mama looked like she was about to say something about my mouth, but she didn't, just opened and closed her hands like she was letting everything go. She stood up.

"I'ma take care of your daddy. We need to have a talk about some things, and we gon get through this like we done got through everything. You just worry about what you wanna do, and how you wanna do it. You got your whole life ahead of you, and you don't need to make no fast decisions. You gotta think through what you doin, or else, before you know it, you'll be stuck in some mess you let happen cause you didn't know it was coming, and when it came you didn't know how to take up room for yourself."

"I know. But I ain't never gon be able to do none of that if y'all don't let me think for myself. I'm tired of all this craziness." And with that, I went upstairs.

I DIDN'T GO TO BED until about dawn. I was up looking at the community college website, all the classes and the application deadlines. They had a couple courses on fashion design. More on business than anything. I knew it would be a lot, but I didn't want to be up underneath Mama all day, or waiting around till Doni or Drina got off work. And I needed my driver's test too. I didn't even know if Daddy was gon let us do that, but maybe Doni or Drina could take me instead of him. Mama didn't need to take responsibility for everything. Plus, I still felt some kind of way about her not believing me about that car, but whatever. It's not like I could change her mind. She'd think what she wanted until she knew better. Before I fell asleep, I wanted to put reminders in my calendar to call Trishelle in the morning and finish my school application, but when I picked up my phone, I saw two missed text messages. First one was from Doni: Ur dad came looking for you. Everything good over here, just wanna make sure you ok. Drina texted too: You make it home ok? I sent the same response twice: Yep. I'm good. Just turning in. Talk about it later. Then I put in my reminders, turned my phone off, and drifted off to sleep thinking, *That's what's up. I can do both.*

BOTTLED WATER

I.

The idea to get head from some rando was Momi's, shortly after we got high off one of her other ideas: weed-infused chocolate chip cookie dough while binge-watching *Atlanta*. I'm a lightweight: even eating weed makes me cough, so I was mid-hack when she started in on Darius and how fine he is. Luckily, Jamarcus was out "on a run"; otherwise, he would have gotten upset, which had a lot less to do with the fact that Momi was still openly lusting after dudes than it did with the fact that LaKeith Stanfield was slightly younger, more famous, and way richer than Jamarcus—unsettling news for a nigga who bagged his current girlfriend by being a young hustler with a little cheese and some local clout. And Momi was probably the prettiest woman who'd ever given him the time of day—young, old, whatever. Her figure was better than mine and most of my friends', and she had dimples and a ponytail full of hair she kept dyed jet black even though it was naturally sandy brown. "I'm fine enough that my shit can look as basic as the rest of these hoes and I can still pull em," she'd tell me while brushing deep waves into it before bed.

Momi already had the munchies, so she'd mixed a few cookie balls into a bowl of ice cream: Blue Bell Tin Roof, her favorite. She gestured toward the screen with her spoon as Darius reddened out the letters on a Confederate Pride hat.

"See, Maple? That's the kinda man you need. He…eccentric." Momi made *eccentric* sound like a dirty word, like it meant you had a big dick or something.

I was still coughing. "Dudes like that don't live here. Shreveport dry as hell."

"That's cause you don't know how to look for nothing. I found Jamarcus." Momi swallowed another bite of her concoction, then licked the spoon like it had balls.

"I been looking. But I keep coming down with the clap."

Momi almost choked from laughing, then thunked me on the forehead with the spoon.

"Next time, slap a condom on him and keep it pushing, because I'm tired of caking your broke ass. I'm really about to start giving you advice instead."

"Like you don't already be doing that."

"And lo and behold, you're still single!" She leaned back so she could look me up and down. "I mean, if I wasn't related to you, I still wouldn't fuck you cause you look like my daughter, and she owe me money. But you are cute. Wonder what the problem is."

"I'm the problem. I haven't figured myself out yet."

Which was kind of the truth. Every halfway-decent-looking hoe in the city had somebody. Momi was right: it shouldn't have been that hard, but I don't think either of us felt like addressing the "a-little-too-tall-and-lanky-for-a-girl" and "definitely-not-supposed-to-be-that-color" elephant most niggas brought into the room. Even though we talked about everything else, that subject was off-limits because Momi didn't believe in underselling your own product by feeling sorry for yourself or believing people when they called you ugly. That, she said, was bad business, but she never said much else.

And the thought of asking her to say more felt like taking a stiletto to the fragile mirror we'd both been looking through since the day I was born. In that mirror, the world considered me as beautiful as she was. There was just one problem: that world had only two people in it.

True to tradition, Momi misheard everything I was trying to say.

"Ohhhh. You should have told me. You not sure you want a man?"

I let out a heavy sigh and tried again. "Naw, I don't mind that. I just don't know what kind I want. But I do know I want the kind that wants me. And ain't too many of them out there."

"What the—" Momi licked the spoon clean and aimed it at my forehead again, but this time I ducked. "Why you stay talking like Eeyore? Ain't no fairy tales out here, Maype. You ain't supposed to *find* love. You supposed to *make* love. You make it up as you go along."

My mama ain't never in her life referred to sex as "making love," so I knew exactly what she meant. See, Momi was the type that rolled with the punches. When life went left, she'd put on a tight dress and some makeup, and *boom*, doors opened. Men paid rent. Sometimes, women too. Or they put in good words and got her jobs. Basically, anybody who was interested got in where they could fit in. When people fell for Momi, they figured out what she needed and became it before she could bat one of her mink eyelashes. It was easy for her to think about love as this glamorous life you could hold your breath for and squeeze into like a girdle. She never thought about the possibility that that kind of life wasn't made to fit everybody.

Momi rolled her head around as she talked, a telltale sign she was reaching a limit and was soon going to stop making sense. She stared blankly at me like she was trying to remember what she was talking about. Then she wrinkled her nose like a bunny and started again.

"Most men ain't smart enough to tell if you don't know what

you doing. So you just gotta fake it till you make it. Right now, you worried about a whole lot of nothing."

"Like real love."

She flicked her spoon in the air, hitting a nail on its invisible head. "Yes. *Instead* of money, which I am tired of loaning you."

"First of all, I have asked you for money maybe twice in the last three months. Second, I'm not worried. I just wanna be happy. While also being realistic."

"You can be happy. You just be looking for it in the wrong things."

"What's the right thing then, Momi?" And I made a point to look dramatically around her big-ass town house with the vaulted ceilings and hardwood floors, decked out in oversized leather furniture and appliances she was still watching YouTube videos to learn how to use. I knew that was a low blow. I mean, I wasn't saying Momi and Jamarcus weren't in love. But I *was* saying it was a match made on, like, OnlyFans or something. Momi was nice to look at and Jamarcus had cheese, which he got from only God knows where. It definitely wasn't from his barbershop, cause that shit stayed empty. Either way, Momi's last two town houses stayed fresh, even the one she lived in before she moved out the hood because it kept getting broken into.

"You a ungrateful little something, ain't you?" she said, turning away from me and flinging her ponytail in my face. "I'm *giving* you the game and you looking down your nose at me? Don't ever ask me for nothing again."

"Chill with the monologues, Taraji. Ain't nobody looking down nothing. I want nice stuff too. But I want to be loved."

"Fine. You got me. I love you. A lot." Momi threw an arm around my neck and smushed her face into my cheek. Her lips were cold from the ice cream. "Now what? Go find a man for everything else. Or, at least, find somebody to keep your eyes rolled back and your bank account out of overdraft."

"Don't start with that."

I'd been out of college—LSUS to be exact—damn near six years and still hadn't found a good job, just kinda drifted between what Momi called penny-enny shit: a waitress at the country club; card dealer at the Horseshoe; all kinds of random jobs at Walmart. And I came to her for help whenever I walked out, no-call/no-showed, or put in my two weeks because I got bored. In college, I majored in marketing with a focus on hospitality because Momi claimed I had the hustle in my blood, and if I learned how to talk to people, maybe one day we could open a luxury hotel that rivaled the riverboats'. Problem was, I didn't always feel like being nice, and nobody could ever make me do it—not for long anyway. Not even Momi, who, at the moment, was grabbing my arms.

"Let me see those hands. They probably fucked up from masturbating all the damn time. No wonder you can't keep a job. You up finger-fucking so much at night, when it comes time to do some real work, your fingers too tired."

I held my hands up for her, then flipped her off.

"Fuck you, too, Maple. Somebody need to. Your vibrator is tired of doing that shit."

When I first got my period, my mom sat me down and gave me the secret weapon she said she never had, the one she said would have stopped her from having a baby two weeks before her fifteenth birthday: a pocket rocket. I was twelve. And from that day on, my mom talked to me about sex the way most women talk to their daughters about skirt length, or the importance of choosing the right color of foundation. She was never pushy about it, but she sure as hell was thorough. And it was clear she was an expert way before she got her first job dancing; although, by the time we had our "talk," she'd been working there for more than a decade, since right after I was born. To be honest, I don't know if my mama was ever a novice at anything that involved getting naked, talking to niggas, and getting money. She swore up and down she never fucked *explicitly* for cash, though. Which might have been true. Like Bun B said, some hoes get down for shrimp and others get down for cum. My mom got down for cum. For access. For a good story. Cash was an occupational perk, but she got it so often it became an unspoken requirement. And niggas stayed trying to outdo each other, so for Momi, fucking them was the lick that kept on giving.

"When's the last time somebody drank from the tap?" She cocked her head, waiting for an answer.

"Momi."

"That long. Damn. What a shame." She was lying down on the couch now, elbows wedged against my left thigh, her feet up in the air swinging a pair of Gucci flip-flops. She rested her face in her hands, pursed her lips tight, and tried to smile regretfully, but she couldn't stop giggling, which was a sign she was done for the evening. I took the lid from beneath the Tupperware bowl of cookie dough and put it back on tight when she wasn't looking. Jamarcus didn't like it when she got too gone. He always thought we were messing around with other people when he wasn't there.

"Are we supposed to be fornicating, though? I thought we were saved?" I narrowed my side-eye and held out my hand so I could play with her ponytail. A few years ago, post–strip club and pre-Jamarcus, Momi and I joined this nondenominational church off West Seventieth. She said we needed some structure and direction. It wasn't even a deep spiritual commitment. She just made the decision and we went. When it was time for the call to fellowship, we stood at the altar with our heads bowed in two of Momi's skirt suits that were too tight and too short on both of us for very different reasons. But my church jab was something not even I necessarily agreed with. Chastity is a lot of shit, but it's also a convenient tool of the patriarchy. I was just tired of Momi dragging me about being alone, because being alone really was insult enough.

"God wants His children to be happy. If you talked to Him more, you'd know that." Momi took my hand out of her hair and flipped over so she could rest her head in my lap and look up at the ceiling.

"On their way to hell?" I joked.

"Hell can be a state of mind too."

"That's what you keep telling me."

"And that's my job, beloved. Cause they don't always tell you that in church. The Lord will, though. Ask Him about it."

"So you want me to *pray*…about sex."

"Why not?" And here's where her familiar logic kicked in. "Listen, talk to God to figure out what you want. If you realize you don't wanna fuck, don't. If you do, do. Then figure out what makes you feel good. Play around a little. Get some head. I mean you probably gon have to give a little to get a little, but that's all right. You know what you're doing. Just, whatever you do, live your life. You're young. You can give it up if you want to, and you can save it if you want to, just don't hold your breath for so long, you forget what it feels like to—" She took in a deep gasp. She was probably about to moan or something, but Jamarcus came in, and we had to change the subject, which, at the time, was a relief, because when my mom started talking about sex, all filters were off. She could go from righteous to ratchet like flipping a phone into airplane mode. Luckily, she was good at flipping back too. We started talking about how we wish there was a Pappadeaux's in the city, and that got Jamarcus back out of the house to pick us up some stuffed shrimp from Orlandeaux's. And I was glad, because we got to sneak in a little more time together. Well, Momi actually fell asleep with her head in my lap, so I ended up half watching TV and playing with her hair.

Two days later, my mother, Brenda May Moffett, was the sixteenth fatal drive-by victim of the killing season, which starts sometime in February and lasts until the New Year. It was early April. Sixteen might not sound like a lot for a city, but imagine a place where nearly everybody knows everybody, and six weeks into spring, a bunch of people you know got shot and a bunch of them are dead. And that shit's gonna happen the next year too. And the next. And the next. Shit, it might happen to you outside the club, or sitting on your porch in your own hood, or driving down 3132.

But sometimes it's not you, but the person who is your whole family: your mother and father, your friend, the cousin you snicker with during service when someone catches the spirit and their wig goes sideways or they lose a shoe. The one person you look like in the whole world, even though everyone keeps telling you you look like some girl who never leaves the house and whose dad owns a car shop. Our faces were our open secret, Momi and me: one in fried-chicken brown, the other in raw-chicken white. Sometimes, if we went too long without seeing each other, I'd forget I resembled anybody else on the fucking planet, but then one of us would swing open our front door and we'd take one look and laugh because we'd both have halos or box braids, or we'd both bought the same color of lipstick at that flash sale at Ulta.

Imagine all that, and you got me.

My mom got hit sitting outside someone's house in the driver's seat of Jamarcus's truck, resetting his radio stations and texting him threats to drive off while she waited for him to do something inside. The police still don't know what happened and they probably never will because my mama was a Black woman dating a dope boy and as far as they're concerned, she probably had it coming. And because he's a dope boy, the streets ain't talking, except every wannabe Al Sharpton in the Ark-La-Tex, including our pastor, who did an interview about how my mama had *almost* turned her life around, found God, and was an active member of his congregation. And that's how it's been since she died. People talk about Momi's past life like it was some kind of fishnet she couldn't escape, one that snagged her by the heel just as she made an attempt to flee. Nobody talks about how she gave to the building fund and served as a greeter and organized the church's Holiday Help Drive. Big-ass church with a parking lot full of Caddies and nobody ever thought of a toy drive till my mama showed up. But that shit doesn't matter anyway. The truth is that my mama got popped and she's gone. She didn't do anything to deserve it and nothing she did or didn't do was able to save her. Not one single motherfucking thing.

SOMETIMES, WHEN SHE GOT SENTIMENTAL (which wasn't often), or when I got sad because I had broken up with someone, or that time I almost died from carbon monoxide poisoning because my landlord was fucking trash, my mom would tell the story of how I got the name Maple Christine. When Momi got pregnant, she didn't get the memo that you lost daughter privileges once you spread your legs. So, one Saturday morning, she comes downstairs after a day and a half on the bathroom floor, damn near delirious from morning sickness. My grandma looked happy enough to see her, and since they were back on speaking terms, Nana asked, "You feeling any better, Brenda May?" Nana hadn't checked on her since she'd put a ginger ale and a roll of crackers outside the door the day before and told her to clean up whatever mess she made. That's how my grandma is: disappoint her, and she'll abandon you.

"I feel better, Mama," my mother said. "Can you make me some breakfast, please? And can I maybe get a glass of water?"

Nana paused her cleaning, put her hand on her hip. "Well, whatchu want, baby? Cereal?"

Momi shook her head.

"Pop-Tart?"

"No, ma'am."

"Oh, you must want something that'll stick to your ribs. Grits? Eggs? Bacon? Pancakes?"

My mama's mouth was raw from dry-heaving, but immediately it started watering. "Can I have a pancake, ma'am? Maybe with some jelly? And bacon and eggs?"

Nana walked over to where Momi was sitting at the dinette table and lifted Momi's chin so she could look her dead in the face. Then she laughed.

"Look here, heifer. You pregnant and you is officially a grown woman now. You gon have to learn how to feed yourself and some-body else too. Sick. Tired. Sad. Don't matter. I ain't obligated to do a damn thing for you ever again, and let me tell you this now: I'm sure as hell not raising no 'nother baby. Cause if you think that, you got another thing coming."

She stormed out of the kitchen and left Momi to make her own breakfast, which she did, albeit, as my grandma likes to point out whenever she's around to hear this story, it was still with Nana's groceries, Nana's stove, and Nana's electricity, so she wasn't as grown as she thought.

Anyway, Momi made exactly what she asked for: bacon, eggs, and pancakes, and she used Nana's expensive maple syrup on them just to make her mad. After heating it up in the microwave, she poured it over a dollop of butter she'd smeared on top of the pancakes the same way she saw folks do on the Bisquick commercials. Then she sat in front of the TV and watched Saturday morning cartoons while she ate: *A Pup Named Scooby-Doo*, *Garfield and Friends*, and later, *Saved by the Bell*, which she loved because people used to tell her she looked like Lisa Turtle. Nana came through the living room to see what she made, and when she asked if that really was her *good* syrup sticking to Momi's almost empty plate, my mom said, "Yes, ma'am. I'm grown, remember? I do what I want." And, just then, Red Herring came on-screen to remind Freddie that he ain't always the one doing shit, and my mom laughed like she didn't have a care in the world. And I guess that was reason enough for Nana to leave her alone.

At the end, I always asked, "But, Momi, why you named me Maple? That's petty as hell. That was y'all's beef. It didn't have nothing to do with me."

She would always kiss my forehead, or, if that was too far away, she would kiss my hand, or my calf, or the phone receiver, and say, "Because I wanted to remind myself—and I wanted you to know too—that sometimes you gotta name your own sweetness." After we started going to church, she would add, "You got to name it and claim it."

And I would say, "Or bang it and drain it." And she would laugh. Her laugh, man.

My middle name was also the name of her two-faced best friend who dogged her like everybody else at school once she started showing. When Christine came by after I was born, trying to be messy because she heard the baby was albino and she wanted to see what I looked like, she grinned in Momi's face, hoping to slide in by saying she'd heard the baby had her name and that was so sweet to do after all they'd been through.

"She sure does," said my mom, "cause she's my new best friend. And you can care your monkey ass right back to wherever you came from." Momi was holding me, standing at the front door, but Nana was on the other side of it, so she had the honor of slamming it in Christine's face when Momi turned away, cooing at me like she hadn't just cursed somebody out. I think that might have been the moment Momi and Nana made up for good.

I'M PROBABLY GOING TO HELL for saying this, but I can't stand my grandma. And that shit's been true for a long time. First of all, Lula Belle Moffett ain't never met a person she didn't try to act like she was better than, including me and Momi. For a couple of years, Nana would beg Momi to let me stay with her for the few weeks during the summer when Momi stripped in different cities or went on vacations with whoever she was fucking. And Nana's fake bougie ass would spend the entire time complaining about how little home training I had, and how if I didn't get my act together I was gonna grow up to be a nobody just like my dope-dealing, dope-fiending dad, Reggie. She always stopped short of roping my mama into that prophecy, probably because she knew if she had, I'd have been ghost in twenty-four hours. My mama ran the streets a lot, but one thing she promised me every time she dropped me off somewhere was that if I ever wanted her to come back—from *anywhere*—all I had to do was call her or text our safe word: *vestibule*.

The other thing I can't stand about Nana is how fucking delusional she is. When the kids in her little raggedy neighborhood made fun of me, she would come outside and yell at them for being heathens and for not understanding I was just "light-skinned." Everybody in Cherokee Park heard that shit and it was embarrassing. Not only was I getting picked on, but my own grandma was too ashamed to call me what I was. I could have forgiven her for all the other shit, but I never got over that, especially after Momi explained that folks who are obsessed with keeping up appearances often have to pretend that some parts of their lives don't exist.

"She don't want me to exist, Momi?" I asked, on the verge of tears. That was back when I was maybe five or six, and Nana's opinion still mattered.

"Oh, Maple-bug, that's only cause she don't know you like I do," Momi cooed. "To know you is to love you. And to love you is to lick you." And she lapped the side of my face real quick before I could duck.

Anyway, Nana's fuckshit was on full display after Momi died. First, it was the meeting with the detectives. A few days after it happened, they asked if they could come by to talk about some of the stuff they found out, and to see if we could give them any information about Momi's last days. I hadn't stayed at my duplex since the night I'd heard, and it was a good thing, too, because I woke up the next morning at Nana's sick as a dog. Two nights before, when I saw the Facebook Live video with my mama's body half hanging out of the truck's open driver's-side door while some idiot bystander yelled about how it's a shame we can't stop killing each other into a cordless mic held by Jay Shorter the Hood Reporter (who sometimes finds crime scenes on his scanner before the police can even get there), I threw my phone across the room and threw up in my lap. After that, I couldn't keep anything down, not even water. By the time the detectives came back, I was well enough to sit up on Nana's couch in the den without shaking too badly, but I was sure I'd have to excuse myself at least once, go into the half bathroom off the kitchen, and throw up a few more strings of bitter yellow bile.

Nana wasn't too worried about that, though. What she *was* frantic about was her house. It wasn't even seven o'clock that morning, and I could hear her vacuuming the living room. When I came out of Momi's old room, Nana was heating up food folks had brought over and arranging it on the kitchen table next to the pound cakes and pies. When she saw me, she sniffed with contempt: "I know you're not feeling well, but you need to fix yourself up a little before these cops come over here." She walked over to the tiny china cabinet and started pulling out plates.

"Whatchu heating up all this food for?"

"In case they're hungry."

"I don't—" I stopped myself because I didn't feel like explaining. I just went back to the room until I heard the doorbell, then went in the bathroom and swished some mouthwash while I tried to run a comb through my hair. Since I'd slept on it, though, it was no use. I dug around in the closet to see what I could find. It was mostly full of Nana's church suits and gaudy hats. One hot-pink one had a floral-print scarf pinned to its brim, so I used that. I knew she would have something to say about it after they left, but I didn't give a damn. I wanted her to.

When I came out, the two detectives—a man and a woman— were perched on Nana's good love seat in the living room nobody ever sits in, drinking coffee from Starbucks. I sat on the couch with Nana, but on the opposite end, as far away from her as possible. I didn't want her trying to touch me while she was talking.

"So y'all didn't want anything to eat?" I looked directly at Nana when I asked.

"No," said the woman. "And we won't be here for long. Just wanted to update you on the case and ask a few questions."

"Excuse her appearance," Nana offered. "She been sick since Sunday night." Nana looked up briefly at the scarf, trying to figure out why she recognized it, then reached across the middle cushion like she was reaching for my hand. I pretended not to notice and looked straight ahead at the detectives, who briefly glanced at each other. Then the man spoke.

"So, we've interviewed Jamarcus Youngblood about the death of Ms. Moffett, since we know they were together on the day of the homicide, and he doesn't seem to know anything about anybody wanting her killed."

I snorted, but he continued. "So, we wanted to ask each of you if you could think of anybody—anything—Ms. Moffett might have mentioned in passing. Is there anyone she might have been afraid of? Even if it wasn't recent. Sometimes people will plan these kinds of hits months in advance, years if they're angry enough. Can either of you think of anything she said that sounded suspicious? Felt off?"

I was about to speak, but Nana beat me to it. "Well, Officers, my Brenda was a good woman. She strayed away a few times, did some things I know she wasn't proud of, but she was never mixed up in drugs or gangs or none of this other violence that's been happening out here. She was good. She had joined a church and everything. She really was a good woman." Nana's eyes teared up on cue and she dabbed them with a handkerchief she probably hadn't used since the '80s.

The woman detective jumped in on this one. "Yes, Mrs. Moffett, we know she was good. She didn't deserve this."

I wondered what you had to do to deserve getting shot eight times in somebody's driveway on a random Sunday afternoon. The woman continued. "But we know she had a past and she met a lot of men as a sex worker."

Nana stopped them. "Well, she was actually a bartender when she worked there, at that club. She wasn't no sex worker or whatever you trying to call it." I laughed outright then. The detectives looked over at me. Not shocked, but definitely uncomfortable.

The woman detective turned to me with a mix of pity and suspicion. "Miss Moffett, do you know anything about your mother's line of work and the people she might have met while doing it?"

"I know she wasn't a fucking bartender. I know that." I sat up a little on the couch. "She was a stripper. She stripped. And she was good at it. And she took good care of me while she was doing it." I started to choke up, so I stopped.

The woman scooted forward on the couch. "Yes, of course there's nothing wrong with that. But it might have put her in dan—"

"Come on." I threw my head back and rolled my eyes. "Y'all gotta be smarter than this. Who's gonna shoot a ex-stripper they met at the club ten years ago? Are y'all serious right now? This is some shit that has to do with Jamarcus. He's a dope dealer and he probably got caught up and owes somebody money. Or he crossed somebody that's banging. I don't know. But don't just take him at his word. And don't assume this was something that had to do with Momi. Investigate his ass. Do your jobs."

The woman had been nodding the whole time I was talking, and when I stopped, she paused for a long time, I guess to give me a chance to get it all off my chest, like I was a five-year-old in therapy or something. When she spoke, she tried to sound soothing. "Yes, Miss Moffett, I completely understand your frustration."

"I'm not frustrated. I'm pissed cause y'all are acting stupid."

Nana's brow furrowed, and she was about to speak, but the woman held up her hand.

"Hold on a minute, Mrs. Moffett." Then she turned back to me. "Listen, I know you're upset, but with all due respect, we're not stupid. We're gonna solve this case, but right now, our job is to get as much information as we can from everyone. Mr. Youngblood, yes, but you too. He told us he and your mother were only casual acquaintances but that you and your mother were very close, so we need you to tell us everything you know, and we're doing that with everyone who knew your mother. When we're ready, we'll go back to Youngblood and interview him about his possible criminal involvement and any suspicious actions in the days leading up to your mother's death. Believe me, we've got eyes on him. He's not going anywhere, and neither are we." She leaned back in her seat and opened her hands, which had been clasped in front of her. I guess she was proud of herself for that speech. "So, you said Mr. Youngblood may be dealing drugs. How do you know this? Were you ever a witness to his selling or receiving illegal drugs of any kind? Even if it was just small deals, marijuana, we can use it."

"No. I mean, he's not stupid. I never saw it. But it's obvious. Like at the barbershop. It never has customers, but he's always flashing money. The nice cars. My mom's apartment. She didn't have to work, but they were always jetting off somewhere. It wasn't hard to guess what he was doing."

"So, you never actually saw him dealing drugs."

"No. I wasn't around him like that."

"What about your mother? She ever talk to you about his activities? Did your mother ever tell you she saw anything? It could be helpful. Jamarcus also said that the relationship with your mother wasn't that serious. If we can prove otherwise, we might have cause to bring him in again for more questioning, before he lawyers up."

"Hell yeah it was serious. He was taking care of her."

"Do you mean he was paying her for companionship? For sex?"

"No. They were together. They were a couple."

The woman looked incredulous. I made sure she saw me cut my eyes at her.

"Are you absolutely positive she didn't tell you anything about Jamarcus's dealings? It's okay if she was involved; we're not here to tarnish her memory. We just want justice for you and your family."

"Yes! I'm sure." I started tearing up again because I knew this shit was useless. They were gonna take Jamarcus at his word and presume he didn't know nothing and didn't do nothing, and they were gonna let my mama's past turn her into the unlucky hoe he was now calling her.

The woman leaned forward again, but she had sense enough to put her hand on the table, and not on me. "That's all right, Miss Moffett. If he's doing anything, we'll find out about it. Thank you for sharing what you know." She stopped, and the man started in.

"Miss Moffett, after speaking with Mr. Youngblood, we might have reason to believe your mother's murder could be connected to an unsolved double homicide that occurred about a year ago." He pulled out his phone and started looking for something as he spoke. "We know that, briefly, she danced in music videos for the rap artist Clyde Thomas, who went by the name AK-47. They also recorded an adult film together, along with a woman named Kitty Velazquez. The video was released early last summer." He stopped scrolling and looked up at me. "Both Mr. Thomas and Mrs. Velazquez were shot to death at Thomas's studio in Queensborough in mid-July. We don't know if there's a connection, but as you might know, Mrs. Velazquez's estranged husband was originally a suspect. At the time, sources told us he was angry at Kitty's involvement with AK, as well as with this film, but there was never sufficient evidence to connect him to the crime, and charges against him were ultimately dropped. However, Youngblood believes the ex-husband may have also been after your mother, based on information he said he's overheard in the days since your mother's death. If *you* know anything about Mr. Velazquez, or suspect there's any connection between him and this crime, we want to know. It would help our investigation and might ultimately bring your family—or someone else's family—some justice."

I heard Nana draw a sharp breath, but I motioned for him to finish. He looked mad uncomfortable, but he continued.

"First, do you know anything about Clyde Thomas, also known as AK-47?"

Of course I knew who he was; everybody did. He'd been a local joker with a few regional hits, but I'd never met him and I'd never watched his videos because they were low-budget and I didn't wanna see my mama in them, playing the elder stripper giving the girls tips on how to get that money. I wasn't saying all that, though, so I just shook my head.

"What about Mrs. Velazquez? Did you know her?"

I shrugged. "Momi knew a lot of women. I might have seen her. What does she look like?"

He held up the phone, and, in what I immediately recognized as a still shot from the porno, Kitty was looking straight at the camera, her head slightly tilted. She was beautiful, and probably mid-orgasm, which made her even more beautiful. Plus, it was a full-body shot: you could see her tiny shoulders shrugged with anticipation; her tits sitting straight up with the nipples at full salute under a thin bra; her abdominal muscles flexed; and, although the detective had his finger strategically placed over the bottom of the frame, her hands were deep in the hair of someone who was eating her out, and that someone was my mama. I tried to take the phone, but the detective kept his grip.

"Miss Moffett, do you know who she is?"

I almost amazed myself at how deftly I used what I had. "I…I'm sorry. I have albinism and I can't see great without my glasses. I'm just trying to get a closer look."

The detectives looked at each other, unsure what to do, because I damn sure wasn't gonna confirm or deny whether I knew Kitty until I got that phone. The woman shrugged, like *Shit, let her see it,* so he relented, stammering as he handed the phone to me. "Now, M-Miss Moffett, I only want you to confirm whether you recognize this woman's face."

I pulled the phone away from his hand and stared at the still shot closely. I wasn't looking at Kitty; I didn't know who the fuck she was. I was looking at my mom. Her hair, those caviar curls lost in someone else's hands. I couldn't see anything past her nape, but I imagined her brown shoulders and the magnolia tattoo on the left one—her favorite flower in the one place she said would never stretch with age. Or, as she would always say with a giggle, with a second pregnancy.

"And this was the *only* photo you could get of her. Of Kitty," I asked, and I kinda sounded like Nana when I said it. Go figure.

The detective touched his collar, looking for a tie to loosen, though he wasn't wearing one. "Mrs. Velazquez"—he cleared his throat—"was undocumented, and we couldn't find an official photo of her that resembled what she looked like near the time of her death. We were in a hurry to get here with this information, and we didn't have much time to search for others."

"I mean, you could have cropped—" But I didn't finish. If they had done that, I wouldn't have been able to see my mom.

While I stared, Nana scooted across the couch. I could almost hear the gears grinding in her head: First she looked at Kitty's face. Then she took in the scene. Then her eyes rested on Momi. I could feel her whole body stop breathing, but the best part was that her shock and embarrassment made her recoil, and she backed the hell up off me. She glared at the detectives.

"I don't know who that woman is, and that one on the bottom? That's not Brenda." Like the rest of us hadn't seen it.

"Yes, it is," I said quietly.

"No, it's not! This is foolishness! Why would you even bring that in here?" Nana's voice started cracking and the detective scrambled to get the phone, but I held up my hand and peered again, pretending that I was still deciding on who Kitty was. As he lowered his arm, I swiped—out of curiosity maybe? Who knows? And there it was: a picture of my mama in the same position as Kitty; her posture almost identical, but this time it was Kitty's head that was lowered, her silky brown hair spilling through my mama's fingers. Momi's pink stiletto tips were snagged in it. It only took me a second to lock that image in my mind, and with the detective staring at me, I couldn't swipe again, so I hit the home button and handed him back the phone.

"I thought I knew who she was, but I'm sorry. I don't." The female detective started apologizing for only having that photo to show us, but I shut her down quick.

"It doesn't matter. I know who my mama was. And she—" But this time, I got cut off by Nana.

"She was a good woman! She was a clean woman! And she loved this girl over here!" she screamed, pointing at me. "I don't appreciate y'all coming in here with all that!"

"Nana," I sighed. "They ain't gon never find who did this if you keep lying about Momi to save face." I gathered up the blanket I'd dragged from Momi's room and stood up, then turned to the detectives. "But she's right. Y'all shoulda known not to bring that in here. It doesn't matter to me, but you could have thought about the fact that her sixty-seven-year-old mama might not have wanted to see that shit." They didn't say anything as I stepped around Nana's legs to leave.

When I got to the doorway of the kitchen, I turned to face them one last time, because I knew I'd probably never talk to them again. Cases like Momi's stay open forever. "We don't know who killed her," I said. "And we don't know who AK or Kitty is. That's y'all's jobs. Find out who did this. But also, bruh? Take that shit off your fucking phone."

IT TOOK A GOOD HOUR FOR Nana to bust into the room like the feds. The detectives left a few minutes after I did, and I could hear her sniffling and groaning in the kitchen before she came looking for me. First, she just stood at the door and glared. I had the covers over my head, but I could see her out of the little gap I made for my nose and mouth, to keep from getting too hot under there. Suddenly, she rushed the bed, but I was quicker. I threw off the covers and jumped up. I was enraged too. Whatever smoke she was jonesing for, she was about to get it.

"How *dare* you let them come in here and treat your mother like a…like a—"

"Like a hoe?"

Nana couldn't respond to that. She just fumed, nostrils flaring. I wondered if this was the face Momi saw right before she ate up all that syrup. I was glad they didn't look alike. Nana is high yellow, tall and narrow like me, with two gray-brown braids that hang almost to her waist. Momi was little and brown like the traveling preacher Nana said was her daddy. That made it easier for me to hate Nana in that moment: she didn't look nothing like the person I missed.

"Her body not even cold and in the ground yet, and y'all passing around that filth like a set of playing cards!" Nana hissed.

"If it was filth, it was her filth," I said calmly. "And you right: her body *ain't* even cold yet and you out here trying to make her out to be something she never wanted to be. And you sitting all high and mighty on that ugly-ass couch like the daughter you wanna make them think you lost is better than the one you actually had. Get the fuck out of here."

Nana raised her hand, and I took a step closer. "Do it, if you bad," I said, lowering my voice to a whisper, so she'd know that, unlike her, I wasn't just saying it for the neighbors to hear.

She put her hand down. "Naw, I ain't goin nowhere. That's what you bout to do. I don't know what done got into you, but I want you out of my house after the funeral. I want you *out*."

And I knew she didn't mean it. She'd said the same thing to Momi twice a week until the day I was born and then at least once a week after. Then when we finally did leave she cried and tried to scare Momi into coming back that time the prostitute got raped with a Coke bottle and left for dead a few streets away from where we lived in Cedar Grove. Old folks like Nana always be making threats they don't mean to people they don't know how to love.

But I had time that day. I got closer to her face, close enough to see where her tears had dried in uneven streaks of salty crust on her cheeks.

"Cool," I said. "I'll be happy to." And later that night, while she was asleep, I packed up everything I'd brought from my old place, which wasn't much—just my laptop, a few weeks' worth of clothes that were still in an oversized duffel bag Momi bought for me back when I went to Panama during a semester abroad, a few toiletries, and my phone. When I'd left my old place, I knew I'd never go back; it was where I'd seen my dead mother's body online and it might as well have been the fucking morgue, someplace I won't see again until after I'm dead. That night, I felt the same way about Nana's. I scanned the room to see if there was anything I wanted to take. Most of it was all Momi's stuff from childhood and high school: stuffed bears and a couple of trophies from pageants. Really, anything there could have been a memento, but so, too, could have been most of what I had in my duffel bag. Momi bought just about everything I owned. And she ragged on me a lot, but I knew she didn't mind doing for me, so I never turned it down.

On the dresser, there was a photo of Momi and me as a baby. She was something else: even though they kicked her off the team when she started showing, she was dressed in her cheerleading uniform, in sitting rest position, hands on her hips and flashing her full smile. On each side of her was a pompon and, sitting in the foreground, but slightly to her left so you could see her legs, was me, in a little green velvet dress to match the school's colors. I tucked the frame in my bag on top of my clothes, and, with Nana's scarf on my head, I walked out the front door with my shoulders squared. I wasn't gonna give Nana the chance to put me nowhere. I was done.

THAT FIRST NIGHT, I DROVE around the city, looking for places to sit in my car. I finally went to Waffle House for a while and had a Texas cheesesteak hash brown with a waffle. I was starving, my appetite back with a vengeance, but I ate slowly, still unsure of what I could keep down while watching people come and go: the truckers perched on stools talking shit to the cooks; the homeless folks with loose change coming in to buy a biscuit, and lingering, like me, trying to waste time. Girls coming from the club, all spandex and loud talking for no good reason. I tried to see if Regina or Lett was in one of the groups, but they weren't there. I know they'd been calling, but I'd turned my phone off.

Then, around six, because I hoped Ranjith would be there, I headed toward the airport, to the hotel. And there he was, behind the front desk, doing the housekeeping board with his earbuds in, probably listening to news stations from the other side of the world. I envied him. I'd rather be engrossed in any other disaster than this one.

"Who called out?" I asked, putting my bag down for a minute because it was heavy. Ranjith never worked the desk overnight unless nobody could come in, including his wife.

"Angel. No one to watch her kids." He put one earbud back in.

"And Puja's been up all night with the baby. Ear infection. I didn't call you because…" He didn't know how to finish, so I just nodded quickly. No one needed to try to find the right words for me.

"That's bullshit. That's like the fifth time this month. We need to let her go."

"I agree. Go ahead and take her off the schedule."

"Got it. Listen, I might need a favor from you."

He just looked at me, waiting for me to go on.

"I might need a place to stay for a little bit. Just until I can get back on my feet. Losing my mom threw me for a loop, and I don't want to be in my apartment right now."

He nodded and twisted his mouth a little, like he was thinking. "Well, we can put you in a room. But it's about to be the busy season, and since it takes one of the rooms out of rotation—"

"What about your family suite?" When Ranjith was building this second hotel a year ago, he'd sectioned off living quarters for himself, his wife, and their three kids. They stayed there while their dream house was being built in Southern Trace, and left when it was finished a month or so back. I knew he planned to split up the space into two suites, because it was way too big to book at our regular rates, and no one would pay what he wanted for it—not this far from the casinos, anyway. But I also knew he hadn't started the renovations because he didn't want to be doing any kind of loud construction during traveling season.

"The suite?" He stopped typing and rested his hands flat on the keyboard, looking up at me suspiciously to make sure I hadn't lost it.

"Yeah. Listen, I know it's not fully operational yet, so I won't be taking money out of your pocket. Plus, I'll be on-site whenever bullshit happens, like people not showing up. I'll be here to work whenever. Just give me another week or so off. Until my mother's funeral. Then I can work my regular shifts and be on call. For as long as I'm here. The whole time."

I knew that shit would sweeten the deal. He leaned over the counter for a minute, thinking it over. But Ranjith is a businessman; he's used to making decisions quickly. Didn't take him long to ask again, in a voice that let me know if I balked, he would have me across the way trying to find a room at Red Roof Inn.

"Are you sure? After all this with your mother? You'll want to work?"

"Yeah. I am. It'll distract me, and I need that." I picked up my bag. "How much you gonna charge me?"

"Three fifty for the first week, since you're not on call. After that, you stay on-site and cover shifts when we need it, serve as MOD on weekends, and be on call during the week…" He shrugged, not wanting to commit to saying it was free, in case something happened.

"Maybe we'll just cross that bridge when we get to it," I offered.

"Yeah," he said, pulling out a room key to program. "We'll do that instead."

I DIDN'T KNOW FOR SURE I was lying when I told Ranjith I needed time to plan for Momi's funeral, but I definitely knew I was later that night after the vigil. I didn't tell anybody I was going; just parked downtown and walked over to the courthouse with the drawstring of my hoodie pulled tight against my face. With my half-assed eyeliner and lip ring, I probably looked like a white kid out there on some hashtag solidarity bullshit. I didn't even have a candle, so I kept my hands in my pockets and stayed toward the back of the crowd. Some folks had signs about random shit, like how the city needed to take some of that riverboat money and spend it on fighting crime. A couple of holy rollers even had signs about how the gambling brought an evil spirit that had taken over. Most folks just had your garden-variety slogans, about how Black-on-Black violence ain't the only way we losing folks in our community. They meant well, but they didn't know the half of it. Those dumbass detectives were gonna let Jamarcus and whoever was after him go free and stay free until they killed somebody important, like a cop. Then they'd do everything in their power to put them under the jail, but only if they couldn't get them the needle.

At the vigil, some people were chanting, but most of the time they were just eating snacks and drinking water, yapping about regular shit like what they were gonna do the next day. Frankie Beverly and Maze were in town for Holiday in Dixie, and everybody was wondering if he was gonna do his version of "Before I Let Go" or Beyoncé's. *Ooh, and what if Beyoncé did a cameo or something! You know she be down here. Houston ain't but a hop, skip, and a jump away. And she do that sometimes. She cool like that. Man, if Beyoncé popped up under a tent on the riverfront ain't no telling what people would do…*

They didn't know how disrespectful it was to talk about living their lives. I mean, yeah, they were at a vigil, but they didn't know it was my mama they were there for, or that I was standing right behind them. They couldn't look at me and tell I was hers. And I got so mad about that I almost started crying right then, but I couldn't. I was in front of people. And I wanted them to continue doing what they'd been doing, which was leave me the fuck alone.

All of a sudden, everybody got quiet. Thadious Blackman, our resident Righteously Indignant Black Man, was on the mic, talking loudly about not a damn thing.

Oh, there's too much violence in this city and we have got to stop NOW.

"We know that, nigga," I said under my breath.

And then, *Oh, the mothers, we're breaking their hearts,* and I was just about to leave when she stepped up to take his place, being assisted by a bunch of dudes wearing their "Dead the Violence" T-shirts. She didn't seem that feeble when she told me to get the fuck out, but now, Nana was hunched over, clinging to one of the men, her voice warbled with tears as she thanked everybody for their support. Then she started in, trying to do damage control.

"My baby Brenda—now y'all might hear some things about her, and you might know some stuff firsthand, too, but she was a good woman, y'all. She loved the Lord. She was a regular member at that big church—Pastor McLendon church—and she was working on herself, working on being a better person. All have sinned and fallen short of the glory. But she didn't deserve this."

The crowd egged her on with *Amens.* Two older women a few feet away from me nodded in agreement. I heard one of them say, "Yeah, I heard she was a little…" but I couldn't catch the rest. They'd been holding some of the signs about the gambling spirit. I felt bitter slime creep into the back of my throat.

"And these po-lice officers out here, they telling more lies than the media, and they just as corrupt as the drug dealers. They not trying to solve this; they just trying to drag my baby's name through the mud." The crowd roared with mutual indignation at Nana's slur of SPD. That was an easy one. Everybody out there had probably been hemmed up by them at least once. They pull folks over on the Black corridors—Hearne, Hollywood, Greenwood Road, Lakeshore—like it's a fucking game. When they're not doing that, they're at Southern Maid Donuts eating up all the hot shit before anybody else can place an order.

Nana waited for folks to finish, then kept going. "But I'm here, and I'm speaking on behalf of my granddaughter, and Brenda's father, and my whole family, cause we want justice. Brenda was a good woman. She loved her family. She loved her daughter, too, even though she was *different*. And she deserved—*we* deserve—"

I turned to walk away, but didn't make it ten steps before I puked what looked like egg yolks in the grass. Nobody really said anything, just moved away from me and kept listening to my grandma. It happened one more time, too, right outside my car, and some of it splashed up on the parking meter. I shrugged, got in, and drove back to the hotel, my grandma's voice still booming from the court steps. She finally had the audience she'd always wanted, and the story she'd always wanted to tell about a daughter who was too dead and a granddaughter who looked too much like somebody else's to refute her.

FOR THE MOST PART, IT was usually just me and Momi, but we did hang out with a few people: a misfit clique of sex workers who nobody else trusted because they thought we were all scandalous hoes. Which might have been true, but wasn't as true as it looked. There were the two Pablettas, a mother and daughter who Momi and I started hanging around when I was in high school. And then there was Regina Collier, who I didn't meet until my world history seminar my sophomore year of college.

The first night Momi met the elder Pabletta, who started working at the club just to make a little extra money, she came home cackling. "I can't believe that woman spent her whole life with that name, then turned around and gave it to somebody else. That poor little girl. Them high school heifers probably laugh in her face every day." Ms. P's daughter was in my grade but went to Loyola, so part of Momi's shade about the names might have been because Loyola was a private school, and for all her hustling, Momi only had me in magnet.

The two Pablettas were also one of a kind because they looked nothing like each other. Ms. P was a rich chocolate brown, over six feet tall, and had the biggest natural titties I've ever seen. They bowed the necks of camis when she and Momi ran errands on Saturdays, or when they came to watch me and Lett's summer b-ball games with SPAR. And it was torture watching her dance anywhere that wasn't on the pole. You kept wondering when those titties were gonna pop out like the Kool-Aid Man. And even though I'd been at the club plenty of times on her nights, I'd be one of the main ones waiting to see them in broad daylight for free, just like everybody else.

Lett was something else entirely, and I sometimes wondered if it was one of the things that made the four of us bond: two sets of mothers and daughters whose skins told contradicting stories. Lett was four foot ten and a redbone in every sense of the word. She had curly auburn hair and a spray of freckles across her nose. She was also curvy, like Momi, and boys went just as crazy over her as they did over her mother and mine. I hated her for that.

Regina, our fifth, came from Texas to study history. She was the first person I met who voluntarily left a big city for Shreveport, and I was fascinated by her from the day I overheard her arguing about sex workers' rights with some dude in our class who was just dissenting so she'd keep talking to him. Regina lived life with far more curiosity than caution and nothing ever surprised her. Of course, over time, I found out why. She'd done everything: call girl, stripper, runner, mule. And she was smart in ways that shut dudes down. We used to smoke with this fool named Najid, who came from New York City on a baseball scholarship but didn't do shit else. Hell, he barely went to practice. One day we were parked out by the diamond, watching his team do warm-ups while passing a blunt. I never really liked to smoke, but as Regina's sidekick, I felt like I had to. As usual, the two of them were arguing, this time about how Shreveport didn't have any good international restaurants and, subsequently, no culture.

"Go home then, nigga," Regina said calmly. "You're failing here anyway. In school and everywhere else."

I laughed loudly because that was my job. Najid glared at me in the side mirror, then pretended like I wasn't there.

"Well, what the fuck you doing out here with me, then?" he asked her, which even I knew was a ploy to gauge her interest.

"Celebrating making all As on my midterm exams. I'm averaging a four-point-oh in my major classes and a three-point-eight everywhere else. Cause real bitches can't do anything but win. Everywhere."

"Ma act like she so hard," he scoffed, talking to himself and not me, of course. "But you just hard in the books. Come to the Bronx and test those skills in the streets."

"Who's to say I haven't been there already?"

"You ain't never been to *my* block. River Park Terrace? Segdwick Ave? Bitch, you wouldn't stand a chance on a Tuesday afternoon."

"Nigga, if I can make it here, I can make it anywhere."

Najid laughed, but Regina kept going. "Do you know how many Black people in this city live below the poverty line? The number of suicides by cop? The rate of violent crime–related deaths per capita compared to lager cities like Houston and New York? Like I said, if you can make it here, you can make it anywhere. And I'm *making* it." She passed the blunt back to him.

"What you caping for this raggedy city for anyway? You ain't even from here," Najid retorted between hits.

"Right. But I'm conducting a survival experiment. And my research is going well." Then she turned to the diamond and finally addressed me.

"Maple, do you know when the next game is?"

"No, but I wanna go! Wonder who we could get free tickets from."

"Oh, we gotta find one of the superstars for that. A future draft pick," she said wistfully, and we burst out laughing. Najid silently finished his blunt by himself. After that, I invited Regina over to Momi's house to chill with us on the weekends. I worshipped women who knew how to put men in their place and keep them there. And I spent a lot of time—with Regina, Momi, and the two Pablettas—feeling that powerful, but only by association.

REGINA CALLED A LITTLE BIT after the vigil, with Lett on the phone. I don't think Ms. P was taking it too well, so she wasn't on there with them. Even though she was the older one (and, of course, the taller one), Ms. P looked up to Momi and clung to her like saran wrap, but I couldn't necessarily talk. Whatever Momi thought was a good idea, so would Ms. P. And when Momi gave parenting advice, Ms. P followed it like it was the gospel. That's how Lett got her first pack of condoms and her first set of birth control pills. Lett wasn't the type to stay on the pocket rocket for long.

For once, Lett kept her mouth shut, and Regina did most of the talking, which was good because Regina was way better at keeping calm. Lett talked crazy when she didn't have nothing decent to say, and she had the bad habit of making jokes when she felt uncomfortable. I woulda tried to reach through the phone to slap some of those freckles off her face if she'd tried that then. But all she said was "Hey, how you doin?" and Regina carried the rest.

"Tell us what you need."

"Nothing. I'm at the hotel right now."

"Your nana doing all right?"

"I don't give a fuck about Nana."

"That's okay. You know anything about the funeral?" Regina was asking me because my stuck-up grandma pretended like Regina, Lett, and Ms. P didn't exist. She didn't even acknowledge them when they spoke to her. No way she wouldn't have hung up the phone in their face if they'd called.

"I told her she could do whatever for a memorial, but no funeral. And she can't touch Momi's body. I'm having her cremated."

"Okay. Maybe we'll do something special at the club then. Ms. P said a couple people were talking about a tribute night. Raise some funds."

"I don't want nobody's money."

"You might need somebody's money, though."

"I'm working. Plus I got the hookup on a room."

"Well, invest it. Create a scholarship fund. Put it in a high-yield savings account and let it collect interest. Nobody said you gotta spend it now."

"But I don't *need* it."

"We know that already. The dancers know that already. And the offer still stands."

I started crying, so I had to get off the phone, but Regina held her ground. "Next Friday night," she said. "We're gonna send her off right. Probably the best way to do it anyway: with the people who knew her before she became a fucking hashtag."

"Damn right!" I heard Lett chime in as I pulled the phone away from my ear.

After they hung up, I nestled back into the sheets. Man, Ranjith hit the jackpot with these duvets and pillow-tops. I felt like my body was suspended in cotton, like I didn't have to hold it up, or make sure my heart was still beating or I was still breathing. I turned off my phone and got up to pin the drapes all the way closed with some hangers so that nothing could get through, not even a sliver of sunlight. And when I got back in bed, I tested my theory, holding my breath to see if I could completely release myself from the burden of all my bodily functions. I can't remember how long I held it, or when I started breathing again, but when I woke up, the whole room was black, and not just because of the hangers, but because it was dark outside for real.

I WOULDN'T LET REGINA OR Lett go with me to Winnfield to pick out the urn—I wasn't sure if they were gonna ask me to view the body again and Momi wouldn't have wanted anybody to see her like that. But I did let the two of them come over beforehand to smoke while I popped edibles. I'd gotten the maintenance manager, DeVaughan, to stop by with a box of Southern Classic chicken and a tin full of all kinds of shit: hard candy and gummies, chocolate drops, and even a few lopsided cupcakes. It was way more than I'd asked for, but better than what he proposed: harder shit, like white, which I don't do. But I did accept that generosity because I needed something to take my mind off my grief. If I kept making myself black out, I really would die, which I half refused because I didn't want Nana onstage again. Her ass was already trending on Twitter.

For a while, me, Lett, and Regina just stared in different directions while we got high: Regina perched on the edge of the bed next to her purse, and Lett sat up with me against the headboard, taking the blunt every now and then and looking at her reflection on the TV screen, which was off. I sucked on a gummy while tracing the duvet cover's pattern. After they finished smoking, Regina leaned back on her elbows, and every so often, she would twist the little clasp on her bag. She was nervous, and it was kind of comforting. I appreciated the fact that the calmest bitch I knew didn't know how to get through this without breaking her cool. It meant that, for all my flailing around, I was doing as well as could be expected. We'd been sitting like that for a while when she spoke:

"The planning is going well. For the little shindig."

"Mmm." I didn't know how else to respond.

"Couple girls from Dallas coming. One from Memphis."

"You know their names?" I asked skeptically. "Did they even know Momi?"

Lett jumped in. "One of em is named Ivy. Or Ivory Doll—I can't remember. The other one is Tawnee Rose I think. They both knew her. And my mama. And they donating everything they make."

"All of it? I thought it was just a portion."

Regina shook her head. "No. All proceeds."

"Even from the bar?"

"I'd have to check but I think so. They're gonna look out, though."

"They better look out. Brenda was good to everybody in there," said Lett, a little too loudly. She never said anything somebody hadn't already said before, usually in private.

I reached for the tin again. "I don't want everybody's money."

Regina moved her purse and rolled onto her side, facing me. "We know it's not about that. I just think people wanna help and that's the only way they know how. That's all. People just wanna help you." She was wearing a sundress and, lying in that position, her breasts pushed up over the neckline, and her copper red wig fell in wand curls over one shoulder, grazing her exaggerated cleavage. She closed her eyes slightly, and it made me think of the way Momi looked when we had to identify the body. They'd cleaned all the blood and makeup off her face so we could better recognize her. She looked like it was early morning and she was on the verge of waking up, except she had a small hole in her left temple that looked like a bruise, and a knot high up on the opposite side of her forehead, where a bullet had lodged. It was like, at that precise moment, she was her most beautiful. No shit talking. No makeup. That was all her right there. My knees buckled when I saw her, but Nana was squeezing my arm so tight, I couldn't even pass out without taking her with me. I didn't say or do anything then, but while I was looking at Regina, I wished I'd pushed Nana or something—just to get free.

Regina scratched the comforter leisurely with one hand. Her tips looked fresh and they were blue like robin's eggs. She looked down into the fold between her breasts, then dug into the crease to pull out a stray lock of hair. She looked up at me and smiled the kind of smile only Regina can give you: it didn't mean anything unless you wanted it to. I looked over at Lett, who was looking at me wide-eyed, waiting. She sat up a little so I could see her breasts, too, then grabbed her hair and put it up in a bun. Then she checked herself out in the TV screen to see how she looked.

Me and Regina had messed around once or twice back in college, but it was nothing serious. We were out one night at Koko's and made out in one of the booths while I had my hand up her skirt, playing with her hood piercing. Luckily it was too dark—either that, or niggas was too drunk to notice us. They either love that shit or hate it, and either way, we wouldn't have been safe. I'd never touched Lett and didn't want to. Her smash list had plenty of bodies on it, I presumed, but one of them didn't need to be mine. Anyway, she'd always felt like my rival, while Regina felt like family. But right now my family was dead and I didn't have enough fight in me to have an enemy. The three of us looked at each other for a long time before I got up and grabbed the room key and Regina's makeshift ashtray from the nightstand.

"Guess I better go ahead and get this over with."

"Want me to close the window?" Lett jumped up a little too eagerly for me, looking for her shoes on the other side of the bed.

"Naw. I'll let it air out some more, so Ranjith don't throw my ass out in the street."

"Aw, he'll be all right," Regina said, popping open the tin so she could roll a few gummies in the little empty bag from her weed.

They left without either of them hugging me or saying things'll get better or any of that bullshit, and I was glad they didn't. I even told Lett she could take some edibles too. It felt good to give that, instead of people constantly trying to set me up to give things to me, like I was some kind of fucking charity case.

I DID WHAT I SAID I was gonna do too: I got high enough to make it to Winnfield, signed the papers, and picked out two urns so I could split Momi's ashes. A couple weeks later, when I got back from picking them up, I texted Nana. And, of course, instead of texting back, she called, trying to sound intentionally amicable, like she was doing me a favor.

"Good afternoon, young lady."

"Afternoon."

"I was just thinking about you. You said you got the remains?"

"Yep. Picked em up today."

"Well, what are you planning to do with them?"

I sighed. "I don't know. Maybe scatter some of them in Cross Lake. Keep the rest. I wanted to do Cypress where we went last Memorial Day, but that water's so dingy-looking. Plus, it's too far away to visit whenever I want to."

"Well, if you want a headstone, we can still do one in the family plot. I was gonna do that when the GoFundMe money came in, but I wanted to see if there was something you wanted to do first."

"I don't want any parts of that money, if it ever comes. It's got your daughter's blood all over it, and you shucked and jived at that vigil to get it. Now it's yours."

Her voice bristled with alarm. "Whatchu mean by that?"

I changed the subject. "You wanna come get your half of the ashes? I bought two urns." I was holding one of them—the one I picked out as mine because it felt the heaviest—when I called her. It was the only way I knew how to get through the conversation. The urn was blown glass, turquoise and gold, and I picked out two of the same kind because they reminded me of the water at Galveston Beach, where me and Momi sometimes went for the annual Kappa Beach Party.

"Of course I want them," she said. "I'll come get you. Where you at?"

I almost laughed. "You don't need to know that. I'll meet you at the boat launch over by Ford Park. Tomorrow. Noon."

DAMMIT IF I DIDN'T START puking again at four the next morning. Luckily, I made it to one of the bathrooms, the one closest to the room in which I slept. But then I couldn't get back to sleep because I couldn't tell when I would throw up again. Momi used to tell her friends that's how you know you're pregnant: when you can't feel the vomit coming. *I wish I was pregnant now*, I thought, but it would have had to be by immaculate conception.

Before she pissed me off, I really should have asked Nana more questions about who my mother was as a kid. I knew a lot about the relationship between them, but they always talked in stories, and their favorite ones were about how wrong one got treated by the other. And even those were sus, because when you tried to ask about specifics, they would each avoid you in ways that spoke volumes about who they were, but not much else about each other.

I grabbed an urn and held it while I sat on the couch trying to huff back tears in the early morning dark. The day my dad, Reggie, OD'd on his own supply, I told Momi—and Nana, who'd rushed over, hoping we'd finally need her for something—that I didn't claim people in death who never claimed me in life. And now, Momi's murder felt like punishment for not being sorry for losing him. Now I was left with Nana, somebody who didn't know how to claim anybody either, not unless she could make them sound perfect. *God, if that's what this is*, I sobbed, *then You won. You got me. You took all I had.* And then I felt so angry and sick again I put down the urn because I was afraid I'd throw up all over it.

IT WAS A DREARY, WINDY day, and even windier near the water, which was so choppy it looked like it was crawling with shards of glass. Even though I can swim, Cross Lake scares the hell out of me. It takes two miles to cross it on 220, and that's not even the widest part. And just like they say about the Mississippi, the current can play tricks on you. You might start off in three feet of water, and a few seconds later find yourself in fifteen. Ford Park, across the way, ain't no joke either. Even though it's just as green and tree-lined as every other park in the city, I wouldn't be caught dead there at certain times of the night or day. I do think Momi went to a few impromptu car shows out there, though.

I was late, as usual, and Nana was standing on the pier, her thin coat clinging to her like a wet paper towel. From the back, she looked headless; her now light gray bun indistinguishable from the sky. I walked up behind her, cradling one of the urns like a baby. Noon had been a good time for this. Everybody that had a job was at work, and even the paw-paws were gone, since they did their fishing in the mornings. The trees were swaying, and I tried to remember if there'd been tornadoes in the forecast.

When Nana turned around, we just stared at each other, her face set in a jumble of lines that looked deeper than when I last saw her. She spoke first.

"We should pray, before we do anything." She was standing back from the water, kind of in the middle of the pier because she can't swim.

"Sure. That's fine. Listen, I don't know what you plan to do with these, but you do it. These are yours. Mine are at home."

"Wait. I thought you was gon bring both?"

"I didn't."

"Well, what I'm supposed to do with these?"

"You tell me," I snapped. "It's your daughter, not mine."

I didn't mean to say it like that, but that's how it came out and I didn't try to take it back. Nana started to cry, and my early morning anger swelled my throat. This was my loss, and nobody else's. Not a trace of Nana lived in the body I was holding, burned down to nothing. And Nana didn't live in me either. I was now unmoored from the one person in the world I could point to and people would let me claim, since few other folks wanted me or Momi for keeps. Plus, I'd spent more years being Momi's daughter than Momi ever spent being a daughter in Nana's stuffy-ass house.

"Whatchu crying for?" I spat out bitterly, shifting the urn to my other arm because it was heavy.

Nana pulled out a handkerchief and dabbed at her eyes and around her mouth. "I don't know who you are anymore. I don't know what all this is doing to you."

"Did you ever know me? You sure as hell didn't know Momi."

"I don't know. Maybe I didn't," she said, and then when I didn't have a response for that, she repeated, "Maybe I didn't." I knew I was supposed to somehow comfort her, but I refused. She was all the kinfolk I had left and it felt like a bum deal.

"Are you gonna scatter these ashes?" I was getting impatient.

"I thought you were gonna do it!"

"I'm not. And it's cold out here. I don't want to be out here all day."

Nana's face started to crumple again. "I don't want to put my baby in that water. I don't want to have to do that. That's why I wanted a funeral."

"Well, it's too late for that. Either you do it, or I'm leaving."

"I can't do that, Maple."

I shrugged and started to walk away, but she cried, "Wait!" and gestured toward the urn.

I looked at her like she was crazy, but kept going. "You a fool if you think you gonna get these now. You want em, then come try to take em from me, and I'll put both of you in the water."

ON THE WAY HOME, I had to pull over a couple of times on 220 so I could get out a good enough cry to see the road. Momi always told me never to do that: pull over where a big diesel can just slam in the back of you and the whole car go up in flames. That shit happened all the time here. Flat as the land is, you'd think they could see where they were going. But that day, the road was empty, just a lot of Suburbans and a church school bus, probably Calvary's. During one of my stops, my cell phone rang, and I almost sent it to voice mail because I just knew it was gonna be Nana, but I didn't recognize the number flashing on the radio screen. Instead, it was a white woman.

"This isn't like you to be so behind on rent, Ms. Moffett," she chirped cheerfully. It was one of Mr. Meche daughters, doing the dirty work for him, which was the only time you heard from them. Meche wasn't the business type. He was more prone to come to the duplex to fix the AC than a hired handyman, but he wasn't big on bookkeeping. I paused to give myself a minute to craft a response. It amazes me how little white people know about what goes on in this city outside their own neighborhoods.

"My mother was killed three weeks ago. Brenda May Moffett. You can look it up. I've been having a hard time, and I haven't been back home since I heard."

"Oh no. I'm so sorry. I had no idea. Please let us know if there's anything we can do." Her voice had dropped now—an alto of shock and reverence. But I wanted this to be the worst phone call of her week, her month, maybe her life. I wanted her to remember it the day her father died. If she loved him, I wanted her to know how stupid she was today, when she knew nothing about how this felt, and all she could offer was a few sentences that were so generic they could have been in response to a job loss, or the death of somebody's dog.

I took a deep breath. "Actually, there is something you can do. Consider the unit abandoned and get rid of everything in it. I'm never coming back, so you can clear it out and rent it to someone else as soon as you're ready. I'll probably be dead, too, before the week is out."

And I didn't want to hear any other platitudes, so I hung up.

I watched it. The whole thing. Later that night, after the lake, and after I'd slept the day away. I took the opportunity because I knew I would have to start working again soon; I'd already taken off a week longer than I said I needed, and I didn't want Ranjith thinking

I was trying to play him. Plus, if I did it now, I could piss away a day recovering. I opened my laptop and clicked the download link.

It started like all cheap pornos: guy's sitting alone on his couch being lonely, then he decides he wants someone to cook him an elaborate meal. I fast-forwarded past the dialogue and got to the part with my mom in it. She's one of the hired chefs, of course, but she finds out it's the guy's birthday and she wants him to have a "layer cake." It was hard to hear her voice, which sounded exactly like it did when she was alive: mischievous and full of joy. The sound of it nearly yanked sobs out of me, so I muted my computer and just watched her on-screen, trying to figure out when it was filmed by her hairstyle. The detective said it came out in summer, but it might have been shot around the holidays, right before she flew to Atlanta for those expensive bright red micros and gave me the down payment for my car. I wondered if this was how she paid for it.

Momi did everything in that video: sucked dick, ate cat, took it from the back. Everything. I watched it because, in it, she was still alive, but also, because I could see her whole body for the first time without her narrating what I did to it when she was pregnant, or posing for me, and telling me I was welcome for the gift of seeing her ass for free. If I was ever jealous of anything, it was Momi's shape. Aside from that and our color, we were pretty much the same: same-sized nose, same heart-shaped mouth. Same dimples. Our hair grew the same length and hung in ringlets when it got wet. But where I was long-limbed and narrow, with slivers of breasts that turned down like dog-eared pages in a book, and a behind that teetered above stick legs like a pair of dumplings held by chopsticks, Momi was a vixen. She was compact, with the smallest hands I've ever seen, arms that were both round and thin, and teacup breasts that sat up perfectly. Her waist was still small, even after me, but her hips were wide, enveloping an otherwise small body like a bustled skirt. Her elbows and knees dimpled under the weight of her tight roundness, her electric sex appeal. And AK was doing all kinds of things to that body, cumming on her back and shoving his greasy dick in her mouth, pushing her head between Kitty's legs while he held himself in front of Kitty's face. It was a frenzy for him. But Momi always seemed to be in control. Whatever he was doing to her, he was doing it because she had willed him to. Maybe even in the script, which I couldn't hear without the volume. And I couldn't put my finger on it until it was almost done, and Kitty was kneeling between Momi's legs and, for once, the man was out of the way, touching himself in the corner of the screen while they played. My Momi looked content. She looked…happy. No matter what was going on around her, she was enjoying it all by herself. Kitty and AK could have been there, but it could have also been anyone. The cameras could have been on or off.

And it's true that what I detected might have been rehearsed, but the shit looked real. My mother looked…joyful. She looked like she had found the sweetness of life—something I knew, from the moment I saw her on-screen, that I had never tasted.

AFTER MOMI'S STRIP CLUB TRIBUTE, I stopped getting De-Vaughan to bring me food because he was acting as thirsty as an undercover cop, always asking if I needed anything else besides what I had in the tin. And even though the club had given me enough cheese to stay high until I saw my mama again, I told him no because I was beginning to scare myself. One night, I ate a shitload of gummy bears, and an hour later, I was fifteen again, in Natchitoches at the Christmas festival. Back in the day, Momi and Ms. P would bundle us up and make the hour-long drive down

I-49 so we could stand outside for hours until the town lit up after dark. Lett and I would always wander off to buy meat pies (beer, too, if there was a teenager working the booth), and do our best to appear like we weren't there with our parents, which was easy because our moms usually lost us in the crowd anyway. They were as distracted by the men as we were by the boys, and tipsy off thermoses of cocoa spiked with E&J Cask & Cream. But somehow we always found each other before the boat parade, and watching Momi watch the boats and then the fireworks was my favorite part. It was like all the lives she'd lived since she got pregnant fell away, and she was a kid again, pointing and squealing at a pontoon decked out to look like Santa driving an alligator-pulled sleigh down the Cane River.

But in my hallucination, I was on the riverbank surrounded by strangers, watching a twinkling barge pass under the Church Street Bridge. I squinted. On the deck stood a woman in a white mink, waving like a prom queen. She looked like Momi, and I told myself if I swam to it, I could crawl onto the deck and find out who it really was. So I took off running in my mind, in a crowd of people who wouldn't get the fuck out of the way. I could smell diesel exhaust and sugar in the air, and I was cold, but I kept going until I got to the bank. Then I jumped. The next morning, I woke up on the balcony naked, wrapped in the duvet and clutching an eraser I'd seen in one of the kids' rooms. It was shaped like a laughter emoji.

That night at the strip club was a similar blur—something I regretted because if anyone ever needed to be distracted by titties, it was me. But I can't remember anything other than flashes of blue bodies, the smell of sweet things, sweat, and money, Ms. P's white turtleneck dress, and her second cousin Chad's beard and open-faced grill, which was all I could recall about his appearance, even though when he first stuck out a jeweled fist to shake my hand, I remember thinking he was almost as beautiful as Ms. P. When he dropped us back at the hotel, where Regina had left her car and Lett had come so they could trail Chad and DeVaughan to some after-party, Chad turned to me and smiled, his diamond-studded gumline catching the interior light as I opened the car door.

"Look like you gon be straight with that bag for a minute. I'ma let DeVaughan walk you upstairs, though. Don't forget to put the latch on. And put that up in the safe if you got one. Niggas be out here acting ruthless."

And my ass, three sheets to the wind, smiled and asked, "What kinda moisturizer you put in your beard?"

Without missing a beat, Lett yelled, "She want you to say pussy juice," and everybody in the car burst out laughing.

On our way up, DeVaughan told me I should consider going into business with a real nigga and flipping some of that money from the club.

"In business with who, Chad?"

"Naw, nigga, me!"

I almost laughed, but I told him I'd think about it.

"Bet," he said, grinning wide as a weasel. When he left, he opened his arms for a hug, and when I went in, he grabbed my ass, shaking it a little before saying, "A'ight, then, take it easy, Maple." He paused a little, waiting.

I waited too. "Ain't Chad downstairs?"

"I mean yeah, but if you want me to stay…"

"Naw, fam, you good." I went into the room and, after sobering up a little, pulled up Momi's video. I needed to remind myself whose daughter I was, and what I could be even when everybody and *their* kids were treating me like low-hanging fucking fruit.

II.

A few days later, I worked the desk for the first time in a long time, which I loved because front desk really isn't hard work if you like meeting people and letting them go about their business. Some folks come through wanting a key to a room with a bed, no questions asked. And I don't; I take the money, let them know when breakfast is served and where to get ice, and point them in the direction they should be headed.

And because I never see anything worth remembering, I don't pay attention until I got a good reason to pay attention, and that's exactly what happened the day Chad stepped into the hotel lobby as casually as if he'd just got off a plane from somewhere interesting and had strolled the half mile from the airport across the parking lots of our almost-identical competitors. (And yeah he could have walked. The airport really is that small.) I had just checked in this couple from Minnesota, here to gamble on the boats and maybe drive to the Rose Garden, and Chad walks in wearing a tight-ass T-shirt and some brand-new red-bottomed gold sneakers, looking for a couple of rooms for him and his boys. I didn't know exactly what kind of sneakers they were, but Jamarcus had that exact pair, so I knew they must have been expensive. I got so distracted remembering that bastard, I almost missed getting a good look at Chad's face again. He had large eyes that narrowed to downturned half-moons when he smiled and skin that rivaled Ms. P's with its color and sheen. The beard, of course, looked moisturized, but I kept that shit to myself this time. He nodded politely when he recognized me and opened his mouth slightly, unsure what to say. No grill this time.

"Hey, what's good, fam."

"Heyhowyoudoin." It was my typical on-the-clock greeting. I wasn't sure what else to say without sounding as dumb as I had three days before.

"Been doin all right myself. It's Maple, right?"

His asking me simple shit gave me time to recover my sass. "Yep. I do name changes once a month. Only had this one two weeks." I shrugged my right shoulder, tipping my name tag toward him as I typed.

He smiled apologetically. "Yeah, I thought it was Maple. My bad."

"You're good. You came in here cause you need a room, right?"

"Yeah." He nodded quickly, like I had said something deep. "You right. That's exactly what I'm here for."

It was Mudbug Madness weekend, and Chad wanted a suite for the night. He didn't balk when I told him the price and the deposit, in spite of the fact Ranjith jacks them both up if we're at 80 percent occupancy during a festival. He knows if we're that full, then every hotel in the city must be packed, and he can tell people with a straight face to try to find a better deal on the riverboats if they want. Chad passed me a credit card and asked what I was getting into that night.

"Nothing."

"At all? Not even downtown?"

I shook my head, pretending to concentrate on his registration.

I guess I was supposed to elaborate on why I wasn't going out on some awesome date, but I felt like I shouldn't have to do that to keep the conversation going. I figured if he wanted to holla, he should holla. When I was done, I handed him his keys. "Enjoy your stay, Mr. Freeman."

"Bet." He nodded again as he backed away from the counter. Just before turning to go, he said, "When you off work tonight, why'on't you come chill with us? You got the room numbers."

Something leaped in my chest, but I smiled noncommittally and told him to have a nice day.

I watched him swagger out of the lobby and dap up DeVaughan just outside the doors. Together, they scratched the backs of their heads, made grandiose gestures with their hands, and laughed. When Chad laughed, he threw his head back, his grizzled neck tilting up to the sun and his teeth catching the light. I imagined them biting the pink meat of my inner thigh. He was mad muscular, too, a bodybuilder type, but someone who looked like they didn't take it that seriously—maybe lifted just to keep in shape in case some shit went down. He was also tall, and had to slouch a little as he patted DeVaughan on the back of his shoulder before walking away. De-Vaughan was about six feet himself. So things in Ms. P's family really did run big.

Huh, I thought as he finally walked away.

I WASN'T SURE WHEN THE party started, but folks were already lit. The suite was hazy with smoke and the bodies it nearly concealed moved slowly through it; even the girls who were dancing seemed to drift over the carpet, stopping to sit in the laps of men pretending to be nonchalant, talking to each other while holding Styrofoam cups of daiquiris spiked with lean. Ranjith would have thrown a fit if he'd known, but he was out of town that weekend for a wedding. Plus, all he would have done was take Chad's deposit and get housekeeping to run a wet vac over the carpet, Febreze the shit out of everything else, open the windows, and put in an industrial fan to clear out the rest of the smell.

People were going between rooms, and it was crowded enough that I could have *maybe* blended in if I wanted to, in a tiny black dress Momi must have picked out at some point back in the day and a pair of silver-heeled stilettos I'd borrowed from Regina the night of the tribute. But Jamarcus couldn't. I saw him as soon as I walked in, and I pretended not to, but my arms stiffened, and had anyone there known me better, they would have noticed how my movements became jerkier as I skirted the bodies that unwillingly let me pass. When folks here don't know why you've walked into a room and don't recognize you as somebody they *know* know, they ain't trying to make room for you, not even to stare. Plus, if any of them recognized me from the front desk, they might have thought I was trying to blow up their spot.

Jamarcus was in the living room area, squashed up on one of the couches with some girl in his lap completely blocking his view of me with her wig and her red titties in his face. It had been a good month and a half since the last time I'd seen him face-to-face, but the top of that egghead, his Little-Bill-ass ears, and those designer shoes gave him away. He was out here, on to the next bitch like my mama never existed, and this one was probably gonna fuck him because he had money to flash and a little drip. I was so pissed I felt like I couldn't breathe. My face got hot, and I felt a sliver of sweat slip past my bra band and trickle down my back. But then I got calm. A little too calm, actually. Methodically, I made my way to the kitchen, where I knew I could let myself be distracted while I figured out what to do. When DeVaughan saw me, he nodded approvingly at Chad, who was standing next to him.

"Oh, this my girl right here, so we ain't gotta worry bout hidin all these drugs." DeVaughan held out his arm for a hug.

"Nope," I said, going in, then moving back quickly. "I don't snitch on the hand that deals to me."

He laughed. "That's what's up. Cause all I gotta do is air out this room tomorrow, and won't nobody know a thang."

He and Chad dapped each other up, and Chad hopped up to sit on the counter across from me, pulling a plastic bag out of his back pocket before he did. "Nigga, you coulda told me you was working here full-time, though, so I coulda got that employee discount. Maple wasn't trying to show me no love at the desk." He handed the bag to DeVaughan, who nudged the contents around with his finger, looking impressed. Over Chad's shoulder, I watched Jamarcus lean into the girl as she recoiled playfully, narrowly dodging the kiss he was trying to plant on her neck. I tried to remember what it felt like to be kissed that way, and a small spot on my neck pulsed with warmth. It almost felt as if it were gushing blood.

"What's that?" I asked, though I wasn't sure if I was talking to Chad or myself.

"Shrooms," said DeVaughan, offering me the bag. "You takin some?"

I waved the bag away. "Mmm-mph. I don't know what those'll do to me."

Jamarcus jostled the girl in his lap and tried again. This time, his lips met her flesh, and she narrowed her eyes. I squinted, too, a little, almost lost in thought until Chad's voice broke through, sounding like he was far away.

"That's how it be. But these here is quality. Got em out there in DeSoto."

"Ooh! You hear about Antonio getting robbed out that way?" DeVaughan was back to the j again, tonguing the paper since he was getting ready to close it, but also looking me up and down, just like he did the night of that business proposal. I ignored him and tried to look back over Chad's shoulder, but for a split second, our eyes met, and Chad must have seen something there, because he gave a quick, barely perceptible nod and looked at DeVaughan like he should chill out and maybe stop talking.

Of course, he didn't.

"See the problem was, nigga wasn't strapped up enough." De-Vaughen held up the j to inspect his work.

"Naw, he had one, but it was in the glove box. Couldn't get to it," Chad corrected him quietly.

"See? That's why you always have something *on* you. At all times." Then DeVaughan turned his hip toward me. "You ever held a strap?"

I was still looking through the crowd at Jamarcus and the girl, but I shook my head, and from the corner of my eye I saw DeVaughan reach for the bulge at his side.

"Take it," he commanded. "Sooner or later you gon see one of these in the streets."

I snapped back to attention and looked over at DeVaughan. He cocked his head to the side and impatiently pushed the gun toward me. My hands trembled slightly as I held them out and he placed it gingerly in my palms. It was small, but heavy. No one was paying attention to us.

The gun was warmer on the side where it had been in contact with his body, maybe all day, and I thought about that, holding a thing that could kill someone so close to you. My life seemed as small and as narrow as the j, by comparison. Momi had been everything that had given me substance and heft, even more so in the past few years, as all my college friends got married and had babies, or pushed out more babies, or finally moved to Dallas, where there were more jobs and, supposedly, better men. Meanwhile, I'd stayed in this city to be close to my mama; now I no longer mattered to a single living soul. I could accidentally suffocate myself one night, OD, or flat-out kill myself for real and only Nana would be mad—maybe not even about the death so much as about my being selfish enough to do it so soon after her precious, whitewashed-for-television Brenda May. I could hear her tearfully explaining to skeptical church folks that, no matter how I'd died, she knew in her *heart* I went to heaven, because I was in so much pain I didn't know what I was doing. Naw. I couldn't let her have that glory again, of being the only person left to tell the story. And I didn't necessarily have the heart to kill anybody else.

But I did want to do *something*. Something big. Flashy. Something that would turn a few heads.

I had my hand around the grip, and DeVaughan stepped behind me and wrapped his hand around mine, showing me how to hold it and pull the trigger. It was supposed to be flirtatious, but it made me jump.

"Ayyye," he said in an almost-whisper, trying his best to sound sexy. "Can't be scared of nothing when you the one with the strap." That was the lowest his voice had been all night.

"One of these killed my mom," I said matter-of-factly, but it, too, came out in a whisper, and it took a moment for DeVaughan to decipher it.

"Yeah. Shit, my bad. I hadn't even thought about that. But, mane, for real, you can't be scared of these. Everybody around here packing. Shit, probably everybody in this room, except maybe the bitches." Chad tapped DeVaughan on his shoulder, then signaled for him to cool it. DeVaughan waved him off. "Yeah, right. Females. My bad."

And I don't know what it was, maybe some stroke of luck or

magic, or maybe even my mama pulling pranks from beyond the grave, but suddenly, the crowd parted, and I had a clear view of Jamarcus reclined on the couch, comfortable in his presumption of anonymity. The girl who'd been sitting on his lap was now beside him, holding a red cup with neon claws that glowed even in the haze, and laughing at something he must have said. That bitch looked too much like Lett not to be related to her, but Chad didn't seem to recognize her and neither did I. I raised the barrel and pointed it at them, slowly backing up to the counter between the stovetop and the sink so no one could come up behind me again.

"Jamarcus," I called, not loud, but with enough projection for him to pluck his name from the noise. Even before he raised his head, recognition, panic, and shame hunched his shoulders. So he had seen me, but that motherfucker was gonna pretend like he hadn't, as long as he thought I hadn't seen him. But the jig was up as soon as we made eye contact. He froze, cup crashing to the carpet, purple slush splotching his expensive shoes. The girl next to him giggled nervously, at first confused because her face had been turned toward him, but once she saw me, she scooted to the far end of the couch and onto the floor, out of my range. I would have said "Freeze," or some shit, but that sounded corny. Everyone looked in my direction, and for the first time in my life, I didn't care. I smirked.

"Wait, wait, wait, wait. Whatchu tryna do to ole boy?" De-Vaughan yelled, and I turned to him, arms rigid, pointing the gun in his direction as he talked. He also raised his hands, but I could tell he was poised; as soon as I flinched, he would lunge, so I tried to keep my grip as steady as possible.

"If you move, I'll shoot you first, then him. And it's not even worth all that. He got my mama killed. I only want him." At my command, DeVaughan's shoulders relaxed a little. He wasn't trying to be nobody's hero.

Chad turned his back to me and waved his hands at the crowd, telling them to quiet down before somebody in another room called the cops, and warning the dudes not to reach for nothing—he had it under control. As soon as I saw Jamarcus move out of the corner of my eye, I turned the gun back on him, but I held one hand up at DeVaughan, so he wouldn't forget my threat and try to come closer.

"Who *is* that?" Chad asked in an attempt to distract me.

I didn't even flinch. "The nigga whose car my mama died in. And I know whoever killed her was looking for him." I cocked my head a little and narrowed my eyes like I was trying to make sure I had a good shot. Jamarcus nodded nervously down at the girl on the floor, to let her know everything was gonna be all right.

"Stop fucking moving!" I screamed. Finally, the room fell silent. I guess people thought I'd just been playing until I spoke. But now they froze. Only Chad moved as he turned to face me. He had his hands up, but he took a step closer and started talking.

"Maple? Maple. Listen. It's all right, fam. That dude? He ain't kill your mama. And if the niggas that did was looking for him, he couldn't control that neither, know what I'm sayin? Maple. People stay dying here. If it's one of our fault, it's all our fault. We be wilin out here. That's…that's all it is. He didn't do nothing. And if he did, killin him ain't gon make it right."

I ignored him. "Get up, Jamarcus," I said evenly.

Jamarcus looked from me to Chad, trying to figure out who to take cues from. And I guess Chad was taking too long to defuse the situation, because DeVaughan turned to him, too, and started cursing.

"Nigga, stop sweet-talkin this bitch! She pulled my own gun on me!"

Chad shook his head, turning slowly away from me to face him.

"That ain't even her, though. That's grief, cuz. I know what it look like. Calm the fuck down."

Meanwhile, Jamarcus is motionless in midair, ass halfway off the couch, and maybe that was all I could ask for. I didn't want anyone's family hurting as much as I was then. Not even his. I looked from him, to DeVaughan, to Chad, and I raised the gun again real quick, just to scare everybody one more time, then handed it to Chad. He passed it to DeVaughan, who looked at it in disbelief, almost as if, because it had turned on him in someone else's hands, he wasn't sure he could ever trust it again. Then the room erupted in chaos: girls grabbing their purses to leave; dudes yelling curses of relief and talking about how they wouldn't have waited to pull on me if I'd been a nigga. Chad grabbed my left arm with one hand and staved everyone else off with the other.

"Don't worry about it. I got it," he said to them. "She'll be all right. Her mama just got shot a couple days ago. That's all it is." We walked slowly out the door while some folks stared in shock and others in disgust. How dare I roll up in a party, already a circus freak, face not even beat, and do some fucked-up shit like that? Chad kept facing the crowd until we got out of the door and closed it. Then he leaned over me and said as calmly as if he were explaining rules for a board game, "Look, I'ma walk you around for a while, then back to your room, so don't nobody run up and try to kill you on the way, just to save face. Cause if you go by yourself, I promise you they'll do it."

CHAD SLOWLY CIRCLED US AROUND the back of the hotel strip, out into the empty parking lots along the edge of the airport. "You done pissed off *way* too many people, cuz. What's your room number?" When I told him, he repeated it under his breath over and over again as we walked, until, finally, fifteen minutes after the last carload of loud-talking folks skirted out onto the main road, we circled back to the building, and he led me to my room.

"You work tomorrow?" he asked, shoving me in and squeezing in behind me.

"Not technically. But I got some paperwork to finish."

"Bet. You need to either go into the office early or after checkout. Folks that's still staying here might try to come for your job if they know you work here. And some of em might already know, so they gon do that anyway."

"I don't care about this job," I said flatly.

Chad looked at me and shrugged. "I already know you don't. Don't mean you gotta give it up today, though. Let yourself figure some shit out first."

"Okay," I said, in the tone I always use when people say dumb shit.

"Got a smart-ass mouth too." But he said that under his breath, like he'd repeated the room number. I shrugged back at him.

"What's your number?" He saved it in his phone and sent a text. Then he took my head in his hands and turned it to face me, both palms on my cheeks like somebody's dad, talking slow so I knew he wasn't playing. "Listen. If you can, stay in here till you hear from me tomorrow. Now getcho ass to bed and get some sleep."

We stared at each other for a few seconds, until I started getting uncomfortable.

I closed my eyes before I spoke. "Why did you tell people my mama just died? That was a month ago."

"Cause when it happens, it always feels like it just happened."

And with that, he walked out of the room and shut the door.

I shouldn't have closed my eyes when he looked at me. But I couldn't take it, those big eyes whose whites were pink from smoke, and the way his skin shone in the hallway light, slightly sweaty from pacing but also, I hoped, from worry about what might happen to me next. And his heavy beard hanging like a mask falling off his face. I didn't close my eyes because I wanted to. I did it because I felt myself softening, and I was scared. I did it because he wouldn't look away.

DAWN COULDN'T GET THERE QUICK enough for me to call Regina to get her take on the situation. I knew I'd fucked up, but I also knew she would understand. Maybe even have a solution. Or at least come over and smoke with me while I figured out a way to make myself feel better. I remembered the way she looked at me the day she and Lett came over to smoke. This time, I'd let her touch me if she wanted to. This time, I needed someone to hold me.

I scrolled through my missed calls list, found her number, and dialed.

"Hullo?" she answered after a few rings. And there was another voice in the background, equally sultry, asking who it was. I'd have recognized it anywhere. Lett. I balked.

"Oh, girl, you sound asleep. Hit me back when you wake up."

"Okay, I will. Promise." Then *click*.

Unbelievable. The *one* time I was willing to indulge folks' generosities, and as usual, bitches like Lett got there first.

I DIDN'T WANT TO TALK to either of them after that, but I wondered if I could muster the courage to entertain Chad. I figured if I didn't answer his calls or texts, he might get worried and show up. And if anybody really needed me downstairs, they knew they could call the room, or just come up if it was serious. So I let my phone buzz and glow all day under my pillow while I showered and straightened up. Then I lit a few candles and turned the air on, trying to get the smell of me out: vomit and leave-in conditioner and old take-out boxes stained with fish grease. When I heard a housekeeping cart pass by, I waited a few minutes, then ran outside and quickly dumped my trash into it, snagging a few clean towels before whoever was inside the vacant room saw me.

It was about seven when I heard the soft knock on the door. When I checked the peephole, I saw him, decked out in white shorts, an orange polo, and a matching cap. I opened the door cautiously.

"Damn!" he huffed with relief, pushing past me into the room. "I thought somethin happened to you."

"No—I'm sorry." I faked a yawn. "I was just taking some personal time today, like you said."

"Shit, I was shook." Chad walked around, checking rooms, one hand at his hip and the other fluttering from door handles to the back of his neck, which I guess is what dudes do when they're trying to keep a cool head. "You sure you in here alone? Nobody tried to mess with you?"

"Nope. Been here all day by myself."

He half whistled and then sat down at the kitchenette table. "Good. Man, what you been doin up in here?"

I shrugged. "Getting my head right. Like you said."

He smirked, and then pulled out a cigarette. "Can I smoke?"

"Nobody in here to tell you you can't."

"That's what's up." He took a hit and blew it out of one corner of his mouth. "Whatchu got in here to eat?"

I smirked. "Besides me? Nothing."

He inhaled again and shook his head. "That mouth, though. You hungry?"

"Yeah, kinda." I wanted it to sound like I was looking for something that wasn't food, but I actually was hungry.

"Whatchu wanna eat?"

"I don't care." I finally sat down across from him. "I been eating whatever, really."

"That's the last thing you need to be doing." Chad let the cigarette dangle from his mouth as he talked and played with his hands, which he drummed restlessly on the table. Then he noticed the tin and slid it away from the wall so he could open it. "What's in here then?" he asked, popping the lid.

"Snacks."

"Damn, I can smell em." He shook it a little to better see past the gummies. "Wait—is those cupcakes?"

"Yeah, but you don't wanna eat them without food first. If you do, you're gonna be hungry and irritated as fuck."

"Bet." He rose from the table and pulled up his pants. The handle of his gun flashed dark against his white shorts and undershirt. "I'll be back."

I WAS HALFWAY THROUGH MY fried rice and oysters when I felt it slipping around my tongue, and I pushed it to the front of my mouth and spat it into my hand. Chad looked over and almost hit me on the back until he realized I wasn't choking.

"You got a pearl?"

"Looks like." I held it out in my palm so he could see it. It was tiny, but perfectly round.

He picked it up clumsily between his thick fingers and balanced it in his own calloused palm. "You gotta make a wish."

"Naw. I don't want nothing."

"Nothing at all?"

"Besides my mama coming back? No."

Chad's face fell, and he looked down at the pearl, rolling it around in his palm. He sighed. "Well, if you think of something else, you can always ask for it later." He set it down on the stack of napkins on the table.

I dipped another oyster in tartar sauce and popped it in my mouth so I would sound more nonchalant. "Fine. I want some dick." But saying it felt awkward in a way that surprised me, given who I belonged to.

Chad burst out laughing. "That's too easy. Try for somethin harder."

"Is it, though? I ain't had it in months—hell, probably years."

"If you ain't found it, it's cause you ain't lookin hard enough."

I laughed. "You sound like my mama."

"And she sound like she knew what she was talking about."

I relented. Slightly. "I guess I haven't been looking that much."

"There you go. Tell the truth and shame the devil."

I got up to grab the tin from the table. "You want some of these? I already had one before you got back."

Chad put his fork down and reached for it. "Don't mind if I do."

I COULD ONLY GET SO high, but once I was there, I felt bold enough to start staring at him. We were watching something on my laptop, but I couldn't follow what was happening anyway, so I just stopped paying attention. He tried ignoring me, but I crawled into his lap and put my nose up to his. I didn't try to kiss him. I wanted him to kiss me first. He grinned, and I inhaled the scent of onion and horseradish from the tartar sauce on his breath.

"Cuz, whatchu doing?"

I moved closer, so our lips were perfectly lined up, almost touching.

He shifted uncomfortably in his seat. "Naw, don't do that."

I put my hands on his face and held it still. "I'm not doing nothing. Just looking at you. You're beautiful."

He squirmed and drew his hands together in prayer position between my forearms. Then he opened them quickly, breaking my grip. When I let go, he held me away from him by my shoulders.

"Yeah, you gotta chill. You high, and you sad, and I can't...I can't really fuck with you like this." He laughed a little, as if the answer surprised him. I tried to lean forward and again, he tried to hold me away, but it was a weak grip and I knew it. I've been thrown around by men before. My mother's mostly, but still, I know how it feels when they mean it. Even so, I backed off a little and tried a different tack.

"I'm sorry, fam. I'm just lonely."

He said nothing. I tried again.

"I thought you might be too."

He shifted again. "I am, just not in the way you think."

"How?"

Chad tried to sit up without touching me because, of course, he was hard. Not that hard, but hard enough. You could see the bulge in the white shorts, though the color probably made it look more serious than it was. He coughed a little, watched the screen for a few seconds, then said matter-of-factly, "My girl. She died. About five years ago."

"What girl."

"Kemmia LaCoeur. She died having my baby."

I vaguely remembered hearing the name before, but you know, hearing about folks dying doesn't always register until it's your people.

"Yeah. I kinda remember that. What happened to her again?"

"Her uterus never healed up after birth. Then it started bleeding. And she kept saying something didn't feel right, but the doctors ain't do shit. It was her first baby. Wasn't nothing gon feel right—that's what they kept telling her. But then she started bleeding. A lot. They said it was normal but she was bleeding everywhere—through her clothes, all on the sheets. We tried getting ahold of her doctor, but he was on vacation. Then we called the office, but they said wait a day or two and come in. Then we went to the emergency room. It was a Saturday, so you know they was busy. Stabbings. Gunshot victims. Car accidents. They told us it wasn't a priority, so we waited. She kept having to go change her diapers and shit. Then the last time she got up she passed out. They finally took her back, tried to save her, but—" He shook his head. "She was gone. On a stretcher. In the hallway." He had been looking past me, at the wall, but then he squinted and rubbed his eyelids with his left hand. He had stopped trying to hold me back.

"Oh, man. I'm so sorry." I waited for what I hoped was a respectable pause. "What happened to your baby?"

"Still here. Stay with Mia's mama."

"Do you see him?"

"Yeah, I see her. Not enough, though, if I'm being honest. I been running around. Keeping busy."

"What's her name?"

"Chelsea. Chelsea Chardaé Freeman."

"That's pretty." I sighed.

"Her mama named her."

"My mama named me too," I said. "That's all I got left."

Chad was quiet a few moments before he nodded. "Yep, when people die, it's like, the record gets cut off. They can't come back and change nothing. And neither can you. And you can try to explain who they were, but how can you explain a whole person? Everything get set in stone when they take their last breath. Everything."

No one had ever explained to me a feeling I thought only I understood. I nodded too.

"Yeah. I wish I had known."

He propped an elbow on the couch's armrest and leaned down to scratch the top of his head. "Me too."

"Would you have done anything differently?"

Chad pinched the bridge of his nose and sniffed. "Shit. Maybe. Mighta tried harder to get her back there to see somebody. Might notta messed around on her so much in the beginning with all them randoms. Mighta spent more time at the house with her. Told her how I felt about her. Shit like that. You?"

"I might have asked her more questions about why she turned out the way she was, cause she sure as hell didn't get it from my grandma. I would have tried to figure out why she lived how she lived. And why she loved it."

"Yeah. I heard stories about your mama. She was wild, boy." He laughed and shook his head, then kissed his teeth and said it again: "If what I heard was true, she was wild."

"She was. But I don't think my mama ever did a damn thing she didn't want to. Not once. Here, let me show you something." I grabbed the laptop off the coffee table. When I pressed play, I propped it on his lap so he could hear better. I didn't fast-forward through it like I usually do, just let it play and watched Chad watch it, first with a mask of shock; then a few minutes after Momi appeared onscreen with Kitty, he squinted a little.

"Hold up." He hit the pause button and peered at the computer.

"What?" I asked casually, but my heart was already beating faster. I'd watched this a hundred times. But maybe I'd missed something.

He put his arm up to hold me back, almost as if he thought I'd try to get at him again.

"What do you see?" I demanded, reaching under his arm so I could shift the screen toward me.

He stared for a few seconds more, then leaned back and stroked his beard. "My bad, lady. I thought I saw somebody I knew."

Chad seemed to stay tense at first, brow wrinkled, hand still on his face, as if he was trying to figure something out, but as he got more comfortable, he got more emotional. He laughed at the corny dialogue and cheered when Momi went down on Kitty. I watched the little space between his belt buckle and the keyboard, too, how it swelled little by little as we watched. About half-way through, I placed my hand on it, and it throbbed an uneven pulse. When the credits rolled, he lifted my hand diplomatically as he rose.

"Mane. That's crazy," he sighed, "but I should go. Because I'm good. But I'm not that good."

A FEW NIGHTS LATER I got the text:

u up?

I stared at the number for a minute. Even though I hadn't saved it, I knew who it was.

yeah what's good

might stop by again if you hungry

word i could eat

Hell yeah. Some action. I went through my routine, opening the sliding door to the patio, trying to air the place out, lighting candles. Damn, Ranjith would kick my ass to the unemployment office if he knew all the shit I'd been doing in here. I set the candle on the kitchenette table, letting it light up the dark room while I took down my night twists and changed into a tighter tank top and a pair of cutoffs. When the soft knock came, I was ready.

Chad must like seafood, because this time, he had plates from Orlandeaux's. Stuffed shrimp and fries with the famous tartar sauce, which my mama loved. He must be trying, I thought to myself, even though I did everything but bust it open for him the other night. I thought it was sweet too. He had a backpack with him, which I assumed had clothes in it. I guess these days, when niggas show up for Netflix and chill, they come prepared.

We ate quietly, awkwardly, at the table. I wasn't sure if he wanted me to make the first move and grab it again, or if he had been uncomfortable last time because he thought I came on too aggressively. So I just ate my food and played it by ear. When we were almost done, he started talking.

"Whatever happened with the owner? He ever find out about that party?"

"Not that I know of. Couple folks made noise complaints about when people were leaving. That's about it, though. You get your deposit back?"

"I did."

"I guess DeVaughan aired out the room like he said, then."

"Yep."

"He still mad at me for what I did the other night? I haven't seen him on shift. I feel like he been avoiding me."

"Naw. That nigga on to some other drama as usual. Hustling. Tryna hit a lick."

I laughed. "Well, I hope he find what he's looking for."

"He keep fucking around, he gon find something. Might be another gun pointed in his face."

We both laughed; then he shifted gears. "You had me thinking last time I was over here," he said, finishing a shrimp and tossing the tail into the top half of the to-go box.

I was excited, but I tried to sound casual. "About what?"

"Your mama. Watching her in that flick brought a lot of shit back."

"Shit like what?"

Chad took a sip of his drink and set the cup down carefully. "Mane, when Mia passed I didn't really want nothing to do with, like, her memories. I wouldn't even go up to the casket. I don't go to her grave. Nothin like that."

"Oh, okay." I was wondering what that had to do with me.

"You know, she kinda had a little social media following. Little homemaking business, and she would put up recipes and videos online. Little something here and there about how to decorate for the holidays. Stuff like that."

"Oh. Word? That's cool." I was hella confused.

"Yeah, I ain't really pay that much attention to it when she was living, but the videos and stuff still up, and I— Well, hold on a sec. I got something." He wiped his hands on a napkin and reached behind him for his backpack, which was hanging on the back of his chair. He slipped a hand into it and pulled out—of all things—a laptop. He held it up with one hand, like a serving tray. "I wanted to see if you didn't want to watch one or two of em with me."

I nodded halfheartedly, but inside, I couldn't believe it. I was high the other night when I broke out that porn. But this nigga looked stone-cold sober. I took the laptop from him.

"Yeah, sure. Why not?"

KEMMIA'S CAJUN CRAFT CUTIE YOUTUBE channel was indeed still up and running, and people were still commenting on the success of her recipes and instructions for making things like yarnball snowmen and bedazzled house shoes. Sometimes, a cousin would post their condolences: gurl we miss u so much Chelsea gon be taken care of 4 life u aint never gotta worry bout that on god we got u we luv u. I was bored as fuck—I'd never learned how to be domestic because I'd never spent enough time with Nana. And Momi was a great cook, but I never showed interest in her teaching me, so neither did she. Chad put the videos on auto-play, and we watched tutorial after tutorial: a pastiche of hairstyles, lipstick colors, and weight loss and gain. In one, her hair was honey blond at the tips, and I realized why Chad had stopped Momi's video the night before. Kemmia looked a lot like Kitty when she wasn't pregnant.

The videos were out of order, so in some of them, she was big-bellied and moon-faced, perspiring as she cut patterns for swimsuit cover-ups. In others, she was slender and spindly armed, offering excited hot takes on celebrity drama or general news about her family. In a few, she was newly pregnant, barely showing, but already making blankets and complaining about how few online mommy-to-be groups were really "for us."

In one, however, she appeared on-camera in rare form, bare-faced and somber in a dimly lit room, talking about how hard it was to conceive: waiting for the right basal temperature, coordinating her schedule with Chad's, doing things to get him in the mood. "Big Mama told me anybody can have a baby, but you gotta conceive it in your mind first. And you gotta conceive with love," she said, leaning into the screen, its purple sheen making her lips look slightly blue, almost as if she were already dying right there on camera. In the middle of listing all the home remedies her aunts suggested, from sprinkling holy oil on the sheets to drinking buttermilk, her face crumpled, and she covered it quickly, trying to compose herself so she could keep talking.

"I'm sorry, y'all, but you know what? I told y'all I don't censor nuthin on here," she said between sobs. "I got everything I want. I got a good job and a good man. I got my family and I don't mean to be ungrateful for none of it, but all I really want is a baby." She knuckled the tears as they streamed down her face, her acrylic nails clacking against each other as she did. "And just one baby too," she said, laughing a little, her cheeks shining. "Just one baby, y'all. That's all."

That one was short; there were no how-to instructions—she just needed to let off some steam. There were thousands of likes and a ream of comments, which I wanted to read, but as soon as Kemmia waved goodbye and reached somewhere in front of her to stop the recording, Chad skipped to an ad and the next video. This one was, ironically, one she filmed while heavily pregnant. A recipe for gumbo. While discussing the pros and cons of filé powder, her belly rubbed the counter and chalked itself with a line of flour (since she was also making biscuits). As she worked, Chad sneaked up from behind and wrapped his arms around her waist. "Babe! I'm filming!" she whined playfully, then invited him to say hello to her subscribers.

"Hey, connivers," he said.

I stopped paying attention to the instructions and watched the two of them, then her, as she cooked. She glowed in a way I've heard pregnant women glow, though it felt like something else to me; she couldn't stop smiling, even when Chad lowered his baseball cap to the camera and disappeared from view. Her dimples and the diamond studs in her ears and on her top lip sparkled as she worked. Even though she was heavier, she seemed buoyant in a way that didn't exist in the older videos we'd watched. She was a woman who'd gotten her miracle, and she looked completely fulfilled. In that way, she looked a little like Momi.

It took awhile for me to realize Chad was crying, and once I did, I still didn't look at him right away. From the corner of my eye, I saw him reach up quickly to take off his hat, and then he cleared his throat once, twice. I shifted uncomfortably and discovered we were sitting super close together: for him, it was so we could both see the screen; for me, it was so I could touch him when the time was right.

Before Momi passed, other people's sorrow annoyed me, or it made me nervous because I'd been raised by a woman incapable of sorrow. I'd never been taught how to deal with it. When Momi passed, Nana's sorrow morphed my anxiety into anger and a lot of possessive shit even Momi would have called out because, as she always said about relationships, "Nobody owns you just because they claim they love you. Don't forget that." But this time, I didn't have a good reason to get angry, or even antsy. This time, I completely understood what the other person was feeling. I quietly moved my shoulder from where it was tucked slightly under Chad's so I could put my arm around him. It wasn't the way I had planned on touching him that night, but it felt like the exact thing I was supposed to do. And as soon as I did, he buried his face in my neck and wept like the child he hadn't seen in eleven months.

AFTER HE LEFT, I SPENT a long time awake in bed, thinking about Kemmia's face and how happy she looked. It felt wildly unfair for her to die only days after her biggest dream came true. But life is a crapshoot in which you're lucky to get, even briefly, something you want as badly as she wanted a baby—that is, if you ever figure out what your "something" is in the first place. I for one had been out there gambling with Momi's dice. But I'd done it because I thought it was the best way to keep loving her the same way I had when she was alive. I thought it would keep me from forgetting how it *felt* to be alive with her. If I did it any other way, I was afraid that love would die, and then after that, Momi's memory.

But I couldn't be her Ying Yang Twin like I used to believe. I never had been. The truth was, me and Momi were different as fuck. Both good. Both fly. But different. And the moment I realized that, my heart broke, because not being her meant she really was gone from this world.

For the first time since the night I'd picked up her ashes, I sobbed, just like Chad: loud sobs that ripped through my chest and shoulders like coughs. I lay flat on my back so I could breathe; then I put a pillow over my head and screamed into it. I didn't, however, try to suffocate myself, which, even as my chest whooped with grief, I knew meant that, somehow, someway, I'd be all right. If the pillow had been a mirror, I probably would have held it up and stared into it like I was looking at a stranger because, in a way, I was. I fell asleep that night as someone I knew nothing about, except that I didn't want that person to die.

you got time to ride with me a little?

It was one of the last mildly warm days of the season, and I was sitting on the balcony of my room, looking at apartment vacancies. The air outside was humid and smelled like dust and car exhaust, which is how I knew the season was changing, and with it the promise of something. I was ready for anything, just not more killing. Maybe more time with me turning corners in somebody's loud car: candy paint and rims glaring, then dimming in the fading sunlight, then coming alive again under fluorescent streetlamps. Speakers rattling against trunks, barely able to stomach all that bass. Taped-up daiquiris in the cup holders. I wondered if Chad was texting because he wanted something similar.

yeah, I could do that

A few minutes pass.

cool. I'll be over there round six

I stayed outside at the little table, looking for places until then. Mr. Meche probably wouldn't give me a good reference, but maybe Ranjith could. And I'd been a fool for losing all my furniture in the process. I'd need a couch at least. Coffee table. Hell, a bed frame. It was getting close to the time Ranjith switched out mattresses, so I could get one of those from here, but I didn't want to have to put that shit on the floor. For a moment, I felt a little overwhelmed, but then I decided I wasn't gonna beat myself up over anything I did after Momi passed. That was my grace period. Only the stuff I did from here on out counted.

It wasn't until we were halfway there that Chad told me where we were going. He wanted to see his little girl, and he didn't want to go alone. Chelsea lived with her maternal grandmother, Ms. DeeDee, over in Allendale. That let me know what kind of money Kemmia's family had. When you're rich, it's lakeside, better known as Long Lake, with big-ass houses and gates and security guards. When you're making it do what it do with the white man's dollar, it's the other Lakeside, sometimes known as Allendale, with dopehouses and twelve and the police tape. Well, it wasn't like that everywhere. In fact, most hoods in this city are catchalls for the folks who can't afford the gates. And the quality of the houses on your street depended on how you and your neighbors chose to spend money. When we pulled up, it was clear Ms. DeeDee spent at least part of hers on her lawn. It was a neat green square whose borders were exploding with flowers. All of them looked intentional, and some of them were your standards, like pink rosebushes, but there were also those orange and yellow flowers I used to see everywhere as a kid without ever knowing the name until recently, when I was high one day and Googled them. They were edible canna. Imagine—I could have been eating flowers every day of my life.

"So, Ms. DeeDee know we ain't…you know." Chad motioned his hand between us as he turned off the car. "But she might ask you anyway, cause she always been kinda nosy."

Ms. DeeDee was already at the screen door when we walked up the narrow, crowded sidewalk, blades of feathergrass slicing our calves and making mine itch.

"Well, look who it is," she said without joy or malice as she held open the screen door for us. Chad didn't really respond; he just hugged her and handed her an envelope. She didn't even bother to look inside, just slipped it under one of the twelve Precious Moments statues that adorned a little side table tucked between a massive couch and a slightly less massive love seat.

"I'm shole happy to get this in person," she said, before turning back toward us. Chad tried to introduce me, but she cut him off right after he said "friend."

"I know who you are," she said. "How's your family doing?"

What did I know to say, other than, "Fine, ma'am. Thank you for asking"? She nodded and started walking us through the kitchen, where she pointed out that she was cooking, and through the den, where an old man slouched in a recliner, watching television. "That right there is *my* friend, Mr. Rudolph." He nodded at us as we passed by. Ms. DeeDee was wearing a wedding ring, but after that introduction, it was clear it wasn't from him. All along the wood-paneled walls, Kemmia smiled at us from different ages. She must have been an only child, I thought, like me and Momi.

The backyard was a little less well kept, with patches of dirt exposed and a doghouse in disrepair way in the back along the fence Ms. DeeDee shared with the house on the back street. A few kids of various ages were out there playing; one who looked to be about twelve held a toddler on her hip while she bossed around the other children, some of whom were already headed toward the back fence so that they could jump it and run off toward home. At first, I thought the toddler was Chelsea, but Ms. DeeDee said to the older girl, "Tammielle, put that baby down so she can walk." Then she called to a spindly little girl dashing toward the fence, "Chelsea! Chelsea Chardaé! Look who here."

Chelsea turned and ran just as quickly toward us, but stopped a few feet away and stared timidly. She put her hands behind her back, and of course she was Mia's daughter. She was the same buttered brown as her and Ms. DeeDee, with the same waify frame.

"Agnes, why don't you come back in the kitchen with me so Chad can spend time with his little girl?" Ms. DeeDee was already holding open the door, so it really wasn't a question so much as a stage direction.

"Okay," I said, but when I passed her, I whispered, "My name is Maple."

She patted me on the shoulder. "Child, who was I thinking about? I'm sorry."

Once we got into the kitchen, she explained, "Chad don't come over here often, and I didn't want us breathing down his neck and making him feel like he had to hurry. So me and you gon have a nice little visit, and he can stay out there as long as he wants."

"Yes, ma'am," I said. I hadn't addressed anybody her age in a while.

Ms. DeeDee pointed to a cake stand on the table. "It's pound cake in there if you want it."

I could already smell the salted butter crust from where I sat, and I realized I was hungry, but I wanted to act like I was raised a little better. "Okay, thank you. Maybe in a little bit. You need some help?"

Ms. DeeDee cut her eyes at me over her shoulder as she washed chicken in the sink. "I been doing this long enough not to need no help."

"Yes, ma'am."

She turned back to clean a leg quarter under the stream of water, her black-spotted elbows moving back and forth and her hair shaking a little as she did so. I think Nana had the same wig. Strawberry blond and flipped at the bottom. She used to call it her Whitney Houston.

"Yeah, you don't look like one who eat too many sweets," said Ms. DeeDee.

I laughed, thinking about the tin back in the room. "I do sometimes."

"Lord, when Mia died"—she paused as she threw a piece of chicken into a colander—"I couldn't eat nothing, especially not nothing sweet. Couldn't keep food down and didn't really like the taste of it." The man in the next room flipped the channel to what looked like a basketball game. I could hear Chelsea outside, her voice rising with insistence—"Yes, I did!"—as some other child refuted, and Chad's deep bass refereed.

"Me too," I said to Ms. DeeDee. "I'm like that too."

"I guess losing somebody'll do that to you. And for a while, I didn't even care. I figured if I starved to death, I'd be better off. You hear about that man who had a heart attack two days after the cops shot his daughter?"

"No, ma'am."

"You ain't got to say *ma'am* every time. I'm not that old." She picked up another piece of chicken to wash. "But yeah, when it happened I thought, 'Man, why don't God just take me too?' I woulda loved to go like that. But then they brought Chelsea over here and she look so much like Mia. So much like her. And at first, it was almost like I had her back again, but, you know, they is two different people. Kemmia? You looked at her wrong and she would cry. That one out there?" She pointed at the patio door for emphasis. "She got a strong will, like me. And smart too. I say, 'Chelsea, time to hit that bed,' and she go hit it with her hand and come right back out the room."

I laughed. "She does sound smart."

"Yep, she say she wanna be a lawyer. Something like that. And you know, over time, I had to realize she was her own person. She won't never be Mia. Nobody will. Know what I mean?"

She paused and looked over at me this time, for emphasis. I got fidgety, and I was gonna tell her I wasn't trying to be the replacement girlfriend, but she was a sly one. She only asked to see how I would react, then slipped into a different conversation altogether.

"I know what you might like instead of that cake, cause they a little lighter. Why don't you look in that basket on the table and get you some pralines? They wrapped up in saran wrap in the bottom there." And since she insisted, I dug around salad dressing packets, desiccated onion skin, and loose pecans until I found one. I unwrapped it carefully, taking a small bite. It melted immediately, and I took another. Damn, they were good, but I tried to slow myself down. Nana would have been mortified if I hadn't.

"Yeah, those are good," she said, reading my mind. "I *been* making them, but I found this Down South recipe that called for a little PET Milk, and I outdid myself on this last batch. I keep em hidden in that basket, though, cause otherwise, Chelsea will eat every last one." She looked out the patio door again, and I couldn't see what she saw, but I guess it satisfied her, because she kept talking.

"That's good he came by to see her. You can't run from your

pain like that. God'll make you relive it if you don't live it the first time."

"Does she ask about him? When she doesn't see him?"

"Yeah, sometimes she will. But she into her friends now and school and this little dance team she joined. Sooner or later, he not gon matter. That's what I'm worried about. And she'll start looking for him in every Tom, Dick, and Harry she can find."

I nodded. Not having a daddy meant I'd heard that before, and I didn't believe it as much as I understood how it could be logical.

"But I don't want her to forget Mia neither. I try to take her out to Greenwood every now and then to the graveside, put a bouquet of flowers on it. And I tell her stories. But she bounce around so much, sooner or later, she gon wanna stop hearing all that too." Ms. DeeDee was prepping the chicken to fry now, shaking bottles of onion and garlic powder into a bag of flour before throwing them in. "Where's your mama buried? Y'all Moffetts, right? Y'all come out of Mansfield?"

"Keithville. But she was cremated."

"Oh, you scattered the ashes?"

"No, not yet."

"Oh, okay." She opened the cabinet to look for more seasoning. "Where are they?"

"I have them."

"You keep em with you? Ain't you staying at a hotel somewhere? That's what Chad said."

"Yes, ma'am. I am."

"So they not with your grandmama?"

"No, ma'am. I keep them with me," I said again, this time with a little less pride.

She paused before transferring the chicken to a plate to rest. "Child, I don't know if I could do that. Have her *around* me. But I did keep a wreath and some of her jewelry. Look." She walked over to me, holding her gunky hands away from us to show me the necklace she was wearing. A slender class ring set with a garland stone hung from it. "So, I guess it's the same thing, keeping a part of them around. So long as you let go of *them*, you know. And how they died too quick, before you felt like you was through loving them."

"Yes, ma'am."

"That was the hardest part. I didn't think I was gonna wake up from no nightmare or nothing like that. Nothing like what they tell you on TV. My thing was, I couldn't let go of what happened to *me*. I would see pregnant women and get mad. Like God coulda took one of them instead, you know? Or," she said, lowering her voice, "I would look at Chelsea and think about how I got left with a grandbaby I hadn't even asked for. Not that soon anyway; I thought Mia needed to finish school. So I would wonder if Chelsea was worth it. And God don't like that kinda ugly."

I nodded. I recognized the feeling.

"So I had to learn how to raise her cause I thought she was worth it, not for Mia or to try to help that boy out there or to try to relive the past—nothing like that. I had to start doing it for Chelsea. No other reason."

"Do you still want to?"

"Not always. I have my days. But most days I'm glad she's here with me."

I dug around in the basket for another praline. "Does having her here make it easier?"

"Nope." She was back at the stove now, and she laughed a little as she settled the chicken into the grease. Her wig trembled as she shook her head. "Having Chelsea here makes having Chelsea here. It's its own thing. It don't make nothing easier. Cause, you know, Mia was a lot growing up. She got sick a lot. When she was little, it was asthma, and she loved running around, so it was bronchitis, bronchitis, bronchitis. Pneumonia a couple of times too. Then, when she got older, it was bad cramps. Then, soon as I got her on birth control, she started running round with some of these little dope boys out here in the neighborhood, and I damn near lost my mind trying to keep her out of trouble. I just knew she was gon end up either dead or in jail. Then she met Chad. And I figured she was safe. Whatever he did, he never brought it around us. So I let up worrying a little. Worst-case scenario: something might happen to him and she would have been devastated, but he wasn't mine to worry about. But then *she* died. And I didn't know what to do with myself." She wiped her hands on a towel. "And then when Chelsea came here, I figured I'd just do with her like I did with Mia, but that's not how it worked out. Chels is Chels, honey. She a handmade original. She don't worry me in the same ways. She don't get into the same kind of trouble. So I had to figure out how to be somebody else besides Kemmia's mama. Cause Kemmia gone. If that's all I was gon be, I couldn't be no good to nobody. I can *be* her mama. I'll always be her mama. But I can't mama a ghost. That's the difference."

"Wait, what's the difference?"

She looked at me, like she was reading my face, and when she got to the last sentence on it, she said, "The difference is whatever Chelsea need, and whatever I wanna give her." She thought for a minute. "But it might be different for you, as a daughter, figuring out what that difference is. Especially if you ain't got no siblings. Or if you ain't got kids, somebody to keep you busy. But even they can't distract you for long. One way or another, you got to heal. But I can't tell you what that's gon be like for *you*, though, know what I mean? And if I did tell you, and it turned out different, you might think something is wrong with you when it's not. So you gotta figure it out for yourself."

I wasn't sure she would give me a straight answer, but I took my chance. "So...will I ever be happy, even if it is just me?"

"If you've ever been happy before, I reckon you can be again. If you've never been happy, right now is a good time to start trying. And the faster you can do that, the better. Not the being—that's a process. But the trying. Cause *real* happiness is like trouble: you look for it long enough, it'll find you. Even if you started out looking in the wrong places." And she laughed a little at that.

"What makes you happy right now, Ms. DeeDee?"

She started shaking her head before I could even finish the question. "Uh-uh. I'll tell you mine as soon as you can tell me yours. Next time you come back, maybe we can ask each other." She looked over at Mr. Rudolph for a long time, but she didn't say anything to him. And I took another bite of my praline and didn't say much after. Ms. DeeDee had my number, area code and all.

CHAD HADN'T SAID MUCH EITHER when he came back into Ms. DeeDee's house, and he barely said two words to me during the drive back to the hotel, but he followed me back to the room, sitting down and looking around at the objects in it like he was seeing them for the first time. His gaze settled on the newspaper I'd thrown onto the coffee table while passing through from the patio. He reached for it.

"Weren't you reading this when I came to pick you up?"

"Yeah. I been looking for a new place."

"Ole boy tryna put you out?"

"Not yet, but I don't want to give him the opportunity. Plus, I'm tired of being on call all the damn time."

"That's what's up." He flipped through the pages without reading them. "Sound like you moving on." And he said it with such finality that I wondered if he meant I'd be leaving him too.

"I'll be around," I said cheerfully. "I ain't going nowhere too fast." When Ms. DeeDee said goodbye to us, she hugged Chad first and then me, holding me tightly for a few seconds—just a beat longer than normal—so I knew she meant it. I could feel the wet spot from the chicken on the front of her apron as she pressed.

"Don't be a stranger, Miss Maple," she said. Then to Chad: "And you already know how I feel about you."

"Okay, goodbye, Ms. DeeDee," I intoned as we turned to the driveway, and she turned to go back inside.

"Nope. We don't say goodbye around here. We say 'see you later.'"

"Yes, ma'am; see you later." And I'd meant it.

I didn't want Chad to think any different, so I moved to sit next to him on the couch and took the paper from him. "First I gotta figure out what to do about my credit. I walked out on my last place when Momi died. I don't know who's gonna want to lease to me now."

Chad nodded. "I bet you can still find something, though."

And we sat quietly like that for a while. I wasn't sure what was supposed to happen at this point. Maybe he'd ask if I wanted something to eat. Maybe he finally wanted to fuck. I couldn't tell.

He cleared his throat. "Thank you for going with me to see Ms. DeeDee. I really appreciate that."

"No problem." I picked at something on one of the couch cushions, trying to act like his gratitude wasn't a big deal.

He sighed. "That shit hard, though. Seeing her face. She look just like Mia. And that shit? That shit crazy. I know she mine, but she look like Mia spat her out. But it was…it was good to see her. Gave me something to look forward to." He laughed, but then his face changed. He started rubbing his knee. "You know you the ringer, right?"

"What's that?"

"The one on the team who come in and change the game for real."

"Okay. I don't mind being that." I nodded with satisfaction. "A little while ago, I would have wanted you to say I was fine." I laughed.

"I could say that too," he said, laughing with me. "You want me to say it now?"

"Let's let it happen spontaneously."

"Bet."

We smiled at each other; then Chad leaned back on the couch and rubbed his knee again. "But yeah. Like…that's why I asked you to go with me. Maybe my mama woulda went, but she and Ms. DeeDee ain't cool like that, so she mighta caused more problems than anything. And my mama ain't seen Chelsea in bout two years, but she keep sayin that's cause I won't bring her over there." He stopped and cupped his mouth for a minute, letting his hand slip down into his beard so he could scratch it before he continued. "But if it's been two years, maybe it's not even that important to her. But you? You watched videos with me when you ain't even know me. You chilled wit me. You saw my pain. My mama really ain't about that life. Just about running the streets with Ms. P and them. Fighting to stay young. Fighting not to change."

"That's another way of grieving, too, though, I'm learning," I said softly, because I didn't want it to seem like I didn't understand his frustration. But I followed up quickly with, "Do you think Ms. DeeDee will let you take her to see your mom instead?"

"Maybe. I gotta work up to that."

"Is that what you're trying to do now?"

"Well, for me, yeah. Cause I can't let her grow up not knowing who *I* am. She gotta know me first, cuz."

"Yeah, she does," I said. Then reluctantly, "And her other grandma too."

"And you know…I know you right about that. I know it."

Then more silence. I wondered if Chad felt about his mama the way I was starting to feel about mine. I loved Momi for all the things she shielded me from. She never gave me direction because she wanted me to find mine. She told me shit straight with no chaser because she never wanted me to live like Nana, inventing one lie about myself after another, and believing them. She wanted me to be free, but her free was the only one she knew. It was the only free I'd ever known too. I'd never really tried to see if there was a different kind.

After a few minutes, I said, "I want to start over. I haven't done that since Momi died. I never made a plan for living without her."

Chad drummed his knee with his fingers. "Me neither. And I feel you. But that's a hard thing to do."

"Hell yeah it is."

"Cain't always be like that, though." Chad was looking me in the eyes, just like he had the night of the party. But this time he was the one who looked terrified.

I leaned back for a minute and tried to think of what I would want someone to tell me if I was that scared. Then suddenly, I remembered.

"You know what Momi used to say to me?"

He shook his head.

"If you ever get stuck, talk to God about it. And while you talking, you'll figure out what you want. But you gotta come correct. She would say, 'Talk to Him like you talk to me, just without all the cussing.'"

Chad laughed. "That's wild."

"Yeah. She was always like, people say God hate hoes. But He can't, cause hoes know how to come to you without all the bull-shit. They'll remind you of what it is before you do. She said

God appreciates that. When you just come real. That's how answers come to you."

Chad looked up at the ceiling. "Damn. That's deep."

"Yeah."

He opened his mouth to say something, then closed it and stood up. He hitched up his pants and looked down at me.

"You wanna try now?"

"Try what?"

"Talking to God about it. You wanna do that now?"

This dude gotta be king of the plot twist. I paused.

"Uh. I mean, I guess?" I felt myself getting agitated, but I took a deep breath. "I don't really pray like that. I mean, in front of people."

"I thought we was just supposed to talk."

"Well, she did say that." I laughed, relaxing a little. "Wait, who going first?"

Chad looked at me like I should already know the answer, so I sat up and offered my hands. He knelt in front of me obediently and grasped them. I tried to think of what I would want said over me if I ever had the chance to ask. Then I just started saying stuff for the both of us, and thinking of Nana, and that I should probably try to call her. I didn't know if I was ready to apologize, but that was okay, because I come from women who don't do that anyway. They just call and announce they want to check on you because it's been awhile, and nobody talks about who made "awhile" happen. Maybe, as a peace offering, I could give her her half of the ashes.

Behind Chad's bowed head, the photo of me and Momi I stole from Nana's house sat on the coffee table, and the fading sunlight coming through the open blinds made a slicing pattern on the glass. One long, white beam cut the image in half, right past Momi's folded legs. I was on one side of it; she was on the other.

I had gone quiet by then, and Chad leaned forward, resting his head on my lap, his breath warming my thighs. My hands were on his head, and the fresh-cut hairs pricked my fingers like brush bristles. His hair smelled soothing and familiar. Blue Magic. The dark skin on the backs of his ears gleamed with it, and I wondered what it would feel like to grab them and pull his face up to mine. Or into my crotch. I laughed. His head snapped up.

"My bad." I waved it off. "I just remembered something my mama told me right before she died."

"What she say?"

"Aw, it was an inside joke. I'll tell you one day, though." And I leaned down to touch the back of his head with my nose. We stayed like that for a long time, as the day sealed shut around us: him breathing on my lap, and my breath cascading down the crown of his head and mingling with his. And it was good. So good, I thought to myself, *This* might be *its own kind of water*.

MIND THE PROMPT

I.

    ———

Agnes Cherie Kirkkendoll always panicked a little when she wrote her name in perfect capital letters in blocks at the top of a Scantron. That extra *k* always threatened to keep it from fitting in, the same way it had two decades before at her high school in Louisiana, the first place where someone made a connection between her name and her skin.

"You white as a sheet. You *must* be the KKK," said Dennis Drummond on the fourth day of classes during their freshman year. Dennis did double duty as both the class clown and the boy other students were most afraid of. He wore blue Dickies suits to school every Friday, and the pants would be creased within a millimeter of cutting his forearms when he bent down to tie his shoes. Agnes had heard whispers he was in the Rollin' 60s.

For Dennis, it was a one-off act of cruelty, but it didn't matter; the moniker's wildfire appeal killed any of Agnes's hopes for popularity or, at the least, blending in. By the end of the second week, everyone knew her as KKK, including the seniors, most of whom were friends with Agnes's sister, a cinnamon-colored spitfire named Berniece. Agnes wasn't sure if Berniece ever used the name herself, but she'd watched her learn about it firsthand. One morning, as students

milled about, waiting for the bell, Agnes happened to be walking a
few feet behind Berniece and her two best friends as they chided the
older girl about her unfortunate kinfolk. When they explained what
the rest of the school called Agnes, Berniece laughed so hard she
tripped over her iridescent platform sneakers and had to collapse on
one of the stone benches near the courtyard to catch her breath—
a dangerous spot, since the white boys played hackey sack there
in the mornings and were indiscriminate about where they kicked
the footbags. Agnes shuffled past Berniece and company without
a word, slipping into the A-Wing bathroom to force a pee and
kill time by voraciously reading graffiti on paint-blistered walls that
were textured (as Agnes noted with resigned satisfaction) just like
Berniece's pimple-pocked face.

From that day forward, the two sisters passed each other in the
school's hallways like perfect strangers who just happened to have the
same bulbous nose and last name. And even those shared traits were
only true for a while. At the beginning of her junior year, Berniece
began dropping the infamous third *k* from all her signatures. It got
so bad that, just before she graduated, the office had to ask their
mother to double-check her birth certificate, since her diploma had
to match it perfectly in order to be legitimate.

The school secretary and the girls' mother chalked it up to an
adolescent ploy for individuality. Agnes presumed it was Berniece's
attempt to disassociate herself from her outcast of a sibling. But
the truth was that such splits had been part of their bloodline
before either girl was born. Family lore was that the Kirkendolls,
a large brood with branches throughout the Ark-La-Tex, split after
Theodore Roosevelt Kirkendoll committed the fatal robbery of a
father-and-son-owned tackle shop in De Berry, Texas. The crime
happened so long ago, even Agnes's paternal great-grandmother after
whom she was named couldn't remember the exact year. But some

of the family had been so aghast they added the extra *k* to distance themselves from the convicted. By the time Agnes's father was born, the split was complete, and he grew up on the "respectable" side, among Negroes who built such a strong rapport with whites, most Black folks wouldn't fool with them. Though some three-*k* Kirkkendolls thought he'd fallen off by marrying a dairy farmhand's daughter from Greenwood, Agnes's father would redeem himself soon after Agnes started high school, and he would do so by leaving his almost-raised family for Sabine, a saddity Creole woman from Down South, somewhere near Lacombe, and damn near white. Agnes longed to point out the irony of Berniece's folly—regressing back to the "bad" side of the family in an attempt to save face— but she comforted herself with the (incorrect) presumption that Berniece was too stupid to understand what *irony* meant.

And soon, it no longer mattered how Berniece spelled the name because, two weeks after graduation, she completely abandoned it and eloped with Keswick Anderson, the tall, fair-skinned son of a local orthodontist who had frighteningly white teeth and drove his father's old ragtop Mercedes. And after PT school, rhinoplasty, and a second marriage, she changed her name again, and Berniece LaVergne Draper (née Anderson) disappeared into the Jack and Jill balls and sorority brunches of the life she'd always wanted, posting photos of the holiday cotillions she organized with Sabine and the rest of Sabine's high-yellow friends. In a rare show of open irritation, Agnes's mother once told a second cousin that Berniece looked like a penny in a bag full of washers. Agnes, who was in earshot but was supposed to be listening to a French lesson, was shocked; her mother never commented on either of her daughters' skin tones. But Berniece had captioned the Facebook post: a wonderful evening serving our young ladies of the community with Mama Bine. Agnes understood her mother's indignation.

Agnes was thinking of all this twenty years later because she was sitting in an ice-cold room with a blanket wrapped around her legs, grading high school students' nearly illegible handwritten essays for a few bucks an hour for the next seven days. Unlike some of the graders around her, Agnes thought bitterly, she had advanced degrees and had gone to good schools. But the result was the same, if not worse. She was so broke she could barely afford the refundable deposit for her room, the requirement of which left her with $18.16 of available funds in her bank account. Everyone who'd heard the KKK story—from her mother to her algebra teacher Mrs. Woczniak—had told her she would one day employ people like Dennis. They'd promised that the ones who made fun of her then would one day need her generosity and eat off her bounty. In short, they'd bamboozled her, and probably intentionally. There's no telling what she might have done to herself as a teenager, had she known this would be her fate now.

Agnes arrived in Utah with the long-shot hope of having a hotel room all to herself, and getting her wish would be the first thing that had gone right for her in a long time. Agnes could not afford to relinquish a portion of her honorarium for a single, so she'd been randomly placed with someone she didn't know. But as soon as night fell with no sign of her roommate, Agnes began envisioning coming back to the spacious double and spending her free hours—that is, after doing some freelance editing—alternating between figuring out what she would do if she didn't get the executive director's job in Boston and quieting her thoughts. While other graders planned to go hiking or dining or to see some important cathedral, Agnes planned to sort out her brain in hopes that, by doing so, she could sort out her life. Lately, her thoughts had begun to swell with the clanging of what had been, up to that point, only white noise: the noise of her mother's laconic bewilderment at Agnes's bleak career prospects;

the noise of her father's nonchalant distraction with his replacement wife; Berniece's equally distracted preoccupation with buying things with her new money; and the noise of Agnes's newsfeeds on social media sites, which were clogged with posts of old high school classmates, their balding husbands, and their fat-legged children, who toddled around cluttered living rooms when Agnes had yet to even buy a house, let alone find someone willing to live with her in it.

On the night of her arrival, Agnes placed her suitcase on one end of the unclaimed bed, and on the other end she laid out her clothes for the first day of Reading Week. She wanted to look nice, but fun. She wanted to look casual, but not desperate to make money. She wanted to appear as if this were a thing she was doing to pass the time, get more certifications, or squirrel away cash for a down payment on a condo or a vacation with chic, single friends. She held up a long-sleeved cropped sweatshirt for consideration. It was a castoff Berniece had ordered for herself from one of those clothing lines endorsed by a hip-hop artist. As Agnes considered the kind of statement it might make to the rest of her table, she did a few elocution exercises. She tried hard to speak with perfect diction most of the time, though her accent often tripped her up, and she would stumble over some words and have to repeat them. She hated when that happened, so she started running through the exercises every time she met someone new. They seemed to train her tongue, which was prone to deeply flattening all of her vowels into a kind of Southern dialect she thought sounded uncouth.

It was the least she could do, she told herself, given that she had so few of her other tried-and-true disguises. And though Agnes refused to admit it, she learned some of that from Berniece, who worshipped their father and stepmother and picked up most of her own self-hatred from them. One summer after the two girls spent a week with the newlyweds in Biloxi, Berniece came home and doused her hair with lemon juice, determined to get the same streaks that ribboned Sabine's wavy tresses with more and more gold each afternoon the three of them spent lounging on the beach. A day later, Berniece marched into Agnes's room.

"Does it look okay? Normal?" she asked timidly, bending down so Agnes could fully see. Agnes didn't know if she was too shocked to reply because Berniece was speaking to her for the first time in weeks, or because Berniece's dark hair was splattered with bright orange patches that looked like bleach stains on black clothing. But before Agnes could stutter out a bewildered response, Berniece rolled her eyes and walked out, sucking her teeth.

"Ugh. Look who I had the nerve to ask."

Similarly, Agnes was no stranger to pitiful attempts at remaking herself into what she considered a more palatable public persona. She was now too broke for the spray tans and heavy wigs she once wore in various shades of auburn, but every morning, she slathered on drugstore bronzer with religious zeal, and when she had time, flat-ironed her strawberry-blond hair within an inch of its downy life, so determined was she to capture what Sabine had achieved by virtue of genetics and leveraged into snagging somebody else's husband: a kind of startling racial ambiguity that made everyone want.

Of course, Agnes failed at it, even before she was broke. Men— and everyone else for that matter—saw through her disguise: the white seam of skin at her temples; the sometimes unevennesss of her orange color; the way her eyes moved. And the questions they posed, first about her race and, when she told them, her condition, triggered a silent mortification that surged through her body like a riptide, shifting the center of gravity in every room. Some people were luridly intrigued. Others were slightly insulted at the ruse. And just about everyone was uncomfortable in ways they had no language to name. So was Agnes, who drowned her discomfort in schoolwork and serial love affairs that all ended the same way and left her reeling with loneliness, which she combated by applying to another graduate program. She read books and wrote unpublishable papers until her eyes were perpetually half closed with exhaustion, and she was pleased because, although she was now much better at looking at herself in the mirror than she was that distant day in Caddo Parish Magnet High's dirtiest bathroom, she could never do so without hearing Berniece's sardonic laughter.

EVERY MORNING AT THE TESTING site, despair be damned, Agnes had a routine and she stuck to it as best she could. She awoke at 5:15 a.m., which gave her just enough time to say a quick prayer, read a daily devotional with its one or two Bible verses, and write exactly three pages in her journal, which promptly ended at 6:00, at which time she showered again for five minutes. Next, she put on her makeup and hastily dressed herself so she could head off to breakfast early. At the convention center, she'd fill two paper cups with hot water, select one packet of oats and one decaffeinated tea bag (usually lemon and ginger), and sit outside at one of the covered tables. While stirring in a few spoonfuls of oats and eating distractedly as she watched readers file into the center, loudly slapping plastic trays against tabletops and yawning even more loudly in the faces of their roommates and friends, Agnes tried to figure out how to pull off the week while convincing the world she had more than $18.16 in her bank account.

It was early summer in the mountains, and the mornings were still stiffly cool, so only a few other brave souls ventured out to the patio where Agnes chewed her oats and stared over the hedges onto the sidewalk and beyond that, at the snow-sharpened peaks of the Rockies. The Reading Room was, after all, an icebox, and the cafeteria air, humidified by steam tables of powdered eggs and limp bacon, was a much more logical option. For that reason, Agnes was, for the most part, outside alone.

The term *Reading Room* was actually a misnomer. Like every other subject's space in the convention center, it was, in fact, a series of large rooms whose partitions had been retracted to create more space and where curtains had been erected to separate each question's graders from each other, and the graders themselves from the graded exams, which were boxed and stacked and stayed in the room until the last day. The heavy doors of the room were locked from 5:45 each evening until 7:45 the next morning, and private security guards patrolled the convention center around the clock, even though the main doors were also locked later in the evening, after roundtable discussions, readings, and the annual keynote address. Years before, a rumor circulated that the guards were added after a disgruntled reader threatened to blow up one of the rooms. Agnes hadn't paid much attention to any of it before this year, and the truth was that she only noticed it now because, after their shifts, the guards often helped themselves to meals alongside the readers, their walkie-talkies sputtering at their hips as they squirted black coffee into cups and held grim-faced conversations with the administrative staff. After her first day out on the patio, one of the guards started taking his break-fast outside, making a series of figure eights as he paced between the tables, still on some kind of duty, even as he pawed sticky Danishes with one hand and flimsy paper cups with the other. On the first day, he said nothing to Agnes, but on the second day, he stopped at her table, gesturing with a pastry that looked to be oozing jelly.

"You ready to go to work, Teach?"

Agnes's mind snapped to attention, and she readjusted her gaze and smiled politely. She'd learned to look people in the eye since her days at Magnet High, but she would often look down quickly, which she did then, into her spackly oatmeal.

"I guess so."

"You *guess* so? You teach high school, right? You do stuff like this all the time. You can't be nervous. Are you?"

"No, I don't teach high school. I used to teach college, though. But not anymore."

"Wait—you're a professor?"

"Well, no. I was a lecturer. Not a professor. But I don't do that anymore. I work for professors, though."

The security guard looked as if he wanted to ask the difference, but he didn't. Like other men Agnes knew, he opted for the tangent that would make him appear the most knowledgeable.

"Yeah, so you're feeling a little rusty. But you'll get back into the swing of things real soon. That's how it usually happens around here. Where ya from?"

"I live in Tennessee."

"You been there your whole life? Where were you born?"

Agnes got this question a lot, and she didn't want to answer "Louisiana," because people often associated her pale skin and coarse red hair with being Creole, and having to explain that untruth often meant having to explain herself. But this man seemed too self-confident to ask genuine questions about things he didn't understand. He was not timidly apologetic for his presence either, unlike other security guards she'd encountered around the center. His large arms strained the sleeves of his gray uniform shirt, which was itself unbuttoned at the top, far enough that she could see his white wife beater beneath, and a few strands of dark hair curled over the top of it. The sight made her feel imposed upon. Still, she took her chances.

"I grew up in Louisiana."

He grinned. "Yeah. New Orleans. I knew you were something like that. I never seen someone who looks like you."

"Oh," Agnes replied, dragging her spoon through her oatmeal while pretending to be in deep thought. "You must be from here."

"Yep. My whole life. But my family moved here from Texas. Before I was born." He squared his shoulders a little and smiled as if he were posing for a photograph. "My name is Edwin. But everybody calls me Prime, like Prime Time."

He was muscular, though not very tall, and his reaching over the large table to shake her hand made him resemble a small child who had seen something he wanted to touch. In closer proximity, Agnes could see the name "Primus" on a badge just above one of his shirt pockets. Prime had a sparse goatee sprouting from his chin that gave him an elvish look with his otherwise clean face and low fade. Agnes thought of a term she'd heard years ago, back when she loved watching trashy reality shows on MTV: *juicehead*. That's what this man made her think of. Not Italian, but Black, and a juicehead nonetheless. She almost gave him a completely false name, but then remembered her own badge, the paper name tag printed with her subject area at the bottom, dangling from the lanyard around her neck.

"I'm Agnes. But you can call me Cherie. It's my middle name." Agnes looked down quickly at the tag, which conveniently featured her middle initial.

"Ohhhhh, Cherie. That's so pretty."

"Thank you." She smiled coquettishly. "It's French."

DAYS INSIDE THE READING ROOM were structured with an alacrity Agnes couldn't achieve anywhere else in her life. From the moment a small bell rang at 8:00 a.m. until it rang again at 5:00, she rose and sat, donned earphones, or laughed in response to various stimuli: the question leader's jokes, the bells that signaled meals and breaks, her own biological needs. In the mornings, the question leader would tell a bland joke or offer a pun about *Silas Marner*, then someone pre-chosen for the task would reread the question's prompt, after which readers were reminded of its importance and offered tips for endurance before resuming their reading. Then it was silence and hushed tones until the next break, which was perfectly fine with Agnes, since by Day Two she either indifferently tolerated or openly disliked most of the people at her table. She overheard them chatting during meals and breaks, and unlike her, everyone seemed to be there on missions that involved the most trivial of financial crises. One woman wanted to decorate an outdated nursery for a coming baby. Another was raising money to move closer to a boyfriend. Everyone seemed optimistic and casually happy, sentiments Agnes hadn't felt in years and loathed having to witness in close proximity for eight hours a day. Nine hours if she sat with people at lunch.

But she reserved her most seething but silent hatred for one person, Cathy, who made a point to excitedly greet each of the table members as they arrived on the first day. Cathy wore a T-shirt emblazoned with some blanket slogan designed to endear her to progressive folks while infuriating others—something banal like "DemSocialists are Lit," with the Statue of Liberty pushing the lettering to each side, and her torch splitting the *Socialists* and *Lit* in a way that made Agnes's frenetically analytical mind seize. She hated when designers did such things; the torch could indeed be an *i*, but it also looked like a *t*, and that didn't make any sense at all. The choice of shirt was reason enough to despise the woman.

Agnes had avoided Cathy's introduction on Day One by excusing herself to the bathroom before the bell rang, but both women had come to the table early on Day Two.

"Hi again! I'm Cathy. So you teach at Vanderbilt?"

Agnes taught her last course at the university that winter, when her lecturer's contract expired and wasn't renewed. Since then, she had been working as a "logistics coordinator" for the department; a position that meant, besides little else, that she was a research assistant with considerable leeway to take off to parts unknown during the summer months—if she could afford it. And she couldn't; that's why she was in Utah. But the grading invitation required a current teaching appointment. Agnes could lie on paper, but she didn't want to do so outright, so she nodded once, trying to make the gesture look as affirmative as possible.

"What a wonderful university," cooed Cathy. "My son follows their baseball team religiously. He's a shortstop. Their recruiter comes to his high school every year because his team is the best in the region. It's his senior year, so our fingers are crossed, but…who knows?"

Agnes smiled, waiting for her to make a point, but Cathy shifted subjects.

"I teach at McClarenden A&M, a small HBCU—the fourth oldest in the Carolinas! It's pretty thankless work, but I love it. The students are so eager to learn, even if they're not really cut out for university life." She sighed. "But those are the ones that end up at HBCUs. We're the only places that'll take them in some cases! And I do my best to help however I can, but it's so sad that, in some ways, they'll never catch up because the schools they're coming from are just terrible. You'll understand once you start reading these essays. Sometimes, the language alone will tell you who is who. And at McClarenden, like I said, I try to catch them up, but some of my colleagues…" She held up a hand and rolled her eyes. "They mean well—I won't deny that—but when you come from the same communities with the same resources? Well, that's why *I'm* there." She smiled, and her lips stretched to an uneven pink thinness, the smoker's lines around them momentarily disappearing.

"Okay," Agnes replied noncommittally.

"So I've got my hands full; plus I'm finishing up my graduate work at Liberty, in the online program. I was ABD back in the Stone Age, but then I had kids and I'm just now getting back to it. Are you adjuncting at Vanderbilt? No, wait—if you're doing this you're probably still just a GA, right?" She kept saying the name of Agnes's university with such a deferential air that Agnes had to retaliate somehow.

"No. I got my PhD back in 2013. So, I'm Dr. Kirkkendoll—to the uninitiated." Agnes smiled again, this time a bit more genuinely.

Cathy gasped with a show of surprise reserved for small children and animals who successfully retrieve balls from behind couches. "How wonderful! So you've lived in Nashville for quite a while! What a lovely city."

"I've been there since undergrad. I went to Fisk."

Cathy froze. Her face deflated a bit, like an old cellophane birthday balloon, and she was about to explain herself, but the bell rang and everyone had to put on their headphones to hear their instructions for the day. When Agnes returned a little early from lunch, she overheard Cathy trying to amend her earlier gaffe by bragging loudly to one of the newbies about Fisk's world-famous choir, whose first members were the descendants of slaves intent on saving the only school that would let them study noble subjects like philosophy and Latin, as opposed to more menial ones, like agriculture and mechanical sciences.

Cathy might have understood the historical differences between Black institutions, but she was still too stupid to know about another of Fisk's practices, which, quiet as it was kept, was the real reason Agnes enrolled. Up until a few decades ago, Fisk admitted its students via the paper bag test. Although that had been abolished by the time she sent in her application (with the still-required photo),

Agnes had chosen Fisk because she fantasized that, perhaps during the years the Kirkkendolls were changing their names, she would have been admitted based solely on her appearance and could have disappeared into an upper-crust marriage and genteel respectability, while the darker-skinned Berniece would have had no such luck. With a bit more reflection, Agnes might have realized how that fantasy completely disqualified her from looking down on Cathy. But she figured that, since she'd never told it to anyone, her blatant hypocrisy didn't even halfway count. Instead, she glared at the woman, who glanced over at her sheepishly as she chatted, certain that the loudness of her praise would serve as the apology she didn't have the guts to offer directly. In response, Agnes angrily flipped the switch on her radio and put on her headphones, even though it would be ten minutes before the bell rang and someone would be there to tell her what to do.

AGNES'S MOTHER CALLED AROUND 8:00 on the evening of Day Three, which meant it was already 9:00 back home. Agnes was editing a jittery graduate student's dissertation, hoping the woman wouldn't email for the umpteenth time for updates. Agnes needed the money as badly as the student needed to finish, so she was working as quickly as she could without making mistakes, though she often got distracted by her own worries. Agnes didn't realize she was staring off into space until her phone began vibrating with obscene pulses on the nightstand.

Agnes's mother, who worked full-time at a day care and part-time as a nurse's aide at the same hospital as Berniece, was yawning before Agnes could even say hello. "What it look like out there?" Doyce yawned again, knowing nothing about how much Agnes detested the sound. Her mother's yawns were always accompanied by a satisfied roar, as if she were happily blowing out all the words she would never say to her daughter.

"It's all right. Kind of flat in the downtown area, but you can see the mountains in the distance. And there's a hiking trail somewhere close by."

"Oh, that's nice. You get a chance to do any sightseeing?"

"No. I've been working. And after work, I've been doing some editing." Agnes hoped it didn't sound as desperate as it was. She needed to wrap up this dissertation by Friday so she could do an instant transfer from the payment app to her bank account, then pay her portion of the rent online and hope the former posted quicker than the latter.

"What about that job you applied for. Any word yet?"

"No, not yet." Agnes had done her final interview with the staff during her lunch break earlier that day, pressing the earbuds into her ears as tightly as she could to drown out the sound of the readers' clattering cups and chatter drifting up from downstairs. She had marched back to the Reading Room feeling a little whittled by the experience, but proud. She'd sacrificed to attend that call, and she made as much clear to the board members, frequently apologizing for the background noise and her sometimes-flustered answers. After all, she was hungry. She hoped it glowed as an act of dedication on their radar.

"Well, like I always tell you, your gifts will make room for you."

"Yes, Mama. I know."

"Well, I'm glad. And things'll get better."

And with that, the Kirkkendoll women settled into the silent, uncomfortable knowledge that Agnes's mother had been saying that for both of their benefit since Agnes was fourteen, with no luck. Doyce herself was still single and struggling, just like her daughter, she presumed, though she never asked for particulars. Questioning the current state of things, the older woman believed, would be an affront to God's will, which was apparently bent on making them both suffer without reason and without even the commiseration of witnessing each other's pain, since each woman kept mum about what she thought about her own life. Instead, Doyce peppered the silence with questions about what Agnes thought about the president, details about the tailgating weekend Berniece was meticulously planning for the Krewe of Centaur's Mardi Gras parade (a full six months in advance), and the pastor's recent anniversary celebration, which included a string of visiting speakers, a potluck banquet, and a children's play.

It wasn't often Agnes felt a longing for places that weren't immediately accessible, but she did then, sitting in a room whose floor she didn't want to touch with her bare feet. Agnes hadn't initially intended to leave home; her anachronistic collegiate fantasy had lured her away. But once she was gone, she discovered it was much easier to flee than to return. In fatter years, she'd driven the nearly six hundred miles for both Thanksgiving and Christmas, but road anxiety and the expired tags on the car that desperately needed new brakes had ground her year-end sojourns to a halt. And the last time she'd gone, she and Berniece got into it because Agnes had pointed out that Bernice's second husband, Algin, wasn't as well-heeled as he pretended to be in order to constantly compare himself to the first. Berniece pointed out that a genetic freak who would be lucky to find even one husband shouldn't comment on anybody else's. And Agnes swore never to return until she had enough money to afford staying at an Airbnb or was married, and then she and *her* husband could rent out a compound on the lake, where they would make pans of corn-bread dressing and banana pudding just the way she liked them, and invite folks over to their place if they didn't want to put up with Berniece's attitude or her throat-clogging broccoli cheddar casserole.

But those things hadn't happened. Agnes was as lonely as ever, and just as stubborn. No, she wouldn't go back home, even when she got back on her feet, she told herself. And Berniece could just kill herself with envy over how fabulous Agnes's life must be going, since Agnes was clearly too busy to trek back to their boring little town to show her. But then, on a random warm day, Agnes would think of the drive-through daiquiri shops, or the sno-cone stands, where she would always choose some wistful flavor like Dreamsicle or Wedding Cake, squinting at the laminated menu taped to the side of a trailer at the edge of a parking lot. The air emanating from the open window felt almost arctic as the cashier leaned to one side, dragging a scoop through a gallon of Eagle Brand Vanilla to place on top of the syrup and ice. Or she would think of driving to her mother's house and never having to ask to be fed; her mother heaping dirty rice and hard-fried pork chops onto paper plates with the plastic plateholders underneath, which had only barely escaped complete meltings from a distracted cook who'd placed them on top of still-hot burners.

Being broke meant that none of those things were possible, a truth that made Agnes both indignant and sad. She thought of Berniece, planning a barbecue spread and perhaps not even asking if their mother could make the jambalaya or baked pork and beans. Algin would probably be burning his gummy-crusted cobblers while oversalting the ribs and watching some traveling cooking show on the too-large television in their too-large house. Berniece could never appreciate having access to their mother, to their food, which was a history of their childhoods, back when Dad was still around. Doyce's cooking was a remnant of her old self, before the desperation of hyper-religiosity and a general reticence about any conversation that went deeper than news headlines and funerals took root. And, remnant though it may have been, it was a kind of love Agnes would have bought outright if she had the money, whether she was ready to admit that to herself or not. Her mother had long hung up, and Agnes was staring at her laptop screen, trying to latch on to a sentence, a clause—anything—to edit. But her eyes kept losing focus and she kept drifting off to some other place, where warmed-up plates and ice-cold treats could be fixed, if nothing else.

SINCE HER CHILDHOOD AS ONE of a handful of Black children at a pilot magnet school tucked in the bayou-bound suburbs, there were many times in Agnes's life when she found herself with white men, and a few times she felt genuinely attracted to them, but always with a kind of surprise that made her react formally, like handling a snake trapped in a pillowcase. Agnes felt that same sage shock when she met Jacob, her table leader. He was dark-haired and bearded, with a regular build, but one Agnes predicted would soften with age into meaty arms and a paunch—all of which would stretch T-shirts printed with puns that were indecipherable to anyone not obsessed with *Star Wars* or geometry. Jacob had an affect that was casually dapper without the requisite tinge of vanity. Like her, he kept his folders neatly stacked, reaching over absentmindedly to right a sliding tower as he back-read the entire table's work. He wore tamely colored button-down sweaters and navy or oxblood leather sneakers, which were clean but not fastidiously so. He liked to pause while explaining things, holding his hands open in midair as he searched for the kindest way to identify an error in a score, or he'd skirt classified information while answering a reader's questions about how the sample essays were chosen, which they all graded together as part of a calibration exercise on the first day.

Agnes told herself she would get zero sendbacks this year, so she refused to get his attention by improperly scoring exams. Instead, she wooed him drily with requests for double checks, which always ended with confirmation that she was scoring correctly. She would begin by whispering his name softly, savoring the way it began with the palate, boomeranged to the back of the throat, and ended with a kiss of the lips—*Jacob*—before she called it louder and he startled to attention, no doubt alarmed that the sound he'd heard several times before without recognizing its significance was, in fact, for him.

Agnes had slept with many of his ilk, but seriously dated only one in her life, and she was dating him at that very moment: a fellow lecturer who first caught her attention at faculty orientation during her first year out of the program, which she spent teaching at her alma mater while grudgingly making the job circuit, as yet unaware that she would never get a job she didn't really want because not wanting it meant she never worked hard at securing it. What Agnes wanted was to fall in love, to be swept away, to be kept, and in so doing, to get a reprieve to figure out what she *actually* wanted to do in life since, through all the years she'd spent studying things like Reformation literature and the metaphysical poets, she'd never taken up the subject of herself. Not knowing who she was meant that every other task felt like a distraction from something very important she absolutely would have been doing if she'd known what it was. It's not that Agnes didn't want to work at all. She did, just not hard, and not for the money that would be used to take care of her. She wanted that responsibility to fall to a man who spared no expense in his doting and who indulged her whims, like, say, taking a year off to study the great Russian novelists. What she wanted was a partner whose love language was benefaction. What she got was Colin.

By happenstance, Colin sat next to her in the lecture hall for the morning session of last year's employee orientation. He was quiet but rolled his eyes enough times during presentations about 401(k)s and tenure—things they would never have access to in their lecturer positions—to make her giggle, so he came back during the afternoon and whispered obscene jokes at her shoulder as she hunched over her rickety foldout desk, hiding her mirth by pretending to take notes about faculty discounts for football season tickets.

"Hey, you still hungry?" Colin asked at 3:30, already standing but looking down at her quizzically as he gathered his new-hire folder and stuffed it carelessly into his messenger bag. "That lunch was bullshit. All those salads and fruit—fucking rabbit food." When he spoke, his blond beard bobbed like a puppet's.

Agnes surprised herself, though not Colin, when she perked up at the possibility of a dinner invitation. "Sure! Wait. Maybe?"

"When you make up your mind, I know a good place. By the time we get there, it'll be open for dinner." Colin stepped into the aisle and started down the steps without bothering to check whether or not she was following. With confidence like his, who wouldn't want to keep up? Agnes walked briskly—but not so briskly that it looked desperate—after him.

WITHOUT ASKING, COLIN TOOK HER to his house once they made it back into town. And Agnes had assented by saying very little and moving in soon after, eating exotic but blandly seasoned meals and struggling to make conversation with the roommate's girlfriend, a spindly German woman named Valda whose hair was dreading, though not intentionally; she simply never combed it.

Sexually, Agnes and Colin were wholly incompatible. Agnes still thought of the act with a sense of awe and reverence. She believed there should have been some kind of ritual surrounding it; Colin should take the entrance into her body seriously, like men who removed their hats when they entered sanctuaries, or made the sign of the cross whenever they passed churches. She imagined that, somewhere, others must feel the way she did, but Colin treated sex the way he watched soccer games: generally bored until something was at stake; then he yelled or cheered loudly, demanding people do things exactly as he wanted and being implacably angry when they didn't.

They had done things together that Agnes considered terrible, but she could tell no one because no one knew about him. The two of them were rarely together at school, and if someone from back home called while she was at his place, Agnes wouldn't answer the phone. No one suspected she made so little money that living with a man was more of a financial than a romantic decision, which still wouldn't be a good enough reason for a mother who grew up in segregated mid-century Louisiana and had never met a white man she fully trusted. Agnes had built the narrative of a busy woman who made reasonably good money but was working to find a better job, didn't always enjoy discussing the search, and had scarce time for idle conversations. After a few months, her mother still left voice mails, but Berniece gave up altogether, and, just as it had in high school, their relationship dissolved into a stony silence.

Colin's family had no idea she existed either, not even his half brother, who attended a boarding school a few hours away.

"Trust me, no one is ready for that," Colin once said as casually as if he were predicting who would score in an upcoming game. "It'll be hard enough for them to digest that you're Black. Having to explain *this*?" He waved his hand up and down her body, taking in everything, from her hair and her bronzer-smeared face to the off-color of the rest of her, all of which contrasted pitifully with itself when she undressed. She was, in fact, naked at the time, though Colin was looking at his phone and not at her as he shook his head and concluded, "Not sure I could even find the words. That's a tall order." It was information he offered without being asked, and Agnes made it a point to avoid creating the illusion that she cared, although she was deeply offended.

After that night, she spent the next few months looking for a job that would either rid her of him and the city, or give her enough confidence to say, in words she once heard Berniece scream into the phone during an argument with an old boyfriend, "*I'm* the prize. You hear me? I'm the *prize*. Your mother should be happy I fit fucking you into my schedule." Agnes felt exactly that way, she thought to herself; although, of course, she might have said it a little less raunchily.

AGNES WAS THINKING OF WHAT to do about Colin when Jacob called her name over her left shoulder. It was midmorning of Day Five, and it was the first time he asked her to reread an exam. The amount of time it took for that to happen might have been a source of pride for most readers, but for her, it was a blemish on a record she had hoped to keep perfect, if not as a validation of her own precision, then as confirmation that she was deserving of better jobs because this one was too easy. Jacob apologetically explained that he had given one of her exams a different score, then sheepishly asked her to reread it and tell him what she thought. Agnes was mildly irritated by his vagueness; after Jacob returned to his seat, she read through the essay twice and still couldn't remember what number she'd given it. The one she slid across the table along with the essay didn't seem to impress him as she'd hoped.

"A five? Well, you gave it a four the last time," he whispered before coming back over to her.

"What do you think it should be?"

"I think it's a high seven. Maybe an eight."

"An eight?" Agnes pointed out a grossly misspelled word in the first paragraph. Jacob smiled sympathetically and she couldn't tell if it was for her or the student. She bristled.

"Well…yes. It is misspelled, but it's used in the right context in the sentence. Remember what the Chief Reader talked about in his welcome address: 'Not every kid knows the name for a demitasse spoon, but he still knows how to use it.'"

Agnes stayed quiet for a long time—enough time for her to sigh, then Jacob, and then, finally, he placed his hand on top of the exam and handed her the scoring guide.

"I certainly don't want to argue about this, but I do want to come to some kind of agreement. Maybe you could take a look at the benchmarks again?"

Agnes skimmed them briefly before taking his offered pencil and changing the score. He returned to his seat, and she shifted uncomfortably in hers until the bell rang, signaling their midmorning break. As she bit into a slightly overripe banana, she turned the conversation over in her mind, and she knew she hadn't exactly been defiant, but her body language, her questions, her silence—she felt a shift in the small space between them the moment she'd given Jacob the wrong number. Even in the midst of true confusion, she was somehow hubristically wrong. Colin had pinpointed her problem once when she complained about an admin who treated her shabbily whenever she retrieved her boss's mail from the departmental office and complained about its always being moved to different mailboxes. When she finished the story, he groaned and shook his head.

"I know how you are, Agnes. You're like our new diversity hire in American studies, the one who wants a minority mentorship program and all this other shit that's gonna take more work than it's worth when she's already got tenure and she just needs to do what we hired her for. Just…chill the fuck out on this one. Keep your mouth shut. You're the help. Your only job is to play nice and not fuck anything up. Once you understand that, people will stop treating you like shit."

Agnes wanted to ask why he thought the onus should be on her. She also wanted to know the race of that new hire, but she was on Colin's time and his turf. He could one day tell her to get the fuck out and she couldn't do a damn thing about it, no matter how evenly they'd split the bills since she'd moved in.

Back at the conference center, she threw away the banana and grabbed a muffin instead, which was sweeter but clotted not with blueberries as she thought, but large raisins, which she hated. She spiked it into the trash can and headed back to her seat.

"THEY TREATING YOU BAD IN there, Teacher? You look mad enough to fight somebody."

It was lunchtime, and Prime had been hovering near Agnes's outdoor table, waiting until he could get her attention while she checked her empty notifications. Agnes put down her phone and rubbed her temples. She wasn't prepared to talk to anyone who needed her to be lighthearted or interested in them.

"No. It's just been a long day."

"I hear that." He paused, waiting for her to respond before continuing. "Yeah, I didn't work graveyard last night, so I got a little bit of sleep, but it feels like that little bit made me even more tired today."

"It's like that sometimes." And Agnes meant as much, even though she hoped he'd go away.

"You ain't lying about that." Prime hooked his thumbs into his belt loops and looked around casually, then behind him, shielding his eyes with one hand, almost as if he was searching for something in the distance. He turned back to Agnes with a grin. "Wiggins ain't lurking today like he usually is. Mind if I sit down?"

Agnes would have said yes either way since (by her own estimation) she was rarely impolite, but she liked the fact that he asked, annoying though he might have been. She picked at a limp but over-filled roast beef sandwich while he chatted aimlessly about himself, and she let him. It was a welcome distraction from thinking about Colin, money, and being wrong.

She learned that Prime worked security, but he liked to paint. He showed her a few pieces he'd photographed with his phone: majestic mountain scenes, one of which featured a Black cowboy. Agnes's awe surprised even her; she couldn't remember the last time a man had done something praiseworthy. Despite all of his so-called standards about his family's racial sensitivities, Colin was decidedly average. She also learned Prime had a young son whose mother, an ex-girlfriend, was in rehab, so he and his parents took turns taking care of the little boy.

"Whenever I'm not at work, that's where I am. Right there with him." Prime leaned back in his chair and smugly clasped his hands behind his head. Agnes sensed that he wanted her to be impressed.

"Really? That's good of you. What's his name?"

"Jackie. Jackie Dale Primus. Middle name from my mom; first name from my dad."

THAT NIGHT WAS DINE-OUT Night, when the cafeteria closed after lunch and the readers could be reimbursed for outside meals and nonalcoholic beverages up to $30. It would have been a fine idea if Agnes had $30 to spare. She'd slipped two cups of instant oatmeal and a few green bananas into her backpack during breakfast and hoped they could tide her over until morning, but during lunch, Prime had offered a far more appealing alternative.

It was after seven now but still sunny out, and Prime was slowly turning the wheel to make a corner in his large, older-model sedan, reminding Agnes of men back home: the ones who took great pride in their driving skills and well-kept vehicles. Prime's car was pristine inside; the red seats stainless, stiff with upholstery cleaner and protectant and their cushions fragrant with the chemical smell, which battled with the scent of the tree-shaped deodorizer. Agnes hadn't realized they still made those. Prime himself was as old-school as the car, opening doors and asking Agnes about her favorite music, then programming his phone to play a list of it. Agnes said "jazz" because she assumed Prime would have expected her to. She didn't know anything about it, and neither did he, so she nodded her head with confidence when certain songs started playing. She wanted him to believe he had chosen correctly, even though the truth was that Agnes hadn't listened to music in a long time.

"You like living all the way out there in Tennessee?" Prime asked as he cut a piece of his cabbage steak and ceremoniously dunked it into a ramekin of Beet-One, the vegan restaurant's version of steak sauce. When they'd pulled up to the converted auto garage, Agnes's heart sank. She had been hungry since shortly after her afternoon break, and she wasn't sure this would fill her up without her ordering half the menu. But since she didn't want to be rude, she followed his lead and also ordered a cabbage steak, cauliflower rice, and a salad. Even though the steak was drowning in something called a groundnut aioli, it felt light as air in her stomach.

"It's okay. I've been there for a while. I could leave."

"Where would you wanna go? Back home?"

"I…No. There's nothing there for me."

"In New Orleans? They got all kinds of stuff there. Mardi Gras. Food."

"I lived in a different city. Shreveport. A little farther north."

"Oh…okay. My fault. Well, what would be your dream city? You wanna live in New York? LA? Out in the sticks somewhere?"

"I don't know. I applied for this job in Boston. I could live there. I've visited a few times." Agnes didn't like to talk about possibilities with people. She'd learned from dealing with her sister that some folks laughed at your dreams right in your face. Others, like her mother, would ask about them over and over again, until you had to tell them you'd failed to get the thing you yourself had thought about obsessively since the day it became possible. But Prime was a stranger. After Saturday, they'd never have to see each other again.

"What would you be doing?" he asked.

"Heading a nonprofit organization for kids. With after-school programs and stuff."

"Okay, that's cool. That's real cool. I love kids, man. Ever since my son was born, that's all I think about, having more kids. You got kids?"

"No. It's just me."

"How old are you?"

"Thirty-four."

Prime scoffed. "You must got some good birth control. How'd you get to be this old without any kids?"

Agnes smiled a little. It was true: she'd had an IUD for years, but she couldn't tell him it was because a childhood of difference had made her terrified of children—hers or anyone else's. She wasn't even sure how she was going to work with them if she got the job. In truth, she imagined herself as the kind of boss ensconced in a cozy office, while her administrators handled the little ones. She might occasionally walk the halls of the foundation, waving at groups of them from afar and perhaps being tackled by a hugging girl who was grateful for her leadership, and who would be immediately shooed away by other staff and admonished for bothering Dr. Kirkkendoll, who was so busy, so very, very busy. She could tolerate a job like that, where people treated you like you were somebody whose time shouldn't be wasted. She could even learn to enjoy it, especially if she took home a nice salary. Boston was expensive, but she could sell her car. She could even live a little ways outside the heart of the city and walk to a quaint little train station like she did that one year she'd attended an academic conference and stayed with a friend of a friend. It was blisteringly cold, but the snow was pristine in that neighborhood, the glittery crunch of it so satisfying beneath her boots. She liked that person as she remembered her: bundled up and headed for warmth with a little money in her pocket and something important to do. That person could be happy, and she was so close to meeting her again. No way the foundation could say no this far into the process.

Agnes was drifting again. She turned her attention back to Prime: "I don't know why I haven't had any kids. Just lucky, I guess. Or unlucky, depending on how you see it."

"Yeah, cause you want kids, right? Maybe you'll meet someone in Boston and have some."

She sighed. "I don't know about that. But I'm open to whatever comes. I'll live anywhere as long as I can be happy."

Agnes's noncommittal response emboldened Prime. He forked another piece of cabbage into his mouth, flecking a dab of sauce that had lodged in the corner of it with his bright pink tongue.

"Boston sounds cool, but it's nice out here too. Pretty quiet. Good schools. Folks aren't too racist. My son is mixed and when his mom and I were together, they didn't give us too much trouble. And they don't give me and him trouble now, except when they mistake him for a girl. His hair is really long."

"Well, that's good…you know," stammered Agnes, "that it's a good place to raise a kid."

Prime nodded enthusiastically as he finished chewing. "See? I told you. That's all I think about." He shifted in his seat a little. "So, if you're not looking for a man in Boston, that means you've already got one. What's his name?"

Agnes thought briefly of Colin, and his refusal to name what they had. She shook her head.

"Nobody. Like I said, it's just me."

Prime beamed as he pushed his empty plate to the side for the server to pick up on her next lap.

"Well…I'm sure that won't last for long. Somebody's bound to pop up and make an honest woman out of ya."

Agnes thought of all the lies she'd told during her job interview and all the lies she might tell before she got wherever it was she was supposed to go. For the first time that night, she beamed right back.

"Maybe so. Anything could happen."

AFTER DINNER, PRIME OFFERED TO drive her around the city, showing her some of its highlights: an art installation of a collage of street signs that he admitted he didn't quite understand, the huge cathedral, and the underground mall, where people were still loitering in the waning dusk of 9:00 p.m. The two scooted along from street to street until, finally, Prime turned to her and said, "You know what? I'm not gonna lie to you. I'm still hungry." They'd spent enough time together for Agnes to feel comfortable enough to agree. Prime put both hands on the steering wheel and squinted at the road as he spoke. "Well, since I'm offering to feed us twice, I recommend we eat someplace a little more casual." He glanced over quickly to gauge her reaction.

"Yeah, sure. That's fine. I could eat a hamburger or something."

"I should have known you really are my kind of woman. You like In-N-Out?"

"I've never been."

"It's good, but my favorite one is outside the city."

Agnes remembered her first date with Colin. "That's the closest one?"

"Yeah, but right next to it there's this really good lookout point where you can see the valley." He laughed and patted her shoulder. "Don't worry. I'm not a serial killer."

"Only a serial killer would think to say that."

"And a good man. A good man would say that too."

THE VALLEY WAS STARKLY BEAUTIFUL. The mountains cradled its muddy green expanse, which was scarred with roads and stubbled with lights that, between the dark outlines of squat trees, made her think of glowing lice crawling in a patchy beard. Prime rubbed his own with one hand as he reached into the bag for another French fry, which he ate without fry sauce, chewing thoughtfully. Agnes bit into a burger that was much larger than she expected.

"This is good," she found herself saying without irony.

"I wish I had known you'd say that. This is my favorite spot, really. I come out here all the time, sometimes to just sit and get my thoughts together." Agnes nodded in agreement, her mouth full. He looked over at her, then playfully shook her shoulder.

"See? If you lived here, we could come here together. You got In-N-Out where you live?"

"I don't think so. It's a West Coast chain, right?"

"Yeah. Well, I guess it is. I wouldn't know. I've been here my whole life." It sounded like an admission he was ashamed to make, even though Agnes already knew it.

"Nothing wrong with that. Especially if you like it here. If it feels like home for you."

Prime rubbed the steering wheel excitedly. "It does. Like, it probably seems weird because there aren't that many Black people here. I just— All I wanna do is buy a little house here, start a family. That's all. That's why I'm busting my ass with all these shifts, you know? Just trying to save a little money. Get me and my little man out of that apartment. Get him a yard and a dog. Cause that's what he wants now: a dog. Then, when I find a good woman, she'll have a nice kitchen to cook in. Big enough table where we can eat meals and my parents can come over. Room for everybody."

"That sounds nice."

He shifted in his seat so he could face her. "Wait—you want that too? You know what? This is fate. You should move here, Cherie. Once I get a house? I'll be set. And you could find a job here, even though you don't like teaching. You could work with kids or something, like that job in Boston. And you would already have a house. You wouldn't have to save for it or nothing. I'm doing that."

Agnes laughed, her lips slick from the greasy meals, and her belly, for the first time in months, not passively churning with hunger or disappointment. She was giddy with the feeling of fullness.

"But...you just met me."

"I know. But listen, my parents knew each other for six weeks before they got married. Six weeks! Then the next year they had me. And they've been together ever since."

"Do they live here?"

"My parents? Yep. Been together forty years."

"Are they happy?"

"They must be. They're still together."

Agnes would have asked more, but the look on Prime's face gave her pause. He was in awe of the kind of life he'd been imagining, the kind he had been a part of for a time. And, maybe, having grown up and left his parents' house, which, as far as Agnes could tell, was a love bubble that encased him from the world, Prime longed for a similar thing even more. Or maybe it was the drug-addicted girlfriend whose thwarting of that hope made it seem sweeter. Agnes had enough dreams of her own, tottering like raw eggs on a spoon, to know how precious they felt, how vulnerable, in a world where everything and everyone seemed determined to knock that egg right out of your hand. She said nothing, but she fished for one of the still-warm napkins from the crumpled bag and wiped her fingers on it before patting his knee, noting how the crease of his khaki pants was so pronounced, she knew that if she bent down to sniff him, she would still smell the hot metal and starch. You can't argue with someone who believes they deserve something, and that, if they are simply good enough, well-enough prepared, they will get it, no matter the odds stacked against them. It is a confidence so strong, you start to believe them, too, in the hopes that, together, your sheer will can make that thing true. This, she now understood, was what her mother meant when she said she prayed for Agnes. But Prime's crease also reminded her of Dennis, with his offhanded cruelty. And Colin, too, who was white and came from wealth, who had no affiliations and no creases, and yet... With a sudden, glaring clarity, Agnes realized something that came to her in a flash so piercing she immediately put it out of her mind, shutting the door on it and stumbling forward in a consensual dark. Prime was looking down at her hand, and impulsively, she lifted his face to hers and kissed him. In her mind's sanctuary, her mother's voice hissed in the dark: *What have you done?* And it wasn't a question so much as it was an accusation. And it wasn't as much about that moment as it was about the entire balance of Agnes's life. *What have you done?* the voice asked with a flippancy that made Agnes want to cry, but also scream.

PRIME WAS NO COLIN; HE kissed Agnes with the same deference with which he'd treated her throughout the night, and she knew enough about his type not to push things, or seem too eager to go any further. Nevertheless, he kissed her deeply, rubbing her back and, briefly, her breasts. But when he stopped, she stopped, and he drove her back to the hotel at a speed much faster than he'd retrieved her, talking excitedly about the future. She could come back to visit in August, just before his son started preschool, and they could spend some time getting to know each other, she and the son. Prime would keep an eye out for jobs, too, maybe in a day care or something, say if someone quit at the last minute and they needed a replacement fast before school started and parents went back to work. They could stay together in his apartment for a couple of months, but of course, he would start looking for a house. He hated to borrow money from his parents, but since things had gotten pushed up, maybe he could, just this once, then pay them back quickly. Well, maybe he just needed to pick up some extra overnight shifts.

"That'd be overtime, and my parents can watch Jackie, since he'll be asleep for most of it," Prime mused, already calculating the profit. "Maybe I just need to start working nights from now on. But

Wiggins got his favorites. I don't know. *But*…if I work a couple nights in a row, I can prove I'm good for it long-term. I can do it." He schemed until they reached the hotel, where Agnes kissed him once more on the lips, and he leaned back and admired her as she gathered her purse and the empty cups and bags, which she'd promised to discard in the lobby.

"Your kids. They'd be light-skinned, too, like my boy. That's good, though, cause that way, he won't feel any different from them." Agnes shook her head ruefully and waved him away as she turned toward the revolving door. She liked both his enthusiasm and his hesitant desire, which were contradictory in a way that could be endearing. He felt upright, and Agnes had felt so dirty, so misused of late. But there was also Boston, and she was so close. She was flattered, but she couldn't possibly be his One. She had said nothing in response to his presumptions in the car, but she'd figure out a way to let him know before she left. Or she could just disappear once she got home. Agnes didn't know nearly as much as she thought she did, but she was right about one thing: she knew how to disappear. Doing so with Prime would be easy.

THE CALL CAME EARLY, AROUND six (eight Eastern time), just as Agnes was opening her journal and putting the date at the top right-hand corner of a blank page. She had awakened late but was moving slowly through her routine, hoping to miss Prime at breakfast.

"Is now a good time?" The chair of the board's voice was chipper, much more so than it had been during the interviews.

"Yes…yes, of course, it's fine," stammered Agnes. Her heart began that two-stepping orbit, like a drum major spinning and pounding on the field, his coattails billowing behind him, his face sweaty with performativity and pride.

"Wonderful. Well, the board has made its decision, and we're sorry…" Agnes couldn't hear the rest so much as she sensed it: the woman's voice dropping with a note of pity and tenderness that sent the drummer into a free fall, then rising again in what Agnes assumed was well-wishes for her continued search, and maybe even a request to stay tuned for the announcement of the chosen director and the exciting new initiatives and…Agnes went through the motions too: her voice rose cheerfully, shrill in her ears as she thanked the chairwoman and agreed that yes, yes, it was an exciting new beginning for an org that Agnes herself cared so deeply about, which was most evident in her stellar application and impeccable interviews, and she would most surely remain an advocate for it in any way she could. *Yes, yes, yes*. Agnes's head nodded and the word spilled out of her, as it often did during sex, a time when she said it constantly, not just as an acquiescence to Colin's kinks, or even an acknowledgment of his insults, but to convince herself that, somehow, all of what was happening was right.

AGNES HEADED TO THE READING Room, hoping she could finish her day's journal entry since she'd been too distracted to go back to it after the call. She'd almost gone to breakfast before realizing she absolutely couldn't face Prime now without the buffer of hope the job had given her, which had made his boyish devotion charming and her fulfillment of his dreams impossible.

Agnes had just settled in her seat when she heard a low squeal behind her and turned to see Cathy and another of her table's readers coming toward her, no doubt here early because they had been every other morning. Agnes's irritation with the woman swelled again; Cathy's excitement at performing such a meaningless job made

Agnes think of all the enthusiasm she'd manufactured and wasted in the interviews. The women spoke and so did Agnes, but Cathy's face soon creased with concern. Of course, she knew nothing about the desperate job search, but must have felt the residual bitterness in the room, like a darkness Agnes was pumping in with every audible sigh she made as the two women prepared noisily for the day.

But instead of lowering her voice, Cathy attempted to fight the black cloud with even more sound. She narrated her every movement as she gathered the things she needed, and as she rubbed a squirt of sanitizer into her hands, her conversation turned toward her skin.

"That run yesterday. I'm so used to running at night, but it gets dark so late here. I think I got a tan."

The other woman hadn't said much up to that point, only hummed in agreement, but this time she ventured:

"Oh, that's nice. If that's what you wanted."

Cathy pulled down the collar of another politically themed T-shirt to examine the deeply browned skin on her chest, then shrugged, placing the bottle of hand sanitizer back on the table.

"Well, at least I don't look like an albino anymore." She picked up a bite-sized Snickers and ripped it open.

Agnes looked down at her journal and carefully finished the date: June 17. Agnes had never told Cathy what she was, and Cathy had never asked, though Agnes presumed she must have known, with Agnes's schooling and her accent and her…Surely she knew. But what Cathy didn't know was how much Agnes despised the word or, at the moment, herself: the hair and skin undoctored by expensive disguises. The lack of both wigs and job prospects. The overbearing presence of unsuitable men: one who didn't know what to call her and another who was afraid to say the word in front of his family. She had a history with the word that reached back further than Dennis and Berniece, back into the recesses of her childhood, when children sang "white honkey" to the tune of "Brass Monkey" and garbled the name of what she really was—so much so that it sounded more like Alabama, a place she had never visited but hated for its homophonic proximity alone. But Agnes hadn't been a child in a long time, and while she might tolerate Colin's dismissals, she no longer took kindly to ridicule.

Because, surely, Cathy knew. If so, why would she say such a thing? The possibilities made Agnes's head swell: first with anxiety, and then seething rage.

"I see," murmured Agnes to herself, nodding.

THE WEEK WAS DRAWING TO a close, so Cathy was collecting money for Jacob's gift, and for gifts for the runners, and for gifts for the new readers at the table, and for a gift from the table to the question leader. Each person was supposed to donate $5 to each—$20 total—and envelope after envelope was passed between laps or kited quickly across the table when Jacob took bathroom breaks. Agnes passed them along without even looking at them. Question 2 was perfectly on schedule, said the question leader, his voice as calm as ever as he reminded them to keep working at their regular pace, since a prematurely celebrating reader is always a distracted one.

Agnes kept her head down, flipping through books until she finished a folder, and then handing it off to the runners as she took new ones. Some had already been graded by readers from the other groups, their employee numbers written neatly on the folder's back flap. Agnes wondered about those readers as she graded. Did they feel as utterly hopeless as she did right that minute? All around the room, envelopes bulged, filled to the brim with money. Mothers slipped into bathrooms to watch videos of their children learning to swim while others stayed at tables, speeding happily through exams, dreaming of vacation sands or the keys to a cozy cottage. Agnes lived in a crowded house in a town that felt too metropolitan to be Southern, but she still ached to leave because both felt empty. She didn't have a bustling city life with friends and nights at the bar that ate all her coins and left her hungover, broke, and happy. Instead, she was drowning in a shallow pool, flailing for solid ground on which to stand when it should have been directly under her feet. She shook her head to clear her thoughts and opened another book.

"hEy yOu sWeAtShOp FuCkIng lOsEr," the words leapt out at her from an otherwise blank page. "FuCk CoLlEgE iM gOiNg 2 tHe ARMY NeWaY sO eNjOy DiS DiCk!!" Underneath the scrawl was a surprisingly accurate rendition of a man, drawn only from the waist down, holding an erect penis, with a woman, bound and blindfolded, kneeling in front of him. A rip of flesh had been carefully sketched across her chest, and one of her breasts was hanging by a thread of black ink. The artwork had been signed with a name, Matthias Granado. Agnes flipped to the front of the booklet and confirmed the student's initials: MOG. She gestured to Jacob, but his head was down, reading.

"Jacob." Nothing.

"Jacob!" Agnes looked around briefly and tried a bit more projection. Still, nothing. Agnes would have stood and walked over to him, but she hated the sound of the chair's scrape against the concrete floor. "Jacob!"

It was clear, after a few tries, that Jacob heard her. He finished a booklet, placed it carefully back into a folder, double-checked the Scantron and initialed it, closed the folder, and placed it gingerly on top of his stack before rising slowly and walking nonchalantly over to her chair. The two women at the narrow end of the table exchanged a glance as subtle as the decreasing temperature in the room—lowered, as Agnes suspected, to keep them all awake and working quickly. Agnes stammered through her explanation of the booklet's breach of anonymity, the offensive nature of the drawing, and her desire to report it to the higher-ups. But Jacob simply told her that no action should be taken because the student had posed no real threat to anyone. The revelation of his name meant nothing; she should give him a zero and keep working. As Jacob stood at her chair, he never once leaned down to meet her at eye level or gestured in that elaborate way he often did. Instead, he stood with his hands crammed into his pockets, and though she initially turned toward him as she spoke, once she realized she was face-to-face with his crotch, she talked instead to the booklet, gesturing at it frantically as if she were trying to get the blindfolded woman's attention so that, if the gash in the woman's chest wasn't so deep, she could perhaps speak on her own behalf.

ONCE SHE MADE THE DECISION, Agnes marveled at how quickly her mind worked out the logistics. Before her lunch break, she emptied her backpack, leaving most of her belongings in a canvas grader gift bag under the table. Then, when the bell rang to signal lunch, she hid in the bathroom and waited for the room to clear before emerging to check the recycling bin for empty bottles, which she refilled in the bathroom sink. She screwed the lids onto each one tightly, then checked to make sure they weren't cracked and leaking, as some of the store brands often did. Then she left the backpack on her chair and tried to grab a quick meal, but her stomach vaulted inside her. Instead, she took off her hoodie and walked the perimeter of the convention center, letting the sun first dry, then heat, then pulsate with a bright warning on her bare shoulders. She ducked into a drugstore for a brief respite and slipped a protein bar on clearance into her pocket, waiting until she crossed the street before she bit into its treacly rubber. When she finally looked at her watch, she realized with a gasp that she was only a few minutes away from being late for the bell, so she jogged huffily, flashing her badge at the security guard as she bounded up the half flight of steps to the room.

"Hey, woman! You lost track of time, didn't ya?" It took Agnes a minute to recognize his voice. By then, she had already passed Prime, so she twirled, and, in a rush of adrenaline at the thought of what she planned to do, she blew him a kiss. She spun back toward the Reading Room, but not fast enough to miss his face, which broke out into a grin, confident that whatever had happened between them the night before was a real thing, like a child they were both eagerly carrying.

"RUN THIS BY ME AGAIN? What did you leave in the room?" Prime had his thumbs hooked into his belt loops, a look of genuine concern laced with frustration deepening the lines that framed his upper lip like a set of parentheses. It was almost midnight, and he'd met her at the locked main door looking flustered, no doubt worried to get a text from her so late. Agnes licked her lips, briefly tongue-tied by his question, but she took a deep breath and started again.

"I left my inhalers in there. My regular one and my rescue one. I'm supposed to keep one with me at all times." She was panting with anxiety and hoped that gave him reason enough to believe the lie and let her in the room.

"You sure you can't wait for one night? I'm not supposed to let anyone in there. *We're* not even supposed to be in there. And I can't leave my round to go get it for you."

"You wouldn't need to do that—it'll take me two seconds. Come on. I'm not supposed to be without it."

"Cherie. You're killing me, baby. You're the only reason I'm out here working graveyard, and now you're trying to get me fired? What about going to the pharmacy?"

"The pharmacy's closed; plus they're expensive, and I have two free ones ten feet away. I'm just trying not to die from an asthma attack."

"Mannnnnn." Prime spun around on his heels. It was an act of exasperation, as well as to see if anyone was nearby.

"Prime, you know me. I'm not gonna touch anything but my backpack and come right out."

He spun back slowly to face her but didn't make eye contact. First, he looked over her shoulder, then up at the ceiling. After a few long seconds, he spoke. Agnes sighed with relief so loudly she missed the first few syllables.

"…but you gotta hurry. Wiggins makes pop-ups on night shift. He can't see you going in or coming back out."

"I understand. I won't get you in trouble."

Prime muttered a few more protests under his breath and then held her by the shoulder, guiding her to the locked double doors of the Reading Room. He looked around once more, then pulled out his key ring and unlocked one of the doors. Before she slipped through it, he touched her shoulder one last time, and they kissed awkwardly.

"It's quiet enough in here for you to hear me talking to Wiggins if he shows up. If you do, slip out the back door. It's only locked from the inside. And the fire alarms are disabled so you guys can get out to smoke during breaks." Agnes nodded emphatically, her back already to him. He turned her around again to face him.

"And you can't turn on the lights because people will see it over the tops of the partitions. You got your phone?" Agnes held it up for him to see. "Good, use your flashlight. And don't take too long."

"I won't. When do you get off?"

Prime smirked a little and, for the first time, looked her in the eye. "Not until seven. I get an hour break at two-thirty, though. You gonna be up?"

"I might be. Text me."

"Sweet." He kissed her again, this time with a bit more intention. Agnes let him, then pulled loose from his grasp and started running. He eased the heavy door closed quietly, and she could hear his keys jingling joyfully as he strolled away.

ONCE AGNES FOUND THE CURTAIN encasement labeled Question 2, set back farthest from the door in the middle of the space, its location buffering her sounds, she worked with an efficiency that even she thought ironic, given her recent bad luck with finding employment. She was made for this kind of thing: brainstorming, audacity, execution. She pulled the backpack heaving with water from her chair and put it on facing the front so she could remove each bottle with ease. As she worked the perimeter of the room, she thought to herself that perhaps the question leader had been dishonest in his cheery announcements about pace and progress. The runners' tables were covered in boxes; why had so few been hauled away to the loading areas? There were even boxes hiding under the tables' thin paper skirts. It was almost as if fate had offered up a surplus for this moment, after years of nothing for Agnes. Suddenly, she thought she heard voices outside and stilled for a moment. Maybe it was Prime talking to his supervisor, but she knew it was a waste of time to await confirmation, so she shook herself out of it and went back to working quickly.

As she approached each runners' station, she unscrewed a bottle carefully, pouring its contents into the boxes with one hand as she pulled another bottle from her backpack. She didn't bother to try to wet the boxes under the tables. Instead, she kicked them from underneath, and then knocked them over with a final punt as she went from one skirted hiding place to the next. Of course she understood that this grading system, precise as it was, couldn't be toppled by a few wet exams and the inconvenience of having to reassemble trampled folders. She knew that she could only disrupt things, and she settled for that, content to imagine the myriad ways people might react: the somber-voiced question leader; the agitated readers; the wary table leaders affirming everyone's dedication while explaining that they might have to stay a day longer. People, thought Agnes, cared—or at least pretended to care—about the most trivial things. She was over it, as Berniece would say.

And what would Berniece say about this? Be impressed by the fact that she had become unbuttoned in such a bizarre way? Berniece knew nothing about Agnes's life, about her letting men drive her wherever they wanted her to go. Agnes wished Berniece had told her what that could do to you. Or failure, although Agnes wasn't sure Berniece could articulate what that felt like. Their mother either. Both were the kind of women who refused to feel—either by self-distraction or by pretending that the hurt, which was the origin of the small knot slowly loosening in Agnes's chest with every box she kicked, was really nothing sentient at all. Agnes had done it too: with every rejection, with every scathing aside Colin threw in her direction. But she was tired. And what of it? She was still broke. She was still lonely. What good would this violently joyful moment do?

Water poured from the bottles with loud sucks of gravity: first a few fat gulps, and then a small cascade until they emptied. Agnes had to move them around quickly for maximum impact, and still, they emptied all too soon. She shook out the last bit of water in the bottles, recalling briefly how Colin would sometimes finish oral sex by pulling himself out of her mouth and, without asking, spray the final pulse directly into her face.

Agnes was near the front of the room when she heard the heavy door whine open and saw the weak beam of a flashlight, strangled to a faint glow by darkness. She couldn't hear the footsteps, and she wasn't sure who it was, but she froze for a beat before sprinting toward the back door. It flew open as she threw herself against the bar, and the chilly night air wrapped around her as she stumbled on the doorstep, then took off running. Her lungs ached with a pain that radiated from her shoulders; she was sorely unused to such exertion. She ran a distance she thought was far, though it wasn't, then stopped in the parking lot of a gas station to assess the situation. She had nothing now—not her clothes or work laptop, which were still in the hotel room—only her wallet and phone. To get home, she'd probably have to call Berniece to borrow money before anyone got wind of what she'd done. She looked around. A long-haired man was pumping gas into an older pickup truck from the '80s, blue with white paneling on the sides. Agnes's father had one just like it when she was small. The man had already glanced at her before looking down again, shaking the nozzle a bit inside the tank and returning it to the pump. She approached him cautiously, her hands raised as if she were surrendering.

"Excuse me? Excuse me, I'm a little lost. I was wondering if you could point me to the airport?"

The man looked her over, furrowing his brow before speaking. "Yeah. It's not far from here. You're not going to be able to walk it, though, unless you wanna get hit on the interstate."

"Could you…take me? I…really don't have any cash. But I am trying to get home."

He looked around and then down at his watch, a thin plastic band with a coin-sized face.

"No, not tonight, ma'am. I got someplace else to be."

The man got back in the truck and pulled out into the street. Agnes pulled out her phone, feeling slightly insulted. If she could just find directions and get ahold of Berniece, she could make it to the airport in enough time to board an earlier flight before anyone knew to look for her. As she walked, cars sped past and she wished herself in one, or anywhere else besides a city where no one had a good enough reason to take her in.

She was walking aimlessly, wondering whether her phone's rideshare app would let her call a ride with no money on her credit card, when one of the cars approaching from behind stopped next to her. She kept walking, intent on ignoring it, but it lingered, matching her pace as she crossed each intersection. She thought maybe the man in the truck had changed his mind, but, having come to her senses, she hoped he would give up and move on. She had done far too many dangerous things these past few months, and getting in his truck wasn't going to be one of them. But then the horn blasted, and she looked up in annoyance. It was the Cutlass. Prime.

They both stopped moving and stared at each other for what seemed like minutes. Agnes could barely make out his face in the darkness of the night and of the vehicle, but she knew he could see her, and for the first time in her life, she wasn't afraid of being seen: of the way her skin glowed bluish in the contrast of the clear night, or of the way her eyes moved rapidly in the dark, straining to make out the shape of his body. She stared back, then hoisted the empty backpack and kept walking. Prime followed, cars skirting him angrily as the two of them crawled up a nameless street. He gave her one block, then another, then blew again. This time, when she stopped, he threw the gearshift into park and got out. He didn't lunge for her, or even say anything. He simply came around to her side and stood, hands crossed in front of him as if he were posing for a photo with his ride. Agnes looked from him, to the car, and back at him.

"What do you want from me?" she snapped. Her backpack felt heavier than ever, even without water in it.

"Cherie," he said, his voice shredded with something that Agnes, for once, couldn't name. "I just want you to get in."

THEY WERE ON THE HIGHWAY now, and Agnes was delirious with momentary relief. The heat was hissing from the vents, and for a while, it was the only sound in the car, but it was as soothing as music. Agnes soon stopped shaking from adrenaline and the cold.

"Are you on drugs too?" Prime's voice was calm.

"No, I'm not on drugs," she said quietly, folding and refolding her arms.

"Then why would you *do* that?" Prime spun the wheel toward an exit: Timber Creek Way. It sounded like one of the neighborhood streets back home.

"I'm just— Listen, there's a lot going on in my life right now, and I'm tired." Agnes rested her head against the cold window. She hoped that, wherever she was going, there were blankets. She wanted to crawl under one and sleep indefinitely.

"Then, why didn't you tell me? I could have helped. Now…man, this shit is serious. I'm dropping you off at my place and then I'm gonna see if I can straighten all this out. I thought…Damn. I thought we were in this together. If you were gonna do something like that, why would you do it on my watch? Now I *know* I'm gonna lose my job. At least. Ain't no telling what Wiggins is gonna do when he finds out. I can't believe you did this to me."

They pulled up to a small complex with blunt, boxy buildings: the square kind—half brick and half shingle, most likely built during the '70s. Prime lowered his head to the steering wheel before turning to Agnes. "Go on up. No one's there. It's 214. I don't know when I'll be back, but I'll try to call you first chance I get. And even if you don't hear from me, *don't* leave." Agnes got out of the car quickly, hoping he didn't want to embrace her, then trudged up the stairs. A dim green light lit the breezeway as she fumbled to find the lock and twist the knob. It wasn't that late, but every unit around her was eerily silent: no ambient noise from televisions, no thumps of bodies moving toward bed and sleep—nothing. Agnes wondered disinterestedly if this was the place where she was going to die.

PRIME'S APARTMENT EXISTED BETWEEN TWO chaotic worlds— single father and bachelor—and it showed. The living room was almost overtaken by toys and two heavily bowed bookshelves that were mostly crowded with encyclopedias and old magazines. A book on single fatherhood was pulled out slightly. She shoved it back into its place and headed toward the back.

The kitchen was filthy. Bowls and dishes still holding their dinner contents were tossed haphazardly in the sink. Next to a small table, a mousetrap rusted in the corner, its clamp snapped down on the neck of a mouse in mid-crawl. Sleep drained out of Agnes. No way she could rest knowing this place had more occupants than the tenants.

The only rooms in the house that looked to be regularly cleaned were Prime's bedroom and an adjoining bathroom. Both reeked with the competing smells of bleach and aftershave, and everything seemed neatly put in place in an order that suggested convenience.

Agnes checked the medicine cabinet. Mostly over-the-counter items: cough syrup, something pink for stomach upset, and nasal spray. But one bottle bore the name of a local pharmacy and a set of instructions to "take as needed up to an hour before sexual activity." Agnes Googled the name, but not without noticing that she'd received no callback from Berniece. The medicine was for erectile dysfunction. Agnes tried to put the bottle back exactly as she found it and checked underneath the sink for cleaning supplies.

Prime's bed was the largest object in his room and the most ornately adorned. It was an old model, from a different decade, its headboard a half-moon of black lacquer with gold trim, and when Agnes kneeled on it, she was surprised it wasn't a waterbed. The sheets were black satin beneath a gold embroidered comforter set, which was complete with cylindrical bolsters and a wrinkled bed skirt. A few stuffed animals rested atop the pillows: one was a brightly colored unicorn, the other a dirndl-clad mouse whose skirt was embroidered with the word *Landstuhl*. Before seeing the real mouse in the kitchen, Agnes would have crawled into bed and tried to sleep her terror away; instead, she stood up and smoothed the comforter flat. She was on a mission. She could rest after she cleaned.

BACK IN THE KITCHEN, SHE scrubbed in silent but apoplectic zeal as her thoughts drifted like plucked feathers over the Rockies and the dismal plains, and down the Red River to the house on Sunset Lane, which her mother made Agnes and Bern clean every Saturday morning after *Soul Train*. If it was the second or fourth weekend, they'd have to do it earlier, before she took down their shampooed and dried braids and straightened their hair for Sunday service. Berniece went first, because she was easiest, then Agnes, who was notoriously tender-headed. Agnes's mother would blast gospel music from the local AM station loud enough for anyone in the neighborhood to hear. It was louder than the kids outside and the cars passing through. Louder, Agnes imagined, than her mother's thoughts. There would be Andraé Crouch and Shirley Caesar, LaShun Pace screaming "IIIIIIIIIIIIIIIIIIIIIIIIIIIIIIII *KNOW* I been changed" in a way that made heaven sound frightening. But Agnes's favorite was Tramaine Hawkins's "Thank You," where, during the bridge, the singer declares what her life might have been like without divine intervention. Originally, Agnes loved the way the song made her family's circumstances feel luxurious. It was true they had fallen on hard times when her father left. The small house they settled into after Agnes began high school was in a dingy but respectable neighborhood surrounded by more dangerous ones, and the house itself was in the early stages of disrepair: plumbing problems, peeling walls, buckling floors, roaches that were small but annoying. Agnes saw her first colorless roach one day after school, camouflaging himself on a roll of toilet paper she was about to use. His pearlescent body was exquisite, and the way he froze, his antennae searching the air to detect the proximity of his danger while perched on a mound of paper in broad daylight, pricked Agnes's empathy. He was the only insect she'd found there that she didn't kill.

Agnes's mother didn't seem to mind any of it and had, in her own words, "handed it all over to God," while the father and Sabine and Sabine's always-visiting family members ran the floors ragged in their old home only a few minutes away, which had real wood floors and not the cheap vinyl they now had to scrub down weekly because it scuffed easily and was visibly filthy again by Tuesday morning. Even so, there was love in that small place and a sense of order that her mother imposed with an iron hand. And there were small joys on which they could count: Little Caesars Bigfoot pizzas on payday and Blockbuster movies. Money left on their dressers for field trips or down payments for choir dresses. And, on her off days, Agnes's mother would take them to the mall where she always got them at least one item of clothing, even if it was from Rainbow.

As she reminisced, Agnes tried desperately to stay aware of her current situation: she was far from home and guilty of a punishable crime with nowhere to go. She would at least be charged with the destruction of property, though Agnes wasn't familiar enough with the criminal justice system to know if that would be a felony or a misdemeanor. And she'd certainly be on the hook for some kind of restitution if she was caught, and she had no money to speak of. What, then, would they do to her? Agnes's mind toggled between memories of home and the possibilities of being stuck in Utah in varying states of incarceration, a disordered slide show that made her almost gag with panic and faint with relief. She couldn't believe she'd blown up her life in such a way, but it had been a life she'd been holding together with spit for years—sometimes literally, she thought to herself, when she remembered her raucous nights with Colin. Now it was such a mess she couldn't even touch it, and maybe that's what she'd wanted all along. She wondered briefly about the possibility that even in her chaos, she was calculating. But thinking about that while standing in the kitchen of a man who'd, in some ways, saved her made her think of Berniece, and she outright refused to acknowledge any resemblance. She was smart enough to get out of this on her *own*, she told herself. She just had to figure out a way, after a good night's sleep, of course. In the meantime, there were things that needed tending to. So she scoured the stove until it shone, convinced she could somehow rid herself of this place, perhaps as efficiently as she dislodged crust from the greasy drip pans. She wondered if, all those years before, her mother hadn't been trying to do the same thing.

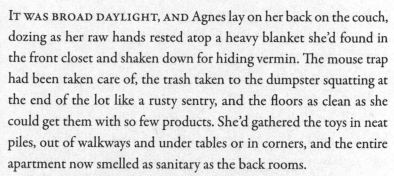

IT WAS BROAD DAYLIGHT, AND Agnes lay on her back on the couch, dozing as her raw hands rested atop a heavy blanket she'd found in the front closet and shaken down for hiding vermin. The mouse trap had been taken care of, the trash taken to the dumpster squatting at the end of the lot like a rusty sentry, and the floors as clean as she could get them with so few products. She'd gathered the toys in neat piles, out of walkways and under tables or in corners, and the entire apartment now smelled as sanitary as the back rooms.

She startled awake when the door opened slowly, and Prime came through carrying his security jacket and a bag of food, which he placed on the table before collapsing heavily onto the couch. Agnes sat up quickly to give him room, clutching the blanket to herself like a frightened woman would her purse. Prime folded his arms and didn't speak.

"How'd it go?" she asked quietly, pulling at a loose thread on the blanket.

Prime sighed heavily and looked around the apartment.

"It went how it went. Wiggins came in, yelling. The Chief Reader dude. Everybody. I told them I heard someone leave out the back door, and I tried to chase them down, then went out in my car, looking, but couldn't catch them. Now they wanna review the security cameras. It might get bad. It might get real bad, Cherie."

"But they let you leave, right?" She sat up taller, hoping it was a good sign.

"Yeah, but not without questioning me for six hours. They're gonna call me back too." Prime leaned back into the cushions and rubbed his temples. "I didn't tell them it was you, though. I said I didn't see who it was. But they wanna check those cameras. They think that's their ace in the hole." He squeezed his eyes shut so tight

Agnes thought a tear might trickle out of them. "Damn. And you're not there. Maybe I should have made you go in. As a cover."

Agnes reached for her phone to check the time and was startled to see all the missed calls, mostly from numbers she didn't recognize: some of them from Utah, others from someplace in the Carolinas. Nothing from Berniece. Nothing from Colin. She made a note of it and turned back toward Prime.

"Well, I can't show up there now. It's too late, and...anyway, it's gon take em some time to go through the footage, and the truth is the cameras might not even show everything. Else, why would y'all have to be there? Why would they need so much muthafucking security?"

Agnes herself was starting to panic; cleaning the filthy apartment alone had been like spinning in a cocoon, where time stood still in a vacuum of dust particles and stale chunks of food. But now, reality had walked in wearing a Rent-a-Cop suit and black sneakers. Her fear was palpable and her home accent was leaking into her normally precise language, but she was too frazzled to bother starting over or correcting herself.

Prime certainly didn't notice; instead, he took up her theories, sighing and nodding again as he scratched the side of his face. "Yeah," he said slowly, his jaw going slack for a minute as he rolled his bottom lip against his teeth. "You just might be right about that." He sighed again, finally looking around the apartment. "You cleaned?"

"Yeah. I was bored. Also, it was way too dirty in here. Oh, I emptied one of your mousetraps." Which was a partial truth. Agnes had actually tucked the occupied one into one of the trash bags she hoisted into the dumpster, then hunted down an empty one and put it in the same place. He didn't need to know all that, though. Prime smirked.

"I guess it was. Haven't had a woman in here for a while." He scratched his face again. "I keep my room clean, though," he added, almost defensively. "That's where me and my little man sleep. I keep it real clean."

"Yeah," she said reassuringly. "I didn't have to do a lot in there."

He nodded in approval and looked around again, then reached over for the fast-food bag on the table. "Here. Brought you a sausage biscuit. I didn't think to get any orange juice."

Agnes thought it best to respond as if it was the most brilliant decision. "Thank you. I don't drink that anyway. Do you have any tea?" She already knew the answer.

"Yeah, in the cupboard over the stove," he said.

She rose, reaching for the bag, which he was clutching like a chicken whose neck he was about to wring. "I can heat those up. And I can make you some tea if you want."

Prime nodded, leaning back on the couch, now thoughtfully rubbing the place where he'd scratched his face.

AGNES COULDN'T FALL BACK TO sleep after breakfast, and she was too terrified to turn on the television, convinced that her face would pop up in breaking news reports on every channel. So, instead of day-time talk shows (which were what was actually playing), she listened to Prime's steady, droning snore and tried to avoid her phone, partially out of indignance that Berniece hadn't bothered to return what was obviously an emergency call made in the middle of the night. But even if she had called, Agnes wouldn't have known what to ask for because she was now completely without a plan. There was no way Prime would simply drop her off at the airport and sort everything out on his own, although Agnes wished he would. Why on earth had she come here? She could have kicked herself at her gullibility. Just as she had done in Nashville, she'd ended up in a place that wasn't hers and hoped the person who'd brought her there would treat her kindly. He had, but Agnes had no idea how safe she actually was. She wondered what Prime might make her do to return the favor. Remembering Colin's sexual proclivities, she started to panic again but calmed herself by scanning the bookshelf for things she could read, and finally settled on a stack of magazines, a few of them published earlier that year. Some were almost exclusively about bodybuilding, others about music, and still others simply filled with stories someone thought would be interesting to men, wedged between ads featuring scantily clad women selling vitamins or cologne.

When Agnes got tired of reading, she hobbled to the kitchen on her fallen-asleep feet to see what was there. She should try to cook something, as a way to make Prime's day a bit easier and to perhaps prove that she was good at something other than what she suspected he'd want. He'd calmed down as they ate breakfast, drinking the pumpkin spiced tea that probably tasted as strong as it did because it was both old and out of season. But as he got sleepier, he seemed to get more nervous. Agnes comforted him from her spot on the floor, surprised at how confident and maternal she sounded. A few minutes before he rose to take a shower, she reached over to rub his knee and promised they'd figure something out.

Hesitantly, he toyed with the idea of leaving.

"I got this uncle in Texas owns a locksmith company, and he's been telling me to come out there cause I'm good with my hands. I never did cause I didn't wanna leave Shana up here all by herself without Little Jackie. But I might have to."

"Would the job pay well?"

"It might pay okay after a while. Or I can work there until I find something better, or until this all blows over. My uncle owns it. So I could be a manager or something. Plus, it's cheaper to live in Texas. Well, in the part where he lives anyway."

"Where does he live?"

"Tyler."

"Oh, I know where that is." Agnes's mother and aunt used to take the kids to the zoo there every summer, usually right before the Fourth of July. It was an easy road trip: ninety or so miles west on I-20.

"Yeah. Pretty decent-sized town. He's got a nice house out there. And a smaller place on some land right outside the city where we could crash for a little while. Not that I wanted to leave here. Still might not. But it might be time. Might be a good move." Prime balled up his sandwich wrapper and free-threw it into the open bag on the coffee table.

"I understand that," she said slowly. "It may be for the best. If you stayed there, it'd be easier to save, buy a house. Even buy one back here, maybe, after all this blows over. And if you make enough money you can always send your son back to visit his grandparents. Or Shana."

"Nah, I might not do that until she's clean again. But yeah, I could send him to my parents. They could let her see him if they think it'll be okay."

"See? It's already coming together."

Prime smiled. "Yeah." Then he rubbed Agnes on the shoulder. "You coming to Texas too? We'd be close to Louisiana, right? Where you grew up."

"Yeah, we would be," Agnes said noncommittally. The prospect seemed even more dangerous than being in the apartment. Traversing the country with a stranger? But the thought of starting over completely while not being alone was alluring. Agnes's and Prime's fates certainly seemed tied together indefinitely anyway, with the loom of trouble lurking in the room, splashing them with alarm as they chewed on oily biscuits and salty sausage.

"Yeah, I might look into it after I get up," he said. "See how much I got saved up for gas. We'd need a good amount of money to get there, for sure. And money for the hotels too. On the way."

"Sounds good," said Agnes, relieved that his spirits were lifting.

"To me too," he said. "I love a sturdy hotel bed."

He stood up, kissed the top of her head, and left the room.

WHEN PRIME STUMBLED INTO THE kitchen several hours later, Agnes was in a rapture of sorts, the greasy air savory with the smell of frying chicken, and her face and the delicate skin at the back of her neck glowing with a thin sheen of perspiration. She had pinned up her frizzing hair as best she could with a few black bobby pins she'd found in one of the kitchen drawers, still tangled with strands of dark hair. She'd also stripped down to her undershirt and underwear, since her joggers had been splashed with dirty dishwater, mop water, and in a few places, bleach. As Agnes moved around, sweat slicked her inner thighs and she could smell the fragrant pungency of her underarms. She needed a shower but didn't care, and she chuckled at the thought of how much she had changed in eighteen hours. Perhaps she had slipped so far into a different life that the grading officials might not recognize her if they came looking.

Prime sneaked up behind her and wrapped his arms around her as she forked a pan of fried leg quarters onto a plate. Cooking had aggravated even more memories from those lean years after her father left. She'd found a half dozen or so small potatoes and had peeled the sprouts and black spots from them before dicing them up to mash, opting for butter and water instead of the warm carton of milk she'd found on the stove that morning. While rifling through the cabinets for salt, she found a pack of potato toppings so old the lettering had begun to rub off, but they were unopened. When she tore the top off and shook a few in her hand to taste, they immediately reminded her of her mother, who would sprinkle them over a glob of instant mash and serve with ranch-style beans. Until now, Agnes had never seen either product after leaving home. She licked her finger and dabbed a few more toppings out of the pack. It was a different brand than Agnes had eaten in her childhood but they tasted the same: salty, with the musty artificial bacon flavor that also dusted her favorite childhood potato chips, Andy Capp's. She had long ago abandoned such food, scared away by education and privilege, but God, it was comforting now, as the scent of fried chicken filled the air, chicken she had quick-thawed with warm water, like her mother used to do when one of the girls forgot to take a pack down out of the freezer after school.

She was finishing the meal when Prime came in, timid, but obviously impressed with her culinary skill, which even she admitted people couldn't tell just by looking at her. Timid and easily flustered, Agnes was not matronly like her mother or commanding like Berniece; she seemed hardly capable of coordinating the completion of a meal without burning something or breaking down. But that night, she spun fussily out of Prime's embrace with the declaration that she needed both hands to finish what she was doing, and distracted him by ordering him to open and heat up the green beans. As he twisted the can opener, she asked about his sleep and how he felt, which was code for whether or not he was still worried about what she'd done.

"I'm all right, I guess. I can't think about it now. It'll be there tomorrow. I did call my uncle, though, and told him I might be down there, maybe with my girlfriend. He said it was all right. I haven't asked him about a job yet. I wanna see what Wiggins and all them are gonna wanna do first."

When they sat down to eat, he tasted the food first and nodded his approval. After a few bites, though, he looked directly at her and smiled. Agnes's stomach lurched, and she stifled an acidic belch with her hand. As a child, Agnes always stared at Berniece, who, in some ways, looked exactly like her, just deep brown, which had given her her childhood nickname: Cookie. Berniece would buck her eyes at Agnes and ask, "Can I help you?" Agnes chuckled a little, then posed the question to Prime. He nodded knowingly.

"I read up on you."

"What about?" Agnes asked sharply, now terrified. So there was a news story out about her after all.

"That thing you have. You're albino, right?"

"Yeah," she said quickly, forgiving Prime the slight and telling herself that someone of his intelligence shouldn't be expected to use a phrase like "person with albinism": both its importance and its letter count were beyond his reach. It was an old defense mechanism, that arrogance, but it kept her mouth shut. He continued.

"Yeah. I think it's cool, though. I always knew you looked different, but now I know all this other stuff. Like, that you have powers. You bring good luck."

Agnes almost choked on a flaccid green bean, its salty juice resurging into her mouth as she coughed it down. "Powers?!"

"Yeah. Like, most of you are witches. And you can see in the dark. That's how you were able to get to the tests so fast and do all the stuff you did." Prime shook his head. "You couldn't have been in there more than ten minutes. And yikes." He shook his head vigorously. "But it also means we might not get caught. Cause you're magic."

We? Magic? Agnes laughed in spite of herself. Last night had been the one moment she had acted, not for the sake of appearances, but on emotion alone, and here she was, being forced to listen while the possibility of her crime was attributed to her physical difference.

"I...don't know about all that."

Prime gulped down a forkful of potato and broke off a drumstick from one of the flaky leg quarters on his plate. "You don't have to play it simple with me. I read about it online a little while ago, after I woke up. I didn't even know until one of the testing officials asked, after I described you. They asked if you were the albino one. Or just white."

"Wait...described me when?" Agnes's stomach heaved again.

"When they asked for a description of folks who'd been in the building after hours. I said I saw a couple people who left right after the lecture. I made one of them sound like you."

"Prime! But that would make them think it might have been me who did it! What the fuck?!"

"Wrong," he said calmly, after chewing slowly and swallowing. "I said you left and never came back. It's supposed to clear you. I put you there in case they saw you on footage I couldn't get to, so they'd know you left before anything happened." He flashed a slow smile of satisfaction and kept eating. Agnes was so dismayed she only heard part of what he said—otherwise, she might have been a little relieved. Instead, she thought he must have lost his mind.

"Prime, how *could* you—"

"Listen, I got it under control. After you split—"

Suddenly, there was a sharp rap on the door. Agnes had never been visited by the police, but she knew the sound of authority when she heard it in the staccato urgency of those five raps. The person knocking was doing so as a courtesy, to give whoever was on the other side a chance to open the door before it was opened for him. Prime's eyes widened, and he instinctively grabbed his phone, got up, and then, in a move that surprised Agnes, walked calmly over to her and whispered into her ear: "*Closet!*"

Like a carefully choreographed dance, they moved silently around each other. Agnes grabbed her plate and fork, holding its handle down with her finger so it wouldn't clatter as she raced to the back room. Prime grabbed her water glass and set it in the sink, then took her chair and lifted it back into place beneath the table, wiping down the ring of condensation left by her glass with his forearm. As he yelled out, "Just a minute!" Agnes raced to the bedroom closet on her tiptoes, hoping the floor didn't creak as she did so and hoping the downstairs neighbors hadn't been paying too close attention to the two sets of feet making noise in the minutes before.

Agnes crouched on the floor on top of wear-warped pairs of sneakers, flanked by the dank coolness of leather coats. She set her plate down gingerly, her fingers cramping from fright and her attempts to silence the fork. She steadied her breathing and listened.

It sounded like there were three additional voices. One was obviously a detective or local official of some sort, who explained to Prime the reason for their visit and asked all the questions. The other she heard Prime greet as Wiggins. The third said little and seemed to need no introduction. She guessed it could be the Chief Reader, or some administrative person. Prime repeated his story as best he could, saying that an hour after he'd done a sweep, he'd heard a noise in the Reading Room, went to check it out, and saw someone running out the back door. In a split-second decision, he decided to see if he could catch them. The official-sounding person explained they were still in the process of reviewing the camera footage, but there was some kind of issue with the hard drive, so they couldn't retrieve footage from the camera facing the Reading Room. Agnes strained to hear what the issue was, but couldn't. They were probably lying anyway, she reasoned. Cops did so on TV all the time.

In the meantime, they had few other leads, other than the fact that at least two readers hadn't shown up to their tables that day. One left abruptly due to a family emergency. The other was a woman named Agnes C. Kirkkendoll. They'd asked about her earlier. Prime remembered, but hemmed and hawed when they asked if he'd ever spoken to her. Sometimes he chatted with readers when they were on breaks, just asking where they were from, nothing too personal. He did that with just about everybody.

They showed him her photo. He said she looked familiar, but he'd probably just seen her after the reading, like he said before. The official-sounding person said that they weren't sure, but Agnes was a person of interest and they definitely wanted to find her. Then the official said he thought he'd heard voices coming from Prime's apartment as they ascended the steps. Who was that?

Prime explained that he'd been FaceTiming with a female acquaintance, someone he'd been dating from out of town. There was a long pause, and then someone asked if they could look around the apartment. Agnes held her breath and thought of the dim life she had lived the past few years. It was awful, but it had to be better than what was coming. Her life didn't flash before her eyes so much as it blazed, leaving only a few faces in her view. She shuddered and huddled, awaiting Prime's answer.

Agnes heard someone stand. Then: "You got a warrant?"

"Well, no, but we thought it might be a good idea to look around a little, just in case you aren't telling us everything."

"Wiggins, you know me. You know I'm a man of my word. If I don't know nothing, I don't know nothing."

Agnes couldn't hear exactly what Wiggins said, but his intonation suggested that he ultimately agreed. The ensuing roar in her ears might have been her own breath in spite of her attempts to stay quiet, but whatever it was, she couldn't hear what came next. When she could, it sounded like the men were preparing to leave. Wiggins was apologetically explaining to Prime that it would be best if he stayed off duty until this was straightened out, which Wiggins said he knew would happen because Prime was a good egg, covering shifts at the last minute and taking care of his son. Agnes sat stone still until they left, and Prime shuffled around in the front rooms, waiting for them to return to their cars and exit. As she listened, she felt something quick and small graze her bare toe, followed by a small clink of the fork. Agnes stood and groped for the light's string, already certain of what she'd find. At that exact moment, Prime flipped on the bedroom light and flung open the closet door. He was holding a filled glass of water, the same glass he'd dumped in the sink as she fled. The moment she saw him, she leaped over the clutter, and when she reached him, she pounced on him and kissed him. He staggered back a bit, water sloshing out of the glass, but then picked her up, wrapping her sweat-sticky legs around his waist and carrying her first to the light switch, which he flipped off, and then to the bed, which he flipped her onto and stood over her, trying to decide what to do next. As he turned toward the bathroom, Agnes realized his dilemma and grabbed his hand. She knew enough about herself to know that the frantic desire writhing her body into eagerness wouldn't last long enough for whatever he needed to take effect. And Colin had taught her enough of the delicate art of arousal that she knew how to handle herself from this point out.

"Please," she said to him, tugging at the waistband of his pajama pants. "I know what to do. Please. Let me."

LATER THAT NIGHT, AGNES PICKED up the stuffed mouse and asked, only half jokingly, "Is there a camera in this?"

Prime was holding her but staring down at his forearm, where the streetlamps that filtered through the blinds made a blue pattern from his elbow to his fingers.

"Nope. Nothing like that in here."

"Where'd you get this from?"

"Military hospital. In Germany. When I was in the army."

"You were stationed there?"

"No. I was in Iraq."

"Iraq?!"

"Yeah. Thirteen months. Almost finished. But something happened."

"Oh," said Agnes. Although Prime's voice was calm—and seemed far surer of what he was saying than she'd ever heard him be—there was an edge in his tone that made her hold off on asking what the "something" was.

"So what was it like? Being in the Middle East?"

"Harder than I thought it would be. We did good things, though. In the villages. We brought electricity and sewage systems. Medicines. Food."

"Did you miss home? Your parents and Shana? Your son?"

Prime sighed and shifted her in his arms. "All that didn't come till after. Way after."

"Oh."

"I missed my parents, though. A lot. Dad's steaks on the grill. My mom making candy at Christmas. I missed living in a world where you didn't have to draw on women and children if the translators weren't around and nobody understood how you spoke Arabic."

"Oh. Oh no. I'm so sorry."

Prime didn't respond. Instead, he turned himself over and topped her again, his chest still wet with sweat, which gathered in its coarse hair and dampened it unevenly.

"Let's get out of here, Cherie. At least to my parents'. If they get too nosy, I can explain what happened and they'll let you stay. They know how the cops can be. And they wouldn't let you get into any real trouble. They help Shana out like that all the time. Or we can go to Texas, to my uncle's. The testing folks might take awhile to find out it's you and maybe they won't make it a big deal. And if they can't find you, they might just leave us alone. I heard they keep scanned copies of everything anyway."

"But I wasted their money. And white folks don't play with their money."

"It's gonna take money to find you too. And evidence."

It was Agnes's turn to be quiet, because she wanted to believe as much, and she didn't want to ask the questions that would shatter that belief, though she was certain someone would connect the dots soon. They were houseplaying here in a hastily cleaned apartment that was little more than a temporary shelter from reality, but one Agnes had developed a fragile sense of comfort in. And she wanted to stay for as long as she could because the world beyond the front door seemed terrifying. The dingy walls had already suffered a breach only a few hours before in the form of big-voiced men making demands. But now, in the dark, she and Prime could make small talk and big plans with the movements of their bodies knitting them together for as long as they shared the bed with its stuffed animals and inky dressings.

"When do you want more children?" she asked during another break. Prime's penis lay wet and limp at her hip, and she hoped he'd reached his limits. Her body ached with exhaustion, and she was convinced that, at least tonight, she'd earned the sleep of the righteous.

"I guess as soon as we get on our feet," he said dreamily, running a hand through Agnes's now-regressed hair, coily and tangled. "Another boy. Maybe a girl if she looks like you." He yawned with the loud abandon of her mother. "I don't know. But you're magic, though. I know that. Look at all we've done and I haven't even needed that stuff in the bathroom. You could probably make a baby happen whenever you want. You want children now? Boom. You might already be pregnant."

"Prime, I'm not—" She stopped herself. "No—I'm not yet," she said, half in his arms, the other half of her snuggling into the mound of decorative pillows. "But why do you want them so badly?" she asked, presuming a civilian answer, perhaps even a romantic one.

"Because of all the people that died while I was there. Us. Them. Too many to even remember. It felt like if I watched one more person die, I would die. From shock, or offing myself, or whatever. I saw way too much to keep on living."

He pulled her back toward him and sighed. "Half the time, I feel like I'm trying to make up for what got taken. All those months I was there, people were killing everybody. Even the kids. We screwed up their balance of power. And when you do that, people start killing each other. And they don't care how young you are, or how old. I'm not saying I wanna replace them. I could never do that. I'm just trying to put back some of what got lost. Not fix it, but fix the balance of innocence in the world. The balance of good. That's what I miss, being in the army. We were doing good things. It didn't always work out how we wanted, but we did good. I miss being the solution to somebody's problem." He took a long pause. "I still miss it."

"Is that what made you come looking for me?"

Prime readjusted himself and held her even tighter. The muscles in his arms locked, and one forearm held her jaw askance as its fine hairs tickled her cheek, near her ear.

"Nah. Well. I mean, maybe. You just…When I walked in and saw what you did, I wanted to know what made you do it, you know? Maybe something happened to you. I needed to know. I've snapped before. And maybe I could try to protect you. Keep you from mucking up your life like I did mine. Or like Shana did hers."

Agnes tapped his arm a little, and he loosened his grip immediately and apologetically. Even so, it took her awhile to speak, and when she did, the words came, haltingly at first, but soon they flowed, and she found herself rattling off the ruin of her career in Nashville and how inconsequential she felt to everyone on campus, including her former professors. Her monetary woes. At one point, when she had trouble recalling a word spat at her in a terse conversation, she sucked her teeth in exasperation, and Prime responded, "Hmph." The mutual unspoken sentiment in the exchange was comforting.

But Prime's arm tightened when she talked about Colin. When she was done, he sat quietly before asking in a tone dripping with disgust:

"So, you lied. You *do* got a boyfriend."

His disappointment made Agnes feel remorseful and small. "I told you how he treats me. He's not my boyfriend."

"But you live with him. And you do stuff together, right?"

"That doesn't mean anything. Especially if half the time I don't want to."

"Wait. What are you trying to say? What else did he do?"

It was Agnes's turn to sigh. "If I told you, what could you do about it now?"

Prime went silent before slowly shaking his head. "Damn. Well, I guess we've both been through it."

More moments passed, and this time, he held her firmly but without constriction. And she stayed in his arms.

A FEW HOURS LATER, AGNES rolled him toward her so she could face him.

"What happened that made you leave Iraq?"

"I messed up. Snapped. Like you did. I lost it too."

"But what does that mean?"

"Just showed up for patrol one day buck naked. Doc thought I was bullshitting, but when I started talking, I wasn't making sense. Well, that's what they told me, since I don't really remember. I can barely remember the night before. I was lying outside, smoking hash, watching the sky, thinking, 'Man, this isn't the same sky up here as back home.' I was on the same planet, but it felt like being on Mars. And then I wondered, what if all this was a simulation, like a video game? What if I could just get up and walk away from it? All these dead people. What if all I had to do was walk away?" Prime paused to readjust himself. "That's the last thing I remember. They held me for like two weeks at Landstuhl, and then back here. I got better eventually, but…" He shrugged. "Sometimes I still overthink everything. Still not always sure I'm living in the world."

"How do you cope with that? Do you go to therapy?"

"Nah. Just take things one day at a time, like they say in Nar-Anon. I map things out a lot before I do them. Make sure all the pieces fit. Or I gotta pace. Or drive. Like I did with patrol. I work for Kettleman cause I get to pace. If I'm moving, I'm thinking. I'm figuring things out."

"You map things—is that why you like to paint?"

"No. That's different. Been doing that my whole life. But there's not enough light here for all that, you know? See, Cherie? That's why I wanted a house. With a sunroom maybe, and I could set up my easels. Man, I feel like everything I love is in these little pieces I'm trying to get all in one place. My paintings. My boy. A good woman. I just want a place where I can put all the pieces. Some people gotta have everything. But all I want is my pieces."

"But it sounds good. It sounds like enough," said Agnes.

"Yeah. It would be," he said quietly.

IN THE HALF-LIGHT OF morning, against the sound of Prime's sonorous breathing, Agnes crawled out of his grasp and hobbled to the living room on unsteady legs, kneeling in front of the couch cushions and running her hands along their seams. She found her phone, its battery low, with missed calls from Berniece, Colin, and more from several unrecognized numbers. She dialed Berniece first.

"Yes?" It sounded like she was driving, probably home from work. Bern often took home-health gigs for extra money, when she and Algin were saving for vacations or new gadgets. Agnes proceeded with caution.

"Hey. Are you alone?"

"Yes."

"Okay." An awkward silence followed.

"Hey, what's going on? Some people have been calling looking for you. They said I'm your emergency contact." Berniece's voice sounded strange, like a piano being tuned by ear. Maybe it had just been too long since they'd spoken.

"Yeah. I'm in Utah doing the grading thing again."

"Again? I thought they didn't pay that much money."

"Not really. But I needed it."

"Huh. Okay. Mom said you had a job interview in Boston or something?"

"Yeah. I didn't get it."

"Oh. Okay." More silence. "Well, what's going on? Who's looking for you?"

"The testing people. I ditched work on the next to last day. Just got tired of doing it."

"Why would you do that? Are they still gonna pay you?"

"I don't know."

"Well, that was…" Berniece trailed off.

Agnes's chest tightened. "Yeah. I just got frustrated I guess."

"Well…" Berniece hung on to that first word for a long time before letting the others follow. "You called me the other night, didn't you?"

"I did."

"Okay? Is there something you need help with?"

"I'm not sure. Listen, I'll try to call you back, maybe later today if I can't take care of everything. But thanks for offering."

"Okay. And if you haven't called Mom, do it now. I called to ask about you and now she's worried. She acts like she knows something's up. But I didn't ask if they called her because then I'd have to tell her they called me, and that'll just stress her out. She doesn't need that."

"Okay. Thanks again."

Just as Agnes was disconnecting, she heard Berniece exhale with disgust. "Dumbass."

Agnes rose from the couch and carried the phone back to the bedroom, hoping to find a charger. She knew she wasn't going to call her mother back right then; she needed a convincing enough story and a convincing enough tone, and at the moment, she had neither. Prime was sitting up quietly, rubbing his eyes with the heel of his palm. She crawled into bed beside him, and he kissed her.

"We should leave. As soon as we can," she said.

"Who was that?"

"Nobody…My sister. But we should go to Texas. Tyler, I mean. Wherever your uncle's house is."

He smiled slowly, turning to her. "My kind of woman." It made Agnes think of their first and only date, and how much had transpired in less than three days.

"First thing, though. We gotta get you out of here." He yawned again, this time without blowing out. Agnes thought that was strange, but she agreed with him.

"Yes! And if they want us, let em come find us. Like you said, maybe they won't even care."

"Yeah, but I mean out of this apartment. To my parents' house."

"Your parents?"

"Don't worry about it; they're really sweet. They live out in the boonies, though. Kinda isolated." He said it quickly, like it was the fine print of their unfolding agreement.

Agnes balked. "But…I don't know them. How far away is that from here?"

"Not too far. And they won't let us take Jackie if you don't. And I'm not leaving if I can't take Jackie."

She said nothing in response to this, so he continued. "Might need to go soon, too, in case they come back with a warrant, or somehow that backup SD card turns up."

Agnes stared at him blankly, then quizzically. Prime was staring at his dresser, at all the cologne bottles lined up in one neat row. His gaze was so intense he might have even been counting them.

The SD card. She was tempted to ask, but the truth was, she didn't actually want to know. If Agnes's mother deserved oblivion as a form of grace, then dammit, so did she. And what might her life have been like had there been things she'd never found out, like Berniece's reaction to her nickname, or Colin's thoughts about introducing her to his parents? How might she be spending this morning, had she lived in total oblivion to what other people made—or wanted to make—of her? It was an unanswerable question, but when Prime turned to look at her, she nodded.

"I think that makes sense," she said affirmatively.

Prime looked up at her hair and smoothed it a little. "It sure does, Magic Girl," he said evenly. He was a man who'd decided she was the last piece in a puzzle he'd been trying to put together while walking the halls of empty buildings, or eating French fries while overlooking the city like a god, waiting for a chance to make something move. Then one day, she walked into his life, did a thing she thought was only for herself, and handed him the final, perfectly fitting blip of cardboard. Maybe Berniece was right: she was a dumbass. She sat perfectly still while the realization bloomed in her, a tangle of devastation and indignance. Berniece had been telling her who she was her whole life. Some of it—dammit, at least part of it—had to be false.

But she also concluded that, if this was a time for people to show their cards, she might as well get her share of what was on the table.

"No—it's okay. Your parents' house is fine. Just one thing, though."

"What's that?"

"If we get to Texas, can you also take me home?"

"Home like Tennessee?" he asked incredulously.

"No. Shreveport. Where I grew up. It's not far from where we're going. A couple of hours, tops."

"Oh," he said. "Yeah, of course, baby. I can do that. We can meet your family. Is that why you want to go?"

She nodded. Then they stared at each other intently. Suddenly, he rolled her over, putting his weight on her pelvis, nudging her legs open.

"Thank you," she said. Then again, "Thank you, baby." She relaxed a little as he pushed himself inside her. "For agreeing to take me. I've got some loose ends I need to tie up."

"Loose ends?" He was already panting, sweaty.

"Yeah. Family stuff—my sister. Plus," she said, stroking the back of his neck, "for my magic. I think I left some of my magic there."

II.

The bed on which Agnes slept in a double-wide mobile home east of Tyler was far nicer than the one she left in Nashville and every hotel room they'd booked during the three-day trip from Utah to Texas. Beds had become the linchpin of Agnes's discomfort since she and Prime left Salt Lake with his parents' promise that they would look in on his apartment and look after the one thing Prime had initially refused to leave behind: his son. They'd also intimated they'd keep Prime's rent up-to-date, but only if he needed them to. With their sprawling ranch house and several cars, Jackie and Dale Primus certainly looked like they could afford it, which Agnes slyly noted for future reference. Agnes herself had never been lucky enough to have a parent who both wanted to help and had the means. Being an in-law of the pair wouldn't be a bad way to end up, even though their generosity still stung her with a jealousy-tinged guilt. She thought Prime was too simple to even understand how fortunate he was, let alone know what they could both do with that kind of support.

Tonight, hundreds of miles away, she stared at a smooth, somewhat low, but impeccably white ceiling of the prettiest home she'd called her own since before her father found someone new. The trailer wasn't much to look at from the outside; it resembled many of the units she'd seen as a child for sale on the sides of highways, or perched on the backs of tractor trailers with flags flipping in the backdraft, warning of the oversized load. But Agnes gasped a breath of awe and relief when they crossed the threshold and she saw the neat living room with its beige couches facing each other, separated by a coffee table and a small fireplace on the back wall. Almost instinctively, she looked down at the floor, which was made of a cheap grade of wood planks, but it was spotless. The whole place looked (and smelled) as if it had been scrubbed for their arrival: the glass coffee table as transparent as air, the scent of room deodorizer still heavy, though under it, the faintest hint of cigar smoke.

Prime's uncle Hubert met them there to let them in but refused to stay. He lived in the family's house in the city and wanted to get back to bed—it was already after eleven—but promised to return in the morning so he and Prime could catch up and shoot the breeze. Nothing in his voice betrayed how he felt about their presence, or about Agnes specifically, but Agnes guessed that that was more Hubert's nature than anything. Surely Prime's mother had filled him in on her misgivings before Agnes and Prime ever left Salt Lake's city limits, and Agnes had no doubt he was as suspicious of her presence as his sister, Dale, who, during the first instance when she and Agnes were alone, brushed little Jackie's hair away from his ears so she could cover them as he sat in her lap, playing with a large red block.

"Listen, I don't know what your intentions are with my son," Dale began in a deceptively casual tone, a hint of Southern drawl still present in the way she drew out *son*. "But I don't trust you. I'm only agreeing to this because Prime's been through the ringer these past few years, and we've all been thinking a move back home might suit him. Now, I'll do whatever it takes to keep him happy, keep him on an even keel. This one too," she said, nodding toward her lap. "But if you aim to run him into the ground, like that other one? Just know I aim to take care of what's mine."

There was no time for Agnes to convince her otherwise, which she might have tried to do if the patio door hadn't opened and Jackie Primus hadn't yelled that the goodbye steak dinner was served. Dale jounced Little Jackie on her knee before picking him up and heading toward the kitchen for his high chair, while Agnes sat on the couch, momentarily stupefied. As grandmother and son brushed past her, the little one threw his large red block with both hands, and it hit Agnes squarely in the head, just above her right ear.

Like his sister, Uncle Hube was stocky, redboned, and dimpled, with an easy smile and an ample paunch, but he was far less demanding of the senses. He unlocked the trailer's front door with nary a jingle of a key, and once Prime lugged in their bags, he disappeared without a sound. In her exhaustion, Agnes wondered if he'd been there at all. Maybe she'd just imagined him.

The weary travelers were in bed now, drifting, and Agnes's body throbbed all over: her back bucked with spasms from sitting in a car for days on end; her skin ached from the sunlight glaring through the windshield; and her pelvis thrummed from bearing Prime's weight every night, almost as soon as the sun went down—sometimes before she was even done eating her dinner. In the mornings, she awoke hungry, bed-lagged, and so sore she thought something must have gone wrong in her body. Maybe her IUD had been jostled by Prime's frantic thrusts. Some nights she was sure it was going to slip down, maybe prick him while he was inside her. Or maybe it would get caught on some part of his penis and bisect the whole organ. *Ah, to be so lucky*, Agnes mused with a half snort before covering her mouth. She didn't want to call attention to herself, since Prime was so quiet, no doubt already half dozing. But she was curious about their mild-mannered host, and she had questions. So she took her chances, beginning with the obvious and, hopefully, the least suggestive.

"How does this place look like this?" she whispered cautiously. "It's…it's beautiful."

Prime adjusted the leg he often swung over her, the one that pinned her in place once he was fast asleep. Away from the familiarity of his small apartment, Prime suffered violent night terrors, and any movement in the room could trigger his waking up with a scream or, worse, searching the room frantically for his weapon. Agnes learned quickly that unlimited sex and keeping still kept the peace.

"That's my uncle," he said dreamily. "He's always been like this. Nice stuff, even in a trailer. Just like in Harlem."

"Harlem?"

"Yeah, he lived there a long time, till my grandma got sick. Then he came back to take care of her, and until she died he lived out here, on our land. We used to have a little farm, but he wasn't cut out for that life. And the government did all kinds of stuff to Black farmers back in the day. Denying loans, penalizing you if you didn't do farming programs or use certain pesticides. That's why some of the family moved out west. Life was easier."

"Yeah. That makes sense. So who was staying here before then?"

"One of his buddies, I think. Somebody who came up from Harlem when my grandma died. But that guy moved to the big house to make room for us."

Agnes was intrigued. As sophisticated as she presumed herself to be, she knew few people who'd moved to New York City. There was a mousy girl from her high school drama class, and another who became a dancer for Alvin Ailey, but most folks got out of Shreveport by moving west like Prime's parents. They often went to closer places like Dallas, a city the couple crawled through during a late rush hour, the traffic jam moving so slowly Agnes had enough time to identify the fabric patterns of abandoned couches on the freeway, even in the dark. Or folks went to Houston, a place she'd never been but wanted to visit. Berniece went there often, if her Instagram was telling the truth. She and her friends loved going to the masquerade balls or to elaborate dinners at restaurants run by Katrina transplants. But New York? Geographically, culturally, it seemed like a place out of reach for Ark-La-Texans. This was one reason why Agnes had never tried to get there herself.

"What was his place like?" she asked. "The one in Harlem?"

"I never went; just heard about it. Real nice, though, if my mom tells it. Lots of art."

"Your uncle painted too?"

"Nah, he was more like a collector. Of famous people, you know? Sculptors too. Fancy stuff."

"Is any of that at the big house?"

"I dunno. My mom said when he found out my grandma was sick, he left most of it at his place since he owned it. Just kind of abandoned his whole life and started over. Like us." He squeezed Agnes a little in the vise grip of his heavy arms. "But maybe the friend brought some of it with him. I don't know. We'll see when we go there, I guess. Whenever we go." With that, Prime drifted into the sleep of the satisfied, while Agnes spent the rest of the night thinking about Uncle Hube and his collectibles. She wondered what kind of man could live such a decadent life elsewhere, then come back here and somehow make a home.

AGNES DESPERATELY WANTED TO TALK to Hube about this—about anything, really—but to her disappointment he abided by the social laws of the land, treating her with the same deference and avoidance he treated their luggage with the night he let Prime roll it into the trailer, offering only a gentle directive about where their bags might best be stored until they were unpacked.

"Please, mind the couches," he said when Prime tried to unshoulder Agnes's dingy backpack onto the eggshell-colored love seat.

And Agnes might have struck up a casual conversation, but Prime never gave her enough time to linger. He sprinted toward doors and chairs with a speed that belied his compact bulk or the way he'd once leisurely strolled around her breakfast table at the convention center. Now he rushed everything. Even the drive, which could have taken seven days instead of three had they stopped to take in some of the sights. But Prime always refused; they had to get where they were going, and fast.

"What if they're following us?" he asked one day when Agnes meekly suggested they take an excursion to a spa Berniece once visited in Santa Fe. "Nope. Can't chance it. We're safer at my uncle's house. He's a business owner. He's got clout and he could help us out if it turns out we're really in a jam. We're Bonnie and Clyde, remember?" He winked. "We're on the run. But we can relax once we get there."

"When will we go to Shreveport? To visit my family?"

"We'll have to see about that once we're there. But don't worry! We'll figure it out, Sherry Berry." He groped her thigh as they sped along the highway, and Agnes fumed at the horrible play on her middle name and the irony: he was spitting back at her the same hollow words she'd told him a week before, back at his apartment.

As wary as he seemed about being pursued, Agnes had come to understand that Prime wasn't running from something so much as he was running toward something else. The thought of what it might be made her nervous. She wanted to talk to Uncle Hubert, see what it took to live how one wanted in a place where so much seemed predetermined by other people. So when he invited the couple into town for dinner, Agnes was convinced she finally had her chance.

Uncle Hube lived near a golf course, and his house was surrounded by two large gardens in the front and back. On the path to his front door, roses crawled over themselves in a line of neat bushes that flanked the cobblestones. She'd paused, waiting for her eyes to adjust to the bright dusk well enough to see what kind of roses they were, but Prime tugged at the puffy sleeve of a blouse he'd bought for her from a Marshalls in Albuquerque.

"Get the lead out, Magic. We're already late."

He'd taken to calling her that too. She hated it.

When Hube opened the door, he pointed them toward a small parlor off the living room. The room's furnishings hearkened back to the Victorian era.

"Please sit, and Griffin will bring you an aperitif."

Griffin, who Agnes knew was Hube's partner the moment Prime mentioned him, caught Agnes with her neck craned, marveling at the chairs she and Prime sat in as they waited for dinner. The backs were high and curved over their heads like canopies, the upholstery a rich red paisley. Agnes might have picked out a similar style for her own house if she had one. The chairs suggested their owner liked things that were ornate but not gaudy, with flair but not flashy. People like Agnes knew the difference, she told herself confidently.

The same could be said for Griffin. He was tall—very tall, actually—with a neat, square face and an even neater gray goatee, which clashed subtly but brilliantly with his gold wire-framed glasses. He was bald, and the top of his head shone like finely blown glass, though his face was dotted with small black moles. He was beautiful, thought Agnes, and graceful to boot. He held the silver tray with one hand and filled the stained crystal glasses on it with the other, not spilling a single drop on the lace doily. His movements were deliberate and effortless. This was the kind of man, thought Agnes bitterly, she could see herself with.

Like his partner, Griffin said little about anything, including Agnes and her color, but as he set the stemmed glass on the table beside her, he looked her directly in the eye, blinked, and smiled a small, knowing smile. Agnes was familiar with what such glances meant to convey. Griffin was saying, *I know what you are, but I am polite enough not to ask you to elaborate for me.* Agnes hadn't thought much about this since Prime introduced her to his parents, who each awkwardly shook her hand, gape-mouthed, openly curious but eager not to aggravate their fragile son. Agnes was silently grateful for their reticence and, here, for Griffin's laconism.

Had the men known how much she coveted their lives and unmatched taste, they might have engaged Agnes in more conversation, but again, there was neither time nor space. Almost as if on cue, Prime took it upon himself to fill the quiet, exquisite home with so much noise, Agnes thought his chatter might rattle the china cabinet. The beef Wellington with its flaky crust and blushing interior was barely on the table before Prime launched into his well-practiced spiel about how they came there so abruptly, after months of both Hube's and the Primuses' suggestions. It was the exact version of what he told his parents: He and Agnes met in the convention center during one of her breaks. She was getting over a heartbreak from a live-in boyfriend in Tennessee, and he was finally considering being done with Shana for good—well, except for coparenting and supporting her sobriety, of course. Then there was some kind of shake-up at the testing site: one of the guards let a male grader back on-site and *something* happened. Prime wasn't sure what. He was on break at the time, but everyone on the shift was placed on leave until the powers that be got to the bottom of it. So he was out of a nine-to-five for the time being, and he needed something to keep his hands busy and his mind clear. Everyone in the family seemed to understand that Prime didn't fare well when he had little to do, and he used that to his advantage, needing only to justify Agnes's presence in Tyler, which he did with the explanation that, now that things were on the outs with her boyfriend, she had nowhere else to go. Though he would often pause to lean back in his chair and grip the table's edges, leaving faint impressions from his fingertips on the white, starched tablecloth, the men at the table seemed none the wiser about the ruse.

As Prime chattered, Agnes distracted herself with wine and the curated beauty of Hubert's home. Prime's description a few nights before did it very little justice. There was art, yes, and beautiful onyx sculptures throughout, but also furniture of all kinds. There were antiques and replicas in the parlor and dining room, but some rooms had a cozier or a modern flare. The den resembled a man cave, with large leather recliners and colorful acrylics on canvas, whose palette hearkened back to the Afrocentric art of the 1990s. One of the downstairs bedrooms reminded Agnes of a romance book cover: a canopy bed was draped with filmy white curtains and its eyelet duvet was embroidered with tiny pink flowers.

The covered patio featured wicker seating and faux-suede pillows, a complicated-looking grill and outdoor range, and a fire pit. The patio was clearly one of the house's add-ons, its wood still blond and bright with fresh stain, the flagstones of the steps an unblemished, unbleached red. Raised boxes held the bristly sprouts of all kinds of herbs. Several trellises were studded with tangles of wild berries.

"Some of the house has been redone over the years," Hube explained softly as Agnes stared. "Griffin has a bit of the carpenter in him."

Griffin smiled his knowing smile at Hube's back as they continued their after-dinner tour. Before following him inside, Agnes gave the patio one last look with a quiet, reverent nod.

But her awe burst forth in the master bedroom, with its imposing four-poster bed, a wood-burning stove, and—to Agnes's surprise when she looked up—an elaborate mural on its recessed ceiling. She gasped in recognition.

"After Aaron Douglas," Hube explained with just a dash of pride.

"I know," she replied breathlessly. "I went to Fisk."

"Ah, did you, now? I have a few old friends who are alumni. I used to visit them on campus back in the Ice Ages, and I fell in *love* with the murals. A friend—my dearest Carl—came down, locked himself in here for a week, and left this. I fall asleep gazing at it every night."

And who wouldn't have, with the greens, blacks, browns, and muted sun yellows? It was the perfect choice for such an intimate space. Agnes craved something similar to look at while in bed with Prime. It might have made more of their nights bearable. She shook herself out of her trance by lightly touching the bedspread, which was a quilt of similar hues but accented here and there with bright blue squares.

"This was Mother's," Hube said, touching it as he talked. "Carl slept under it his first night here, and I suspect it brought the mural to mind." Griffin sniffed contemptuously in the background. Hube slipped glibly into another subject.

"My mother was a complicated woman; we didn't agree on everything, but she was immensely talented. She could take the scraps from anything and make beauty. I suppose everyone had a woman in their family who could do that with a needle and thread, but look here at how the fabrics complement each other. And the stitching!" Hube traced a pattern as Agnes leaned in close to better see it, but Griffin had already turned away from the group and headed for the bedroom door. Prime followed. With the wind knocked out of what Agnes had hoped to turn into a fruitful conversation, she and Hube did the same. Though she could see nothing but the raw silk shirt rippling on his back, she imagined Griffin was sporting that same knowing smile.

THEY'D ONLY BEEN IN TYLER for a week, but Agnes and Prime had developed the nightly routine of sitting on the wheelchair ramp Hube built for bringing his late mother out to the country for fresh air. The landing was wide enough for two kitchen chairs (which might have greatly displeased Hube if he saw how they dragged them through the trailer to the front door), so it was a perfect erstwhile porch from which they could watch deer scuttle woozily between the bushes in the mornings, and fireflies burn in and out of the air at night. Agnes loved that porch until she saw the one Griffin built, perhaps in an effort to rival the bedroom mural. Now the one at the trailer seemed silly. But that night, after dinner at Hube's, Agnes herself felt silly, with wine sloshing in her belly and dreams of a beautiful home swimming before her eyes. She was sitting in Prime's lap, something she'd never done before, but it was a cool night, and he seemed subdued enough by his own profligacies at the dinner table. The extra shot of whiskey he'd taken in Hube's study as they talked about Prime coming on at the locksmith company freed Agnes to be wistful in his arms without fear of expectations. Prime held her loosely as his chin rested on her shoulder, and they both looked out contentedly into the thicket.

"What did you think of that house?" he asked, without envy or excitement.

"It was beautiful." Agnes knew he shared the sentiment; she didn't have to pretend one way or another.

"Yeah," he said. "Yeah. I would fill a house like that with art just like him."

"Or your paintings. You could fill it with those too."

"Yeah," he said again. "Yeah." He shifted her in his lap, straightening his leg so she rested squarely on his meaty thigh. Then he drifted again into his own thoughts. Agnes searched for something to say to bring him back.

"How much is the art in that house worth, you think?"

He rubbed his chin on her shoulder, and the stubble itched like mosquito bites. "I don't know. Probably a fortune. That's over a lifetime, though. Of collecting. People giving you gifts. Building things."

"Yeah, that's true."

"That's what houses are for, though. You know? That's... That right there is the main reason I want one."

"I remember. You said that on our first night together. Or maybe it was on our first date."

"On the hilltop? Oh man, if I did that, I really was into you. I never tell people that the first time I meet them."

"Well, technically, the date wasn't our first time meeting."

"That's true." He scratched her shoulder again with his stubble. "But I musta known then, right away, that it was you."

"Me? Me for what?"

"For being my One."

Agnes wanted a lot of things at the moment, and some of them might have even been contingent on that declaration. Still, she was bewildered at the finality of it. *His One*. It sounded so permanent. So eternal. She smiled weakly and nuzzled his stubbly cheek with her chin, but said nothing. Prime read her silence as assent.

"I can't believe we're so close to our dreams right now, Cherie. Like, I can just work here, and build, and bring my boy out, and we can have a house just like that one. I'll even paint you a mural if you want. What was that guy's name again?"

"Aaron Douglas."

"Yeah. I'll paint you a mural. All cowboys if you want, like that picture I first showed you."

Agnes's heart sank a little. She would have preferred something a little more classical. Still, she agreed. "Yeah. I'd love that."

"Yeah. Art. Family. Everything I love in one place, like my own little museum."

Agnes felt a chill like a thin electric shock travel up her arms. She distracted herself by returning to an old request. "When do you start work, though? Should we visit my family before then? Cause if you're working doubles, it might be hard to get time off for that."

Prime sighed and worked his mouth a little. Then he squeezed her tighter and whispered into the dip of skin just above her clavicle. "You gotta get your family to approve me before we settle down?"

Agnes rubbed his back playfully. "There's certainly nothing they could do to change anything now," she offered. "But I do want them to meet you."

"You really mean that?" Prime beamed. "Maybe I could ask them for your hand."

Agnes closed her eyes tight at the thought, but behind them played snapshots of Hube's house: the furniture, the aperitifs, the patio, the mural. A dream swelled in her, one that almost looked like Prime's. "Yeah! Yeah, baby. Of course you can."

Then, Agnes simply gave in. She thought briefly of what Berniece might do in the face of such circumstances, then leaned back and blew Prime a kiss, then two. Next, she blew into her hands and rubbed them together, warming them. Colin's hands were so cold sometimes, and he never asked if or where he should touch her. Agnes held hers up for Prime, and with the left one, pointed down. He nodded eagerly. She slipped both of them into his boxers.

Prime let out a breathy moan, and as she worked him, she thought of all the times she'd gasped as men entered her, in shock at her own audacity as well as theirs. She had either duped or dared them to take her body thus far; she had even tried to chicken some of them, but they'd held out. So did Colin, with his laughable unkindness. She worked Prime harder, but not faster, thinking, *If I do everything the exact opposite, I can show him a tenderness neither of us has known.*

Agnes stood and stripped completely naked there on the porch. Prime did, too, and they stood awkwardly, the night air closing warmly around their bodies as if it had drawn them into its mouth like a breath awaiting release. For the first time since the night back at the apartment, it was Agnes who initiated things, and Prime was briefly frozen, unsure how to respond. She reached for his shoulder, pushed him back down on the lawn chair, and straddled him.

Their eyes locked as she rose slightly and sat down on him slowly. But it didn't feel the way she thought it must have felt when Colin thrust himself inside her. She'd presumed one got drunk on that kind of unchecked power—careless and swept up in the bitter wine of it. But she didn't. In fact, she saw everything now with brutal clarity. It was Prime who seemed adrift as he stared. So she played with him, taking him into her one inch at a time, resisting, wrapping herself around him carefully like a boa: tighter, tighter, constricting as she held her breath. Then she relaxed, loosened, and let him completely in.

She rocked slowly at first and waited until their breaths synced before she put her mouth to his ear and asked, "Where are you taking me?"

At first, he didn't answer; he simply breathed harder, holding her by the waist to push himself deeper. She brushed his hands away, determined to keep her own pace. Prime's head flopped back, his eyes a glaze of wet; his mouth open slightly, the pink tongue now dark from dinner's gravy and ganache. A slender spool of his breath met her nostrils, and on it, the charred-earth smell of whiskey.

"I'm okay," he said, answering a different question.

She sped up a bit, lifting and lowering. "But where are you taking me?"

It took him awhile to answer, so long that Agnes slipped, too, into the nebula of her own self-awe. That her body could be capable of bringing someone something other than disgust or satiety? Now *that* was something—dare she say it?—akin to joy. But she also felt sorrow at how fleeting the feeling would be. It made her think, as she often did during sex, of duende.

"Lorca," she breathed inaudibly. She knew that Prime, if he was listening, wouldn't understand. And she didn't want him to know she was anywhere else. So she returned to herself and looked at him with intent. But "Lorca, Lorca" fell sloppily out of her mouth—so sloppily it almost sounded like "love."

It's not clear what Prime was thinking of, or what he heard, though he might have stepped through some portal, perhaps into the Iraqi desert heat, then out, returning to the southern summer's mouthwarm breeze. Wherever he'd gone, he gripped her, panting, and she felt, for a brief moment, the full expanse of her power over him, with his hands rolling like tires over her hips and up her back with crushing urgency. She gave one forceful thrust. Then another.

"Where are you taking me tomorrow?" she asked.

Agnes had been stuck in duende all her life. The duende of what was there. What was not there. The duende of who loved her and who didn't. Agnes lived on the edge of these things at all times; it was where she was, in fact, her most comfortable, though she didn't know it. For years, she'd tried to flee the feeling, but she could never find a place outside it. What was wrong with her? Where did she belong? Then Prime said the word that shifted the longing in her legs.

"Home, baby. I'll take you. I'll take you home."

Home.

That was the only reason she came.

THE SCENIC ROUTE ON I-20 East was okay, but Agnes half wished they'd entered the city from another direction. Any of them really. Had they come up from the southern part of the state, the highway would have widened and neatened, and they could have gotten off on Kings Highway or Line Avenue to drive through the nicer parts, the ones originally built with old money and infused with Katrina wealth and opportunities. Maybe they could have had lunch on Youree Drive or Industrial Loop, which were now both filled with strip malls, restaurants, and car dealerships. Had they come from the east, the cheap motels and truck stops would have disappeared as they sped through Bossier with its big-box stores and mall, then to the Red River, where the casino lights insulted the dark with their dazzle, the Horseshoe rising like a glittery tidal wave out of the water. Even from the north might have been fun, taking 220 over Cross Lake, the miles of nothing but water and trees that made the small ponds they now passed seem like teasers for Agnes. Whenever she thought nostalgically of the landscape of home, she thought of that lake, the houses surrounding it on all sides—some upscale, others modest, depending on the location. And of the boats that dotted that massive body of water, pulling fish and sustenance from it, or bobbing along for the beauty of the view. Sportsman's Paradise, they called it. Home really was a place where everything depended on what side of the water you called yours, and whether you went out on it for necessity, crime (because sometimes bound bodies washed ashore), or pleasure.

Coming from this direction, she was eager to escape the dingy monotony of the heat-cracked highway, so she asked Prime to exit. They drove the last few miles on the surface streets she'd memorized as a child, ones that were close to the neighborhood in which she'd lived out her high school humiliation. But that, too, was a disappointment. Everything about the city had seemed to deflate in both size and cleanliness. Even the enviable mansions of her youth were now just large ranch-style houses, some of which were in grave disrepair. The only well-kept thing she noticed between Pines and Lakeshore was a shop that looked like it serviced luxury cars. Elkins Custom Auto, the sign read.

What had not changed, however, was the land. Every house had a generous front yard, and usually an expansive back one. Agnes missed that: green lawns with their blond mower lines, where the dead grass bleached in the sun, giving off the archaic, sweet scent of a dying thing. It was an aromatic buffer between where you slept and the roads that led somewhere. She wondered if Hube had missed that, too, while he was away, and if the ways he had settled into his ancestral space was his way of taking back the privilege of spreading out, of taking up occupancy in a place, not just perpetually passing through.

But her fantasies dampened when they pulled under her mother's carport. Agnes was relieved Prime didn't mention the house, which was small. And her mother looked smaller when she answered the door and smiled slowly. Her life had been such that Doyce Kirkkendoll was rarely surprised.

"Hey, girl. I was just thinking about you." It was the strangest way to greet someone you had no intention of seeing that day, but somehow it fit.

"Hey, Mama."

Doyce looked off into the distance of the driveway, where Prime was unloading bags from the car.

"That's just my friend, Mama. His name is Edwin. He drove me down here. To surprise you." Agnes didn't want to say from where just yet.

"Wasn't you somewhere doing grading or something?"

"Oh, I finished last week. And I'm on vacation for the Fourth of July." Which was a complete truth if you believed the parts she told, and not what any of them implied.

Doyce started fumbling for the burglar bar door keys, which Agnes couldn't see, but knew from memory that they sat in a bowl on top of a defunct stereo speaker, along with the mail. "Well, come on in, girl. Good to see you." It had been seventeen days since she'd last spoken to her mother, and for Agnes, it had felt like a lifetime, but her mother didn't care. And Agnes knew this wasn't the end of the story, or of the questions, but for now, she was relieved.

BERNIECE'S HOUSE. ALL AGNES'S MOTHER could talk about was Berniece's house, which, in a way, had once been hers but would soon belong to her daughter and son-in-law in a twist of fate even Agnes considered cruel. The neighborhood in which Agnes and Berniece spent part of their childhoods was undergoing a Procrustean level of gentrification. It had already been well-enough-to-do—an enclave for the Black folks who could afford to live on the western lip of the city going toward Greenwood. But over the years, its inhabitants had grown paranoid and persnickety, enclosing the subdivision with a gate and creating a neighborhood association, who had lately been pressuring folks to sell so land developers could tear down and rebuild, or pestering the stragglers to renovate their comfortable homes into more opulent—and sometimes Frankensteinian—places to bolster the neighborhood's overall curb appeal. Sabine had used the pressure as an opportunity to convince her husband they could find something just as nice in the suburbs around Baton Rouge without having to renovate, so the couple packed up and moved sometime that spring. Agnes hadn't even known they were gone.

But Berniece and Algin were well aware; they'd bought the girls' childhood home and immediately gutted it, reconfiguring and repurposing rooms, adding an extension in the back that would give Berniece a makeup room and a small gym on one side, and a test kitchen for Algin on the other, complete with a walk-in freezer for large game. He had ambitions of hosting a local live cooking show. The master bedroom would now be twice as large, taking over part of the living room, which would, in turn, steal space from the eat-in area in the kitchen. Their father's study was now a movie room. Agnes's room was a walk-in closet that opened into the makeup studio. Only the dining room and Berniece's room—which was now "guest quarters"—would stay the same. There would have been a mother-in-law apartment out back, but Berniece had opted for an in-ground pool instead.

The remodeling seemed to bring Doyce and Berniece closer, though Agnes had her suspicions about why. Since Doyce's houseguests were unannounced, she made no bones about having important errands to run before shops closed for the holiday, and she enlisted Prime and Agnes for the tasks, all of which turned out to be for Berniece. Agnes suspected being a Girl Friday made Doyce feel like part of her eldest daughter's life again, so she humored her, as did Prime, who liked being helpful. Having a to-do list and now a crew seemed to imbue Doyce with renewed strength, or rather, a returned obsti- nance of opinion that made her—a woman who seemed to have lost her voice in the outside world the moment she lost her husband—a force to be reckoned with in every specialty shop in the city. Doyce double-checked paint chips against sample cans Berniece wanted to try on the cabinets because she didn't like the color she'd picked out before. Doyce inspected the frosted glass on a few custom-made light fixtures, almost mistaking the designs for cracks. And sometimes she simply marveled at things, like a set of fireplace doors with Berniece's and Algin's initials engraved on the handles. Then she would order Agnes and Prime to hold her phone while she looked through her purse for Berniece's credit cards or receipts, or instructed them on how to haul things to her late-model Suburban, one of Berniece's castoffs gifted to Doyce when Algin surprised Berniece with a showroom-new Cayenne two Christmases before.

While they drove through the city, Doyce talked about the house while Agnes looked at the changed landscape around her. It stood in stark contrast to the beauty of what Doyce said Berniece was building, but that depended on what part of the city you were in. The design studios were in the bustling southern loop, studded with strip malls clustered around big-box stores and the new hospital, and subdivisions that were so new the concrete had a sickly blue sheen, like it had dried too quickly. The masons' workshops and paint warehouses, on the other hand, were in the shabbier and mostly Black neighborhoods that served as a buffer between downtown and the mostly white suburbs.

On their way back from picking up the fireplace doors, they cut through Sunset Acres, a neighborhood where Agnes remembered the family attending church shortly after Doyce's abrupt divorce. Agnes had loved watching the yards from the rear-facing seat of her mother's station wagon on Sunday afternoons. They weren't the boring, unearthly green of the more expensive neighborhoods, but pluckier, with lime-hued grass, brightly colored garden decorations, and flags sprucing their exteriors. Sometimes you saw a house painted a lovely seafoam, or another with subtle but striking accents, like sienna shutters and doors. Agnes often fantasized about who lived inside. Young couples, maybe, with a few small children and grandmothers who came over on the weekends with fresh vegetables and another pair of hands to help wives tend their tiny gardens. All of that was gone now, and the very color had been sucked out of the neighborhood: drab lawns sprawled in front of shabby-looking houses, some of which had expensive cars parked out front, some with clusters of cars in various stages of repair, and others with no vehicles at all, just dark oil stains where cars had been. Men sat on porches with their feet propped on the railings, drinking liquor from brown bags near their cheap lawn chairs. Others walked briskly in dingy, oversized shirts and cutoff shorts from house to house, in a hurry for no obvious reason. Prime took all this in, too, as he bounced along in the backseat, holding a chandelier in place by snaking his arm over the backrest.

"This neighborhood didn't use to look like this," said Agnes, her accent returning again in fits and starts. "What happened?"

"Time I guess," said Doyce. "Neighborhoods don't get better. They get worse." That was a thing Agnes's dad used to say. Maybe that's why Berniece moved so much.

"Do they? What about Youree Drive? That place got way better."

"Of course it did. That's where all the Katrina money went. When folks started moving up, starting businesses, shooting pictures they couldn't no longer shoot in New Orleans, that's who got the money. White folks. And when the opportunities dried up, that's who kept it. Prime, you still got a good hold of that fixture, don't you?"

"Yes, ma'am."

As they drove, Agnes watched Prime out of the corner of her eye. It had only just occurred to her that his family was better off, probably the kind of people who would drive through these parts with the windows up and call the inhabitants "niggers" with intention. But he seemed oddly calm, watching through the window as Agnes did, seemingly unruffled by not driving or being in charge, and instead being ordered around by Agnes's mother like a small boy. It both surprised her and endeared her to him. His adaptability would bode well for him in this family, where people who just met you tended to treat you like they treated the person who brought you in. In Doyce's case, that meant you were loved, if not a little harangued with tasks and occasional yelling, though that was proof of the affection. In Berniece's case, Agnes wasn't sure. Berniece didn't waste a great deal of energy on love. Especially if she thought the person who was looking for it was beneath her. Agnes told herself she was thankful for not being that way. She caught Prime's eye in the rearview mirror and he puckered his lips at her in an air kiss.

EVEN THOUGH IT ONLY SHAVED a few seconds off their arrival, Doyce liked to return home by cutting through neighborhood side streets, preferably ones with the shabbiest houses and most derelict lawns. She'd done so since Agnes was in high school, and Agnes half suspected it was an act of audacious pride, to remind the whole family of where they now lived. But as soon as they hung their final right turn, flashing blue lights blared and a white van blocked them from going farther than Mrs. Hamilton's house on the corner. Agnes tried to make out what was happening. So did Prime.

In the street, a dozen tent cards had been placed around a large lump covered in a white sheet. Mrs. Hamilton was in her driveway in her house shoes, hands on her hips, glaring out toward the road. Doyce pulled in and jumped out. Agnes protested.

"Wait—don't be nosy! Le's juss *go*!"

"Girl, what is you talking bout?" Doyce gave a half glance over her shoulder as she swung one foot out and handed Agnes her purse, which had been in her lap the whole time. "I need to know what's happening. We ain't never had crime like this over on this side."

Agnes groaned as Doyce slammed the door, and the chandelier's hanging crystals tinkled like wind chimes as Prime whipped back and forth, checking behind him, then staring at the sheet. By "this side," Doyce had meant the side that clung to respectability and the false belief that crime couldn't cross major thoroughfares. Agnes tried to keep her eyes in front. She didn't want to see the terror on Prime's face or try to address questions she didn't have answers to. Instead, she counted the flowers on Mrs. Hamilton's dress, remembering how the woman had been her French teacher in elementary school and had snitched on her for falling asleep in class, for not paying attention, and for generally being bad at the language. She'd once rapped Agnes's hands with a ruler because Agnes couldn't remember the French word for "living room." As if every person in the whole damn state was supposed to be fluent.

When Doyce returned to the car, she shared what details she could. Mrs. Hamilton had heard shots around 2:00, but the police hadn't bothered to arrive until after 4:00. These crimes weren't a priority; they'd photograph the scene, then cart the body away and let the next rain or a prudent neighbor wash away the blood. There might be a Crime Stoppers feature on KTBS, but that was about it. Mrs. Hamilton, who lived alone, was furious that it took police that long to respond to a murder that happened right outside her front door. Doyce had other gripes.

"We just keep killing each other, and we need to stop. Lord Jesus, we committing our own genocide," she said as they backed out of Mrs. Hamilton's driveway.

"People kill people for all kinda reasons, Mama. All races too."

"Not like we do. This city'd'n gone overboard. There's a killing every weekend."

"Well, there's prolly reasons for that, like poverty. Lack of opportunity. If you ain't got nothing to look forward to, and you ain't got nothing to reach for cause everybody else took everything, maybe you'd get mad enough or desperate enough to kill somebody too."

Doyce drove the next block in silence. It was as if she couldn't believe Agnes knew what she was talking about. Or that she, too, hadn't felt a similar way at least once in her life.

LATER THAT NIGHT, PRIME HAD trouble sleeping. At first, Agnes thought he was nervous about meeting Berniece and Algin. After all, they'd already met a few of their things, which even gave Agnes the impression that seeing her sister for the first time in nearly three years was an event she didn't bring nice enough clothes for. But she couldn't bail now. Wasn't it why she'd come in the first place? Agnes had crossed several state lines with something to prove. But she wasn't sure what, and she had a hard time figuring it out tonight, because Prime was pacing. Her usual method for calming him was unavailable, with her mother's head on the other side of a thin wall, but she did convince him to lie with her in the other daybed, and they held each other there: him sprawled between her legs, his heavy chest on her pelvis, his ear on her sternum, the scraggly beard tickling her through her nightshirt. To make room for him, she bunched herself up near the top of the bed like an accordion, with her head slightly tilted to avoid hitting the wall. Her insides twisted in a similar position as she listened to him explain how the sight of the dead made him think of combat. She tried to be comforting, but when Prime turned the conversation to her, she grew furious, even though he wasn't saying anything untrue.

"You sound different here."

"Huh?"

"The way you talk. You sound different."

"How so?"

"Like, country. But people from here—I thought they were supposed to sound different. Like the way New Orleans people talk."

"This isn't New Orleans, though."

"I know, but…when we first met I just thought you talked like you did because you went to school."

"And?"

"Like, I didn't think you were faking it."

"I wasn't. I just talk different around my family. I'm home."

"Maybe." Then he looked up at her expectantly. "But this isn't *home* home. Not for us. That's Tyler." He waited for her to agree.

"Yeah, I *guess*." Agnes rolled her eyes so hard even she felt like she'd gone back in time, to a sassier, less polished self. Maybe middle school.

Prime raised his head and chuckled. "See? The way you say that. You didn't talk like that back in Utah." He shook his head and lay down again. "It's fine, though. I guess everybody's gotta code switch every now and again. When in Rome…"

And with that, he went quiet, though, Agnes suspected, not asleep. She remembered the seemingly distant night at Prime's apartment. She *had* slipped back into the tongue she was using now, though he'd been too distracted by the ensuing crisis and his curiosity about her color to notice. After their first date, he never bothered to ask her about herself. He'd just read a few Wikipedia articles and thought he had her entire story. Agnes brooded as she dozed in an uncomfortable position, wedged against the wall of a house, pinned between two people who should have known her but didn't know her at all.

Sometime midmorning, Agnes unhooked her torso from Prime's grip and shimmied out from underneath him. She felt sluggish today. Unlike him, she hadn't slept well, and by the time she drifted off, her mother's loud phone conversations jarred her with every exclamation. She kept startling herself awake from dreams of policemen barging into the house, demanding to know where Agnes was and why she'd done what she had in another time zone. Instinctively, she checked her messages and found two from Colin.

ok so now some people are looking for you??

goddammit Agnes. At least tell me where you are so they can get the fuck out of our hair. Valda's visa expired a year ago. You know they deport white people too.

Agnes finally deleted the thread and blocked his number. He'd sent a few halfhearted messages the week before, asking her if he'd forgotten to pick her up from the airport and if she was mad at him for doing so, but he didn't seriously care about her or her whereabouts until he thought they might get him or some other woman in trouble. And whoever had come to his door wasn't any closer to finding her just because they'd found him. Agnes wasn't even sure Colin knew where she was from, and he sure as hell didn't know her mother's address. Agnes quietly shut the bedroom door and headed for the kitchen. She smelled coffee, and Doyce was on another call. Maybe Agnes could sneak a cup in peace.

For several minutes, she gazed into the backyard as she drank the dregs of the reheated pot, a thick, dark fluid that was grainy and bitter and tasted the way it felt living in that house for Agnes's last lean years of childhood. It hadn't been big enough for a single one of her dreams, and certainly not for all three women's together. Berniece always acted like the house was unfit for a woman of her station. Doyce thought she should have still been married, or at least married to someone new, though her orbit of work, church, and home offered little in terms of a dating pool. Agnes just wanted to live in a place where someone cared about what other people called her. Her mother had been so busy, and so lonely; Berniece was all Agnes had and Berniece was not one to be had by anyone who didn't have something to offer in exchange. So Agnes was, for all intents and purposes, as alone in that house as she was in the kitchen now. She stared out the same sliding door she used to let out their old dog Bison after school while she watched *Tiny Toon Adventures* or *Animaniacs*, and the same door through which Berniece sneaked in Keswick, who'd ultimately become her ticket out. Maybe Agnes hadn't been paying attention to the right things, and that's how she ended up at square one again. She'd been memorizing Lord Byron and staring into Bison's big black eyes, wondering if he, too, knew how strange she looked. But she should have been looking for a Prime instead. She could have taught herself to be satisfied with someone like him by now, fucking his brains out in exchange for wigs and better handbags, and people could be more distracted by her things than the incongruity of her skin tone. But Agnes wasn't a complete fool. She knew whatever it was she lacked couldn't be bought or bartered. Even when she'd had those things, back in college when she had more credit than bills, she hadn't been what she would call happy.

Agnes was so deep in thought she didn't know her mother was now off the phone, having told the last person who would pick up about the shooting, and how she suspected it was a boy who walked the streets—a nice-looking young man, maybe just "strung out." Somebody's son. Doyce was in the kitchen talking again to no one in particular by the time Agnes realized she wasn't alone.

"Lord, help us. We gotta stop killing our own. And I don't care what nobody say about no 'opportunities.' How we gon have opportunities if all we doing is shooting one another? We gotta have enough hope in *ourselves* before anything. Cause the white people are sitting back laughing. They don't even have to do the work. We doing it *for* em."

Agnes recognized the dig, but she said nothing, like she should have done in the car. Doyce tried another tack. While brewing another pot of coffee, she walked over to the table, lowering herself carefully into one of the chairs, rubbing a knee through a red velour housecoat with an elaborate neckline. Layers of ruffles, like a lothario's blouse. No doubt a last-season castoff from Berniece.

"Does that boy sleep all day?" she asked in a stage whisper, chuckling. Agnes knew what she was asking.

"No. He's a security guard, and if he moves to Tyler he'll start working as a locksmith around the clock. That's good money. He's just off work this week. On vacation." She held her breath and hoped Doyce didn't catch the catch in her voice.

"Oh, okay," Doyce countered noncommittally. "Who stay in Tyler?"

"His uncle. He's the one owns the locksmith company. He's been wanting him to come down for a while to check it out. That's why we came together. Since it was close. He's still deciding if he wants to stay and take over, though." Agnes cringed internally from the lie, but wasn't that how it went with families and businesses? Hubert had no blood heirs of his own.

Doyce nodded, looking over her shoulder to see how the coffee was doing. "And how y'all met again? Online?"

"No, he was working at the place where I was doing essay grading."

"In Utah?"

"Yeah, we would just talk whenever I was on breaks. He seemed like a nice dude. Then we went out later, and we…" She trailed off, having been unable to come up with a convincing tale of the transition from coworkers to something more. Her mother, squeamish about those details anyway, didn't push. Instead, she shifted to digging for more practical information.

"Now, how long was you in Utah?" Then she got up to check on the coffee in case she didn't like the answer.

Agnes quadrupled the time and changed the subject. "About a month. Anyway, you talked to Berniece lately?"

"Not on the phone, not since she called about something, a week, maybe bout two weeks ago. Oh, she say somebody was looking for you. Like a loan officer? I know you ain't gone into debt, have you?"

"No, I think that may have been for a credit check. I was looking into getting a new car."

"Oh, okay, girl. That's nice. What kind?"

"I don't know yet. I was just looking into loans right now."

"Oh, all right then. Naw I ain't talked to Berniece, but I was gon drop them items off over there tonight since she off work today. I think Algin might be out of town too. Maybe we can have a nice time. Have dinner over there. I gotta call her and tell her y'all here, though."

"Okay." Agnes was shocked. So Berniece had shown her some mercy and hadn't told. Either that, or her mother was too tired to remember the details. Agnes's shoulders relaxed a little as she took another timid sip of coffee. Its temperature felt like nothing in her mouth, but nothing felt good. Maybe things didn't have to be so tense after all.

BUT SHE SHOULD HAVE KNOWN better. It was clear the moment they sat on the couch and Berniece peeked out of her bedroom door and then slammed it shut that Berniece had different plans than entertaining her mother and sister on her first night off in ages in the house that rightfully belonged to Doyce and Agnes as much as it did to Algin and Berniece. Doyce rapped on the closed door, and when Berniece opened it, Agnes heard her ask in disbelief, "Didn't I tell you not to bring them here?"

Doyce shoved past her into the room and shut the door. Prime hadn't heard it because Algin, who was not out of town at all but was watching television while wearing an apron that said *Craw Zaddy*, was asking if Prime wanted to change the channel, dangling the complicated remote in front of him like a gauntlet. And damned Agnes's luck; she herself now couldn't hear what was happening in the master bedroom. The insulation in that house had never been so good.

Agnes looked around the den, trying to remember how it once looked, but like the neighborhood itself, which had morphed into something beyond even her most aspirational imagination, nothing was recognizable. Like their old street, which was now gaudy with houses-in-progress with builders' logos plastered all over their unfinished frames, Berniece's house had an overabundance of everything unnecessarily new: fake flowers in vases; jeweled Uncle Sam hats for the upcoming holiday; overstuffed couches with throw pillows perched on their backs and tucked between back cushions and armrests, falling to the floor whenever someone got up or sat down too fast. There were large prints of cartoonish New Orleans jazz bands, and twin four-foot-tall statues of Louis Armstrong playing his trumpet in front of a collection box. Agnes promised herself that she'd have better taste, though she had to admit the house had never looked better. The carpets were a plush, pale Berber (Agnes preferred hardwood floors); the walls respectable shades of eggshell, mauve, and gray (at least one room could have been a nice mint green or marigold); and the state-of-the-art appliances were stainless steel. Some of them were so high-tech Agnes had trouble recognizing them. The refrigerator was almost invisible—a wood-paneled be-hemoth that matched the cabinets. Agnes was bewildered by all of it, but more bewildered when Berniece rounded the corner from the master bedroom suite. She breezed behind the couch, ignoring Agnes, and stuck out a hand to Prime.

"Hi," she said in her best brunch drawl. "I'm Agnes's sister, Berniece. Nice to meet you." Prime turned around, still holding the inscrutable remote in his hands while Algin smirked, gleeful at the game he had been playing and now, with the tension that blustered into the room. Prime was none the wiser; he shook Berniece's hand dutifully.

"Nice to meet you too. I'm Edwin, but you can call me Prime."

"All right, Prime. You hungry? We should be getting dinner started soon." With an irritated gesture, she motioned Algin to get off the couch, and, as if he'd been waiting for the cue, he quickly explained to Prime how to speak into the remote for his favorite channels, then jogged into the kitchen with a half-smirk.

Berniece asked Prime if he liked holiday movies. There was a Christmas in July marathon on and they were playing her favorites. So, for an hour and a half, Prime, Doyce, and Agnes sat staring at a large, snow-spangled screen, in a silence broken only by Berniece's obligatory questions tossed at Prime during commercial breaks: How was the drive, and where exactly did his family live? Had he ever been to this region before? Had he tried the seafood? Gone to Whataburger? After a half hour, Doyce reclined on a chaise lounge and dozed, mouth slightly open and her glasses falling off her face. Berniece kept her eyes up, trained on the screen. Prime leaned back and forward on the couch, poking Agnes playfully every time the couple almost kissed in a comedy of errors that would, of course, end with a wedding. Agnes swatted him away and then stopped respond-ing. She was watching, too, even though she knew how these movies ended: happily, with a blended family finally making amends, or a parent serendipitously falling in love with a son-in-law's widowed godfather, or some other configuration where the horse farm got saved, and everyone got exactly what they wanted. Agnes knew all this, but still she looked on, enraged someone could dream up such stupid, stupid luck.

THE MEAL WAS OVERSEASONED, LIKE every gesture or remark Berniece haltingly threw in Agnes's direction. The hypocrisy was stunning; Berniece was kind to Prime—almost as if she pitied him for his choice of a mate—but she did little to hide her disdain for Agnes, which led the younger sister to resort to her most prized weapon: critique. Agnes could say nothing of the house, as much as she would have adorned it differently. And she could say nothing of Berniece, whose beauty was much like the house's—one Agnes didn't covet but could admire all the same. And perhaps the beauty of the house was a reflection of Berniece's, whose features had hardened into the ageless steel of Black woman adulthood: almond-shaped eyes, an aquiline nose, and wide lips lined, highlighted, and glossed with high-end cosmetics. Her spiky eyelashes and deep-wave sew-in shone under the chandelier's harsh light, and her green silk robe showed off how thin she'd remained; it did not drape across her body like water, but rather like a bag that bulged here and there with the jewels of her breasts and elbows. Every bright bulb caught some angle of her body or face, both of which were flawlessly beautiful and noiselessly percolating with compressed rage.

There was one flaw that no one else noticed, and if they did, they didn't acknowledge it. Berniece and Algin seemed to be on the outs. His questions about what drinks to serve or dishes to use were met with eye-rolls and finally a "Don't worry about it. I'll do it." The thought of marital discord made Agnes smug, though not satisfied enough to keep quiet. She turned her disdain toward the food, which did indeed deserve it. When Algin asked Prime how he liked the fish, Agnes cut in:

"It's a little too salty for my taste."

Algin bristled a bit, though not openly. He shrugged his shoulders. "Really? Maybe you mean 'spicy.' You haven't been home in a while. You might have forgotten how we do it down here."

"No. I meant salty."

"Tastes fine to me," Berniece said before turning to Prime. "Algin makes his own blend of meat seasonings. One for beef, one for poultry, and one for seafood."

"None for wild game?" said Agnes.

Berniece took another bite and didn't look up. "Wild game is beef and poultry."

"Not venison. Or boar."

"There aren't any wild boars here."

Agnes picked up her phone to check. Algin, eager for an opening, turned to Prime. "I learned how to cook in the army. I was stationed in the Philippines for a year. Saw all kinds of stuff you wouldn't believe. You ever traveled overseas?"

Prime took a sip from a can of peach-flavored soda. "Yeah. I have. In the army. I did two tours in Afghanistan and Iraq."

Algin stiffened. "Wow. Thanks for your service, man."

Prime nodded. "Same to you. Hey, I knew a sergeant who was stationed at Clark awhile back. Hutchinson. Blond guy. I wonder if you ever crossed paths."

Algin stammered helplessly before Berniece jumped in.

"Did you make dessert?"

Algin shook his head but said he could grab some ice cream from the walk-in freezer out back. Someone had churned it from a hand-crank maker in his test kitchen. Homemade vanilla with a bourbon brown butter swirl. Doyce, who'd been enraptured by her meal and pouring small amounts of the soda in a red cup, piped up.

"Ooh, Lord, that sound good."

"Perfect. Be right back, Mrs. K."

As soon as he left, Berniece turned to Agnes and narrowed her eyes, which were expertly cat-lined, as if with a ruler. "You would think somebody who showed up unannounced wouldn't care what the food tasted like."

Agnes blinked and pushed her plate forward, though there was still plenty of food on it. "I didn't ask you to cook."

"But you're here. And you're eating it. So…" She shook her head as if trying to convince herself not to finish her thought.

To her own surprise, Agnes's feelings had been worn smooth by time. Unlike in high school, or even a few weeks ago, she didn't care about Berniece's comebacks because nothing Berniece could say could be as disrespectful as Agnes's life felt right now. And Agnes felt heady with the notion that, at least at the moment, it seemed Berniece didn't know how desperate her life had become; in fact, she seemed overburdened with her own troubles, even in her beautiful "new" house. So Agnes felt free to be as arrogant as she wanted with no threat of heartbreaking repercussions.

She took the bait. "Were you saying something?"

"Nope. Sure wasn't."

"Cause if you got something to say, you need to say it. This is *your* house, after all."

"It sure is. Went and filed the deed last week. And what has Dad signed over to you lately?"

"Nothing. Cause I don't spend my free time up his wife's high-yellow ass."

"Better high yellow than…" Berniece chuckled at the joke she kept to herself.

Agnes read her mind. "Better whiter than someone's ass than all up in it."

Doyce looked up, her cheeks bulged with food. She smiled. "I know y'all better be playing, but y'all getting too rough, especially in front of comp—"

"Stop trying to laugh shit off. I'm sick of her," Agnes snarled. Then she turned back to Berniece. "You always thought you were better than everybody in this family. Except Sabine. You spent your whole life putting me down cause that's what you thought rich people did. Keep somebody to look down on. Since you didn't have no real pedigree, that's how you got in. That's how you got on. That's the only thing you had going for you anyway. Not looks. Not color. Not money. Just a deadbeat dad and a stepmama who let you stay around cause you followed her like a puppy dog, licking her scraps. Now you got the audacity to live in a house your own mama got kicked out of. And you got her running around the city like Flo-Jo picking up your shit? That's cold." Agnes shook her head.

"You don't even know what you're talking about."

"Really? Cause we was out all day yesterday running your errands. She ain't the help!" Agnes pointed at her mother, who had finally put her fork down, her mouth sagging like it was still full of food.

"I ain't the one treating her like the help, showing up unannounced with nowhere else to stay."

"I got somewhere to stay."

"Then go back. And before you go, you let me know why them testing people was looking for you. You always been a little evil. Ain't no telling what you did."

"I ain't the evil one. I didn't turn my back on my family cause I was ashamed of them. I didn't do that."

"Oh, but ain't that why you skipped town? Went to college upstate so you could disappear? I've seen some of your Facebook photos. All smeared and done up. Who you trying to fool?"

Agnes peered at her, pretending to get a closer look at her skin.

"I could ask you the same thing bout that too-light makeup on your face."

"You can't afford this makeup."

"And wouldn't want to if I couldn't get it in my shade."

"So whatchu come back for? Does it have to do with the people calling?"

"Stay out of my fucking business."

"You have no business. None that I haven't cosigned for anyway."

"Well, then, congratulations to you for that boost to your credit score. Probably helped you get the loan to remodel this shit. You're welcome."

"I don't need you for a goddamned thing."

Agnes got up and walked over to her. "You've always needed me. You wouldn't have as much self-esteem as you do now if you hadn't had me. Everything you *think* you are you built on my back, making fun of me just like everybody else in school. You'da thought blood was thicker than water. But it ain't. And you. Ain't. Shit."

Prime had stood up quietly and was now holding Agnes by the arm. She wouldn't look at him, so she couldn't tell if he was trying to get her to sit down or leave. Doyce had forked another bite of food in her mouth but was chewing it slowly, looking on in frightened disbelief.

Berniece stood up so she could be face-to-face with Agnes, so close Agnes could see the dark edge of her lipliner—not black like the gangster girls from their childhoods, but a slightly darker red than her actual lipstick, a trick they'd both learned from Sabine.

Agnes thought of the day Bern tried to highlight her hair. That may have been the last time they'd been that close to each other. Berniece stuck a finger in Agnes's face, so close that Agnes's eyes couldn't focus on it. It looked like two fingers at once.

"Me? I thought *I* was always better?" She shook her head. "No. That was you. You always thought you were. Smarter I guess. Whiter. Thought you'd end up better off. But look at you. Got some dude bringing you home cause your car probly got repoed and God only knows where you found him. Finally, you got you a little lackey now. Aside from that, tell me: What else have you accomplished? What do you have that I don't have?"

Agnes had spent the whole time looking at Berniece's teeth, which were as straight as a dummy's and bluish white. When they were little, both girls had silver caps put on their fillings, but Agnes's were on her back molars, which were hard to see. Berniece's had been closer to the front, so Agnes called her Foil Mouth for years, then Fence Mouth when she'd finally gotten braces. It wasn't that Agnes genuinely meant either insult. It was just that Berniece was always getting things that would make her more beautiful, while Doyce seemed to leave Agnes's improvement up to God. And just as she had then, Agnes dipped deep into a well of bitterness and intuitively pulled out the perfect insult, one she knew Berniece couldn't rebut with her house, her expensive smile, or her husband. Ironically, it was a statement that was as untrue for Agnes as it was unattainable for Berniece in the gated community where she hid her worthless goods.

"What do I have that you don't have? Happiness. *Real* happiness," said Agnes.

"Get the fuck out," said Berniece.

"Cool." Agnes spun around, shocked to find Algin standing behind her, holding the tub of carefully made ice cream. Agnes looked him up and down, then said to Prime, "Let's go, before this 'flauging-ass soldier tells us another lie about where he served."

Algin set the ice cream on the table as Doyce rose slowly, tears streaming down her grief-wizened face. By the time they all made it to the front door, he'd been there for several minutes, holding it open.

Just as Agnes was leaving the bathroom, Doyce grabbed her arm and ushered her into her bedroom, hastily closing the door.

"I need you to tell me what's going on with them people calling Berniece. I thought you said it was about borrowing some money."

Agnes was already exhausted, and the weight of disclosure sat so heavy on her chest she almost winced.

"Mama, it's nothing. Don't worry about it."

"Are you in some kind of trouble?"

"Noooo," Agnes whined petulantly.

"Cause you need to tell me."

"There ain't nothing to tell."

"What's happening in Tennessee?"

"Nothing at all." Which was true. Colin counted for nothing.

"And you really just came here to visit."

"Yes, Mama, and to see Prime's relatives in Tyler."

"How serious is this? You bet not be using him. That's not what men are for."

"Tell that to Berniece."

"I'm not talking bout Berniece right now. I'm talking bout you."

"Why I gotta be the one that get the hard time, though? Everything Berniece do, you applaud. You even wearing her clothes. When I do something, it's bad. It's always been that way."

"I never showed favorites. I loved y'all both and I chastised y'all both."

"Really? Cause it didn't feel that way."

"You a lie."

"After Dad left, you forgot about me. You got divorced and I guess you figured you was done raising kids."

The pain that sprang to Doyce's face was like a gust of arctic wind, cracking its earthy brown with windswept lines. "I *never* stopped raising y'all. Or loving you."

"Well, you sure stopped calling."

"You stopped calling me!"

"I got tired of hearing about Berniece."

Doyce could say nothing to such a charge. She had wrapped herself around Berniece's success so tightly it strangled the daughter she assumed wasn't concerned enough to be harmed. Doyce turned away from Agnes and looked at the bed. It was the same bed she'd slept in with her husband for years; almost too big for the comically small room, and now falling apart, its railings having been glued in some places and duct-taped in others. Agnes wept inside for what she thought her mother might be holding on to—not only with the bed, but also with Berniece. Distance had taken one daughter, and an unscrupulous new wife had almost taken the other, but with the remodeled house, Doyce had a fighting chance at getting one back. And perhaps this one too. Out of her pain and confusion about who Agnes had become, Doyce made the most fervent promise she could think of. One of her most honest, and one of her oldest.

"Whatever trouble you done got yourself into, you can always come home."

Agnes said nothing, just turned and walked out of the room. Her troubles were not one, but legion. They had followed her home. Doyce couldn't even begin to understand.

"Cherie, baby. Let's go home."

After she'd insisted he go back to his own bed but before he drifted off, Prime and Agnes whispered across the space for almost an hour as they talked about Agnes's childhood, her high school names, her relationship with Berniece—everything. Agnes hadn't told him this to bring them closer. She'd simply told him because being there and not knowing must have felt bewildering for him, not unlike seeing the dead body in the street.

Prime asked question after question, then squared his shoulders and made an executive decision. Dinner's abrupt end had been anathema, no doubt because his own relationship with his kin was buffered by their concern for his mental health. Families didn't fight in front of Prime, and the sight of Agnes and Berniece exchanging words had pricked some anxiety in him. He was ready to go.

"Maybe since you live closer now, we can try again later in the year, during the holidays," he reasoned. "Right now, though, we just need to leave. We don't need this vibe while we're trying to build a life together." He reached across the divide for her hand, but Agnes wouldn't take it.

"I understand that, but maybe I could at least talk to Berniece before I go." In the hours since the disastrous dinner, guilt had invaded Agnes's arrogance. She needed to apologize to her sister as well as her mother. Nothing had come out right. She'd instigated the fight, then railed about it with Doyce when she should have been grateful for her concern. Even though Agnes understood her mother better than Doyce knew, she punished her for it when the woman was being her most vulnerable, trying to protect a child she didn't understand. There had to be some way to make amends. Maybe with both of them.

Prime's next question brought her back to reality.

"Has your sister always been like that, even when you were kids?"

"Like what?"

"Well, she acts like she was raised in a totally different household. A better one. Better than both of us." Prime spat out the last sentence and shifted in the bed. "Your mom is cool, though. She's really sweet. But I don't know, Cherie. Maybe this can't be fixed in one trip. But they can always come over to Tyler. Maybe we'll have Thanksgiving there. The trailer is big enough. Bigger than this place, anyway."

The thought of Berniece eating a meal in a trailer, even though it was the nicest one any of them had ever seen, almost made Agnes laugh out loud, but she said nothing. Prime was right. Maybe some things couldn't be fixed in a few days.

"Let's leave tomorrow, Cherie. I need to start work anyway, and we need to figure out what you're gonna do, too, at least for a little while, until we get on our feet. I don't wanna take advantage of my uncle's kindness. We'll have to start paying rent, or find our own place soon."

Prime had never mentioned Agnes working in Texas, but not doing so would be impractical, even though she didn't want to. She'd actually prefer to go back and never leave the trailer. For a millisecond, she imagined what it would be like to live there alone, drinking coffee on the ramp on brisk fall mornings, maybe growing a potted plant or two on the windowsill above the kitchen sink. Of course she knew it was impossible. At least in Tyler. But goodness, it would be nice to have something like that of her own. It would be a prefab chrysalis for her body and brain. No men clamoring for her, or using her body as the yardstick by which they measured their virility and success. If Agnes's mother was lonely, it was only because she didn't know what she had: unmanned solitude. Agnes ached for that. More so than for money or stability or maybe even Berniece's sisterly love. She was shocked at the realization, but she clung to it like a raft. If she had a goal—maybe the first one since college—she could forge a plan.

"Cherie!"

"What?"

"I lost you for a second. What about leaving around ten?"

"Yeah, yeah. I gotcha. But I'm gonna try to talk to Berniece in the morning. Maybe I'll stop by on our way out."

IT WAS THE MIDDLE OF the night when Agnes's mother burst into the room, snatching the pullchain to turn on the cluster of dingy lamps on the ceiling fan.

"Get up. Something happened at the house."

Agnes bolted upright in the daybed, terrified, not so much at what her mother was saying, but at the prospect that Prime might awaken disoriented and panicked. Miraculously, he didn't budge.

"What?" Agnes hissed, moving carefully as she stood, hoping to walk her mother back into the hallway.

"Something happened at the house. Berniece just called. The cops are on their way. I'm headed over there now."

"Okay."

"What are y'all gonna do?" Agnes knew that was a cue for her to offer Prime's presence as protection. Algin must have gotten physical. But why?

"I can try to wake him up, but I don't know."

"Well, I'm gonna leave in about ten minutes."

"Okay."

Agnes sat on the edge of Prime's bed. He looked frighteningly peaceful, secure in the knowledge that his plan would go his way in just a few hours. This, she thought, must be how he convinced his parents of the rightness of so many things, including her. But that plan had been thwarted by something that happened in the night, while Agnes lay awake thinking and he dreamed. She gently dug her nails into his shoulder with one hand and placed the other flat and firmly on his chest, so if he awakened, he knew it was her. This is how she touched him when they made love. His muscles tightened; then he opened his eyes.

"Cherie? What's wrong?"

"I think there was a fight or something. Algin and Berniece. My mom is on her way over. Can we go with her? Make sure everything is okay?"

"What? What happened?"

"All I know is they called the police."

"Cherie. The police? We can't go there. What if they're looking for us?"

"For a few destroyed tests? Come on, don't feed me that line again. We'll be fine."

Prime returned to his argument from earlier that night. "Why would we even go over there after last night? They don't care about us. Let's just leave. This isn't our problem. They're married, and it's between them. They'd say the same thing if it was us."

Agnes shivered stealthily but stuck her wrists between her knees to disguise it.

"Listen, I just want to make sure she's okay. Know what? Let's leave for Tyler after we go. We can pack up our things and go straight back from there. She reached over for Prime's phone on the TV stand so she could see the time. "It's already four in the morning. We could be there before sunrise, sleep in, then plan our next move." She pressed her palm firmly into his chest and kissed him, a reminder that they were less than one hundred miles from a house where they could comfortably share a bed.

At that, Prime's eyes widened. He was fully awake now, excited about getting Agnes back to himself. "You sure?"

"Yeah. We can head out after this if you're not tired."

"No. I'm not tired."

"Okay. Good." She kissed him again. "Get dressed."

"WHAT ARE Y'ALL DOING?" Doyce was sitting on the couch in the living room, rubbing her hands, which she had just anointed with holy oil; the green bottle was sitting in front of her on the coffee table.

"We're gonna trail you to Berniece's house, then get on the road. Something came up with Prime's family in Texas, so we're headed back." Prime passed the two women with their bags as Agnes fumbled out a lie. He didn't say a thing. They were leaving. His niceties were no longer necessary.

"But I thought y'all were gonna stay till the Fourth! Why would you leave in the middle of the night?"

"We've already put you out enough, showing up unannounced. We wanna get out of your hair. Plus, what if Berniece needs a place to stay for a few days? You don't want all of us in here at once. And with one bathroom?" Agnes tried to sound lighthearted as she said this. Her mother didn't take the bait. She eyed her daughter suspiciously.

"I am a *mother*. It don't matter how many people are in this house; I'm *happy* to have you here. You're never putting me out!"

"I know that, but we'll just be in Tyler. Right up the road."

"I don't like this. I don't know why they would get to fighting anyway, around the holidays? This is supposed to be a time for celebration. You haven't been here in years…" Doyce's voice trailed as Prime returned to the front door, politely waiting. Agnes stood up and zipped her hoodie, the same one she wore that night at the testing center. Her mother rose slowly, too, and Prime held open the burglar bar door, tossing and catching his car keys with his free hand.

IT LOOKED LIKE EVERY LIGHT in the house was on when they pulled up, and Agnes could see Algin's silhouette inside a rustling curtain. He looked like he was holding something to his face or neck. Berniece was out front, leaning on one of the massive pillars lining the front porch. She was standing on fresh sod in a pair of expensive-looking slippers, and as Agnes and Prime pulled up behind Doyce, she shifted from one foot to the other to inspect the bottoms, then scowled off into the distance, crossing her arms. Doyce got out first, and she, too, stood for a minute, her arms crossed, trying to see what was happening inside the house. Finally, she cautiously approached Berniece.

"Are the police still coming?"

"Yep."

"Why? Y'all can't solve this on your own?"

"No. I hate him."

"What?"

"He's a pathological liar." Agnes and Prime crept up behind Doyce as Berniece spoke. Apparently, Algin *had* been lying about the army, among other things. Something about the renovations. They were deep in debt and Algin's cooking show was another hoop dream that was now an expensive, unachieved accolade that made him feel important. It was hard to grasp the full story because Berniece wasn't offering details so much as she was talking to relieve the pressure of her rage. And Doyce wasn't asking the right questions so much as she was responding to every revelation with "Lord, Jesus." Agnes and Prime stood back and said nothing. It was an awkward exchange between women who never divulged their ugly, unpresentable truths, at least not to each other. Even so, Agnes wanted in. Dear God, she wanted to be a part of this purging. But Berniece wasn't even paying attention to her. She was in her own world, fifteen again, with their mother guilting the truth out of her about sneaking Keswick into the house.

Then Doyce offered her own solution.

"Well, we need to leave before the police show up. Cause they gon try to take you in, no matter what happened."

"Who cares?"

"Me. *I* care. You don't need to spend no nights in jail. You might mess around and lose your license."

Berniece shrugged. Agnes looked up at Prime, who was about to say something when there was a notable clatter inside. The silhouette that had once been standing in the window had flipped another shadow—an end table—then collapsed to the floor.

"What's wrong with *him*?" Doyce screamed angrily, though the pitch revealed she was in fact terrified.

"I stabbed him," said Berniece.

"Lord, Jesus!"

At this, Agnes started laughing, a loud laugh that rang out into the night and she knew the neighbors heard, though they were too genteel to come outside while the police were en route. They'd simper forward from the shadows into the blue light, asking to be kept off the record and snitching with what little information they had: yelling, a glass breaking, someone maniacally cackling. And who wouldn't have laughed? Imagine Berniece, as sophisticated as she intended to be, brandishing a knife like a common thug. Agnes couldn't shake the absurdity of it. She chuckled here and there as Berniece scowled, but not at Agnes; she was too proud to make eye contact. Instead, she glowered at Doyce, who tried again to reason with her.

"I don't wanna leave him, but you'd'n already called a ambulance. And you need to figure out how we gon handle this. I can call my pastor in the morning, but I don't think you need to just be sitting out here. Ain't no telling what they might do once they pull up. You need to talk to somebody in a position of authority first."

Berniece looked around at the dark, quiet houses, perhaps wondering why the neighbors who called themselves friends hadn't emerged. A siren wailed faintly in the distance. She looked back at the house one last time, then turned toward her mother's car. Doyce turned, too, catching Agnes's eye. She recognized something there but said nothing.

While Berniece and Doyce talked, Prime stood behind Agnes, cradling her in his arms. At any other time in her life, she might have thought it endearing, to be held tenderly in front of the two women who, for very different reasons, thought she was unholdable. But now, in the watered-down predawn dark, the weight of his arms felt like they were sinking her. All those mornings in hotel rooms, as they lay entangled, preparing to hit the road again and trace their way to the land of their roots, Agnes felt weighted down by his desire. Still, she clung to it like a buoy, knowing it would save her. But she hadn't imagined salvation quite like this.

Agnes shifted to loosen Prime's grip, and he, sensing her intentions, held her tighter as the two women walked slowly to the car. Prime leaned into Agnes, his chest hard as a tombstone behind her shoulders. He put his mouth to her right ear and kissed it.

"Let's go, Cherie," he said softly. "We can check on them once we get back."

Agnes leaned away so she could look at him. Was he anxious? Aroused? Suddenly, she felt exhausted from the obscene amount of work involved with managing other people's feelings and not being courageous enough to tend to her own. She shifted again, this time thrusting her elbows into Prime's stomach. He buckled, loosening his throttling grip.

"What are you doing?" he said softly, but at that precise moment, Doyce turned toward them again. Next, she glanced back at Berniece, who was a few steps behind, then walked over to the driver's-side door and waited. Agnes hadn't noticed it until just then, but the whole time they'd been outside, Berniece was standing next to a small bag, which she was now carrying as she followed their mother like a child. But this was supposed to be *Agnes's* chance. How could Berniece, who had so much already, take it instead? The bag looked like she'd planned it all along. Agnes jumped forward, out of Prime's reach.

"Wait!"

"No!" yelled Prime, springing after her. "Don't do this." They were now standing a few feet from Doyce's back bumper. Through the window, Agnes could see the chandelier was still in the backseat.

"I have to," Agnes said to him. "I have to be here." Even if she had to stand ten feet away from Doyce and Berniece for the rest of her life, she had to stay.

"No, you don't!" Prime pleaded. "This isn't where you belong. You've been telling me that all night. Come back with me. Stop running out on everything that's ever been good to you."

Agnes heard a cough and didn't realize it was her, sobbing. Her mother and sister stood at the driver and passenger doors, watching, waiting to see if Agnes would join them, though neither of them made a single plea.

"Not 'ever,'" said Agnes to Prime. "No, not 'ever.'"

"I love you, Cherie. I've been loving you. Don't do this to me."

"I'm not doing this to you. It was never about you." And she was hoping he knew she meant destroying the tests too. She hoped that, whatever happened to him, he could forgive her. Maybe even come back to visit if he stayed in Tyler. She would like that. Well, she *could* like that someday.

As if he were reading her mind, he said, "I'm not coming back. You do this, and I'm not coming after you ever again. I've lost too much already. I've lost everything."

"That's not true. You still have everything you need. Uncle Hube and Jackie. Your parents. Your parents love you, Prime. You've got a really good family."

Prime shook his head furiously, like he was trying to unhear her words. Then he pointed a finger at her. "What about the SD card?" he spat petulantly.

"Do whatever you gotta do with it. Clear your name so you can go back to work. Or stay in Tyler, where you have a chance to start over. I want that for you. But I want that for me too. That's why I'm staying here."

"No, you don't. You don't even want a home. If you did, you'd come back with me."

"But I wouldn't be happy. And I want to be happy."

"You're lying. Not if you wanna stay here. You could die here. Or you'll be lonely for the rest of your life."

Agnes didn't know who was giving Prime the liberty to predict the outcome of living in a place he hadn't even been in for forty-eight hours. But she knew reasoning with him was useless. If she didn't stay, she'd never know if she could have come back and reset things. As Berniece opened the front passenger door, Agnes stepped away from Prime.

It would be a different kind of work, this work, but it could be meaningful. Agnes admitted to herself that she would miss Prime's body and its weight holding her in place. Some nights she would even yearn for it. It was very possible no one would love her that way—hungrily, possessively, needily—ever again. That she would live feeling as unwanted as she did during her teenage years. But it was a chance she was finally willing to take. She needed time to decide how she wanted to be loved, and by whom. She looked at Prime. Agnes knew he believed that, if he had her, he had everything, and if he lost her, the loss would be bigger because of all the others that came before: Iraq and Shana and the job at Kettleman. But those weren't Agnes's fault. At least not the first two. And she couldn't spend the rest of her life trying to compensate for all three. Agnes also knew it was either Prime's loss or hers. They couldn't both get what they wanted. They couldn't both win. But for the first time in a long time, Agnes wanted completely to win.

So she walked to her mother's car, opened the door, and got in.

ACKNOWLEDGMENTS

God, thank You for tapping me on the shoulder until I sat down to write about a disgruntled worker at the end of her rope. Agnes's story became these stories, and writing them has changed my life. Thank You for this journey, which has helped me better understand myself and women like me in ways I didn't know I was *not* understanding. Thank You for knowing where I begin and where I end.

Many thanks to everyone in my families—Birdsongs, Byrds, Dotsons, Pierres, Williamses—and especially my mother, whose love, I suspect, has kept me alive.

Thank you, Shreveport, aka Ratchet City, the city that helped raise me, that gave me good people and good food, land, and a history, a place where I will always live, even when I'm far away. You're in my blood and my bones. I'll never quit you.

Claire! You were one of the first people who believed in my prose. You taught me about character and voice, about deeply loving a place and rendering it on the page, about what it means to be a friend to your friends' dreams. I could not have finished this book without you. Shout-out to Zoom writing sessions! Shout-out to long walks in the evenings! Shout-out to terrible, lovable dogs! (RIP Jeja.)

Josh, thank you for rewriting the slurs and making them

affirmations ("What she meant was…"), for the best (and I mean the *best*) food and even better conversations. Love you, fam.

Donika, you were the first person to teach me how to build healthy families not bound by blood. I am a better person because I know you.

Tafisha, who keeps it cute always: Thank you for teaching me how to pitch, how to serve, and how to write outside the boxes people try to put us in.

Many thanks to Christina Stoddard and Chris Allison, who have supported me and my dreams in surprising, miraculous ways. Thank God for you.

Much love to all the folks I've met and fallen in love with along the way: my fellow Fiskite, Selena Sanderfer Doss; Cave Canem fam Maya Marshall and L. Lamar Wilson; my MacDowell buddies, Juleen Johnson and Greg Marshall (and Lucas Schaefer, hubby extraordinaire!); my Ragdale folks, Sheree L. Greer and Leslie Roberts; Jack Jones alum Jenna Wortham; the Callaloo cutie (and one of the funniest writers I know), Tatiana Richards Hanebutte; and the Tin House Summer Workshop crew: Keith S. Wilson, Monterica Sade Neil, Dantiel W. Moniz, Antonio D. López, Jesús I. Valles, Luke Muyskens, David Sanchez, Threa Almontaser, and all the other scholars. (Special love, too, to Mariana Goycoecha.)

Many thanks to Nancy Reisman, whose workshop was the first place I shared Suzette's story. You told me it could be longer and I leaned into that like nobody's business. Thank you so much for your unwavering kindness. And thanks to the other folks who gave feedback: Christina Stoddard (again), Rachel Teukolsky, and Anna Silverstein. Much love to my other first readers, Larrysha Jones and Claire Jimenez (again), who read the entire book (all those damn pages) and treated it with such care.

Thanks to my agent, Kiele Raymond at Thompson Literary, for

reading, believing, and advocating for my work with such poise and grace.

Seema Mahanian! You are a writer's dream editor. You know exactly where to push and where to pull. This book is exponentially better because of you. Thanks to the rest of the Grand Central folks whose hands have touched this book: assistant editor Carmel Shaka; Carrie Andrews and Carolyn Kurek on copyedits and production (thank you for preserving my characters' voices!); and Adekunle Adeleke, Tree Abraham, and Albert Tang, who created a love-at-first-sight cover.

This book is dedicated to every person with albinism on the globe, in sometimes-precarious states of acceptance, love, and safety. Contrary to popular opinion, we are not all the same and we are not all related, but I feel you. It would be easy to say that I hope you see yourself in this book, but what I really want is that you see the possibility to be beheld in nuanced ways. I wish I could have written every story, but I couldn't, so my hope is that, for every person who wants to do so, reading these stories will compel you to tell your own.

For folks who want to learn more about people with albinism, here are a few places to start:

National Organization for Albinism and Hypopigmentation:
    https://www.albinism.org/
Action on Albinism: https://actiononalbinism.org/en/
United Nations Office of the High Commissioner for Human
    Rights (campaign for people with albinism): https://
    albinism.ohchr.org/

READING GROUP GUIDE

DISCUSSION QUESTIONS

1. Having been sheltered her entire life, Suzette is gaining new skills and a greater understanding of her family and friends, and she must finally face the ways people in her life see her. Discuss how Suzette actively learns more about the world around her and accomplishes her goals. Discuss the ways in which the people around her helped or hindered her from reaching those goals. How did her relationships with those people evolve?

2. Maple's story examines three very different women: Maple, Momi, and Nana. In what ways do Maple and her grandmother approach their grief differently? Why do you think that is, and what could they learn from each other?

3. Discuss how Agnes's relationship with her sister, Berniece, shapes her life. What does she gain from the relationship and how does their relationship hurt her?

4. Discuss the way Agnes's section being written in the third person informed how you thought of her.

5. Compare and contrast Suzette's, Maple's, and Agnes's different relationships to themselves, their attitudes toward self-love and

acceptance, and the ways they take on other's perceptions of them as women with albinism.

6. From losing her virginity to Doni to kissing her best friend, Drina, discuss the evolution of Suzette's sexual exploration. What are the similarities and differences in what drives Suzette's, Maple's, and Agnes's needs and desires?

7. Discuss the ways in which Chad helps Maple as she copes with the loss of her mother. What lessons about grief, loss, and life does she gain, and how was Chad able to help her do so?

8. Compare and contrast Agnes's relationship with Colin versus Prime. How does her relationship with these men affect how she sees herself?

9. Discuss the ways in which the men in Suzette's, Maple's, and Agnes's lives help or hinder them from reaching their goals.

10. All three women have difficult, fractured relationships with their parental figures. Discuss your thoughts on the strength of those family ties versus the ways Suzette, Maple, and Agnes perceive them.

11. *Nobody's Magic* takes place in Shreveport, Louisiana. How do you think the setting shapes the characters and events of the story? In what ways do you think the novel would be different if it took place somewhere else?

AUTHOR Q&A

What inspired you to write *Nobody's Magic*, and why tell the story in three parts?

Nobody's Magic began with a joke I told to a friend while I was working as a grader for high school exams in Salt Lake City during the summer of 2019. The grading area is such an austere space, and I said, "It'd be wild if someone just lost it in here." Later that day, the first lines of "Mind the Prompt" came to me, and even after I got back from Utah, the idea stayed, so I said, "Fine, I'll write a short story." I thought it would simply be a one-off thing. But the "short" story came out long—more than forty pages—and my first readers kept telling me it could be longer. By that time, I thought I might be writing a collection of short stories.

Soon, I got another idea for a story about a woman with albinism who was a charlatan and had convinced people she had special powers. That story evolved into Suzette's part of the triptych, and it too got longer and longer as I revised it. Maple came last, and I started writing "Bottled Water" because I told myself I wanted to write about a mother and daughter who were besties, but after completing the opening scene, I had an epiphany: The mother was supposed to be dead.

Before I knew it, I had three parts to a book and no more short story ideas. And the characters in each part were speaking to each other across the sections, even though they never meet in person. This, coupled with their shared subjectivity as Black women with albinism, their complicated family structures/love lives, and their connection to my hometown made putting them together an easy decision. With that, *Nobody's Magic* was born.

Suzette, Maple, and Agnes's sections are written in three distinct voices. What were the choices you made for each woman's narration and why?

Suzette's family's wealth made me want to write her narrative in Northern Louisiana AAVE; her voice works as both a plot twist and as a way to create a character I could relate to. I know what it's like to grow up around adults like Suzette's parents, and to be tragically naïve about certain aspects of life, including oneself. I liked the idea of parsing out those things in a voice that sounded like one of my family members telling a story. I'm probably biased in this, but I think Southern Black women are some of the most intelligent people I know, and it felt fitting to make Suzette sound like the women who raised me, or like me when I'm home and I know my language is understood. I also love the irony of the fact that (in my opinion) Suzette is the most insightful of the three women, even though it's an insight she has to grow into. But the way she talks about what she knows just sounds like someone shooting the breeze. I wanted that.

Maple sounds like me when I talk to my friends, the way she code switches to get things done, and her sarcasm. It makes sense that the spaces she's moved through—college and hospitality jobs—would make that easy for her, so that was a choice that I fell into as I wrote that first conversation with her mom.

In "Mind the Prompt," I wanted Agnes's narrator to sound like

Agnes if Agnes were humble enough to tell her story. I wanted them to sound pompous and academic even when they're describing what's happening in Agnes's head. Honestly, the voice highlights one of Agnes's tragic flaws: her mistaken presumption that she's somehow remade herself into someone completely different from who she once was. I wanted her to sound intelligent while making disastrously stupid decisions, because eventually, she begins to realize how wrong she's been about so many things.

Were there characters that you understood and could write easily, and were there any characters that took longer to reveal themselves to you?

Suzette was the easiest to write, which is ironic because her character evolved the most between my initial conception and writing down her first words. Like I said, she was initially supposed to be a scammer, someone I wouldn't get along with in real life, but as she became herself, I liked her more and more, and by the time I got to the part when Doni starts to show interest, I loved them both so much it was unreal. I couldn't wait to spend time with them each day as I wrote.

Maple was also easy to write but writing her section down and then cutting it was difficult. Even so, I had a very clear sense of who she would be from the beginning, and that didn't change much during the process.

Agnes was the hardest to write because, full disclosure, I hated her! But my hatred intrigued me; one of my favorite books is Toni Morrison's *Sula*, so I'm always down for a character who makes me cringe but makes me want to keep reading—or, in this case, keep writing. But when I got to what is now the halfway point in "Mind the Prompt," I just wanted to destroy her. In the original version, she got into the truck with the man she met at the gas station, and they disappear to parts unknown because that's what I thought she deserved. But when folks (including my editor) kept asking for more of her story, I realized that, at some point, she would find herself back in Shreveport with her mother and, more important, with Berniece.

Who are some of your favorite writers, and did they influence the way you wrote *Nobody's Magic*?

Even though the triptych aspect of *Nobody's Magic* came out of my longwindedness and friends who kept asking for more pages, I know I could not have envisioned it without having read Tayari Jones's debut novel, *Leaving Atlanta*, or Marie Vieux-Chauvet's *Love, Anger Madness: A Haitian Triptych*. They are both powerful books written in three parts.

I'm also a longtime admirer of Charles Chesnutt, the early-twentieth-century writer who, in my opinion, is the best transcriber of AAVE to date. There's an exquisite rhythm to the way the character Julius McAdoo tells stories, and I spent hours combing through Suzette's section, making sure the rhythm on the page matched the one Suzette would speak, just like Chesnutt. I love Toni Morrison's work, and watching *The Pieces I Am* shortly after I began writing this book gave me permission to write about home, to create a problematic character, and to write the book no one was looking for.

As for contemporary fiction writers—goodness, there are so many, but I deeply admire the work of Lesley Nneka Arimah, Deesha Philyaw, Tia Clark, Dantiel Moniz, Tatiana Richards Hanebutte, Morgan Jerkins, and Angela Flournoy. Each of them writes about something deeply important to me, including place, family, relationships between women, terrible men and the violences they often commit, grief, and even humor. They're all amazing.

What was your experience writing *Nobody's Magic* versus your poetry collection, *Negotiations*? Do you have a different approach to writing depending on whether it's poetry or prose?

I'm not sure I have a different approach, but in each genre, different things are possible. With poetry, every word matters. It carries a weight, a beat on a line, and can serve multiple purposes in terms of sound and meaning. I try to do the same thing in prose, but the truth is that there is a little more playing room, more space to add in little anecdotes and gestures that sometimes exist simply because I want them there. But that also happens in my poetry too. On the other hand, sometimes in prose, superfluity is necessary for character development—like with Agnes—but that doesn't always work in a poem.

There have definitely been times in my life when I've been writing books of poetry and prose simultaneously, and when I was doing that, I'd simply spend an hour or two on one, and then would switch for an hour or so on the other. And I didn't necessarily put on a prose or poetry hat to do it. I just wrote what I liked until my timer went off, then set up separate days to revise it. Someone once told me that good, keepable writing usually only happens for about four hours a day, and that's a practice that works for me unless I'm caught up in a new idea or development. Then, all bets are off!

I think the major difference between the two is that writing fiction is physically exhausting for me, and I'm still not sure why! I do think the stakes of writing about women with albinism—my own deeply personal subjectivity—may have played a role, but I'm not totally convinced that that's the culprit. I've written about difficult subjects in poetry too: racist violence, sexual assault, illness. But the revision process for *Nobody's Magic* was draining in a way I've never experienced before. After that, I decided that, unlike poetry, which I tend to write whenever, wherever, I should try to make time for writing fiction on its own, to make space for that intense exhaustion.

Nobody's Magic is an honest exploration of womanhood, but what inspired the creation of the men in the story? From fathers to lovers, what role did you want them to play in their relationship to the women?

Ah, the men! I think I love Doni the most, and he's an amalgamation of many of the men I grew up with: my uncles and their friends, mostly, but also a little of my great-grandfather, and maybe a little of my baby brother. Some of Doni's mannerisms are so…us—my family, I mean. The way he shows love through acts of service, like handing Suzette the mask when he's using the sandblaster, or how he answers a question long after the conversation has shifted to something else. Or his random knowledge about what's best to feed the birds. That he knows how to sew. I love all of those small, endearing idiosyncrasies that make him who he is. They remind me of my blood kin.

Chad reminds me of men I've dated from back home, men who loved to ride you around in their cars, playing loud music, maybe smoking something. Men who didn't have the most honorable ways of making money, but who were good. Men who showed tenderness and vulnerability in unexpected ways. Originally, the final scene with Chad and Maple was supposed to be comical, but by the time I got to it, Chad changed how that scene went down. He was too tender for all that. And he compels Maple to get serious too.

Prime's origins are a bit murkier; he's a lot of men I've known, some of whom are manipulative in dangerous ways, even though he has some sympathetic elements. And in "Drive," Mr. Curtis is actually based on some mothers I've met. Although his need for control is part and parcel of his fragile masculinity, it most certainly isn't a gender-specific trait.

For each of the men, I suppose I wanted them to serve as catalysts for the women to embark on journeys, reject certain things, and embrace others, but I didn't want the men to have all the power to make those things happen. And I wanted them to be complex Black men—not all good, not all bad. I feel like sometimes that's what you get in larger mainstream representations: monsters or angels, martyrs or deadbeat dads and hopeless criminals. I wanted something a little more interesting.

Nobody's Magic takes place in Shreveport, Louisiana, your hometown. Why did you choose to set the story there? What are some of the specific places in the Ark-La-Tex region that inspired the setting of the book, and do you have a favorite place to recommend to readers?

It's wild: The first time I met my agent, I told her I'd never write about Louisiana. At the time, I was much more interested in the spaces I was inhabiting: writers' conferences and retreats in various parts of the country. But when I started to tell Agnes's story, so much of what she was thinking about _was_ home, the place that had shaped her but also scarred her, and perhaps it was the difficult work of leaning into that shared pain that made me reluctant to write about it at first. But I couldn't tell her story without talking about where she came from, and I certainly couldn't have put Suzette anywhere else. And when I realized that Maple's mother was dead and why, I had to make space to talk about gun violence in this place I love so much, and the proximity of that violence to the people I love. So really, it wasn't a creative decision as much as it was an emotive one.

I think the best part of writing this novel was getting to visit the places of my youth at a time when I couldn't get back home (and in some cases, even if I had gone, those places have completely changed). I loved writing about Agnes's high school, Cross Lake, and the parks and neighborhoods Suzette and Doni drive through on their dates. I also loved writing about the shopping areas, like Pines

Road, Line Avenue, Youree Drive, and the Industrial Loop. Some of those places existed when I was a child, and others have come up in the years after. And I loved taking Suzette back to the Cedar Grove/ Eden Gardens South area, where I grew up!

If I had to recommend any place in the Ark-La-Tex, I'd say: Get close to some trees and some water (Louisiana is called "Sportsman's Paradise" for a reason). If you drink, get a carryout daiquiri from Thrifty Liquor with the tape across the lid. Go to the Boardwalk or go eat on one of the boats. Get doughnuts from Southern Maid and fried chicken from Southern Classic. Please eat fried oysters with the Brothers tartar sauce. No place does these things better. I don't make the rules.

Did you learn something new about yourself during the process of writing this novel?

Every book I've written, even the ones that haven't yet been published, has taught me how to be a better writer. They've taught me what I'm good at and what I have to work on to make good, the importance of first readers, and the difference between the story I think I'm going to tell and what the story actually needs to be. *Nobody's Magic* certainly did all of that, but it also taught me how fun—and how powerful— invention can be. It's a wonderful thing to immerse myself in a character who is like me but not me, who doesn't share my wounds or my complete past. She can be anyone; she can do anything. *Nobody's Magic* also taught me the importance of listening to that quiet voice that often nudges me to do a thing. That voice, that instinct, has never steered me wrong. Without it, this book wouldn't exist.

ABOUT THE AUTHOR

Destiny O. Birdsong's writing has appeared in the *Paris Review Daily*, *African American Review*, and *Catapult*, among other publications. She has received the Academy of American Poets Prize and the Richard G. Peterson Poetry Prize. Her critically acclaimed debut collection of poems, *Negotiations*, was published by Tin House Books and longlisted for the 2021 PEN/Voelcker Award for Poetry Collection.